DEAD HEAT

Glenis Wilson

severn
House

This first world edition published 2018
in Great Britain and 2019 in the USA by
SEVERN HOUSE PUBLISHERS LTD of
Eardley House, 4 Uxbridge Street, London W8 7SY.
Trade paperback edition first published
in Great Britain and the USA 2019 by
SEVERN HOUSE PUBLISHERS LTD.

British Library Cataloguing in Publication Data
A CIP catalogue record for this title is available from the British Library.

ISBN-13: 978-0-7278-8858-7 (cased)
ISBN-13: 978-1-84751-982-5 (trade paper)
ISBN-13: 978-1-4483-0194-2 (e-book)

Typeset by Palimpsest Book Production Ltd.,
Falkirk, Stirlingshire, Scotland.

Dedicated to my family and especially to the one where the honour lies.

ACKNOWLEDGEMENTS

Nick Sayers at Hodder & Stoughton. His belief in me and the manuscripts kept me going. Kate Lyall Grant and all at Severn House Publishers. Roderick Duncan, clerk of the course, Southwell racecourse. Nick Kilmartin, manager and all the staff at the North Shore Hotel, Skegness. David, Anne and Elaine Brown, printers and friends. Wally Wharton, jockey, superb horseman and lifelong friend. Phil Ashmore for maintaining my website. Barbara Newsome for her invaluable help with the snow racing in Switzerland. Andrew Pacey. Chris Coley for sharing his knowledge on the snow racing together with racehorse trainers Nigel Twiston-Davies and John Best. The staff at Bingham, Radcliffe-on-Trent and West Bridgford libraries. All the people who have helped me in whatever way during the course of writing the 'Harry' novels. And of course, all my lovely readers, bless you for your wonderful comments and emails. To everyone, may I say a very big thank you – have a great read.

'The legacy of heroes is the memory of a great name and the inheritance of a great example.'

Benjamin Disraeli

'To the one who has gone before, the great master of horseracing novels, Dick Francis, thank you for all those wonderful reads. I offer my sincere gratitude and humbly follow in your footsteps.'

Glenis Wilson

PROLOGUE

'd been kidding myself. Complacency had lulled me into self-congratulations for urging Annabel, my estranged wife, to avoid the murderous intentions of Jake Smith and escape to London. Only she hadn't escaped. Neither had the man in her life, Sir Jeffrey, the father of her unborn baby.

Sitting here on the edge of my hospital bed about to leave for home, I could hardly believe what Mike was telling me. Annabel and Sir Jeffrey were actually here too, in *this* hospital. I'd assumed both were safe; they weren't – nor was the baby.

Mike had come to collect me. I'd been told I could go home after having been seen by the doctor. My X-ray had shown no deep damage to either patella, the teeth of the electric Alligator saw, wielded by a crazed Jake Smith, having bounced off rather than grinding into the bone. I'd been grounded while the soft tissue healed but it shouldn't take long. There was no lasting damage and I could get about with crutches. A massive relief. Sitting on my bed, bag packed, I couldn't wait to go back home. And I'd happily related the good news to Mike. Until, seeing the grim expression on his face, I'd stopped enthusing about my good luck. 'What's up?'

'Have you seen or heard the news since you came into hospital?'

I shook my head. 'No, drugged up mostly, and because of the bash on the head, I've been asleep a good deal.'

'I've some bad news – truly awful news.'

I picked up the depths of his depression. 'Tell me. Something happened to Pen?' Penelope was Mike's partner.

He waved a hand. 'No, it's Sir Jeffrey and Annabel.'

I stood up. 'What's happened?'

'They were setting off to drive to London—'

'Yes, I know, I persuaded Annabel to go with him; she didn't want to, but I told her she'd be safe with him.'

He shook his head slowly. 'I'm so sorry, Harry. Sir Jeffrey was driving. Annabel, apparently, was lying down on the back seat—'

'She wasn't feeling well,' I put in.

He nodded. 'Well, that's what saved her. They had a crash on the M1 just after they'd joined the motorway at Leicester Forest East.'

'Oh my God! What injuries have they got?'

'Sir Jeffrey's pretty bad, I gather. He's got spinal injuries . . .'

'And Annabel?' My fists were clenched hard.

'I'm sorry, Harry. She's lost the baby.'

I closed my eyes. She had so looked forward to the baby. 'How is she?'

'I think she's shaken and bruised, but otherwise she's escaped injury. It was the offside front wing and door that took the brunt of the impact. Sir Jeffrey had to be cut free. Then they were flown in by air ambulance.'

'To this hospital?'

'Yes. They were here before you were brought in, although I didn't know about it then. Sir Jeffrey had an emergency operation, they say.'

'And just how *bad* is he?'

'Don't know,' Mike said, miserably.

We were silent, taking in the implications of what he'd just told me.

'I'm going to ask if they'll let me see him.'

'I'll wait here, Harry. Don't think they'll let two of us in.'

'No,' I agreed, 'and it will only be a five-minute job, probably.'

I left him sitting beside my bed and, stiff-legged, slowly hobbled off.

'Two minutes only,' said the nurse, eyeing my crutches.

I thanked her and sat down gratefully on the chair beside his bed. He was conscious, head held immobile in a brace.

'Jeffrey, God, I'm so sorry . . .'

'Harry . . .'

'Mike tells me you've had an operation on your spine.'

'Yes, T-six, seven? Likely a wheelchair job,' he said in a weak voice.

I shook my head in sympathy but couldn't find the words to say how gutted I felt for him. 'They say Annabel's lost the baby.'

'Hmm, my poor Annabel, she wanted it so much . . .'

The man was amazing. In the face of his bleak future, maybe as a cripple, he was all concern for her. I could see how right Annabel was when she said he was a good man, good for her. I felt utterly helpless to do anything for him.

'I don't think she, herself, is injured, Jeffrey.'

'Thank heavens.' His eyes closed.

'Amen to that.'

Out of the corner of my eye I could see the nurse hovering.

'I think I have to leave; they said only two minutes.'

'Wait!' His voice was urgent. He made a big effort. 'Nothing's changed, Harry. We're still sharing her. I've got her affection, her company, but you've got her heart and soul.'

I didn't know how to reply.

'Look after her, while I'm in here; she needs you to lean on . . .' His voice weakened, trailing away with exhaustion.

'Don't worry, Jeffrey. She can rely on me to look after her just now.'

'Thanks . . .' His eyes closed once more.

The nurse walked up to the bed. She didn't need to ask me to leave. I'd already risen from the chair. I needed to see Annabel.

She was sitting in the chair by her bed, taking sips of water.

'Harry! Oh, Harry.' She put the beaker down and stood up, holding her arms wide. I reached for her and we held each other tightly. It was debatable who needed the most comfort. We hugged . . . and wept . . . for several minutes. When we broke apart, I wiped the tears from her cheeks with a tissue.

'Darling, I'm so, so sorry. It's my fault. If I hadn't insisted you went with Jeffrey—'

She put fingers to my lips. 'Hush. Of course it wasn't your fault. You were trying so hard to protect me.' Her eyes widened, taking in the crutches. 'Did that monster attack you?' She gently traced a fingertip down the side of my right cheek where the edges of the knife wound had been drawn together.

'Yes. But let's not talk about it.'

She shuddered. 'He said the baby wouldn't be born. Where is he now?'

I put my arms around her and gave her another recovery hug. 'Not around to hurt you. The police have him. He's safely locked up.'

She slumped against me. 'We're all a lot safer now, then, and it's thanks to you. Well done, Harry.'

'With all that's happened, that's insignificant. I'm gutted for Jeffrey.'

Tears flooded her eyes and ran down her white cheeks. 'I don't know what to do, Harry. Help me . . .'

'You know I will. You don't need to ask.'

She clung to me for several minutes. I tried to inject some of my strength into her.

'I'm coming out of hospital today. Are you?'

'Yes. Take me home with you, Harry. Please.'

I stroked her hair. 'Of course. Do you mean to your home?'

'No, back to the cottage with you. I don't want to be by myself just now. And,' she gulped, 'it is just me. The baby's gone, Harry.'

'Oh my darling, I know, I know.' I rocked her gently until her weeping had eased. 'Let's get your things.'

'Jeffrey! I must speak to Jeffrey before I go.'

'I don't think you can at the moment, Annabel. He was having an injection to put him out when I left him. You can visit him tomorrow.'

She bit her lip and nodded. 'Home, then.'

'Home.'

Mike dropped us at Harlequin Cottage and drove off.

Leo greeted us warmly. Annabel clutched him to her, burying her face in his warm ginger fur. There was safety and undemanding comfort in loving the cat. He submitted to the embrace, squeezing his eyes shut and purring for England. Animals offered therapy just by being themselves.

I left them sitting on the settee and went to turn up the central heating and put the kettle on. While it was boiling, I poured us each a whisky and took one over to Annabel. It was, of necessity, a one-thing-at-a-time job. I was very much reliant upon my crutches because Jake's antics, even if they had not broken any bones, had badly bruised the patella on each leg. He knew, of course – the entire horseracing community knew – that my left kneecap was vulnerable. No doubt, it had been that knowledge that had spawned the evil thought of how best to exploit it. As champion jump jockey, I was in a high-risk occupation; one in every eight races, or thereabouts, ended in a fall, the damage from which varied from being winded to being killed.

The crashing fall I'd sustained at Huntingdon racecourse had landed me in a hospital bed with a raft of injuries; most seriously, it had shattered my left patella. Falls were the risk I accepted –

they were part of the job – but it was this inescapable fact that had, finally, convinced Annabel that she couldn't take seeing me suffer any more, and although she'd let me have the cat, Leo, she had left.

The other inescapable fact was that now she was with Sir Jeffrey, not me – his gain, my loss. And it was my justified concern in trying to keep Annabel safe so Jake Smith couldn't find her that had led to her being in Jeffrey's car, heading for London when the crash happened.

Jake Smith was a hardened criminal, convicted of GBH and an acknowledged main player among the low life both in and out of prison. When he pulled strings, the others jumped. It was my unpleasant luck that our paths had not only crossed but become hellishly entangled when I'd been forced into tracking down Alice Goode's killer. Now, in retaliation, knowing she was my Achilles' heel and what hurt her hurt me even more, Jake was gunning for Annabel.

Alice, who had been a prostitute, had also been a caring human being. She'd helped me in the past – the only one who could, when I'd been badly beaten up. After her murder, I'd felt morally obliged to track down her killer.

But if you will go into the jungle after tigers . . . And there was no bigger tiger out there than Jake Smith.

I held out the glass to Annabel.

'Thanks, Harry.' Annabel sipped at her generous slug of whisky; within a very short time, I was gratified to see her body relax and a slight colour return to her face.

I made coffee and together we sat on the settee, coming to terms with the events of the last two days. I knew Annabel's safe, protected, ordered life with Sir Jeffrey steering the ship was gone for ever. That she would cope with the change I had no doubt. Once the shock had worn off, she would rise to it magnificently. Jeffrey was now a dependent, vulnerable man himself. Annabel was by nature a carer, a healer. I knew she would nurse him and look after him for however long it took.

That thought gave me an unpleasant jolt. Sir Jeffrey's injuries were on a par with those of Mousey Brown's late wife. Not so severe, it was true: his injury had occurred lower down the spinal column, but just how bad we would have to wait to find out. None of us knew what was up front on the road we travelled, but in so many cases it seemed brutally unfair how life handed out its lessons.

Sir Jeffrey had travelled the same roads – the M1 in particular – up and down to London all the time. It must have crossed his mind that the law of averages might one day catch up with him. But it was entirely my fault that this particular time Annabel had been travelling with him. And because of that, she had paid a heavy price and lost her unborn child. Guilt was sitting firmly on my shoulders and I didn't know how to throw the heavy burden off.

'Harry' – Annabel put down her empty glass – 'I have to tell you something. I know you're blaming yourself – about the baby, I mean.'

'How could I not?'

She gripped my hand. 'Harry, the hospital have explained the facts. I knew something was wrong because I was feeling so poorly before we started our journey. The hospital said the baby had died before we had the car crash.'

'*What?*'

'Yes, it's true. They think the umbilical cord had looped around his neck. Nothing anybody could have predicted. Even if I'd stayed at home that day, it wouldn't have altered anything. The baby couldn't have been saved. He'd already died inside me, probably even as much as three or four days before. They couldn't tell.'

'Annabel, my darling, I don't have words to tell you how sorry I am . . .'

'I know it's awful, but I'm the one who's sorry. It's *not* your fault. It was already too late before you told me to leave with Jeffrey.'

'But you were involved in the crash, too: *that* was my fault. And I can't forgive myself.'

'You must, Harry. If I'd stayed at the house – and it would have been just me on my own, because Jeffrey was definitely going to London – I would certainly have gone into labour, the hospital said so. And I might very well not have survived because the baby wasn't in the right position for birth. So, I'm glad – and grateful – that you insisted I went with Jeffrey. It might actually have saved my life.'

'Annabel . . . the whole episode is so traumatic for you and yet . . . you seem to have already accepted it . . .' I waved a hand helplessly.

'Dear Harry' – she pressed my hand to her cheek – 'what else is there to do?'

I looked into her beloved face and knew I would love her forever.

'We simply don't have an alternative, do we?'

She shook her head. 'No. The baby will be fine now. I must think of Jeffrey.'

I remembered Annabel was a spiritual healer with strong beliefs. I'd felt that incredible power flowing through her to me, via the palms of her hands. It had helped heal me and there was no way I could deny it. We didn't have all the answers to life and some things couldn't be explained – but they did exist, without any doubt.

'I haven't told you about Aunt Rachel's baby yet, have I?'

Her eyes widened incredulously.

'Yes, it is true. A baby she had as a young girl – not George's.'

'*What?*'

I told her the whole story and how it had, later, become intertwined in the hunt for Alice's killer.

'Gracious! It's all about families, isn't it?'

I nodded. 'Samuel has already coined that phrase. But yes, you're both right. And this case has similarities to the other ones. They were all about families, too. It would have saved me a great deal of time if I'd considered that aspect in the beginning. It's one thing the police fall down on – they can't get close enough to access family bloodline secrets.'

'But what a wonderful thing to happen to Aunt Rachel. There's a kind of wild justice – I've lost my baby and she's been given hers back.'

'Only you could think such a magnanimous thought. You are the most generous woman I've ever met.'

'Nonsense.' She gave me a wan smile. 'Life is so unpredictable. That's what makes it magnificent. But, Harry, I've been so wrong.'

'You're never wrong, my darling.'

'Oh, yes. I've always thought your work the most dangerous sort in the world. Stupidly, I've been so fixated on that I've totally forgotten that life itself is lived dangerously, at the sharp end, all the time. I found that out two days ago.'

Before I could reply, the horseshoe doorknocker banged against the back door. It was Nathaniel Willoughby, the racing artist, returned from Switzerland. As gently as we could, we filled him in on the developments.

'It's so sad; you won't be needing a portrait now.'

Annabel looked bewildered so I quickly explained I'd commissioned him to do a painting of the new baby when it was a few months old, and now, of course, it wouldn't be painted.

'My dear' – he patted Annabel's hand – 'life gives . . . and it also takes. You have to stay strong.'

'Yes.' She nodded. 'Jeffrey needs me.'

He turned to me. 'I've really come to collect my keys, Harry. I take it the, er . . . "lodger" has departed?'

'Of course.' I went to find my jacket and fished his keys from my pocket. 'Thank you so much, Nathaniel. Don't know what I would have done without the use of the studio.'

Nathaniel's generosity in allowing me to use his rural and isolated studio where he painted his masterpieces of horseracing art had solved a major problem for me when I'd been landed with a most unwelcome house guest. Without alternative accommodation at that point, I was deep in it. It wasn't too strong to say he had probably saved me ending up on a police charge that might even have led to me being convicted and going to prison. I owed him big time.

'And you, Harry,' he said, '*you* have to keep going. We need you to keep sorting us all out.'

'No more! I've had enough with this last case to put me off for life.'

He stood there smiling, somewhat sadly, and shaking his head. 'I don't think so. I may need your help. I've discovered something over in Switzerland. It involves Mike's late wife, Monica . . . But I'll tell you at a later date. You look after this lady.' He bent and kissed Annabel. 'She needs comforting right now.'

He made his way across the room and I saw him out. Then I closed the back door firmly against the world.

'You see,' Annabel said, when I returned to the lounge, 'we all need you, Harry. And I need you more now than ever before.'

Later that evening, although neither of us felt much like eating, I cooked a light supper, which we merely picked at, but it was sufficient.

At nine o'clock, I took her to my bed.

She put her arm tightly around my chest and pressed her cheek to my shoulder. And in safety, comforted by each other's presence, we slept, chastely, like spoons.

ONE

From the tall chimney a curl of smoke wound its way up into the sharp blue sky. Unseen, in the bowels of the crematorium far below, the furnace burned efficiently, fired by unfeeling flesh. The escaping smoke signified more sombrely than the tolling of a bell the departure of a human soul being sent off on its journey.

I stood and watched. Felt the now familiar, totally unfounded guilt settle heavily on my shoulders before walking on up the steeply rising hill for the cremation of one John Dunston, former horsebox driver.

His body had, finally, been recovered from the merciless North Sea. After protracted police investigations, including inquest and post-mortem, the coroner had now released the body.

Without my intervention in solving a murder some months ago, John's recently deceased son would still be alive. That alone would have given John sufficient reason to live. I couldn't escape that fact. The barrel I'd been over at the time was not, to me, sufficient to excuse my actions. Which was irrational and stupid, but didn't make one jot of difference to how I felt.

We all did things we felt were right at the time, but so often the ripples from those actions continued to spread, widening and becoming far reaching in ways totally undreamed of. And, as we could never undo those actions, we had no option but to live with the results.

Life, like a horse race, demanded we go forward. We could never go back.

As a parent, John's responsibility had been hard-wired into the contract that came with his baby son's birth. That responsibility was sufficient to make continuing to draw breath a priority. Certainly, suicide wasn't an option when someone was relying on you being there for them.

But when the last member of your family was gone, you had to be strong to get up off the canvas and continue. I'd thought John very strong – I'd been wrong.

In the absence of any surviving relations to mourn and pay

respects, racing's own extended family stood in. I joined the rest of the mourners in front of chapel number three, the designated one. There were four others. All were in use and business was ongoing. The smoke, obviously, was from an earlier cremation.

My appearance produced a few approving nods and, conversely, there were also two or three tight, condemning glances. The guilt crept coldly up the back of my neck and I repressed an involuntary shiver.

What *they* didn't know was that I condemned myself.

TWO

'Harry.' Ted Robson, the Yorkshire racehorse trainer John Dunston had worked for, acknowledged me. 'Pity you weren't around to save John this time. Still, they do say, if you're going to commit suicide, nothing will stop you, but it's a bad business.'

'Have to admit, when Pete told me, it was a hell of a shock.' Pete was the valet from the weighing room who looked after my clothes and kit. 'Could hardly take it in . . .'

Robson gestured towards the other mourners. 'Reckon we all feel the same. John had got himself together again after losing Lilly . . . thought he was going to be all right.'

'At least there's a good turnout.' I scanned the faces – all very familiar to me as racing colleagues, jockeys, other box drivers, one or two trainers – and finally my gaze came to rest on an unfamiliar person. Although the majority all wore suits – jockeys as a breed were keen on sharp suits – the tall, thin man was wearing a definite City pinstripe. I wondered vaguely what his profession was.

But there was no way to satisfy my curiosity. We were being ushered as a group, gently but firmly, through the double doors and into the small chapel where muted strains of Bach's 'Jesu, Joy of Man's Desiring' played through unseen speakers.

Dunston's coffin was placed on the raised dais at the far end, tall candles, lit on either side, guttering madly in the stiff breeze generated by the open doors that allowed in the bitingly cold wind.

The crematorium being sited on the top of a hill, it caught the prevailing west wind.

I'd no idea who had arranged the funeral, but it had been done very correctly with 'Order of Service' sheets placed in front of each seat, along with a small, discreet card asking for mourners to write on their names and contact details.

While we shuffled and settled ourselves, I filled out my own card. Since, to my knowledge, no family remained, it seemed odd that the cards had been issued. Of course, normally, it was a comfort to the next of kin to be able to see who had taken the trouble to pay their respects.

Had Dunston made a will setting out his wishes? Since his death had been by his own hand, and premeditated, the answer was, probably, yes. Just who the cards were going to be handed over to after the service was the question.

Unaccustomed singers, we nevertheless made a fair fist of both hymns – predictably 'The Lord's My Shepherd' and 'Abide with Me' – giving them volume if not tuneful harmony. Robson gave the eulogy. He drew on Dunston's ability for hard work and, when under extreme pressure, caring for his sick wife, his tenacity to hang in and keep going.

I ventured a swift glance across the body of mourners and wondered if any of them, apart from me, noticed the irony of Robson's words, given the circumstances of Dunston's death. But it seemed no one had.

The final prayers over, the gates swung closed and we mentally said goodbye before trooping outside to stand in small knots of twos and threes, talking in low voices and viewing the sparse floral tributes.

'Well, he's got his wish . . .' Pete came to stand beside me.

'Hmm . . . joined his family.'

'At the end of the day, what else have any of us got?' Pete said glumly, reaching for a cigarette before thinking again and sliding the packet back into his pocket.

I winced as his words hit home. I'd lost most of my immediate family and could appreciate how John must have been feeling before he threw himself off Flamborough Head. I wished Pete hadn't said it. My own family had dwindled in recent times and in dire circumstances. But even if I had no family left, I couldn't envisage myself doing what John Dunston had done.

It's been said that it takes guts to go on living, and no doubt the cliché is true. But standing inside the chapel, looking at the coffin containing his body, I knew it must have taken even more courage to throw himself from the top of those cliffs, knowing that below waited the jagged, unyielding rocks and the wild seas that raged and foamed around them.

Whether it had been guts or just desperation, his actions didn't fit the man I'd known. The man who'd struggled to keep breathing with a knife buried in him and, from the brink, had forged his way back to life when it would have been so easy to take the way out being presented.

I shook my head sadly. He'd come through the toughest of times only to chuck away all that effort.

It made no sense.

THREE

The tall man in the City suit cleared his throat. 'If I could have your attention . . .' he said in a slightly raised voice. The subdued murmuring faded away and we awaited his next words.

'My name is Caxton, and I am a partner in the firm of Caxton, Blithe and Attewood. I act for Mr John Dunston. I am his solicitor. His instructions were to offer all the mourners free drinks and refreshments after the service at the Mulberry Bush public house. The undertakers' cars are at the disposal of anyone requiring transport.'

'I was wondering who he was,' Ted Robson muttered.

'Hmm, me too,' I said.

Caxton was busy marshalling the straggling group, and Ted and I made our way to our respective vehicles, allowing the big funeral cars clear access out on to the main carriageway before following the rest of the cars in convoy. It was only a short journey to the pub.

There was a cheerful log fire crackling away inside the Mulberry Bush. Everyone's mood had now lightened – elbows were being lifted and drinks sipped. In company with most of the men, I'd

ordered a whisky. The cold at the crematorium had been
bone-chilling.
    'Please feel free to help yourselves to the refreshments.' Caxton
waved a munificent hand towards the loaded table opposite the
bar.
    Mousey Brown, trainer and alcoholic, quickly downed his double
whisky, waved the empty glass aloft and voiced the thoughts of
all of us.
    'Good on you, John. It's a bloody lovely spread.'
    And it was. We loaded our plates with cold meats, pies and
quiches along with accompanying salads and pickles, found seats
and got stuck in. Clive Unwin, who trained in Leicestershire,
together with his travelling head lad, Phil, joined us at our table.
    Mousey, predictably, went to the bar for a refill before starting
on the food. It was a good job his son, Patrick, was here to do
the driving. Mousey had lost his licence a long time ago.
    I flicked a glance at the other jockeys enjoying their meal and
knew that none of us were likely to eat anything else today. For
myself, I had five rides booked for tomorrow at Leicester – two
of them for Clive and the rest for Mike. That was assuming the
temperature didn't drop any further overnight and result in a severe
frost. It was a tricky time of year for jump racing. We were booking
rides and hoping. But the weather was in charge, and if it turned
dirty, it could halt racing.
    'Mike not here, then?' Clive said.
    'No, probably is in spirit, but he couldn't be in person. Pen was
taken ill in the early hours so he's stayed to look after her.'
    'Nothing serious, is it?'
    'Don't think so. Nothing he's calling in a doctor for, anyway.
Says he should be going to the racecourse tomorrow afternoon as
normal.'
    'You riding for him as well as me?'
    'Yes, three actually.'
    'I'll make sure I ask after Pen when I see him. She's a lovely
woman.'
    'Oh, yes,' I said, 'the best.'

Phil dug into his well-filled plate. 'Pity the do's because of John
topping himself,' he said, indulging in a massive piece of pork pie
and loading his fork with pickles to accompany it.

'Never know, do you?' Clive shook his head. 'I mean, what constitutes a man's breaking point, eh?'

'What, indeed.' Ted chewed thoughtfully. 'He never gave any indication it was all too much. Yes, I know, his son died and he was the last of the family, but John wasn't a stranger to death and tragedy. He'd lost Lilly . . . Now if anything was going to prompt a quick exit, you'd think it would be his wife dying, but John seemed to accept that.'

'Terrible to say it, but Lilly falling downstairs was a mercy in the end,' Clive put in.

'I'll second that,' said Mousey. 'By God, I will!'

We all buried ourselves in the business of eating. None of us knew quite what to say.

Mousey's wife, Clara, had certainly paid the full price after the horrendous accident that left her paralysed and clinging to life for the next two years while every day saw her fighting a battle that could only end one way. I knew for sure that Mousey saw her death as a blessing – he had told me so. But that was between Mousey and me, and I wasn't going to air it. Before her accident, Mousey hadn't been an alcoholic. Coming here today, I suddenly realized, couldn't have been easy for him. Memories could be stirred up by other people's events. And they weren't always good ones.

'It certainly ended Lilly's suffering,' I said, trying to restore conversation to fill the tense silence.

'That's right.' Mousey nodded fiercely.

'Anyone ready for a top-up?' Phil volunteered to go to the bar with the orders. He knew Mousey certainly wouldn't turn down a drink and that the atmosphere needed lifting. But he added diplomatically, 'Got to see John off right. An' don't forget, he's picking up the tab.'

His attempt at humour brought smiles to our faces. Of all of us, Phil was the one who had seen most of John, both being horsebox drivers out on the road all day long, using the same box parks for their vehicles at the different racecourses up and down the country. He was going to miss a familiar face.

'Oh, go on then.' Ted laughed. 'It'll see us along on the way home.'

'One more's not going to put us over the limit,' said Clive, 'so, yes, same again, please, Phil.'

We all opted for another whisky. My first one had hit the spot and I could actually feel my toes again. But a second one would certainly warm the journey home. And it was a fair drive from Yorkshire back home to my cottage in Radcliffe-on-Trent, in Nottinghamshire. The fire was laid ready to have a match tossed on to it and the Rayburn would be ready to produce a scalding mug of tea. But, like John, I had nobody waiting there for me. I paused in my thoughts. Not a person perhaps, but Leo would be there. Leo, my enormous ginger tom cat. Having saved my life not once but twice, he was pretty special.

'To be honest,' Phil said, seamlessly continuing the conversation when he returned with a loaded tray, 'I reckon John was relieved. OK, it was a hell of a shock an' all that, but she was never going to get better, was she?'

We all nodded in reluctant acknowledgement. Poor Lilly had been facing a drawn-out period of suffering, and the end result would still have been the same. The strain on John must have been tremendous: not simply the physical caring but also the financial burden of paying for live-in carers when he was out working, trying to earn the necessary money to keep the whole show going.

Ted swallowed the last of his food and sighed heavily. 'He never let on that he couldn't cope. Just shows, you never know what's going on inside a man's head.'

'Well, he's out of his torment now an' I think we should give him a toast for how he coped. Well, up until he jumped. An' it must have took a whole lot of guts to do what he did.' Phil grabbed his beer. 'Here's to John.'

We all followed his lead and took a quick pull of our drinks. 'To John,' we echoed.

The pub was just starting to clear. For the mourners from racing stables, work at evening stables was beckoning. Several of the other tables were now empty.

Ted pushed back his chair. 'Reckon I'll be getting back to the stables.'

We all took it as a signal and stood up. There was a general slow drift towards the door, but before I could follow, a voice at my side stopped me.

'Mr Harry Radcliffe?'

I turned and saw it was the solicitor, Caxton.

'Yes.'

'Perhaps we could have a quick word?'

'Of course.'

I followed him to a vacated corner table. He placed his briefcase carefully down on the top.

'Mr Dunston gave me his very specific instructions and entrusted me to ensure the arrangements were carried out.'

'You did a good job. It all went off beautifully. I'm sure John would be very satisfied.'

'Thank you.' He permitted himself a slight smile. 'However, there is one more thing I need to do.'

He unzipped his briefcase and reached inside.

'Mr Dunston asked me to hand this to you personally . . .' He withdrew a foolscap envelope and gave it to me. 'I've no idea what the letter says. I was merely instructed that should you attend the funeral, I was to make sure you received it.'

With some misgiving, I took the letter from him. My name was written on the front, along with the words *Private and Personal – only to be opened by Harry Radcliffe*. The words were heavily underlined, twice. I turned the letter over. It had not been tampered with in any way and was securely sealed.

I felt a familiar shiver run down the back of my neck – maybe I was getting psychic. I'm sure Annabel, my wife, would have endorsed that. Apart from being a psychotherapist, she was also a qualified spiritual healer.

But I was strictly a down-to-earth person, wasn't I? I'd always considered myself practical and not given to whimsical thoughts. However, the events of this last year had seemed to question that assessment. Even I couldn't explain how I seemed to know certain things when there was no logical explanation.

But that shiver . . . it was something I couldn't ignore. Too many times it had warned me that life was about to get bloody dangerous.

And right now I knew the letter I was holding was a time bomb. As soon as I opened it, it would go off.

FOUR

I unlocked the Mazda, tossed the envelope on to the passenger seat and fired up the car. Still unopened, the envelope lay there taunting me all the way down from Yorkshire.

I caught myself casting glances at it as I drove home. Just what it contained would remain a mystery until I'd lit the fire and wrapped myself around a mug of tea. After that, there'd be no further excuse to avoid opening it.

The big question was: why me? There had been upwards of forty people attending the funeral. What made John single me out? Caxton had said he'd been instructed to hand it to me personally. That meant John had wanted to be sure I got it. But the proviso had been that I was only to be presented with it if I actually attended the funeral. What did *that* mean? Probably, if I cared enough to bother going.

However, maybe John had thought I might meet somebody else who was attending the funeral.

I pondered on the variables all the way back to Harlequin Cottage.

As soon as he heard the key in the lock, Leo appeared and welcomed me back by leaping up to sit on my shoulder – his favourite position. He bashed his ginger head hard against my cheek and vociferously demanded some attention.

'Good to see you, too, Leo.' I rubbed behind his ears 'How about a bit of grub? Reckon you could tackle some?'

Damn fool question. He was down on the quarry tiles before I'd even begun to pour him a dish of milk.

I took a mug of welcome tea – and the letter – through to the lounge, placing both on the side table. Taking the paperknife from the desk, I slit open the envelope and left it beside the mug while I squatted down in front of the fireplace and struck a match. I'd buried a firelighter under the wigwam of kindling when I'd cleared out the grate this morning and it caught straight away.

I sat back on the settee, toed off my black funeral shoes, wriggled my toes in relief and relaxed. Reaching for the tea, I sipped the sustaining, scalding liquid. It's what every Englishman or woman does, isn't it? Any sort of crisis or dilemma prompts the making of tea. But I couldn't put off the moment any longer. There was only one sheet of paper inside the envelope. It read: *Harry, if you're reading this, then you've just been to my funeral. Obviously, it seems I'm dead and they got me.* I drew in a deep, ragged breath, my heart now thumping away. So, it hadn't been suicide. To be honest, I'd never bought into the theory in the first place, but it was still a real facer. John was telling me he'd been murdered. I took hold of my mug and drained the hot tea. Pity it wasn't whisky. I read on:

> *I knew they'd make a good job of faking a suicide but, believe me, I want to live as much as the next man. I also want justice, Harry, and you're the only one who can give it me. You saved my life once. Don't let these bastards get away with it.*
>
> *My son, Frank, was murdered, too – in prison. I expect you know that, probably blame Jake Smith. But was it? I don't think so. I do know Frank died because he had a nail stabbed through his eye. The other man had a blow to the head and died later in hospital. The authorities reckon he killed Frank and was thrown backwards as Frank lashed out.*
>
> *I've left a parcel for you with the solicitor. It contains the only bit of proof. I'm asking a lot because these are murderous bastards, but if you want to help, ask Caxton for the parcel – your decision.*
>
> *John*

I sat staring at the letter in frozen horror. No wonder I'd felt a shiver of premonition down the back of my neck. The information I'd just read was devastating. The details of Frank's injuries hadn't been made public. For John to learn that his son had met his death in such a ghastly way was enough to unhinge the man. But then John's own death must have been preceded by sheer terror. Knowing he was to be thrown from the cliffs to die on the rocks in the crashing sea far below . . .

I rubbed a trembling hand across my eyes at the enormity and horror of both deaths. And now John was asking for my help. The very last thing I wanted to do was get involved in any more murders. I'd had more than my fill.

But how did you walk away from something like this?

You didn't.

I'd saved John's life a few months ago. This outrage made a mockery of our combined efforts to help him stay alive. But, like falling into an evil-smelling swamp, it seemed the more I tried to extricate myself, the deeper in I sank. Getting involved in tracking down killers was never something I'd signed up for willingly, but circumstances gave me no choice. And where other people's lives were threatened – people I loved – a man had to find the guts to ensure their safety.

The situation now presenting, however, was very different. John had been murdered. Nothing I could do would alter that grim fact. Nobody's life was in jeopardy now. And that made all the difference.

If I tried to find out who the perpetrators were, undoubtedly the only person facing possible extinction would be me. I should let it go. It would be the sensible thing to do. And yet . . . this was a cry for help from beyond the grave.

I got up and poured myself a much-needed whisky, then mended up the fire, although the extra logs weren't necessary. But I still felt frozen by the graphic details. The drink helped, warming me inside as I sipped. It also helped free me up mentally.

John had said there was a parcel waiting at the solicitor's office with my name on it. Even the solicitor didn't know what was inside. It could do no harm to collect the parcel and see what it contained. The only bit of proof, whatever that meant. It was tantalizing. Why hadn't John said straight out? Had he phrased it in that way to deliberately dangle the carrot in front of me, tempting me?

I sighed and tossed back the last of the whisky. One thing was very clear. The letter itself was dynamite. If the killers got wind of its existence, they'd be determined to destroy the evidence. A second thought followed that: they'd be even more desperate to destroy whatever was sitting inside the parcel in the solicitor's office.

That unpleasant thought brought me up short. I'd been complacent. I was wrong. There was another person in the firing line – Caxton himself. Only he was totally unaware of it.

John had thought he'd given me a choice – *your decision*, he'd said – but having realized the danger, I had no choice.

However, there was nothing I could do this late in the evening. Caxton wouldn't be in his office now; he'd have gone home.

So it would have to be tomorrow – except I had five rides booked at Leicester racecourse. I swore forcibly. The number of rides I had lost through chasing killers was gutting. I was no longer out in front of the other jockeys. And the Championship was looking increasingly unattainable.

I'd have to phone Caxton as soon as his office opened in the morning, ask him to get the parcel into the post. At least that way he wouldn't have it in his possession if he got an unwelcome visitor. But if I couldn't ring Caxton, there was someone else I could – *should* – ring.

Reaching for my phone, I called Mike.

'Hi, how're things? How's Pen going on? Is she feeling any better?'

Mike's reassuring chuckle was a welcome sound. 'Thanks, Harry, yes, Pen's much better.'

'Oh, great. And we're still on for tomorrow's racing?'

'Absolutely. Chloe and Samuel are intending to be there. Chloe told me she's not only putting her shirt on White Lace, but the entire contents of her wardrobe.'

'Oh Lord, no pressure to win, then.'

He laughed. 'We both know with the line-up in White Lace's race, you're going to walk it.'

'What's that saying? The only dead certainty in life is death.'

'Ah . . . talking of death . . . how did Dunston's funeral go?'

'Smooth, no hitches, lovely spread afterwards at the Mulberry Bush pub . . .'

'But? I can hear a "but", Harry.'

'Hmm. John's solicitor was in attendance – a Mr Caxton.'

'And?

'And he singled me out at the end. Apparently, John had left a letter with him to be handed over personally to me, should I actually attend the funeral.'

'Have you read it yet?'

'Yes. It's dynamite, Mike. I don't want to say too much over the phone – rather tell you in the morning.'

'*That* bad?'

'And the rest.'

'Oh.'

'And it also means that straight after racing tomorrow, I might possibly have to get myself up to his office to collect something. I'm hoping he'll be willing to post it, but you know solicitors – they're reluctant to let anything out of their possession without a signature. Don't know whether they're better or worse than the police. Anyway, I'll phone him first thing, get the full SP.'

'We need to be off to Leicester by ten, don't forget, Harry.'

'I expect his office opens at nine. Shouldn't think it will take long to sort it out. But since reading that letter, it is pretty urgent.'

'OK, see you when you get here, then.'

'Yes, see you, Mike.'

I put the phone down and reached for the letter again. It read no better the second time. I decided I wasn't going to take it with me to show Mike; the message was written in my brain. It would be enough simply to tell him what it said. Get his take on it. His view was always practical and sound. I relied on his input and support in life: he was my childhood friend, my boss, and a good mate.

He had, in addition, helped save my life on three occasions. When your back was up against the wall – or, on one hair-raising occasion, pinned to the stable door – there was no finer person to have on your side. I was most definitely in his debt for life.

I slid the letter back into the envelope and stood up, undecided about where I should put it for safekeeping. And it definitely needed keeping safe – somewhere it couldn't be found in case anybody tried tossing the cottage to get their hands on it. Desks and drawers were no good. Hiding it inside books or with other paperwork would certainly slow down anybody intent on finding it, but it wouldn't defeat them. That ruled out most of the rooms in the cottage. Except one. I went through to the kitchen and rooted around in the odds-and-sods drawer until I came upon a roll of cream-coloured masking tape left over from when I'd painted the kitchen window frame.

I took the tape and the letter upstairs to the bathroom. Dropping to my knees beside the hand basin, I felt around for the water outlet pipe. Running from the back of the basin and feeding out through the wall, the pipe was practically invisible unless, like me, you were at an unnatural corkscrewed position on the floor.

I rolled the letter tightly around the cream-coloured outlet pipe. Then I proceeded to unroll the tape and wind it round and round the pipe, on top of the envelope, until the whole thing was entirely hidden. Even though I knew it was there, I would never have discovered it. It appeared to be simply a piece of pipe. Satisfied it was never going to be found, I went back downstairs to the kitchen.

It wasn't terribly late, but I decided an early night was very desirable. Leo was circling around near the back door. His nightlife was out there waiting for him. He had a cat-flap, but when I was around he didn't deign to use it and expected me to act as his doorman. But since, by God, I owed that cat, I played along and was happy to dance attendance.

I slipped off the safety chain and opened the door a few inches.

'There you go. Have a good night.'

He shot out. But before I had time to wonder why he took off so suddenly, the door was slammed wide open in my face. Two men burst into the kitchen. Totally unprepared, I lurched backwards, cannoned into the table, and the first man landed a jabbing punch to my jaw.

'Where is it? We know you've got it.'

Before I could answer or return the punch, the second man, much taller than the first, joined in the fun and delivered an incapacitating punch to my solar plexus. Doubling up, gasping for non-existent breath, I was incapable of speaking.

'Come on, where the fucking hell is it?'

He landed two more body punches into my ribs for encouragement. I knew it was the letter they were after, but with tightly wrapped scarves over their lower faces, I had no idea who *they* were. I needed to play for time. With enough rope, they were bound to let slip some clue to their identity. The only thing I did know was that they were professionals. Their blows were landing in all the right places to bring me to heel.

'Wh . . . a . . . t?' I gasped, feeling like a boxer's punchbag as several more punches battered into my ribcage.

'You stupid fucker. Caxton gave it you; we saw him. Now give.'

He rocked back, aimed and kneed me in the crotch.

Pain seared through me, red-hot and vicious. But ironically, even as I went over, clutching at myself, I knew I had him. Although he had his face covered, with those few words he'd given himself away as being one of the people in the pub this afternoon.

And I also knew they weren't going to finish me. If they did, they would never know if I'd passed on the information contained in the letter. They didn't even *know* what the contents of the letter said. And, even better, I knew damn well they'd never find it. Tucked away in the bathroom, it was safer than in a bank vault. But I could play dirty, too. Judging the moment when he was about to land a right-hander and had all his weight balanced on his left leg, I brought my right heel down hard at a sharp angle and connected with the tall man's kneecap. With satisfaction, I heard his scream of pain as it dislocated.

Ignoring his writhing sidekick, the first man lost it completely. Drawing his foot back, he smashed his heavy boot straight in my face.

My last thought before I lost consciousness was five rides – I'd got to ride five races tomorrow.

FIVE

God knows how long I was out cold. Long enough for at least one of the tossers to trash my desk. I discovered that devastation only after attending to my own physical mess. Consciousness and pain arrived simultaneously.

I found myself flat on the kitchen quarries surrounded by a fair puddle of blood – it wasn't a lake, thank heavens – which had obviously drained down my bashed-up nose. OK, there were other cuts and grazes putting in their pennyworth, but it was a relief to find my skin otherwise intact.

Still lying there, I wriggled toes, fingers, flexed arms and bent knees. They all worked. No limbs broken. It was an each-way bet whether my nose was or not, but with the level of pain in my face, I wasn't going to prod about to find out right now. I just hoped my cheek and jawbone had withstood the battering.

Breathing was reduced to shallow breaths. With the hammering my ribs had taken, it would be surprising if they weren't cracked.

Gingerly, I levered myself up to a sitting position, slewed sideways and sat, suppressing groans, propped up by the table leg. It was simply a matter of enduring the pain until it eased back. I'd been here a hundred times before. But mostly the injuries had been caused by falling off a horse, guaranteed to cause bruises and grunts.

One happy non-event: I'd not been sick. Moving my right index finger from side to side, I was further heartened to only see one finger. It seemed I might have got away without concussion. Had I have fallen on the racecourse and blacked out, the stringent rules would have seen me automatically grounded. But apart from the hoods that had laid me out, nobody knew I'd been knocked unconscious. And I sure as hell wasn't going to tell anyone.

The last thought I'd had as the boot connected with my face came rushing back. It was racing at Leicester tomorrow. I was booked to ride five horses. And it was important. The Jockeys' Championship was slipping away from me. Holding on to that award signified total commitment; to retain it meant daily fasting, saunas, workouts, plus all the rides I could get, if weight – and age – weren't to win instead. Not to mention all the other striving jump jockeys who were hungry for success.

It was the spur I needed. Pushing my palms flat on the cold tiles, I heaved myself up on to my knees. And stared at the floor. No fresh drops of blood splattered down. At least one piece of my anatomy had decided enough, it was going to start healing. The rest would have to follow suit.

Once I was vertical, I clung to the tabletop and listened for the better part of ten minutes. There wasn't a squeak to be heard. I crawled very slowly upstairs to the bathroom. It took several heavily sweating – and swearing – minutes, but I made it.

The corkscrew position beneath the washbasin was quite something in the agony stakes but, having checked, I collapsed on to the toilet seat, choking back relieved laughter. Laughing out loud was not something the ribs could take right now. The water outlet pipe sat there innocently, undiscovered and quite untouched. Whatever else might be wrecked or destroyed, they hadn't found the dynamite. Well, thinking back, it wouldn't have been both men who searched the cottage. One, to my certain knowledge, wouldn't be walking at all without the assistance of crutches for some time.

Fishing in the bathroom cabinet, I took out several powerful painkillers and knocked them back. Closing the cabinet door, I stared at my reflection in the mirror. It would have graced any Hammer film: blood, bruises and black eye.

I bent over the washbasin and swabbed away the caked blood.

The basin filled with pretty pink-tinged water, but the worst of the gore was coming off. It revealed a sorry picture underneath. The bruises were purpling up very nicely and the bridge of my nose was twice as broad as it had been before the attack. The warmth had activated the affronted nerve endings. I pulled the plug and let the water run away.

Filling the basin with cold water, I took a deep breath and plunged my entire face under water and held it there until my lungs rebelled. Surfacing, gasping and dripping, I held a towel to my face and simply let it dry by absorption. A vast improvement looked back at me from the mirror.

Then, stripping off all my clothes, I turned on the bath taps and ran the water high and very hot, added a generous amount of foamy muscle relaxant and finally lowered my screeching, protesting body into the water. The pain soared up the Richter scale to an eye-watering level before very slowly reducing as the healing water got on with its job. I sat and half dozed, added hot water a couple of times, and eventually clambered out awkwardly, wrinkled as a walnut and bright scarlet, but basically back in charge.

I tottered downstairs wrapped in a thick bath sheet – no point in getting dressed, it was so late – and surveyed the devastation. To be honest, it wasn't as bad as I'd feared. My desk had been the main focus. All the drawers had been wrenched out and tossed aside. The contents had been thrown around all over the floor. It was going to take time to sort out the mess, but I was relieved the papers weren't ripped or, worse, soaked in urine.

The kitchen floor looked like a butcher's shop, with a pool of blood congealing and splatters of red droplets sprayed around the front of the sink unit and the Rayburn. If I didn't feel like cleaning up right now – and I most certainly didn't – it wasn't going away, and I would feel even less like it in the morning. Plus, left overnight, the blood would dry and be twice as hard to remove.

I knuckled down to the skivvying and mopped and wiped until all traces had been obliterated. But a bath sheet left a lot to be desired in the keeping-warm stakes. If I got cold, the body would stiffen up in retaliation. With the Rayburn now pristine, I slid the kettle on to the hotplate, brewed up a mug of tea and filled a hot water bottle. Then, making sure the back door was securely locked, chained and bolted against any further unwelcome midnight callers, I took myself off to bed. Only one thing I needed now: sleep – nature's great healer.

'Caxton speaking.' The solicitor answered, my call having been transferred from the receptionist. It was dead on nine o'clock.

'Harry Radcliffe, Mr Caxton. You approached me yesterday at John Dunston's funeral.'

'Ah . . . yes. What can I do for you?'

'You gave me a letter from Mr Dunston.'

'Yes?'

He wasn't going to make this easy. 'It wasn't the only thing Mr Dunston left with you, was it? I understand there's a parcel awaiting my collection.'

'That is correct.'

'Could I ask you to post it to me, please?'

'Oh, no, I'm afraid that's not possible. We're bound by legal restraints and require a signature before relinquishing the . . . er . . . article.'

'I rather thought that might be the case. Do you know *what* it is?'

'I'm afraid not. Mr Dunston didn't disclose any details whatsoever.'

I thought quickly. My last race was at three thirty. Caxton's offices were in York. It was going to be tight.

'What time do you close this evening?'

'Five thirty.'

'If I call around five, could I sign and pick up the parcel then, please?'

'Certainly. I'll ask my PA to have everything ready for you.'

'Thank you very much. I'll see you this afternoon.'

I put the phone down and swore forcibly. Bloody red tape. Now I was facing a long journey to and from York after a full day's racing. In normal circumstances, it wouldn't bother me, but I was most definitely feeling the effects of yesterday's beating, and driving up north after punching out five races wasn't going to encourage swift healing.

I made a strong coffee and took it up to the bathroom and repeated last night's hot soak.

*   *   *

I arrived at Mike's stable yard just before ten o'clock.

His eyes widened. 'What does the other guy look like?'

'Two actually. One's OK. The other is going to need crutches to get to the bogs.'

'Unwelcome callers late at night, I take it?'

'You take it right.'

'What were they after?'

'The letter John Dunston instructed his solicitor to pass on to me at the funeral.'

'Ah, yes. You mentioned it was . . . volatile?'

'Too right. John's death wasn't prompted by grief or depression; he was murdered.'

'Good God!' Mike's eyebrows shot up.

'Hmm, and he stated that Frank's death in prison was also murder. According to John, his son was killed by a nail piercing the eyeball, and that little gem wasn't given out by the authorities, so it's not common knowledge.'

'And the other man that died – what happened to him?'

'Seems he sustained a head injury that saw him carted off to hospital and he passed away there.'

He rubbed a hand over his mouth. 'Open to any amount of interpretation.'

'Yeah.'

'Did the two callers have time to find the letter, after working you over?'

I gave a sideways grin; it hurt too much to laugh properly. 'No. Foxed them there. And if I die before I tell anybody where it is, chances are it won't ever be found.'

'You devious sod.'

'Thanks. I love you, too.'

'So? Give. Where have you hidden it?'

I shook my head slowly. 'Safer if I don't, Mike.'

'They're unlikely to come after *me*.'

'It's not the only hot property. Afraid I've got to shoot off straight after the last race this afternoon. Got to go and see John's solicitor up in York. Bloody nuisance, but nothing I can do about it.'

'You're driving yourself to the races, then?'

'Yes. That way when I've collected whatever it is, I can drive straight home.'

'OK.' He nodded. 'Let's get started. I'll take my car as well, seeing we've got three runners consec.'

I was riding in the one o'clock, one thirty and two o'clock, and apart from the travelling head lad who'd be driving the horsebox, two other stable lads were needed. There wouldn't be room in the horsebox for Mike.

Fifteen minutes later, we all left in convoy, Mike leading the way down the A46 and the horsebox following my car.

Reaching Leicester racecourse, I pulled into the jockeys' car park and took the Mazda round and parked conveniently close to the exit. Getting stuck in the crush at the end of racing would seriously foul up the job I had to do in York.

After dropping off my gear in the weighing room, I wandered through the high-spirited racegoers in search of a sugarless black coffee in the bar. No calories to ingest there. The air was rich not only with the eager, expectant atmosphere of the racecourse, but also with the vying aromas of hot dogs, fried onions, fish and chips, curry and jacket potatoes . . . I indulged to the extent of lifting my nose, breathing in the tantalizing smells, and blessed the fact I could enjoy them without taking in a single calorie.

'Hello, Bisto Kid.'

I spun round. Smiling at me was a lady trainer I'd not seen since the last party Mike had given. Her hair caught back in the nape of her neck by a tortoiseshell slide, and dressed to kill in a striking red, black and cream, checked winter coat topped off by scarlet beret set at a pert angle, was Tal Hunter.

'Hi.' I laughed. 'Yes, sniffing the air – you know how it is.'

'Oh, yes,' she said with feeling, 'I know how it *was.*'

We both laughed.

Tally had been an extremely talented and successful jump jockey in her youth. Not old now, she was around forty, I suppose. It was so difficult to tell with women. Especially when they'd been careful not to put on weight. Her figure now – what I could make out beneath the snow-busting coat – seemed exactly the same as it always had been: reed slender.

'See you're running Dark Delight in the two thirty. She's looking on her toes.'

'Hmm, want to get a race in. If the forecast is right for next week, racing will be called off.'

'Must say you're also looking well-turned-out.'

'Oh, my coat, you mean?'

'Hmm, very smart.'

'I bought it last winter to go to Switzerland. Now there's a place that's cold, my word.'

'Go on holiday?'

'No, no, I went with two or three other trainers who had horses running. I'd just got the one – this one that's running today.'

'I bet it proved interesting.'

'You bet! A marvellous experience. I took Gerard Faulkes as jockey. He really rated it. We didn't come in the frame, just midfield, but it was wonderful to watch.'

'Racing on snow, eh?'

'Yes.' She smiled. 'And not only on horseback either. Gerard has some guts. Even had a go at the skijoring.'

'I don't know what's involved, but from the little I have heard, it sounds pretty scary. Wearing skis and being pulled along by horses.'

'Yes. I think the word for it would be "exhilarating". Gerard was high as a kite when he finished the race. Didn't win, of course, but it's really some experience.'

'Did *you* try it?'

'Me?' Her eyes widened in mock shock. 'Good God, no. I'm much too much of a coward.'

'Give over,' I said. 'Your nerves are made of tungsten – probably titanium.'

'Nonsense.' She patted my shoulder. 'Must go, Harry, racing calls.'

'True enough. Take care, Tally.'

'I'd say the same to you but seems I'm too late.' She raised an index finger in the direction of my swollen, purple nose. 'Doing a Philip Marlow again?'

'Something like that,' I agreed ruefully. 'Bye, Tally.'

She went off towards the racing stables. I followed my nose through the delightful smells, went into the bar and settled for a caffeine boost of black coffee.

SIX

D ressed in green-and-purple silks, Samuel Simpson's racing colours, I crossed to the parade ring with the ten other jockeys. I spotted Mike, together with Samuel and Chloe, standing beside White Lace in the centre of the ring.

The welcoming smile on Chloe's face faded rapidly as she saw the state of my face. 'Harry! What happened to you?'

I flicked a glance at Samuel, who read it correctly.

'Not now, my dear,' he said to his daughter. 'Harry's got to ride. He needs to be fully fit.'

'Oh.' She bit her lower lip. 'Yes, of course, I see.'

'I *am* fully fit; don't worry about it.'

Her beautiful smile reasserted itself. 'And are we going to come first?'

'Certainly give it my best.'

'I know that, lad. The day you don't try will be the day they nail down the coffin, eh?'

'You could have phrased it differently, Samuel, but thanks again for the confidence.'

'We're definitely going home with the prize money.' Mike rubbed his hands together and beamed jovially.

The familiar 'Jockeys please mount' was called and he flipped me up into the saddle. White Lace swung her quarters round, tossing her head. I could feel the keenness to race running through her body and took both feet out of the irons and rode long a couple of times round the parade ring. She had a real eagerness to run which was very much a plus factor in her temperament, but I needed to settle her down so that she didn't use up precious nervous energy before the start of the race. Darren, the stable lad leading her round, looked up at me and grinned.

'Keen, ain't she?'

'Sure is. Have you had a bit on?'

He nodded. 'Reckon most of the lads have.'

'Have to see what I can do, then.'

'You'll win,' he said decisively and patted the grey mare's neck, reinforcing his words. I remembered Mike had said Chloe had put her entire wardrobe on as well. I'd most definitely have to win.

Darren led us through out on to the course and I eased White Lace into a collected canter down to the far-distant starter with his tape. We all circled round, getting into line, only to have one or two break away again. But finally, although somewhat raggedly, the starter was satisfied with the placing and the tape flew up.

It was a two-mile race over hurdles and I held the mare back in second-to-last place. Predictably, Port Wine took the lead in a flat-out gallop. He was a noted front runner, but I knew he couldn't maintain that blistering pace and was certain to fall back at some point. Three other horses were hugging his heels, but the rest of the field was strung out by the time we'd finished the first circuit of the course. I began to urge White Lace on and we moved up into midfield. Port Wine was losing ground now as his jockey gave him a breather, but how much he'd got left in the tank was debatable. I knew my mare had plenty in hand and I continued to urge her to make up ground. We passed another five, her ground-covering strides fluid and her jumping judged to perfection. It was a real pleasure to ride her.

Three hurdles from home, the three horses in front jumped as one, but Port Wine misjudged his landing, pecked badly, couldn't recover in time and came crashing down heavily, sending his jockey, Dickie Flynn, flying over his head. It was a bad fall and I doubted Dickie would be walking back to the weighing room. It had all the hallmarks of an ambulance job. The other two horses were thrown off course as they tried to avoid the flailing hooves of the fallen horse and both lost ground.

I booted White Lace on. She sailed over the hurdle with lengths to spare and we went smoothly into the lead. Her ears pricked with anticipation, she stretched for home and I gave her all the encouragement she needed. A swift look back told me we were about five lengths' clear of the rest of the pack. But Mailbox was putting in a challenge now, his jockey working hard, pushing the head off him. I judged the moment and gave White Lace just one smack of the whip and she found another gear. We flew past the post, a clear winner by two lengths.

Chloe's wardrobe was safe, the stable lads' wages enhanced nicely.

I eased the mare down to a walk, leaned forward and told her what a great girl she was, pulled her ear and slapped her steaming neck. She was a beautiful ride and I was very satisfied with her performance.

Darren led us into the number-one spot in the winners' enclosure where a euphoric Chloe was waiting. Her smile was as wide as the Trent. Mike took hold of the bridle.

'Told you it would be a walkover.' His smile matched Chloe's.

'By God, lad. Don't even *think* about retiring,' Samuel said. 'Can't do without you.'

Then he slapped me hard on the back by way of thanks and encouragement. Unfortunately, his hand caught the side of my ribs and I had to clamp my jaws together to avoid yelping aloud in pain. The need to prevent advertising my true state of health was paramount.

Mike, realizing, instantly bent towards me, blocking everyone's line of vision, and motioned me to undo the girths. I did, but it was less about doing what was necessary and more about leaning against White Lace's body while the wave of pain subsided.

And I couldn't spare more than a few seconds' respite; I had to take the saddle to the weighing room to weigh in and get ready for the next race that was due off in about fifteen minutes. It was most definitely a case of being professional and overriding my feelings and just getting on with the job. I simply couldn't afford to show any vulnerability. But I'd just won the first of my five races – that was a very good feeling. I concentrated on that fact, knowing it wasn't only me who would benefit from the win.

In racing, it was never a case of 'I've won'. Behind all the successful jockeys was a loyal, grafting team of workers who made success possible. Judging by the pinkness of Darren's ears, as he sought to suppress his exultation, he – and no doubt all the other stable lads – had benefited considerably. And I was very pleased for them.

I won the next race and, unbelievably, the third of my rides for Mike. It was turning out to be one of those racing days that were usually only a jockey's daydream.

And I still had two further races booked. Both were for the trainer, Clive Unwin. As I came out with the rest of the jockeys for the three o'clock race, Clive waved me over to where he was waiting in the parade ring with the owner of Gunshot, an iron-grey gelding that was giving his stable lad a hard time. I could quite appreciate why: when they'd tacked him up, they'd thought it necessary to put a Chifney on him. Snatching his head up and down and trying to put in bucks, he was obviously very well, and I was in for a taxing ride – the other horses were being kept well clear by their own lads.

I touched the peak of my cap to his owner, and Clive proceeded to give me instructions on how he wanted the race run. I listened dutifully and decided to make up my own mind once I was on board.

'Full of beans, isn't he?' his doting owner said, smiling. 'Or should I say full of oats?'

I smiled and nodded and kept my own counsel. From what I could see of Gunshot, I might end the race thinking he should live up to his name and take a quick exit.

He proved a battler from the off and set his jaw at an aggressive angle. With reins bridged, we proceeded down to the start with Gunshot cantering sideways, head to the rails, and me sawing at the reins to try to stop him from bolting. We were both in a lather of sweat by the time we joined the other horses circling for the start.

As the tape went up, so did Gunshot, in an impressive rear, front hooves thrashing the air. With the horse all but vertical, I was left hanging on to his mane, trying desperately to keep my weight over his withers. If he went over backwards, he would take me with him and I'd most likely be crushed underneath. Crashing down on to all four plates, to my immense relief he took off after the other horses that were now several lengths in front.

At seventeen hands, he was a massive horse and had the strength to match. Even wearing a Chifney bit, he was proving a major handful. The more I tried to settle him down, the more he wound himself up.

Galloping at a manic pace, he closed the gap, swept past several of the horses at the back of the pack and proceeded to clear the hurdles with air to spare. At this stage, I was little more than a passenger, simply steering.

There had been eight horses in front when he'd landed back on to all four racing plates. Now, only two remained in front. But with the amount of energy he'd already expended, the question was could his fiery spirit continue to propel him as far as the winning post? I'd thought the race was blown well before the halfway mark and was waiting for the ineluctable dropping back when his petrol gauge hit empty.

We came upsides the next horse, Turnpike, ridden by Jamie Furlough. He jerked his head towards me.

'On bloody rocket fuel?' he yelled.

I didn't answer, just shook my head and waited for the inevitable.

It didn't happen. Whatever was stoking Gunshot's boiler – rocket fuel or sheer guts – it saw him clear the last hurdle cleanly, if not with air to spare now, almost as though the horse himself knew what the gauge was reading. I'm damned if I did. It was a magnificent performance he was putting on.

All that remained now was to see off Butterdrop, the one horse still in front. And Gunshot made it his mission in life. I hadn't slapped, booted or even used my hands up to now. I hadn't needed to – the big-hearted horse had done the lot. His will to win was infectious. I simply threw the reins forward and shouted encouragement.

Butterdrop had now started to hang to the left – a sure sign of a tired horse – and I knew the race was Gunshot's if he could keep up the pace. I yelled encouragement and flung the reins forward, and we came upsides. Two more strides with both horses straining for supremacy, and then Gunshot was in front. Stretching his neck forward, living up to his name, he shot across the finishing line.

The applause rippling up from the stands and then from around the winners' enclosure was very sweet. I'd thought he had no chance. But Gunshot had proved me wrong. Inside the winners' enclosure in the number-one spot, I slid off his back and slapped his sweating neck, almost enveloped in the steam coming up off him. Other hands reached forward to take hold of his bridle, pat his neck, pull his ears. He tossed his head up and down proudly, well aware of his victory and accepting all the accolades.

'Well done!' Clive was smiling broadly. 'What a race, Harry.'

I nodded, too breathless to make conversation. It had been an incredible race. From certain disaster to overwhelming victory, the horse took all the credit.

I undid the buckles and pulled the saddle off, allowing even more clouds of steam to rise, the smell of hot horseflesh like perfume to my nostrils. I was living my dream. It was all I'd ever wanted: to be a successful jockey. Not many people could say they were living *their* dream. I was a very lucky man. And I knew it, acknowledged it and offered up thanks and gratitude. It was something I did, almost like a mantra, after every win.

And this win now made it four rides – four wins. However, Sod's law wasn't going to lie down and die. I ended the last of my five races second to last. I was sorry for the disgruntled owner of the horse, but losing didn't diminish my pleasure. It had been a great day's racing. And throughout the whole afternoon, I hadn't given a single thought to yesterday's beating. In the white-heat concentration of riding and winning, I hadn't experienced any pain, barring the moment Samuel slapped me.

But as I trotted across to the jockeys' car park to collect my car, the body's woes came back in full force. I unlocked the Mazda's boot and stashed my saddle and gear, then slid into the driver's seat and reached for a bottle of mineral water. Popping open the dash compartment, I took out three painkillers and washed them down gratefully. Pity I couldn't simply drive home to a hot soothing bath and bed, but duty called and I had to face the drag of a drive up to York.

I reached on to the back seat and dragged up a thick fleece. The car had sat here for hours and was well cold. Switching on the engine, I turned the heater to full. It wouldn't do to get chilled, especially after the rigours of the afternoon that had seen me so hot I'd sweated pints. The last thing I wanted was for my bruised body to start stiffening up.

I found myself thinking it was a pity I hadn't got a hip flask of whisky to hand, like Mousey Brown, to warm me up and keep me going. But then again perhaps it wasn't a pity but a blessing, because I would surely have downed some right now.

I turned out of the racecourse car park and headed north up the A46 before branching off on to the A1. Despite the fleece and the car heater going full blast, it wasn't until I took the A64 heading for York that I began to feel a bit warmer and more comfortable as the three painkillers kicked in and began to do their job. It was a good thing I'd packed them in the dash before leaving home. The pain level had zoomed up the scale after the afternoon's exertion.

But I didn't regret a single moment.

Winning four races was a very satisfactory tally and would send me further up the Championship stakes. Whether I stood any chance of retaining the title was an unknown.

I'd lost so much time, so many race opportunities this year, it was a massive ask. But if I was stripped of the title in April, I couldn't complain.

I knew those things I'd done, had had to do, were the cause of losing my chance to have a fair crack at winning, but I would do them again, no question, to keep the people I loved safe from harm.

Reaching the city of York, I found a multi-storey car park and then walked to the solicitor's offices. It took me much longer than I'd estimated and it was well after five o'clock when I finally found the office, but there were still lights on in the impressive building. I went up the steps to the heavy wooden door and into the reception area.

'Harry Radcliffe. I'm here to collect the parcel Mr Caxton has been holding for Mr John Dunston.'

'Oh, yes. Just one moment.'

The receptionist reached into a drawer and handed me some paperwork to sign. 'We were expecting you. It's typed ready for your signature.'

I signed it and gave it back to her.

'This is the parcel. There's only the one.'

It was about the size of a small shoebox. Wrapped in brown paper and with about half a yard of sticky tape holding it firmly in place, John had obviously not wanted it to come undone before it reached me. On the top, in large black letters, he had written: *PRIVATE. NOT TO BE UNDONE EXCEPT BY MR HARRY RADCLIFFE.*

SEVEN

The car tyres crunched over the yielding gravel as I reached home. Parking near the cottage door, I heard the telephone ringing as I slid the key into the lock. Opening the back door, I was met by an unfriendly glare. Leo, looking like a ginger bolster – he was certainly too big to be described as a pillow – lay curled in his basket on the worktop above the Rayburn. One green eye was open the merest slit. The wall-mounted landline was sited a couple of feet above his head.

His tail flicked in annoyance.

'Shame,' I said, ruffling the fur between his ears. 'Dreaming of lady cats, were you?' I reached for the offending phone. He glowered at me before burrowing deeper into his basket. The eye closed and a 'do not disturb sign' was put firmly in place. Fair enough; he had been out all the previous night entertaining the local queens.

With my free hand – the other one was clutching Dunston's box – I lifted the receiver to my ear. Before I could answer, I heard Annabel's voice. Her tone was high-pitched, taut. Something was wrong.

'Annabel, what's the matter?'

'Oh, Harry, thank goodness. I've been wanting to ring for hours but I knew you were racing.' Her words were tumbling over themselves.

'Steady, girl, just tell me what's happened. Is it Jeffrey?'

Although Annabel was still officially married to me, we had been living apart for nearly three years. Sir Jeffrey was the partner she had chosen to spend her life with when she left me. Leo's green eyes had nothing on mine – I was extremely jealous of Jeffrey. I wasn't jealous because of his title or his considerable wealth and position, but simply because Annabel was no longer in my life – she was in his. Yes, I was jealous, or had been, until his accident. How could you remain jealous of a man who was now bound to a wheelchair?

'No. No, it's not Jeffrey. Well, he hasn't been taken ill. But I am very concerned *for* him.'

'Why?'

'Oh God, Harry, he's been threatened. He doesn't know. I've kept it from him, but I need your help. I . . . I don't know what to do . . .'

I felt a cold clutch at my guts. I'd been on the receiving end of threats several times in the last year, but that was one thing – Annabel receiving threats was a different ball game. And to threaten a man who, for the most part, was paralysed and helpless, was beyond comprehension.

My feelings towards Jeffrey were ambiguous. On one level, I wished him anywhere but sharing Annabel's bed, and yet the irony of it was that I liked Jeffrey. He was an extremely likeable chap with a dry humour and, despite the bizarre situation, we had become friends. We were both united in our love for Annabel and the wish to look after her.

And since his horrific accident – indeed, after he'd come round from the anaesthetic following his operation – he'd made me promise to look after her until he could. Even as I stood beside his hospital bed and assured him he could rely on me, we both knew he would, in all probability, never get better.

The reason Annabel had left me wasn't because she'd stopped loving me, it was because of my obsession. No way to get round it: racing was an obsession. Plus my flat refusal to give up riding and get a safe job. Not one where every eight or ten rides I would get pitched off half a ton of straining horseflesh at around thirty miles an hour, with the accompanying risk of getting kicked by the other horses coming from behind. It was rare to find my body bruise-free; mostly it didn't happen. To me, it was the price I willingly paid to be a jump jockey.

But I could see how it affected her. If it had simply been bruises, I dare say Annabel could have gone along with my lifestyle, but the days came, with frightening regularity, when I didn't get to walk back down the racecourse and was taken off by ambulance to hospital. Danger was always present; it was really a question of accepting the degree on each day. *That* was what had driven Annabel away – she simply couldn't bear seeing me suffer.

And I was damned if I was going to allow anybody to make *her* suffer. Although she was with Jeffrey, I still felt protective of her – always would.

'Can you come over?'

There was fear in her voice and my anger began a slow burn against whoever was putting pressure on her.

'I'm on my way. You stay with Jeffrey and I'll see you both in about twenty minutes, OK?'

'Thank you, darling.' The relief was obvious. Whether I could sort it out and maintain that relief when I saw her, however, was an unknown.

I put the phone down and realized that I was still clutching the cardboard box. No time now to start undoing the wrapping to discover what John Dunston had entrusted to me. Nor could I leave it unguarded. The letter had cast-iron security up in the bathroom, but where should I hide this new unexploded bomb?

Briefly, I toyed with the idea of burying it in the garden – surely the safest place. But there was no time for such activities with Jeffrey under threat. Eventually, I decided it would be safer, temporarily, in one of the brick outbuildings rather than in the cottage itself.

I picked up a torch and pair of scissors and took the box into the store shed. It was half full of the usual paraphernalia that tends to accumulate: lawnmower, wheelbarrow, a wall hung with garden implements and yard brushes – and a big new bag of cat litter.

I tugged the bag into the middle of the floor, slit the top of the plastic and thrust the box down nearly to the bottom. The absorbent granules shifted and settled around the box. I folded down the top of the bag and forced it out of sight under the workbench. It was the best I could do. I doubted anybody would find it there tonight. In the morning, I'd find a suitable spot in the garden and bury it deep.

After I'd opened it and seen just what it contained.

A full moon lit up the Leicestershire countryside as I drove fast along narrow country lanes, silver frost glistening on each blade of grass and leaf. Passing one five-barred gate, a fox shot across in front of the Mazda, escaping being flattened by a fraction of a second. His white-tipped brush whisked away to safety into the dyke on the far side. The frosty night was probably increasing his gnawing hunger and forcing him out hunting. I wished him well and was glad I'd not smashed into his russet body. Life was an ongoing battle – and a gamble – for every living thing on this earth.

Twenty minutes saw me approaching the entrance gates that heralded the start of the long tree-lined drive leading to Annabel's home. A magnificent listed mansion, complete with scrambling Virginia creeper and tall chimneys, I had been a visitor here on quite a few occasions.

The last time was as a recovering patient just discharged from the Queen's Hospital in Nottingham. The three of us had had dinner – Jeffrey, Annabel and me. Annabel herself had just been discharged from the same hospital, albeit, in her case, from the maternity unit. We had been considerably fortunate to escape with our lives at the hand of a knife-wielding killer. Jeffrey had, solicitously, waited on us, and was overwhelmingly grateful and relieved that we were alive and able to enjoy a meal together. He'd played a significant part in our rescue. It was situations such as this that had bonded the three of us as an unlikely triumvirate.

Thinking about his toss-away quip about if there was a third case that had had us all laughing as I was taking my leave that night, I was swamped with pity for him as he was now. Humour would be hard won right at this moment. But he wouldn't want pity. I forced the feeling down. It would be bloody selfish of me to show any sign of it in front of him. He had the battle of his life on right now, and pity was lowering – he could do without it.

I swung the car around in a tight circle in front of the house. Lights blazed out into the night from a great many windows. Annabel's defiance against whoever, whatever, might be circling outside? Out here in the sticks, north of Melton Mowbray, there were no streetlights to pollute and the blackness was absolute.

She had been watching for my arrival and came rushing out down the steps to meet me, tugging open the driver's door.

'Thanks for coming, Harry.'

I stepped out of the car and her arms were around me, holding on tightly. I hugged her back.

'It's OK, I'm here. If I can help, I will.'

'I'm scared, really scared. Jeffrey's so vulnerable, so helpless. He's only been home just over a week. I think he feels . . . fragile, you know? While he was in hospital, all he could talk about was coming home – he couldn't wait. Now,' she spread her hand, adding, 'it would have felt very safe in hospital. Doctors and nurses on tap twenty-four hours a day in case anything went wrong. Whereas, here at home . . .'

'Here at home Jeffrey has you, Annabel. That's enough to reassure him, surely.'

'I'm not a doctor, Harry.'

'If he needed the constant attention of a doctor, they wouldn't have sent him home.'

'No, no, I suppose not.'

'Anyway, let's get inside; it's too cold to stand out here.'

'Wait.' She grabbed my arm. 'I have to tell you about the threat. It was a phone call, made to the landline.'

'When?'

'This afternoon, around three o'clock. I've written down as much of what he said as I can remember.'

I nodded. 'Show me.'

She took me into the kitchen and pulled out the cutlery drawer. 'Jeffrey wouldn't find it in here.' She passed me a small sheet of paper torn from a pad. Running fingers through her long blonde hair in agitation, she waited while I read the short message.

If you don't want to see your posh bloke in a coffin instead of a wheelchair, get Harry to hand over the letter. I'll ring tomorrow for the where and when.

I raised my gaze and met her anxiety-filled eyes.

'Well?' she demanded.

'Nasty.' I shook my head. 'Did he give a name?'

'No.'

'OK. Two things come to mind. Does Jeffrey have nursing assistance?'

'Yes, twice a day – getting up, putting to bed at night.'

'Right. You need to hire a full-time nurse. I think you'll find if he's feeling insecure, having a nurse in the house will shore up his confidence and he won't kick against it.'

She nodded. 'Yes, makes sense. And what's the second thing?'

'When this piece of pond life rings again, you tell him where to meet me and at what time.'

'Harry.' Her blue eyes were deeply troubled. 'He could try to kill you.'

'Yes,' I agreed, 'he could. But forewarned and all that, I think he'll find it a much more difficult job than finishing off poor old Jeffrey.'

'Oh God, you're so flippant.'

'Come here . . .' I reached for her and pulled her close, running my hands up and down her back comfortingly, feeling her shoulders shaking as she tried not to break down and cry. 'This is not your problem, Annabel. You've just got caught up in the crossfire.'

'Again.' Her one word came out muffled.

'Let me handle it, OK?'

She nodded, her face still pressed close to my chest.

'Now, let's go find Jeffrey, cheer him up a bit. And you can make us all a coffee or something. Then, while you're doing that, you can source the number of a nursing agency and arrange immediate help.'

She drew away from me and rubbed her eyes with a tissue.

'You've got until tomorrow before this man rings again, so you and Jeffrey are both safe tonight, right?'

She gulped and nodded. 'Yes, of course we are. I'm being silly.'

She drew her shoulders back. 'Thanks, Harry. You can always get me back on course.'

'Like all the times you've done that for me.'

We stood and gazed at each other, and the depth of our feelings was practically tangible. Had been from the first minute we met. However, we both knew where the line was drawn. And with the condition Jeffrey was now in, that line was dug deep in concrete.

Then she frowned. 'Your face . . . I thought earlier you must have come off. But he's already had a go at you, hasn't he?'

'Yes.'

'If you didn't give it to him then, what are you going to do now?'

'I'll think of something. Come on, let's find Jeffrey.'

'Don't breathe a word about the threat, please.'

'I promise. He needs complete peace of mind right now.'

'He'll be pleased to see you.'

She led me up the broad staircase and along the galleried landing.

We found him in bed. The nurse had obviously been this evening and he was comfortable for the night. His back rest was at an incline, propping him up, and the television was tuned in low to an episode of *Lewis*.

His eyes lit up when we entered the bedroom.

'Good to see you, Jeffrey.' I gripped his hand. 'Bet you're glad to be home.'

'I am.'

Annabel bent and kissed his cheek. 'I'm going to make Harry a coffee. Do you need anything?'

'No, I'm fine.'

'Leave you two boys together, then.' She smiled brightly at us and pulled the door closed behind her.

'Busy, Harry?'

I nodded and sat down beside his bed. 'Had a great day – four winners.'

'Any chance of retaining it?'

I laughed. 'Can't say. I'm way behind at the moment. Most likely it will be injuries that sort us all out.'

'Strange. Driving a motor car can have just the same effect as being a jump jockey. Luck of the draw, Harry.'

'I'm so sorry, Jeffrey.'

'Don't be. All my life I've done what I've wanted and enjoyed it. The scales are balancing all the good years.'

'What does the specialist say?'

'The prognosis is far better than they thought at first. I'm in the hands of the physio now. And we're making a bit of progress. How much improvement is up to me and how the body responds. But yes, not so bleak as was originally thought.'

'That's wonderful news.'

'And, of course, Annabel is giving me healing every day.'

'And we both know the X factor involved there. Without Annabel sending me absent healing when I was grounded in hospital, I doubt I would have healed as I did.'

Annabel had studied for nearly three years on top of being a qualified psychotherapist and was now also a spiritual healer.

The door opened and she came in with a tray and two coffees.

I stood up and took one from her. I didn't need to ask if she'd put in a spoonful of honey; she knew my preferences. 'Thanks.'

'I've arranged a bit of help, Jeffrey, darling. I hope you think it a good idea.'

'What sort of help?'

'Well, really for me. I've engaged a nurse to live in for a little while. It will free me up a bit.'

He studied her face. 'I'm sure you need a hand looking after me. I think it's a most sensible idea. Let you get a bit of rest . . .' He smiled fondly at her.

Annabel flushed a little and took a sip of coffee.

Her words didn't fool me: she was feeling as guilty as hell telling a white lie, but it had had the required effect. Jeffrey wasn't objecting, plus he was getting an additional bodyguard.

Even though he didn't know it.

EIGHT

Six thirty in the morning and bone-chillingly cold. The horses' deep snorts threw out clouds of white vapour as their stable lads sat hunched in saddles preparing to leave Mike's stable yard for the all-weather gallop.

The frost had really come down last night. I had intended to unearth Dunston's box when I got back to Harlequin Cottage. But I was pretty sure there would be no midnight callers. Having fired a broadside at Sir Jeffrey, it was now a waiting game.

An additional safeguard was that the opposition had no idea about the parcel. The letter, yes; they'd certainly seen it handed over to me. But unless John had told anyone else, only his solicitor and I were aware of another item. So with that reassuring thought, coupled with the earth in the back garden hard as the bisecting concrete path, I'd held off getting out the spade.

Joe, the head lad, gave the signal for the string of racehorses to pull out. I squeezed Penny Black's sides and kicked him on, following the others out on to the road leading up to the gallops a quarter of a mile ahead. In company with the other lads, I was cold right now, the icy wind cutting my face in two, making my nose drip, but by the time we had put in a half-speed gallop, we would be sweating.

Above us, a flock of seagulls wheeled in great circles, mewling to the wide grey sky. Snowbirds, Annabel called them, saying it was a sign of bad weather that fetched them so many miles inland from the coast. She could well be right. If the weather forecast turned out to be correct, we were in for some sub-zero temperatures and considerable falls of snow soon. All racing would be off.

Tally Hunter's words came back to me. Ironically, it was only when temperatures plummeted in Switzerland and the lakes at Arosa and St Moritz froze over that racing could take place on the snow.

Meanwhile, the horses filed through the opening on to the gallops and circled while Mike, who had driven up from the stables in his four-by-four and was now struggling with the driver's door in the strengthening wind, issued his instructions. I'd had no chance yet to tell him about the threat to Sir Jeffrey. He would be horrified.

But I needed his input on the delicate matter of the proposed handing over of the letter. It would have to be broached after breakfast because later I was racing at Huntingdon.

The horses moved off into a loosening, warming canter prior to doing some work, and Mike lifted binoculars and watched with intense concentration. I was only riding first lot today because I had to be away smartly after breakfast for my drive to Huntingdon racecourse.

Mike would be charting the progress of his horses in the second and third lots, too. It was essential to know the potential of each horse in order for him to decide on the right races for each, and rather like a class of youngsters in school, their abilities were not uniform. In addition, I knew that he was expecting two or three owners to turn up to watch their expensive investments going through their training schedule.

Owners were the essential element in racing. Without their involvement and regular payments for the care and training of the horses, racing would come to a full stop. And, as such, they were given respect, deference and, in some cases, downright pandering to smooth the unpleasant fact that they were pursuing a dream and any possible wins would in no way cover the substantial costs of owning a racehorse.

Of course, the cash outlay was offset by the joy and jubilation they would feel when standing in the winners' enclosure if their horse did actually win. Something that money could not buy. Plus, there was always the hope that their horse might just prove to be the next Frankel. Slim to non-existent, but there all the same.

Penny Black, Lord Edgware's horse, was warmed up and eager. I shortened the reins in company with Josh on Floribunda and we moved smoothly into an upsides gallop. The dusty kickback from the all-weather topping flew up from beneath the blur of hooves that pounded in a satisfying thud, thud, of raw power. The icy wind cut into my cheeks, but the goggles prevented my eyes from watering or being blinded by the cloud of disturbed dust.

The seagulls lifted in an alarmed screaming cloud of white and powered away on strong wings, outlined sharply against the clear winter sky. We galloped up the all-weather, chasing their progress in the air above us. The creak of oiled leather and smell of steaming hot horseflesh were all part of the exhilaration and feeling of freedom.

I spared a thought for all the suited and booted office workers who would soon be streaming into towns and cities for a desk-and-chair job. And gave thanks that my personal seat was a saddle. I might have felt cold on the trot-up from the stables, but by the time I reined in Penny Black I felt the trickle of sweat run down between my shoulder blades.

All the horses, having completed their gallops, were being

circled at a walk, and Mike was waving the string back to the stables. He drove away and we formed a line and began the hack back to the stables at a sedate walk to allow the horses to cool down from their exertions. It not only gave the horses time, but it allowed me to run through the plan that had been forming in my mind about what the hell I was going to do.

I had to hand over Dunston's letter to safeguard Sir Jeffrey, and yet John Dunston had gone to a heck of a lot of trouble to ensure that nobody but me saw its contents. Having taken a beating to protect John's message, it would be stupid to meekly hand the letter over on demand. But what to do was a problem. I had to ring Annabel before I left for Huntingdon. The man, when he rang her later today, was expecting to be told a time and place. I couldn't risk leaving it until after racing because I might not make it back. Not an overdramatic thought. Last March I'd gone racing at Huntingdon and awoken in hospital. I hadn't made it back home for quite some time.

The string clattered back into the stable yard and split up as the lads dismounted and led their horses to individual stables. I took Penny Black back to his and untacked. Once he was rubbed down, rugged up and pulling at his hay net, I went back to Mike's house for breakfast myself.

'Hello, Harry. Scrambled eggs suit?' Pen, Mike's partner, smiled a greeting.

'That'd be great, thanks.'

She poured me a mug of coffee, pushed the jar of honey towards me and slid a further piece of bread into the toaster.

I stirred my coffee and debated whether to tell Mike about the threat to Sir Jeffrey in front of Pen. But she pre-empted me.

'How's Annabel coping, Harry? Is her new partner out of hospital yet?'

'Yes, came home about ten days ago.'

'What's the prognosis?' Mike queried. 'He was in a dire state after the crash.'

'Actually, Annabel telephoned to ask if I'd go over last night. I spoke to Jeffrey. He's surprisingly well, spirit-wise.'

'And otherwise?' Mike raised an eyebrow.

I gulped coffee and nodded. 'Seems the injury isn't half as severe as was originally feared. He's doing well on physio and improving all the time.'

'Is Annabel giving him spiritual healing? Could that be what's making the difference?'

I smiled at Pen. 'It most certainly makes a difference. I know. I've been on the receiving end myself. It's powerful stuff – can even start bones fusing. That's why, when I was in hospital, Annabel had to ask the ward manager for permission, and to check if my bones had been set before she gave me some healing.'

'Wow!' Pen looked impressed. 'A good job he's got her on tap, then.'

An unwelcome but familiar wave of jealousy swept over me. The feeling wasn't wanted, was enervating and uncomfortable, but it couldn't be denied. It was a familiar reminder that I was still hopelessly in love with Annabel, probably would be for the rest of my life. And there wasn't a thing I could do about it.

But from the moment of the accident, it had placed her in a very different situation. Not only was she Jeffrey's live-in lover, but she was now his carer as well. It put her totally beyond my reach, if indeed she would ever have succumbed and returned to me.

'Yes, it's fortunate for Jeffrey she's qualified.' I gritted my teeth as I said it, knew what I needed was a good kick up the backside to restart my private life, get myself a new woman. And I remembered that when I came back from Huntingdon in the evening, I'd arranged to take Georgia out for a meal at the Dirty Duck at Woolsthorpe. It would only be our third meeting, but maybe I should kick on with Georgia. In no way did I want to use her, but perhaps it was the way to get over Annabel.

'More coffee, Harry?' Pen's enquiry broke into my thoughts.

'No, thanks, not for me.' I pushed my chair back. 'Have to get moving.'

Then I remembered I'd not filled Mike in about the threat and the demand for Dunston's letter. But Mike, also through with breakfast, was now on his way to the door. We went out together.

'Mike, got a sec?'

'Hmm . . .'

'Didn't really want to say anything in front of Pen.'

He nodded – and waited. It flitted across my mind that by now, having involved him so much in the past – mostly dangerous stuff – he was braced to hear just about anything. Predictably, he blew a gasket about Jeffrey being promised a coffin if I didn't comply.

'Look here, Harry, John Dunston's dead. OK. I'm sorry, really extremely sorry, but he's beyond further harm. Sir Jeffrey is a wheelchair-bound shoo-in for uncontested violence. He would be totally unable to defend himself. I think you should just hand the blasted letter over and be done with it.'

I'd been going to mention the box but, following this outburst, I kept quiet.

With no roadworks and relatively light traffic, it was an unusually smooth and swift journey to Huntingdon racecourse. I drove into the jockeys' car park and dropped off my saddle in the jockeys' changing room before slipping through the buoyant crowd of racegoers, all muffled up to the eyebrows. My objective was the bar for a black coffee, but before I got there, I bumped into Nathaniel Willoughby. As usual, he was wearing an eye-blasting choice of waistcoat.

'Don't need your lights on going home, then,' I bantered, pointing to the buttercup yellow garb.

'Jealousy,' he said, sighing, 'is such an unattractive thing.'

'Buy you one?' It wasn't so much a question with Nathaniel as a forgone conclusion.

He beamed. 'D'you know, Harry, I really don't mind if I do.'

If I bought him a drink on every racecourse every time I saw him again, it still wouldn't balance the debt I owed him. Without his help the last time I'd got embroiled against my will with an unscrupulous criminal, my still being around to breathe and race would be highly unlikely. As a man, like the rest of us, he had proved to have feet of clay, but as a professional artist specializing in racing paintings, he was a class above anyone else.

We walked into the bar and I went to get the drinks while he found a couple of seats.

'Thanks very much. Your good health. May you have a winner.'

'No thanks needed, but I'll take your good wishes.'

'How many today?'

'Three.'

'Still aiming for the title, I take it?'

'Yeah,' I agreed. 'Could be pie in the sky after losing so many rides this year, but it was all for the right reasons.'

'Ah, yes. The right reasons.' He looked into his glass and pursed his lips.

'OK, Nathaniel, what are you trying to say?'

'Remember when I came round your place to get my keys back, after I got back from Switzerland?'

'Yes.'

'I believe I mentioned there might be a . . . problem. A problem that your skills might be called upon to help with.'

'No.'

'Eh?'

'You heard me. No dice. I'm up to my ears in a "problem" right now. And I don't know what the devil I'm going to do about it. Anything else, I don't need. Sorry, Nathaniel, but the answer's no. I hate to turn you back, especially when you've helped me out, but I can't.'

'Well, if you say so. But it does concern your mate, Mike.'

I took a deep breath. 'Is it a life-or-death problem?'

'Not Mike's, no.'

'There you go, then.'

'But it might have been why his wife died.'

NINE

I gaped at Nathaniel. 'Monica died from injuries after she had a skiing accident.'

'Hmm,' he agreed, making inroads into his gin.

'She fell down a glacier.'

He gave me a sideways glance. 'If somebody falls off something – say, a balcony – it's questionable whether it's an accident or not. A case of did they fall or . . . were they pushed?'

My jaw dropped further. 'Are you saying Monica's death may not have been an accident?'

He shrugged. 'That sort of question is one you're more able to answer than I am.'

'Now hang on, Nathaniel. As far as Mike's concerned, her death was a tragic accident. Are you saying it could have been murder?'

'All I'm saying is that it's possible someone organized the "accident".'

'No. I don't buy it.' I shook my head and drank some steadying black coffee. 'Monica was a lovely person. No reason on earth why anyone would wish her harm.'

'I don't think her personality is in question. But she might have been in the wrong place, seen something she shouldn't have seen.'

'Like what?'

'Harry, I don't know, I'm speculating. But she was there in Switzerland when it was the snow racing that year.'

'So?'

'I don't know much about the actual racing side, but I generally go over for the piano recitals. Well, last year there was a new young talent, Jackson Fellows, an amazing pianist. I was hoping to hear him play this year.'

'And?'

'He's the only son of a businessman. Between the lines, I'd guess that's where his funding comes from. His father's madly proud of Jackson's talent. But he didn't come over to play this year – just to attend and be part of the audience.'

'I'm listening.' There was something coming that I knew I didn't want to hear.

'I'd met Jackson last year. Told him how much I'd enjoyed his playing. Said I'd be here again this year and hoped to hear him play. He asked if I played and, anyway, we got on very well, had a drink – quite a few actually. I think this was why he opened up a good bit. I won't say he got merry – he most certainly did not. He told me he was also into White Turf racing, comes every year to watch. But his main interest, obviously, is the piano recitals, so it made conversation easy – common ground, y'know?'

I nodded. 'So, if he was all set to take part this year, why didn't he?'

'Because he'd got two broken fingers.'

'Go on.'

'I commiserated, asked him how he'd broken them. He said somebody broke them deliberately.'

'*What?*'

'When I asked him what the hell for, he said, "Sorry, can't tell you. They're my price for some silence."'

'Blackmail?'

Nathaniel nodded grimly. 'Seems like it.'

'Did you ask him anything else?'

'I asked if his father could help. His reply was, "God, no. That's why I need the silence. As far as *Dad's* concerned, I don't know this man, never met him."'

'Do you know who he was referring to?'

'No. But Jackson said if it hadn't been for some stupid tourist and her bloody camera, it would never have surfaced. Still, it didn't matter about her anymore; she wouldn't be taking any more pictures. Then he added – a bit ruefully, I thought – "nor playing piano".'

'Are you talking about Monica?'

He shrugged. 'She was there at that time.'

'So were thousands of other tourists.' I took a deep breath. 'And don't forget, Monica's friend, Clara Brown, was there, too. She was badly injured at the same time.'

'Yes, Mousey's wife, I know; she died recently.'

'After suffering for three years. Another bloody tragedy.'

'You think I'm overreacting to what Jackson told me?'

'I think you're reading too much – far too much – into it.'

'It's been worrying me, Harry. Thought perhaps Mike should know.'

I shook my head. 'Definitely not. There's nothing that ties up. I'm sure Monica's death was just a ghastly accident.'

'I sincerely hope so. Thanks for settling my mind. I'm glad I've told you. With your track record in nabbing "baddies", you're the expert.'

'Give over. Anyway, must go.' I drained my now cold black coffee. 'Races to ride.'

'Of course.'

I took a couple of steps, then stopped. Curiosity prompted me to ask, 'What nationality was Jackson Fellows?'

'English.'

'Right . . .'

Lady Willamina Branshawe, the smiling owner of Lucy Locket, my first ride of the afternoon, was waiting in the parade ring together with the Midlands trainer, Jim Crack. I took one look and winced. The ocelot fur must have looked stupendous when the big cat was alive and wearing his own coat. Not that Lady W didn't look stunning; the fur made a big statement on the dreary, overcast day. And her long blonde hair, contained within a fancy tan clip at the nape of her neck, added a further touch of colour. In her late thirties, the young widow of Lord Rudolph Branshawe was certainly feeling merry.

I walked across to them and touched the brim of my crash cap. 'Your Ladyship.'

'Hello, Harry. So pleased to have you riding again for me.' She flashed me a wide smile before turning to Jim. 'Are we going to beat Midnight Sun, do you think?' She nodded towards our main rival, the favourite in this race. The bright chestnut was stalking grandly round the parade ring – definitely all presence: arched neck, erectly pricked ears.

'He's certainly a strong contender, but with Harry on board Lucy Locket, we've more than an even chance of beating him.'

Her smile grew wider. 'There's nothing to beat the feeling a win gives you, don't you agree?'

We nodded.

'And I've had a little flutter – well, a little bit more than a *little*.' Her blue eyes sparkled with mischievous excitement. 'So you have to win for me, Harry.'

Her high spirits were infectious. And I wasn't immune to her gentle flirting. She was a lovely woman; it was a great pity about her taste in clothes.

'Do my best.'

Then, hearing the summons, we followed the other jockeys' example and Mike flipped me up into the saddle.

Holding the eager horses to a walk from the parade ring on to the course, we cantered down to the start. Joseph Williams, Midnight Sun, jockey, was having a job holding the big horse. The rest of us gave him plenty of space as the chestnut bucked his way over the sad tussocks of the winter-blasted turf. The wind had risen to near gale force, whipping tails and manes, increasing the horses' skittishness.

We formed a ragged line behind the tape, still avoiding Midnight Sun, who was playing up big time and had added cow-kicking to his repertoire. Joseph turned him in a tight circle and, as he came back to the tape, the starter let it fly high and we were away.

The manic chestnut bolted in front and flew the first fence, leaving the rest of the field trailing and trying to sort itself out. I opted for two in front of the back-marker and let Lucy Locket find her stride. She lobbed along comfortably, judging the fences with a measured, efficient accuracy. She was a perfect example of a stayer – could go for ever – but I knew she had no finishing burst of speed. I needed to keep creeping up the pack ready for when the front runners began to tire from the exertions that had initially taken them into the lead.

Lucy Locket's sure-footed jumping was a big bonus and we gained ground at every fence we cleared. By the time we were on the second circuit, three fences from home, we were lying joint second from a field of eight starters.

We chased along upsides Pixiecap – one from Mousey Brown's stables, ridden by Davey Marriott – a very consistent horse that regularly came in the frame. But the only horse out in front we both needed to beat was Tal Hunter's taxing ride, Midnight Sun. The gelding was still a good ten lengths in front and going like a train. It was easy to see why he was the outright favourite with the betting public.

We all cleared the next fence safely. If we held the same placings when we passed the winning post, at least we would be in the frame. Not a bad outcome.

But not a win – and racing was all about winning.

With two left to jump, there was nothing in it between me and Davey. It was going to be a battle between us for second place.

Midnight Sun galloped up to the second-last fence, took off half a stride too soon and raked his way through the brushwood top before pitching forward, throwing Joseph out the side door.

I'd seen the misjudgement as we chased up behind, but for a brief second, after clearing the fence, I saw a brightly coloured red-and-blue-striped ball rolling on the ground – Joseph – and the inert form of the horse stretched flat out close by.

Not what you ever want to see.

However, as a professional jockey, Joseph knew the risks, as we all did, and the lucky ones still in the saddle could not afford to lose focus. It was now a contest between just the two of us.

The rest of the horses were strung out behind, the nearest one some six or seven lengths behind.

With one fence left to jump, we were now working on our horses and, with both safely over, were scrubbing the head off our mounts. As the winning post came up, we flashed past, and it was all on the nod.

But I was sure Lucy Locket had the race. She had reached forward with her head a split second before Pixiecap had done the same.

We eased back the horses to a circling walk as the commentator gave out the winning number, and I reached out and shook hands with Davey.

'Bloody close there, mate,' he panted.

'You're so right.'

We walked our tired mounts over towards the entrance leading back to the winners' enclosure. I glanced back down the course and saw with a jolt of dismay that there were screens set up three fences back. I knew behind those screens there was a horse receiving veterinary attention, a horse ambulance standing by, the crowd in the stands holding their breath for the outcome.

However, I had to walk Lucy Locket away from the course and go on through to the winner's spot. But the very moment I turned my head away, I heard an almighty roar of approval from the crowd followed by much clapping and cat-calls. A grin settled on my face. Quite a few times in the past I'd encountered the same miracle myself. I knew the prostrate horse, far from suffering life-threatening injuries, had only been winded. He'd recovered his breath and stood up, all was OK, and the vet had nodded for the removal of the screens, to the rapturous relief of the people anxiously awaiting the outcome.

It made my win now a cause for celebration.

But the celebration had to wait until after my third and final ride of the afternoon. My first win had been backed up by a couple more, and going into the owners' and trainers' bar later, I accepted a glass of champagne from Lady Branshawe. If I was on a high, which I was, she was fizzing more than the champagne.

'A wonderful day's racing. Thank you, Harry.'

She chinked her glass against mine in delight.

'Your horses are the ones we should be thanking. They're class acts. I'm only as good as the horse I'm riding.'

'Oh, I agree with you – my big babies are splendid,' she gushed, 'but they can't do it by themselves. You sell yourself short, Harry.'

'Very true,' Jim Crack put in.

He himself had been an accomplished jump jockey before eventually turning trainer. Eventually, because in the interim he'd been in business as a private investigator. I accepted his praise because he knew all about race riding – and what it took to win. Praise from a fellow jockey was always sweet.

'I want you to ride for me again,' Lady Branshawe said, nodding. 'You will, won't you?'

'Be my pleasure.'

Her horses were always top notch and Jim was a talented trainer who brought them to perfection for each of their races – winning was then so much more achievable. Suddenly, the Champion Jockey title appeared more doable. I took a satisfied gulp of champagne and was pleased with the day's work. Three wins and a promise of more work – couldn't be better.

We sat and chatted a little longer until Jim heaved himself to his feet and declared it was time to go; he needed to oversee the loading up of his horses for the journey home.

'Me, too,' I said, following his example. 'Best get back.'

'Wait, Harry.' Lady Branshawe caught my arm. 'Just one thing . . .'

'Yes?'

She leaned in and whispered, 'The coat's not real; it's faux fur.'

As I felt the flush redden my cheeks, she laughed. 'I saw your grimace in the parade ring.'

'I'm sorry . . .'

'Oh, don't be silly. I'm glad. You're obviously a caring man.' Her lips brushed my cheek very lightly. 'And thank you again.' She swept out of the bar, taking her coat with her, leaving me to return the chairs under the table.

As I walked towards the door, a familiar figure came in.

'Harry, congratulations on the wins.'

'Oh, hello, Tally. Thanks.'

She brushed her hands down her coat; it was dusted in snowflakes.

'Snowing?' I queried, and looked out of the wide windows.

'Oh, yes, coming down like a punctured quilt out there.'

'Not what the doctor ordered. At least the racing's at Southwell tomorrow.'

Southwell was an all-weather course. When the rest of the racing was called off, the all-weather ones kept going. Even so, Southwell had been the victim of extreme flooding in the past which had resulted, unfortunately, in a complete shutdown.

But Southwell, I'd already decided, wasn't simply the venue for racing; it was where I intended to hand over Dunston's letter.

TEN

The journey back to Nottinghamshire from Huntingdon took a lot longer than getting there. Drivers obviously took note of the weather and were all intent upon reaching home before it worsened.

By the time I drew up on the gravel outside the kitchen door at Harlequin Cottage, the snow lay almost two inches deep, but for the last twenty minutes no further flakes had drifted down.

As I turned the key in the back door, a big ginger streak bounded across the pristine white snow and launched itself at me. With wickedly sharp grappling hooks, the cat clawed his way up my jacket to reach my shoulder. He bellowed a greeting down my ear.

'Hiya, Leo.' I reached up and rubbed his chest. His fur felt cold. 'Come on, let's get indoors.'

The Rayburn gave out a welcoming warmth that wrapped itself around us and shouted 'Home!' in a loud voice. Leo leaped down on to the red quarries and sought out his food bowl – empty.

'So impatient.' I shook my head at him as he bellowed again, glaring with emerald eyes.

Pushing the kettle on to the hob, I dug out the can opener and found a tin of his favourite pilchards in the pantry. His mood changed instantly as the metal teeth pierced the lid and let forth the pungent smell of fish.

I left him to it and took my mug of tea into the lounge. Now that the snow had stopped, the evening was looking good. I was due to collect Georgia from her parents' house in Plungar – Vale of Belvoir country. Again – this would be the second time – because it was conveniently near and the food excellent, we were having dinner at the Dirty Duck in Woolsthorpe. Belvoir Castle, situated on the top of the hill that towered above the pub, dominated the landscape with its grandeur.

The pub was situated on the bank of the Grantham Canal. In spring and summer, the punters liked taking walks along the side of the canal that stretched for miles in each direction. I doubted anybody would be tramping along tonight. What the rest of the evening would bring, after our meal, was an unknown. It was ball in her court.

I'd met Georgia when I was trying to discover the identity of the person who had placed white roses on my mother's grave. The only clue had been the card tucked in with the flowers that gave the address of a flower shop, The Trug Basket, in Grantham.

I'd followed it up and discovered Georgia, not the person who had sent the flowers, but the girl who owned the flower shop. I suspected that for her, like me, work had taken the place of a special person. In filling that gap, however, work had its limits. I was looking forward to seeing her again.

But before that there was something I needed to do. Draining the mug of tea, I went into the office and took out a buff foolscap envelope. I needed to implement my idea of what the hell I was going to do about John Dunston's letter. The original that Caxton, the solicitor, had handed to me, which had been clocked by the men who had attacked me, had been an identical buff envelope, the sort that was available countrywide. It was exactly this wide availability that had given me the idea.

In desperation, before I called Annabel in the morning, I'd hatched a half-baked idea that might or, more probably, might not work.

Tomorrow, at Southwell racecourse, I'd find out.

I took the A52 almost as far as Bingham, then swung off on the right towards Langar, the first of the many small villages that snuggled into the Vale of Belvoir. Threading my way along glistening white back lanes that linked the picture-postcard-pretty dwellings, I drove at a steady thirty miles an hour. The snow had fallen thickly out here in the sticks and in places had drifted up into soft banks at the base of the hedges.

Arriving at Plungar, I followed the directions Georgia had given me and nosed the Mazda through a pair of wide iron gates that allowed access to a broad tarmac drive. The outside lights beamed out over the wheel tracks that showed someone had driven away a short while ago.

I parked and rang the bell on the mahogany front door. Georgia opened up and smiled when she recognized me.

'Harry, you found me.'

'Indeed, I did.'

We stood and smiled at each other. Then, peeping round me, she looked down to the gates.

'You've just missed Mum and Dad. Now it's stopped snowing, they decided they'd carry on with the usual routine. Once a week, they go round to Aunt Josephine's for dinner.'

'I'm glad it's not because of me. Did you say I was coming?'

'Yes.' She laughed at the recollection. 'It made their eyes widen.'

'You can't leave it at that.'

She sobered up quickly. 'Well, since you're the first man to "come calling" . . . since' – she hesitated – 'they were intrigued.'

I nodded and didn't press her for any more. 'Are we still on for dinner at the Dirty Duck?'

'Oh, yes, please.' The smile returned to her pretty face. 'I was busy at the shop today – so busy there was no time for lunch – and I'm starving.'

I laughed. 'What would you have done if it was still snowing?'

'Dug something out of the freezer for both of us. If you had actually made it, of course.'

'I'd have made it,' I said, looking at her, liking what I saw.

A blush pinked her cheeks and she stepped back into the hall. 'Come on in, out of the cold. Sorry, I've kept you standing there. I'll just get my coat.' She led me through to a massive lounge with original dark beams against the cream ceiling. 'Have a seat. Would you like a drink before we go?'

I shook my head, 'No, thanks. It might have stopped coming down out there' – I inclined my head towards the heavily draped windows – 'but driving is a bit tricky on these back lanes. I'll save my intake for some wine with our meal. The food will soak it up.'

While she was fetching her coat, I glanced around the lounge. It was obvious that her parents were well off. The pieces of furniture were mostly antiques and the soft furnishings top quality. The house itself was a substantial property. I wondered how much land there was. Georgia, I knew, had adopted two horses, Pegs and Jacko, from Bransby Rescue Centre in Lincolnshire. Maybe there was a paddock and stabling attached.

She reappeared snugly wrapped up. 'OK, Harry?'

'OK.'

I stood up and we went out into the cold night.

* * *

The Dirty Duck was ablaze with golden lights reflecting off the water of the canal and making the shimmering snow gleam.

The barman acknowledged us with a smile and Georgia wiggled her fingers in a familiar greeting. We were lucky. 'Our' table – the one we'd sat at once before, closest to the open fire – was free and we claimed it. The fire had recently been made up and orange tongues were reaching far up the chimney, heat roaring out. All along the walls, scores of assorted and highly polished brass pans hanging there reflected the dancing flames. On a cold snowy night, it was definitely the place to be.

'White wine?' I queried.

'Yes, please. You've remembered; how good for my ego.' Her smile was a little on the smug side.

'Oh, yes.' I grinned and went to fetch our drinks. The barman, in anticipation, had already poured Georgia's out. I carried the glasses back and together we scrutinized the menu.

'I'm going for the same as last time,' Georgia decided. 'I'll have the vegetarian lasagne. And,' she warned me with a flash in her eyes, 'I'm paying my half.'

I took a pull of my lager and studied her. That so attractive pink blush crept up her cheeks.

'Yes, it does mean no dessert,' she added.

'What a shame,' I said, shaking my head and smiling broadly. 'I shall make sure that doesn't spoil our evening.'

Now she was laughing out loud. 'You're a lovely man, Harry Radcliffe.'

'And, as they say in America, back at you.'

I went across to the bar and ordered the food – and paid with my plastic. The barman keyed in the details before saying in a low voice, 'Good man.' He nodded almost imperceptibly in Georgia's direction. 'She needs someone who can make her laugh again.'

Our eyes met. 'She obviously comes here regularly.'

'Used to,' he said dryly.

'Ah . . . before Peter—'

'Yes.' It was said abruptly – a definite end to the conversation.

I slipped my card back into my wallet and returned to Georgia. 'Madam's lasagne will be here shortly.'

'Good, can't wait. I'm so hungry I could eat a horse. Oops! Can't believe I said that.'

I laughed. 'Hunger makes savages out of us all. But how are they, the horses, Pegs and Jacko? Both OK?'

'Oh, yes. Fancy you remembering their names.' Her face lit up. 'I'm so lucky to have them.'

'Don't you think that the reverse might be true?'

'To an outsider.'

'Fingers rapped.'

'No, not at all.' She reached across the table and stroked the back of my hand to prove her words. 'You're not included. The horses are a lifeline. Yes, I've got the shop, and, thank God, it's a success, but that's just my business life, isn't it? Horses are . . . personal, aren't they?'

'Yes. They engage your emotions.'

'Even though with you, Harry, horses are your business life?'

I took a deep drink of my lager. 'If I were a farmer, say, I'd drive a tractor, get from A to B down the field. No emotions attached to the tractor – it's just made of metal, albeit metal which moves and takes me to where I want to be.'

'Whereas?' She took a sip of her Chardonnay and relaxed back against the padded seat.

'With horses, any jockey will tell you, it's personal. You're sitting on their backs and they're talking to you, with their bodies as well as through their minds. I suppose telepathy describes it. But they're living beings, and to get the best result, you engage with them. So, yes, I understand exactly what you mean by "personal".'

'Knew you would.' She released a tiny sigh and smiled with satisfaction.

The waitress eased her way through the tables and the now increasing crush spreading out around the bar area. She placed two delicious-looking dinners before us. 'Enjoy.'

'Thank you,' we said in unison.

The food smelled good and tasted better. Georgia tucked in enthusiastically. I took my chance and flicked a quick glance across the room towards the barman. He was looking at Georgia with unmistakable fondness.

I returned my gaze back to my plate and continued eating my own superb steak. But I wondered . . .

We spent an enjoyable evening: a superb venue, good food and drink, light-hearted conversation and the company of each other.

Easy, relaxed and with the fizz of sexual attraction between a man and a woman lurking just underneath the radar. The chemistry between us was never mentioned, but nevertheless we were both keenly aware of it.

But Georgia had made it quite clear how far she was prepared to allow things to develop between us tonight. I wasn't worried. There was no hurry, none at all. We both had baggage that would no doubt need talking out before any further moves were made – by either side.

I dropped her off at the gates outside her home at Plungar. No more snow had come down; in fact, it actually felt a little bit warmer than it had earlier. There were no returning car treads imprinting the lying snow, which meant her mother and father weren't back yet. I wound down the driver's window and leaned out.

'I'll hang on until you get inside. Let you flick some lights on.'

'You're a lovely man. I know I've said that already tonight, but I do mean it.' She bent down and gave me a gentle kiss on the lips before straightening up. 'Thank you for a super evening. I've not had one I've enjoyed so much for such a long time.'

Before I could reply, she walked smartly away up the drive, sinking a little into the snow at each footfall, but reaching the front door safely without slipping over. She opened the door, switched on the hall light, turned to wave goodbye to me – then closed the door behind her.

ELEVEN

By morning, most of the snow had melted and gone.

I pulled back the curtains and looked out on a soggy garden. Leo was stalking along the hedgerow. A bird squawked a warning and flew off. Leo watched it fly away to safety, flicking his tail in frustration, before lifting a back leg and giving it a quick shake. I was headed for the National Hunt course at Southwell today, and the going would probably have changed from soft to heavy. For flat racing it didn't apply. The all-weather fibre-sand track would be standard.

I wasn't driving over to Mike's yard first thing. Southwell was very close to where I lived, and Mike's stables were in the opposite direction. He wasn't expecting me; I'd prompted him the previous day that I'd a heavy date that night and would meet him at the racecourse at about eleven. Racing at this time of the year started early and finished early, unless the course was floodlit.

I was not only meeting Mike. I'd left a message with Annabel to pass on to the unknown man when he telephoned her that I'd see him at two thirty, after my last race.

I grabbed a mug of scalding coffee and took it through to the office. A free couple of hours first thing were rare and I could best fill them by switching on my computer and writing up my copy for the racing column in the newspaper. It was a second string to earnings as a jockey. The job wasn't one I particularly enjoyed, but in the past I'd had cause to be extremely grateful for the extra cash it had brought in. No real need now, of course. The necessity to earn a lot of money was no longer relevant. I pushed the thought to the back of my mind. The memories it brought were still raw and painful. So I sipped coffee and tapped away at my three hundred words. I'd just finished, checked it and pressed send when Leo slid sinuously through the partly open door. For such a huge cat, he moved soundlessly. Spotting me, he immediately dispelled that observation with a bass bellow that rang in my ears.

'OK, I know, breakfast. I was thinking that myself.'

We repaired to the cosy kitchen for sustenance. Then, leaving Leo to his vigorous paw-washing routine, I went back to the office and found the buff envelope I needed for Southwell and took a drawing pin from the corkboard above the desk. It was a complete toss-up if the handover would work. There was no point in dwelling on the outcome. At best, it would buy me some time – at worst, it left Sir Jeffrey vulnerable.

Very carefully, I slipped the single sheet of paper into the envelope and noted the position of the signature. On the outside, I carefully inserted the pin at the correct place, so that it pierced only the envelope and didn't penetrate through to the paper inside. I withdrew the pin and smoothed the edges together. Unless you were aware it had been pierced, you would never know; it was barely discernible. But I knew and, even without looking down at the letter, when I ran my thumb across that corner, I could feel it. It would need split-second timing at the actual handover, but there was no more I could do.

However, before that, I had four races to ride. I needed to focus.

I found Mike at the racecourse, saddling boxes.

'Seems we've escaped the white stuff, Harry.'

'Yeah. But don't forget this is England. Could be six foot deep by bedtime, you know.'

'You're a cheerful sod.'

He was about to saddle up his runner in the first – Mudpie. The gelding was well named. He was a real mudlark and came into his own in heavy going.

His lady owner, Mrs Portly – a most appropriate name for the generously rounded woman – lived near Southwell and had asked Mike to let him have a run there. Mike, of course, had the last shout on which horses ran where and in what races. But owners paid the bills and he tried to comply with their wishes – sometimes really bizarre ones.

Her request for me to ride Mudpie wasn't something I was going to turn down. Even if we didn't win, I'd still earn my riding fee. And jockey fees were what ran Harlequin Cottage – and provided Leo with big tins of pilchards. A win, on the other hand, put the jam on the top of my bread-and-butter fee.

I left Mike to it and made my way over to the jockeys' changing room and swapped my civvies for Mrs Portly's silks with colours of orange clashing horribly with fuchsia pink. However, if at the end of the eleven forty-five race, those colours flashed past the winning post ahead of the rest of the field, I'd be delighted. Pete, the valet, handed them over, freshly washed in all their striking vibrancy.

'Go off all right, then, d'n't it? Reckon old John would have been OK about how it was handled.'

'Oh, the funeral, you mean. Yes, it did. No hitches at all. And I suppose it's difficult for the undertakers when there's no family left to give instructions.'

Pete was the man who had given me the shocking news of John's death. I recalled I'd seen him among the mourners at the crematorium.

'Where did he live?'

'Near Bridlington. Moved out from his other place when Lilly went. Reckoned he couldn't stand the memories, y'know.'

I nodded.

'He shared a rented place with Keith Whellan. Think it was only going to be temporary, like.'

'Keith's a box driver, isn't he?'

'Yeah. Down with flu at the time of the funeral; otherwise he'd have been there to raise a jar an' all. See John off properly.'

I nodded again and let Pete get on with his job of handing out gear. It was a useful bit of information. Like most jobs, there was a kind of kinship in a shared occupation and, with no family, John had probably spent time after work in Keith's company, whether down the pub, most likely, or flaked out in front of the television. And they would have talked, swapped racing gossip, maybe even opened up a bit personally.

I made a mental note that after I'd unwrapped the box, still buried in the cat litter, a word with Whellan might very well uncover some facts or theories. He was box driver for Mousey Brown. John Dunston had worked for Robson and both stables were based in south-east Yorkshire.

Robson had helped me in the past regarding another murder.

I put thoughts of the past very firmly out of my mind and pulled on the racing silks, then followed the other jockeys as we all trooped outside to the parade ring.

Mudpie was waiting with his stable lad, Mike, and Mrs Portly. She was wreathed in smiles, scarf and tweed coat.

'Harry.' She beamed coming forward to greet me. 'We shall soon find out if my little investment can pull it off.' Her little investment, all seventeen hands of dark bay, tried out a couple of bucks for the hell of it, much to the delight of the crowd around the rails.

I touched my cap deferentially. 'Indeed, we shall.'

'Now, I know you weren't at all sure, Mike, but I do so want to try him in a race on home ground. And he's very well, isn't he?'

Mike agreed. Mudpie certainly was well. So well that he was practically jumping out of his skin. I could see I was in for a lively ride.

'Jockeys please mount' was called and Mike flipped me up. The moment Mudpie felt my weight on his back, the hooves went up into the air. But it wasn't from evil intent; I could feel the excitement running through him. This was what he had been born to do – race. And he couldn't wait.

'I'll see you in the winners' enclosure afterwards, Harry.' If anything, Mrs Portly's smile was even broader.

An owner's enthusiasm is a very positive, warming thing. And she was here to enjoy the day. She infected us all with her bubbling optimism.

The stable lad led Mudpie off towards the course and I took him down to the start at a respectable canter.

Circling round with the rest of the runners and riders, I pulled down my goggles ready to deflect the kickback of the mud splatters that inevitably flew up from the score and more of racing-plated hooves. For a brief couple of minutes, the sun actually appeared, weak, watery and lemon yellow, but nevertheless it seemed an omen of goodwill.

And so it proved. Mudpie claimed the race as his own right from the off, flying the fences with aplomb and banishing any fears regarding his ability to pull it off. Mrs Portly's faith in him was fully vindicated.

We returned, plastered in muck, and I had to push my goggles up on to my crash cap in order to see where we were heading. That place was one a triumphantly clapping Mrs Portly had staked out as her own as soon as the commentator announced that number five, Mudpie, had won by three lengths.

Mike reached up to take hold of the reins, his face full of happy disbelief as he laughed out loud, shaking his head. He slapped the horse's neck and congratulated Mrs Portly at the same time.

'I knew he was going to come first,' she declared. And she went on to make us both laugh. 'A mother always knows.' Adding, 'Mudpie is my late-in-life baby.'

The crowd around the winner's spot heard what she said and they good-heartedly joined in the fun. I suspected, having seen his high-spirited bucking in the parade ring, they'd risked a flutter on the big horse and it had been justified. His odds were twelve to one. A nice little earner for them.

I carried my saddle to the weighing room and had my weight confirmed. Outside, the punters around the winners' enclosure heard, through the loud speaker, the words they were waiting for – 'Weighed in, weighed in' – and let loose a roar of approval.

I endorsed every cheer, but the next race was coming up fast.

Colours had to be shed and handed to Pete, and new silks put on for the next horse with a different owner. There was no time to spare. Races were set at half-hourly intervals which, no doubt, the racegoers might think a bit of a wait, but the jockeys involved had a regular schedule to fit in and couldn't have managed tighter timing.

I ended midfield on the next two horses: the first hadn't the speed to do better and the second was boxed in on the rails. But racing is full of such races, and having had a winner to begin with, I was philosophical about the results. However, my two o'clock race was on Nightcap, a horse owned by Lord Edgware, and he was odds-on favourite. He could very well show the rest of the field the way home. I'd ridden him several times before and knew his capabilities. He was a front runner who had done very well last season.

As usual, Lord Edgware had spoken to me in the parade ring prior to the race.

'Just get round safely, you and the horse,' he'd said, nodding gravely to emphasize his words. 'Very nice if you win, of course, but don't take any unnecessary risks, eh?'

I'd touched my cap and smiled agreement. I'm quite sure the noble lord realized it was an impossibility to win without going all out for it – which meant taking risks. But jockeys are paid to please owners, and agreeing with them went with the territory – even when their words were nonsense.

Lord Edgware was one of that regrettably rare type of owner who actually wasn't bothered about winning as long as the horse came back in one piece. He was there predominantly to have an enjoyable day at the races.

Nightcap was a seasoned jumper and judged all his fences with precision. He was a class horse and riding him was a joy. Not only was he a superb jumper, but I knew he had a turn of speed in a finish. However, Nightcap didn't know that his owner had suggested throttling back if it was needed to play it safe. He gave his usual outstanding performance and we took the race in some style – eight lengths in front.

Lord Edgware, red-faced with obvious delight in the winners' enclosure, insisted when I'd weighed in, showered and changed, that I join him for a drink. He went on to compound the situation further by saying he'd also invited Mrs Portly.

'I understand she's a local lady, and as owners of winning horses, it will be very pleasant to celebrate all together, won't it?'

I flicked a glance at Mike. He was nodding encouragement. It was another one of those 'keep the owners sweet' moments. I hadn't banked on this happening. With dismay, I could see no way of getting out of it. Between them, they had five horses at Mike's stables, and that number generated a great deal of income for him. For me, it also represented regular rides. I certainly didn't want to jeopardize the goodwill by appearing unsociable.

However, with both Mrs Portly and the Lord eager to chat, this could take time. They were looking at me expectantly, waiting for my answer.

But it was already two fifteen and what neither Mike nor Lord Edgware knew was that I had an assignation at two thirty.

A letter had to be handed over.

TWELVE

'**O**h, you *must*, Harry. Please, say you will,' Mrs Portly entreated me. 'Without your skill, my darling Mudpie might not have won.'

Out of the corner of my eye I saw Mike's eyebrow raise a fraction. He wouldn't want any friction in the camp.

'Of course I'll have a drink with you both. I'd be delighted. Thank you.'

Mike's relief was obvious. My own tension notched up a few more degrees. A pity I couldn't split myself in two – be in both places at the same time and save both situations. Since that wasn't possible, I needed to think on my feet. Excusing myself to get weighed in, I escaped to the jockeys' inner sanctum, desperation whirling my thoughts round like a kaleidoscope.

What was needed right now was a mobile phone – and in the changing room, mobiles were banned. By the time I got out, it would already be two thirty and the contact would be waiting where I'd arranged – in the gents' toilets.

And I didn't have his number. Nor did Annabel. She was waiting for him to contact her. I cursed under my breath. It was Sod's law that Lord Edgware had pressed me to have a drink; how long that would take was an unknown. But one thing was for sure: whoever the contact was, he was already here on the racecourse. Not a pleasant thought.

I disrobed, swilled off mud and dressed at the double. Outside, quickly reunited with my phone, I slid round the corner of the building and put a call through to Annabel.

'Harry? It's gone two thirty. What's happening? You're supposed to be meeting that piece of scum.'

'He rang?'

'Yes, of course he did,' she snapped uncharacteristically. 'I told him what you said, that you'd meet him inside the gents'.'

'Listen, did you manage to check what number he was ringing from?'

'Caller withheld.'

'Yeah, suppose it was bound to be.'

'What's happening now?' Her voice was rising up the scale with stress.

'I'm stuck. No time to explain. He will be bound to ring you back very soon when I don't show. Tell him I'm officially held up and I'll be there at three thirty.'

'And if he doesn't ring?'

'Don't worry, girl. He *will* ring. He's desperate to get hold of the letter.'

'Oh, Harry, for God's sake, give it to the little shit. Get him out of our lives.' Since Annabel very rarely swears, it was a yardstick of her state of mind – right up there in the red zone.

'Three thirty, Annabel, right? Just tell him that. He'll agree. He has no option. Must go. Bye.'

I cut the call before she could reply. I felt a heel, leaving her in such a state, but there was no point in prolonging the conversation. I thrust the mobile into my jacket pocket and went to join Lord Edgware – and appease Mike. I'd allowed one hour. It should be long enough, but the sooner I joined them, the sooner I'd be free to meet the pond life, hand over the letter – get the job done with.

Moving the time on one hour, however, had an advantage. Most of the male racegoers would have used the facilities, if needed, and be streaming out of the public car park. The gents' toilet had been the only place I could think of that was free from crowds, prying eyes and had a solid floor. All essential for what I had in mind.

In the meantime, entering the bar, I returned the greetings from Lord Edgware and Mrs Portly.

'You'll have a flute of champagne, won't you, Harry? We're already on our second.'

'Yes, thank you, Mrs Portly.' I smiled. 'We'll toast Mudpie, shall we?'

'What a horse!' She clasped hands and an ecstatic look came over her face.

'To Mudpie, to Nightcap – and to their jockey, Harry.' Lord Edgware gave the toast, lifted his drink high and chinked glasses with us. 'It's what owning a racehorse is all about,' he continued, 'having a splendid day out at the races and watching your horse enjoy his race. And, of course, today' – he bent towards Mrs Portly – 'winning has amplified that pleasure.'

'Oh, it has.' Mrs Portly, fuelled by champagne, was still on a high cloud.

Mike beamed at his owners. 'That's what we aim for – satisfaction.'

In an atmosphere of general good humour and high spirits, I joined in and managed to forget for a short while what I was facing later.

On the professional front, today had added yet another two wins to my season's total. It was also a sure thing both owners would ask me to ride for them again. Whereas Mrs Portly's horses were possible winners, Lord Edgware's horses were first class, and more winners would be sure to come along.

Winners were what I needed to try to retain the Champion Jockey title. I was beginning to claw my way back up, but it was a mighty big ask. However, whatever the title meant to me, when balanced between winning it or saving lives, there was no contest.

Clearly, in the past, although to my own detriment, I'd made the right choices – three times. Now, possibly facing a fourth, my decision would have to be made on the moment, and from a gut instinct.

On the personal front, last night had gone very well and I knew when I asked Georgia out again, she would say yes. No doubt it was the bubbly lifting my spirits and making me feel much more positive because, apart from the letter, I found I was feeling optimistic about the future.

On arrival at the racecourse, I'd left the Mazda near the exit in the jockeys' car park. Coming in my own vehicle had the double advantage of leaving Mike in the dark about the handover of the letter and also giving me a means of getting away swiftly from the racecourse, should I need it. I'd excused myself from the drinks party after an hour and made my way across the tarmac towards the gents' toilet, five minutes short of the agreed meeting time.

There were three possible scenarios. The man – no way could it be a woman – was secreted somewhere nearby, watching my approach. Second, he had decided not to turn up. Or he was already lurking in the toilets, maybe locked in one of the cubicles. My money was on the last.

Just before entering, I swept a swift glance around. It all looked sweetly innocent. And, importantly, no men needing to use the facilities were making a determined beeline in this direction.

Bracing myself, I went inside. Two men were on their way out. I stood aside and let them go. It gave me the chance to look around with my back safely pressed against the wall. No one was standing around. No one was using the urinals. Which only left the cubicles. Most had their doors standing wide open and were obviously empty. Three, all adjacent, down at the end, had doors firmly shut.

The sight brought an instant replay to my mind's eye of the horrific set-up I'd found at Leicester racecourse earlier this year, the first time I'd got myself into the deadly cat-and-mouse game of chasing a murderer.

Going into the last open cubicle, I bent down nearly to floor level and looked under the narrow gap. The following two were entirely empty. In the last one, butting up to the main wall were a pair of scruffy trainers planted motionless on the ceramic tiled floor. And they were pointing not from pan to door, but across, from wall to wall.

I pushed the door of my cubicle closed with a firm click. And waited. Two minutes went past and then I flushed the toilet. At the same time, I whipped out silently and flattened myself on the hinged side of the door to the last cubicle, my left shoulder tight up against the wall.

And waited.

And prayed.

Prayed no other men would come in for the next few minutes.

Slowly, the door began to open. Just before the angle of the door came into contact with my shoulder and gave a warning, I lunged forward and to my left. My hand instantly grabbing for the dark jacket sleeve, the only thing I could see from this angle. Grasping a firm handful, I yanked the arm back and up.

A satisfying yell of surprise and pain issued from the owner of the arm. I swung the man round and forced his arm even further up his back.

'Bloody fucking hell! Get yer hands off me!' he yelped, struggling violently.

'Who are you?' I lowered my voice and put gravel into it.

The man struggled ineffectively against the restraint and began kicking backwards.

'Get yer fucking hands off!'

I kept his elbow clamped hard against his backbone and pushed upwards some more.

He gave a gargling yell of agony.

'Tell me,' I ground out.

It was an unfair contest. Despite the fact he was as tall as I was, and thin and wiry, I was a race-fit jockey.

'Harry Radcliffe, ain't yer?' He stopped struggling and I eased his arm down an inch. Any further screams could bring someone to investigate.

'And you are?'

I felt him relax, chanced it and released him. He turned to face me, nursing his smarting arm. We eyed each other with mutual distrust. And then recognition came to me. He was the go-between Jake Smith had used to contact me at Market Rasen racecourse a few months ago.

'I'm here for that letter. Give it me.'

'The last time we met,' I said slowly, 'you gave *me* a note.'

He shrugged thin shoulders. 'So?'

'Who are you working for?'

He set his lips together. Shaking his head.

'Was it Jake Smith again, this time? The man who set you up to come here?'

'You've tasted his temper. You know what he can do.'

'Oh, yes.' I nodded grimly. 'I've been on the receiving end from him.'

'So, I shan't be singing, shall I?'

'*Was* it Jake?' I persisted.

'Freelance, ain't I? As long as the readies keep coming.'

'Are you going to tell me who sent you, or not?'

A sly look came across his face. 'Or not, top jock.'

'Right.' I reached into my inside pocket and took out the buff envelope and fingered it. 'This what you want?'

'Yeah.' He held out his hand.

'And if I don't give it to you, what're you going to do about it?'

'If he don't get it, your bird's posh bloke gets stiffed.'

'If *you* don't tell me what this man's name is, you don't get this.' I waved the letter tantalizingly back and forth, just out of his reach.

'Then it's goodbye posh bloke.'

'So you're not going to tell me his name?'

'Got it, top jock.' He was grinning, sure of himself.

'OK.'

I reached into my trouser pocket and took out a cigarette lighter.

The smile died on his face, replaced by apprehension. 'What y'doin'?'

'Well, it's obvious you aren't bothered whether or not you get to take this back to your boss – whoever he is.' I held the envelope between my left index finger and thumb, directly over the pinhole. With my right thumb, I flicked the lighter. The blue and gold flame leaped up. Keeping eye contact, I slowly drew the flame towards the envelope.

'You wouldn't,' he scoffed, swallowing very hard.

'You think not?' The flame was now almost touching the top corner.

'Give it us 'ere.' He lunged forward.

I swung my left hand high, out of his reach.

'His name,' I rapped.

'Get stuffed, Radcliffe.'

He grabbed for it again – and missed. I brought the lighter to the extreme top corner and the paper caught alight instantly.

'Bleeding hell!'

He grabbed again. This time I didn't move. His fingers snatched at the blazing envelope, closed round it. His screech of pain was pure animal. I let go of the envelope at the same moment he did.

While he danced around, cramming fingers into his mouth, I quickly stamped on the blazing envelope where it had fallen on to the stone tiles. Immediately, the flames went out and left the partly charred letter lying on the toilet floor. Seizing his chance, he grabbed for it and waved the envelope in my face.

'I'll drop you in it up to your fucking neck, Radcliffe.'

Then he was gone, running for the door.

I followed him and, catching the door before it swung back, stood watching him race across the tarmac in the direction of the public car park. He disappeared among the cars. I put the cigarette lighter into my trouser pocket and went back into the toilets.

I sat down on the nearest toilet seat and let my heartbeat slow down to normal. It had been a close thing. But then I knew it would be, had to be. It had been a close thing too, not long ago, at the hands of Jake Smith. Shakespeare put it beautifully: 'There is a tide in the affairs of men, which, if taken at the flood, leads on to fortune . . .' Very true. I'd taken my chance once before with Jake Smith at the maximum point of the flood. And then today, against the odds, but it had worked perfectly.

I passed a hand over my forehead, wiped away the film of sweat. And then began laughing. Jake's one-time go-between had got away with the letter, without letting on what his boss's name was. It might be Jake Smith or it could be someone else. After all, as he had said, he was freelance.

I stood up, still laughing. He thought he'd won, got away with it, literally. What he didn't realize was I'd intended him to take the letter back. It wasn't the original one – that was safer than the Bank of England tucked away in my bathroom.

But the important thing was that the boss-man – whoever he might be – *he* would think the letter was the real thing.

THIRTEEN

'Get away!' Mike's face wore an incredulous expression. We were having a quick honey-laced mug of coffee before morning stables the next day, and I was relating the incident at Southwell.

'If I'd simply handed the letter over, whoever is pulling the strings would have smelled a rat. This way, with the non-essential part of the letter burned away, he can still read the contents and he thinks it's the real deal. I must say, my forgery of John Dunston's signature was pretty good. 'Course, it took hours of practice . . .'

I ducked as Mike aimed a swing at me.

'How do you know the signature wasn't destroyed?'

'Ah, because I'd placed it in the envelope directly under the pin hole.'

'Eh?'

Laughing, I explained.

'But how can it possibly save Sir Jeffrey?' Pen's face was screwed up with doubt.

'If I'd simply written a copy of the real letter, of course, it wouldn't. I did have to amend it somewhat.'

'Somewhat?' Mike chortled, pushing his chair back in preparation for getting off down to the stable yard. 'I don't need to hear. As I've said before, you're a devious sod, and I've every faith in you, Harry.'

He stood up. I made to follow, but Pen caught my arm.

'No. Don't slope off, Harry. I want you to tell me. There's Annabel, taking care of Sir Jeffrey, but she must be worried sick. I certainly would be.'

'Leave you two to it.' Mike grabbed his jacket and headed out the back door.

'I've rung Annabel, put her in the picture. I'm sure at the moment he's not in any danger.'

'Well, put me in the picture as well. From the lurid tales Mike has told me about your previous sleuthing, it's pretty scary stuff.'

'Don't worry, Pen, I'm not going to involve Mike in anything dangerous.'

'Hmm . . . that's not what I've heard.'

'OK. Yes, but only in the end game. I've been damn glad of his help before, in that last throw of the dice, but this time I don't know if it will even get beyond the point where we are now. If the unknown boss-man believes that letter is the original one John left for me, I don't see it going any further.'

'But what did you write to put him off?'

'I copied the first part, about him losing his son and saying he knew I thought it was on Jake Smith's instructions. Nothing fresh to get excited about there; the whole criminal underbelly knows what Jake's capable of. Although John didn't think it was Jake, I disagree. Alice Goode, the prostitute who was murdered – her husband, Darren, told me Jake had a long reach, and whether in or out of prison, it made no difference. If Jake saw you as a target and wanted you dead, even going to the moon wouldn't save you. And I know that to be true.'

Pen shuddered. 'You said the first part . . . What else did you write?'

'I omitted most of the rest, particularly the bit about his concern that he might also end up being murdered. That's what's causing all the retaliation. Or I think it is. The boss-man doesn't know what John has written, only that he has given me a letter. As far as he's concerned, John might have fingered him and given me a name. Now, that would be enough provocation to warrant the demand for the letter. So,' I sighed, 'I'm afraid I gave myself some credit and wrote that John was thanking me for saving his life once before.'

'Which you did.' She nodded. 'Mike told me.'

'Well, whatever.' I waved a hand dismissively. 'Anyway, it seemed quite credible that he might have written that.'

'And if this horrible man believes there is no threat to him, he'll back off.'

'I'm hoping so.'

'Did you reassure Annabel?'

'Yes.'

'Good.'

'So, you see, there's no need to worry, Pen.'

'Hmm . . . probably not . . . well, not about that.'

'What else? Is there something?'

'Yes, I'm afraid so.'

'Go on.'

'Oh, Harry, I've been up in the loft, packing away some Christmas decorations, you know.'

I nodded, and waited.

'Mike asked me to look for an ornate table centrepiece that was put up there after the last party he gave – you were there, and Fleur, you remember? Well, he's hosting an owners' drinks party next month and thought it would be good to use it. I did find the centrepiece. But, oh dear, I also found something else . . .' She hesitated.

'Go on.'

'I don't know what to do.'

'What did you find?'

'I think . . . I mean, it has to be hers. It wouldn't belong to anyone else, would it?'

'You're not making any sense. Just tell me what you found.'

'A big sponge bag. A woman's, obviously – it's pink and mauve.'

'Monica's?'

She gulped and nodded. 'Yes, has to be, don't you think?'

'Almost certain to be,' I agreed.

'How did it get up there, in the loft?'

'No idea. Monica died in Switzerland, in a skiing accident, as you know.' She nodded, biting at her lower lip. 'Her body was flown back to England. I assume her belongings from the chalet where she had been staying were sent back, too.'

'I suppose so. What should I do, Harry? Just put it back and keep it secret? Forget I've seen it? Tell Mike I've found it? What?' She spread her hands in distress.

'Depends on what's inside.'

'It doesn't look as though Mike has opened it or even looked through the bag because there's one of those disposable cameras inside. It's not a proper one. This one doesn't have a strap, just a cardboard case.'

I felt a lurch in my solar plexus. 'A camera?'

'Hmm . . . one that takes about twenty-four snaps and you discard afterwards.'

'And it hasn't been processed?'

'No. All the shots have been used, but not printed off.'

'Mike obviously stored the bag away because he couldn't bear to look through it and dispose of the items inside.'

'He's disposed of all her clothes and shoes, that kind of thing. But this is such a personal thing. Her cosmetics and creams are inside. Together with her flannel, hairbrush . . . and toothbrush . . . It's heartbreaking.'

'Yes.'

'It's so selfish of me, Harry, but it feels almost as though she's come back.'

'Don't go there, Pen. Much as we all loved Monica, she's dead. There's nothing you can do about her death other than accept she's gone. Mike's future is with you.'

Pen burst into tears and I put my arms around her. I knew how insecure she felt about her position in what she still saw as Monica's house. It had manifested, much to my surprise, when Mike had booked a singer to attend a party he organized. Mike had raved over the woman's beautiful voice – and she had been a beauty, too.

Pen had known how deep his feelings had gone for Monica and had felt, unjustifiably, second best. But she had accepted that while Monica had died and was no threat to the new-found happiness she now had with Mike, a living, breathing – and singing – beauty might tip that balance.

I'd reassured her at the time and thought she'd realized Mike's love for her wasn't going to be affected by any third party. Now she had unexpectedly come across so personal a possession as Monica's sponge bag, and it had released her half-submerged insecurities.

I was pretty sure something horrific had happened to Pen before she and her brother, Paul Wentworth, had come to live in a nearby village. While Paul was a bachelor, Pen was a widow. She had never revealed her past, and it was only a comment Paul had made to me some months ago that had hinted at a traumatic incident.

Now I held her close as her tears flowed until, finally, they slowed and ceased.

'Tell you what, Pen, how about you put the bag back in the loft where you found it, eh? I'll take the camera to have the photographs developed and printed. See what they show. If they are important, then we'll both tell Mike. How's that?'

'Oh, yes, thanks, Harry. Let's do that.'

She grabbed a tissue from her pocket and wiped her face free of tears.

'Sorry to be such a wimp.'

'You're not,' I said firmly. 'You're like the rest of us: we all need a life raft sooner or later, in whatever situation.'

'Bless you, Harry.' She kissed my cheek. 'Give me your keys. I'll put the camera in your car while you're out schooling the horses. That way Mike won't be bothered with it. At least until we know what the photos show.'

'Good idea.' I took the keys from my pocket and handed them over. 'But if I don't get myself out to the stables, he's going to wonder where I am.'

Racing today was at Wetherby racecourse. I wasn't riding any of Mike's horses. Surprisingly, I had two rides booked with Mousey Brown's stable, although I suppose, technically, it was his son Patrick's. His elder son had taken over when Mousey had been struggling to look after his wife, Clara, in her last couple of years of life. She had died despite the best efforts of the doctors, and it was following that sad occurrence that Mousey had been officially declared an alcoholic and had lost his driving licence.

Racing's extended family had cut him a lot of slack during that time, sympathizing with his suffering and thankless struggle, everybody knowing there was only one outcome.

Personally, I agreed with Mousey. He'd confessed to me afterwards that he'd rather she had died in the accident in Switzerland – like Monica, Mike's wife – than be brought back in such a parlous state and lingering.

Mousey's younger son, Ian, was an accomplished flat jockey. He was rarely to be found on an English racecourse because he was in such demand the world over.

My rides today were in consecutive races at two o'clock and two thirty. It allowed me to school first for Mike and grab an early bite of lunch before driving off up the A46. I had wondered why Patrick wanted me to ride. It was rare. Usually, he put up the younger jockeys. However, when I'd done my homework and discovered both horses were owned by Lady Willamina Branshawe, I wondered no more.

She had obviously been sufficiently impressed by my performance at Leicester races to offer me the rides. However, I wasn't going to hold an inquest. Right now I was up for any – and all – rides offered to me.

The only way to try to retain my Championship title was to go for it relentlessly and hope nothing blew out of the water to foul up my hopes. The biggest worry, of course, was possible injuries that could lay me up and jeopardize my chances. All the rest of the jockeys were in the same boat.

I had no doubt that my nearest rivals – one of whom was actually a few wins in front right now – were also praying they could avoid having a close encounter with cold, wet grass right in their faces.

But apart from the business side of agreeing to the two rides, it would also place me in an ideal situation to be able to speak to

Keith Whellan, Mousey's box driver. I had been intending to make a special journey up north to speak to him. It could have been put on the back-burner for a bit until I saw what results the replica letter produced – or, hopefully, nothing further. In which case, I could kick on with my own life.

However, it was a good bet that Whellan would be at Wetherby and I could get to meet him. What I'd say I had no idea – yet. A case of leap in and see how deep the water was, and just what I could catch.

There was a decent crowd milling about when I arrived at the racecourse, even though the weather was going downhill again and an icy wind was blowing.

It wasn't the only thing that felt icy.

A short time later, when I went inside the weighing room, the coldness followed me. The weighing room was usually a place of good-natured banter and an air of positive expectation, but as I sat on the bench below my peg, I could feel the concentrated stare. It carried all the coldness of Siberia. I took my time and finished pulling on my breeches before I slowly straightened up.

Duncan Rawlson had walked in and was standing aggressively, legs apart, with fists clenched by his sides. He didn't need to say a word. The intense dislike in his eyes directed straight at me was saying it all.

Pete, the valet, apprehensively came between us and placed my boots down beside the bench.

'Everything OK?'

'Yes,' I said.

'No,' said Rawlson.

Pete licked his lips nervously and moved out of the firing line.

FOURTEEN

I cast a quick glance at the time. Very shortly, the early warning would be given. Somewhat like a curtain call in the theatre, the announcement would state, 'Five minutes to go, jockeys,' usually resulting in an organized scramble to get from the changing room over to the parade ring where the owners, trainers and horses awaited us.

I met Rawlson's hostile stare. 'Is there time for whatever you've got to say?'

'Oh, yes, it won't take long. And I've got *plenty* of time. *I don't have a ride.*'

'Ha.' I knew immediately what had upset him. 'I didn't ask for the ride.'

'No? But you're a crawler, a fucking boot-licker. And she's a bit tasty, i'n't she?'

I shook my head in disgust. 'Give over. I didn't jock you off on purpose. I never angled for the rides.'

'I always ride her horses.' His fists clenched and unclenched as he sought to keep control.

'And if I don't win, you'll be back in the saddle. She won't put me up again.'

He snorted. 'We both know, with his form, that gelding's going to walk it.'

I couldn't argue with him. Lady Willamina Branshawe's horses were all top-class. I could well understand his frustration. Being jocked off was potentially going to cost him a lot of prize money. In a similar situation, I wouldn't be too sweet-tempered either. But the owners paid the bills – bottom line. The choice of who rode for them was only negotiable with the trainer. The tannoy sprang into life and gave us the prompt we had been waiting for.

'Take it up with Mousey – or Patrick.'

I bent and pulled on my boots.

'I bloody well will.' Rawlson barged his way through the other jockeys and flung out.

Lady Branshawe was all smiles when I entered the parade ring. In contrast, Patrick's face was dour. It was quite obvious he did not agree with her ladyship's decision to swap jockeys. But, most likely, Mousey had put his foot down on the delicate matter of keeping the owner sweet. Patrick had a lot to learn in the business of diplomacy. He was never going to be the trainer his father was, or, rather had been, until he learned to respect where the stable income came from.

'Lovely to see you again, Harry.' Pimms's owner gave me a dazzling smile that conversely increased the depth of Patrick's frown lines.

'Your ladyship.' I touched the peak of my cap and turned to Patrick to receive riding instructions.

'Hold him up for a breather halfway, but when you get to the front, don't let him take the lead until the last few strides. And' – he glowered at me – 'don't use the whip. OK?'

I nodded. 'OK.'

'Don't do a "win at all costs", Harry.' Lady Branshawe placed a hand on my arm. Clad once again in her warm, ocelot-lookalike fur, she was a strikingly lovely woman. 'I *do* want you to bring him back sound.'

'That's right, Radcliffe,' reiterated Patrick. 'Her ladyship favours safety. Don't forget.'

I shot him a quick glance as he proceeded to help me into the saddle. Not surprisingly, he didn't meet my gaze. Patrick was a far from sympathetic trainer. Duncan Rawlson's flat-out driving style was much more in keeping with his own ideas.

As I cantered Pimms down to the start, I wondered whether Patrick would be better pleased if we didn't win. Almost certainly, Lady Branshawe would change back to the usual jockey, and harmony would prevail in the stables. But a non-winner wouldn't help my Championship chase for a start and, secondly, I liked to win.

As the starter brought the yellow flag down smartly, I let Pimms run freely before settling him in fourth place on the rails. He jumped like a cat, surely and efficiently, and had an engine that purred along, coupled with a long ground-eating stride, absolutely ideal for the easy turns on Wetherby racecourse. He was an easy ride, smooth and responsive. I relaxed and enjoyed myself.

Not everybody was so lucky. It turned out to be one of those races that occurs now and again when there seems to be a jinx on it. The horse third from the front was the first to fall and he was quickly followed at the next two fences by a horse down at each. The field was now reduced to four horses.

I dutifully eased Pimms back just over halfway and let him have a breather. Predictably, two horses gained ground and came upsides. For a couple of furlongs, we raced in a line with just the leader out in front by about six lengths.

At the second-last fence, the jinx kicked in again. The horse in front put in an extra half-stride and blundered through the top of the brushwood, sending bits of twig flying. Unable to keep his balance, he fell heavily, pitching the jockey over his shoulder and out the side door.

I held Pimms steady and jumped the last with the other two horses still upsides. Then I kicked for home and Pimms's response was electrifying. He left the others behind in a matter of strides and kept up his drive right to the post. His dominance was never in any question.

We were greeted by elated cheers from the punters around the winners' enclosure. Most had no doubt had a flutter on Pimms as the outright favourite and he had not let them down. But you would have been forgiven if you'd expected the trainer, as well as the owner, to be pleased. Lady Branshawe had a wide, welcoming smile, but Patrick was as mournful as a bloodhound without a quarry.

Just what Rawlson's reaction was could be guessed at, and I'd undoubtedly find out in the weighing room. My win meant there would be no easy way back for him to ride Lady Branshawe's horses. If I kept riding winners, she would keep asking to have me as pilot. But for myself, I was delighted to have brought Pimms home in the number-one spot – and in one piece. It had upped my score for the current season, not to mention earning me a share of the prize money.

I took my saddle through, weighed in and went through to the changing rooms. I still had a further ride in the next, the two thirty. And, like Pimms, this one was also favourite.

Rawlson collared me just before I was due to go out to the parade ring. He knew I'd got the ride on Masterful Knave.

'All those fallers,' he sneered, 'and you're still standing. Sod's law going strong.'

'And I'm after winning the next race, too.'

He stuck his face within inches of my own. 'Well, lose it!'

'So you can get your rides back? Are you mad? The name of the game is winning.'

I didn't like rubbing it in, but I was getting sick of his arrogance at what he seemed to consider his exclusive rights.

'You're going to come a cropper, Radcliffe. I'll make bloody sure of it.'

Turning, he pushed his way brusquely past two other jockeys who must have heard what he'd said.

I shrugged off his threat; I'd had so many in the last few months that it was getting to be par for the course. Race riding demanded the fullest concentration, and I needed a clear head.

My second mount, although favourite in the betting, was still a bit green and would need to be guided far more than Pimms had done. He was not so sure a jumper either and had come down in his last race. Despite his lack of race experience, Masterful Knave had a devilishly fast turn of speed and could put in a fast finish. It was quite possible we would win, but not such a tied-on certainty as my first ride; I would give it my best effort as usual, but the outcome was unknown.

No horse in any race was a dead certainty. Horses weren't robots or machines; like people, they were better some days than others with no explainable reason why.

Outside in the parade ring, I was given minimal instructions on how to ride the race and then legged up. If anything, Patrick's moroseness was even more intensified, but Lady Branshawe appeared to disregard his attitude and favoured me again with her dazzling smile.

'As before, Harry, it would be super to have another winner, but not before safety.'

'And don't use the whip. Doesn't like it. OK?' Patrick snapped. The hostility was coming off him in waves.

I nodded. 'OK.'

I could feel the excitement running through the horse. He was eager to get out on to the course. He may have been a bit green but he was learning fast. With much head-shaking and skittering around, we circled the parade ring, allowing the enthusiastic crowd of punters to view him up close from behind the safety rails. And then we were heading for the walkway out on to the course. I allowed him a fairly free canter down to join the other horses.

We were eventually called into a rough line to the starter's satisfaction and he brought down the yellow flag. This time, I tried to settle the horse near the back of the field. If there was going to be a replay of the regrettable fallers in the previous race, I wanted to give Masterful Knave every chance to avoid coming to grief in their wake.

Horses will instinctively try to avoid a fallen horse or a rolling jockey. But it isn't always possible and a lot of the injuries jockeys suffer do not come from the force of the impact with the hard ground but from the hooves of the following horses.

One of my most serious injuries had come from the hoof of a following horse which had crashed down on to my head while I'd been rolling on the ground. The iron-shod hoof had split my crash cap almost in two, as Mike had shown me when he'd come to visit me later in hospital.

Given the chance, a horse will twist in the air to avoid a collision, but if they are bunched up going over a fence, it isn't possible. Knowing of Masterful Knave's fall in his last race, I was particularly careful that we should approach each fence with an uninterrupted view and space around us to help increase his confidence.

The strategy worked perfectly over the first two fences and the young horse was going forward eagerly, enjoying his racing. But nearing the third, I felt a slight shift in my position in the saddle. My first thought was that the breastplate, or possibly the girth, had loosened, causing the saddle to shift. If nothing worsened, I could maintain my seat. My boots were in the stirrups and I gripped with my knees and hoped we could get away with whatever was going wrong.

Stirrups, attached to straps, are cinched up with buckles to hold them at the correct length. Just below the horse's withers, the top of the saddle pommel houses the necessary padding and webbing. Leather flaps, hanging down on either side, cover the necessary buckles and connecting parts and provide a smooth surface. Jockeys grip the horse on the outside of the flaps to avoid rubbing sores on the inner side of the knees and legs. Right now, my knees were gripping tightly, ensuring my balance in the saddle.

The horse approached the next brushwood fence and met it perfectly placed. I put my weight down in the stirrup irons as normal as he rose up in the air. It was at that crucial moment of going over the fence the breastplate gave way and the saddle slipped backwards.

Within the space of a few seconds, from holding a comfortable position in the field with a fair chance of winning, we were now a completely no-chance job.

The loss of balance threw me forward on to the horse's neck. He felt my sudden dramatic shift of weight and came down awkwardly on the far side of the jump.

The impact of landing was the final thing that flung me further forward and sideways. I shot out the side door over Masterful Knave's left shoulder and hit the ground with a hefty thump.

Instinctively, I did what all jockeys do: I rolled myself into as small a ball as possible and went with the momentum. I was lucky. The two other horses behind had time to avoid trampling me, and although the earth shook around me with the impact of eight hooves ploughing past inches from my body, not a single hoof struck me. I lay in the wet grass and mud, struggling for breath. Already, I could see the attendants racing in my direction.

But I could wiggle my toes, shift my elbow and wrists, and I knew I'd escaped any serious injury. What I had done was winded myself. Given a few minutes, that would resolve itself, leaving me with just some sizeable bruises.

However, along with the relief of knowing I'd got away with it, the unwelcome thought came into my mind that Rawlson's threat had come about. I'd not only lost the race, but I'd certainly come a cropper.

And on the heels of that thought was a further skin-crawling one – had someone deliberately tampered with my horse's tack?

FIFTEEN

I got away with it: no red entries – no concussion, no broken bones, no standing down. My left shoulder had taken the brunt of the impact of my fall, but it wasn't dislocated. I had had a bang on the head – I lied about that – although the medical officer probably didn't believe me. He was well used to being told tales by jockeys. However, the searching light shone into my eyes had upheld my lie. All was well, it seemed.

As I dried myself off in the changing rooms and began dressing in my civvies, I mulled over the likelihood of the breastplate coming adrift.

Everything on this earth – butterflies to human beings included – began wearing out from the moment of creation. It was a natural law. So it could simply have been an accident. Or, then again . . . it might have been a deliberate act.

If it had been deliberate, the obvious suspect was Duncan Rawlson. I tugged on my second sock – my feet were still damp. He'd threatened me certainly, but only after I was almost ready to ride in the race. Between his threat and Patrick flipping me up into Masterful Knave's saddle, there had been no opportunity for him to vandalize the tack.

It was possible, of course, that he'd sabotaged it earlier. In any case, a deliberate act or an accident, the outcome remained the same: I'd lost the race. I'd still get paid my riding fee, but I'd lost any winnings percentage. More importantly, to me, I'd lost the chance of adding to my season's score. However, the most positive thing was I'd not sustained any injuries other than a painful shoulder and a headache. Wincing, I shrugged on my jacket, squinted in the murky mirror and ran a comb through my unruly dark hair.

I'd been summoned to present myself for a drink with Lady Branshawe. No doubt there'd be an inquest on what had happened during the race. If Patrick had been subpoenaed as well, it gave me the opening to ask about the age of the breastplate. If it was a fairly new one, then the accident could not be put down to wear and tear. I had no further rides this afternoon so I could take my time asking questions. Not that I knew what to ask – as so many times before, it was a fly-by-the-pants job.

There was no sign of Rawlson. Most likely, he'd already gone over to the parade ring. He had a ride in the next. The horse was not one belonging to Lady Branshawe. Whether she'd want to put me up again was debatable. Pete was waiting for the soiled kit I'd just stripped off. I handed the silks over.

'Good to see you're OK.'

'Thanks.'

'Bit odd, that,' he said, eyes gazing down firmly at the bright mud-splattered clothing in his hand.

'Hmm . . . you could say so.'

'Especially after what Rawlson said.'

I knew that conversation hadn't gone unheard. How many ears had picked it up was an unknown.

'Just sour grapes, that's all,' I said, seeking to defuse the situation. The last thing I wanted was an ongoing vendetta.

'Reckon he meant it.' Pete raised his eyes and looked straight at me. 'I should watch your back.'

I met his gaze, held it. 'Why?'

'He had a run in with John Dunston not long ago. And look what happened.'

'John committed suicide.'

'Yeah, I know *that* . . .' His voice tailed away.

'What was the row about?'

'Not sure,' he admitted, running a hand back and forth over the kit. 'Something to do with the horsebox. Patrick had told him to sort it. Well, that's what John told Keith. That time it broke down at Southwell.'

'Something and nothing, then.'

'Yeah, but Rawlson holds grudges, is what I'm sayin'.'

I patted Pete reassuringly on the shoulder. 'I'll be careful.'

He nodded, unconvinced, and walked off.

I made my way over to the owners' and trainers' bar. The ocelot lookalike had been removed and hung up. Lady Branshawe was resplendent in a beautifully cut woollen dress and jacket in a pale coffee colour. Against her upswept blonde hair, it looked good, very good – and so did she. The look of concern on her face melted away as I walked over to her table. I exchanged nods with Patrick.

'Harry.' She held out her hand and I took it. 'Are you all right?'

'Yes, thank you, Lady Branshawe.'

'Thank heavens for that. And I know you'll be pleased to hear Masterful Knave is fine, too.'

'Yes, perfectly sound,' Patrick added. 'Sit yourself down; have some champagne, do.'

This was a different man to the one I'd left glowering in the parade ring. Gone was the mournful bloodhound look, replaced now by a beaming smile.

'I'm very glad to hear it. Horses give us their best shot. Pity if we sometimes don't reciprocate.' I sat down and received a flute of champagne. I could really have done with a strong whisky. My left shoulder was just getting into gear and the pain was increasing all the time. My last words hung in the air awkwardly.

'Patrick tells me the saddle slipped – well, something helping to hold it in place did, and it let the saddle drop back.' Lady Branshawe, sensitive to the atmosphere, sought to smooth the conversation.

'Yes' – I took a sip of the excellent champagne and eyed Patrick over the rim of the glass – 'it seems so.'

'Most unfortunate,' he said suavely.

'Was it an old breastplate, then?' I held his gaze.

'Not especially, no. Not a new one, but perfectly adequate for purpose.'

'I must disagree, Patrick.' Lady Branshawe's perfectly arched eyebrows drew together in a frown. 'The wretched thing came to pieces, it seems. It's more than fortunate that Harry has come out of this unscathed.'

If she could have felt the angry drumbeats my shoulder was pounding out, she wouldn't have said that. However, I nodded and smiled.

'Did you tack up yourself, Patrick?' I asked.

'Of course I did.' His demeanour slipped into truculence. 'I made sure it was perfectly all right. I value the safety of my owner's horses. You must have forced your weight down sharply in the stirrups.'

'Perhaps.'

He took a gulp of his drink. 'Anyway, here you are, walking, so . . .' He shrugged and added, 'No harm done.'

'But I didn't win, did I?'

He glared at me. There was no commiseration on my loss – or his. He wasn't moaning about the loss of his prize money. And I found that very interesting.

'If it was a case of coming back safely, Harry,' Lady Branshawe said, 'or winning, then I'm very glad you didn't win.' She gave us a well-bred all-embracing smile and poured oil. 'Shall we change the subject?'

By the time I reached the horsebox park a fair number had loaded their horses and left for home. But I knew Mousey's box would still be there. He had a runner in the last race.

The two horses I'd ridden earlier would have been hosed down by now and put in the racecourse stables to await transportation back to their home stables. There was a short time before Keith, the box driver, would begin loading up.

I knew the colour of Mousey's box – a distinctive maroon with cream stripes and lettering – it should be easy to spot. With over half the boxes already gone, I worked my way between the rows and pinpointed it more or less straight away.

Keith was sitting at an angle in the driver's seat, feet up on the passenger seat, ratting cap pulled down over his eyes. It was such a shame to wake him. However . . . I rapped hard on the passenger side window. His hand came up and an index finger slowly raised the peak of his cap. We eyed each other across the width of the vehicle. Reluctantly, he swung his feet down, leaned forward and opened the door.

'Yeah?'

'Can I have a word?'

'Thought you were after cadging a lift.' He gestured me inside. It was considerably warmer in the cab.

'Want some tea?' He fished under the dash for a flask and poured a drink.

'Not for me, thanks.'

He grinned. 'Been on the champers?'

'Yeah.' It was my turn to grin.

'Go on, then, Harry, what do you want to ask me?'

'You were good mates with John, weren't you?'

His gaze lifted from the mug of tea and he looked intently at me. I held his gaze and knew he was weighing up how much to reveal.

'S'right.'

'He came to lodge with you after Lilly went, yes?'

'S'right.'

'Do you think he killed himself?'

'Nothing like coming straight out with it.'

'Do you?' I persisted.

'Who wants to know?'

'I do.'

'Yeah?' He leaned forward. 'Why?'

'You didn't make his funeral, did you?'

'No. Had flu.'

'Hmm . . . I was told that.'

'Some things you're told can be dangerous.' He took a deep gulp of tea.

'John left a letter for me with Caxton, his solicitor. He gave it to me after the funeral.'

'I know.'

I shook my head at how efficient the racing grapevine was. You couldn't swap your socks without the word going round.

'Ah, but did you know what he wrote?'

'Some of it. Like the bit about Frank being taken out. Sure, he was John's son, but Frank was a bad lot. *You* know that.'

I nodded. 'Tell me, was John scared – for himself, for his own safety?'

Keith hesitated, stared down into the dregs of his tea. 'Yeah,' he said at last, 'I reckon he was.'

'Did he say why? Mention any names?'

'Are you working for somebody – like, on a case?'

'If you mean, am I getting paid to investigate, then, no, I'm not. I never have been. But I have been paid a visit – a middle-of-the-night job.'

He nodded. 'Sounds about right.'

'When people close to me get threatened, though, I've got to do something.'

'You saved John's life once. The whole of racing knows that.'

I didn't answer. I was hoping he would carry on talking. Maybe unburden himself, if he did know anything.

'So,' he sighed, as if he'd come to a decision, 'I *do* agree with John that you can be trusted – you're one of the good guys. And you've got a reputation for getting results.'

'Only if I've something to work from. I need facts, not smoke and mirrors.'

'Yeah, I can see that.'

'So?'

'I don't want fingering for this, OK?'

I nodded.

'I think John was pushed off that bloody cliff. Can't prove it, o'course.'

'Why do you think he was?'

'I reckon he found something pretty damaging. He hinted it was left in the horsebox that day at Southwell. There was a rumpus. I also reckon Patrick told Rawlson to put the frighteners on John to make him talk. 'Course, Rawlson won't admit it. He's running scared as well, if you ask me.'

I thought about his twitchiness in the changing room, clenching and unclenching his fists, and privately agreed with Keith.

'But John didn't talk?'

'No. What happened was our box broke down at the racecourse. Robson told John to have our horse loaded up in the box along with his own.'

I nodded. Robson was a trainer whose stables weren't a million miles away from Mousey's. Box sharing was pretty standard practice in cases of emergency. Indeed, some trainers made arrangements in advance to share boxes if necessary. It cut down costs.

'And the end of the story?'

'I stayed behind with our box and waited for a mechanic. John drove the horses back, dropped off our horse, then took himself to Robson's yard.'

'And that's all?'

'Yeah, pretty much.' He pursed his lips.

'But?' I prompted.

'OK, yes, there is a bit more. I know somebody'd been in our horsebox. I had to take a slash and it was after I came back, I saw it. There was a smear of blood near the dash.'

'Blood?' I could feel my eyebrows rise.

'Yeah, I know, damned odd. Don't know where it came from, wasn't much but . . . there was another thing. I opened the dash to wipe the blood off and the piece of old tea towel that I keep in there to dry off condensation on the windscreen, that was missing.'

'What did this piece of cloth look like?'

'One of those woolly types, if you know what I mean.'

'Yes, terry towelling?'

'That's right. A striped one, blue and white.'

'Just a piece, or the whole tea towel?'

'Dunno, really. Suppose about half – not a full one.'

'And you got the box fixed and drove it back to Mousey's yard?'

'Yeah.'

'And John took Robson's box back first and then drove his car to your place?'

'Yeah.'

'Nothing else?'

He shook his head. 'Nothing.'

I took one of my cards from my wallet and passed it to him. 'If you remember anything else, give me a ring, eh?'

'Sure. If John was murdered, I hope to God you nail the bastard. Anything I can do to help, count on it.'

'Thanks, Keith. I appreciate it. Until I see what happens following my efforts to calm things down at Southwell, I have to say I don't know which way the cat will jump.'

He grinned wickedly. 'His name's Leo, isn't it – your cat? I heard a rumour going round about him routing Jake Smith at your place. That true?'

'Oh, yes.' I laughed. 'Jake had me by the throat, and just before I blacked out, Leo took a dislike to his face – ripped it to shreds.'

'Better than a Rottweiler by the sound of it.'

'Believe me, I owe that cat. Anyway, I'll be in touch if I need you.'

'Good luck, Harry.'

'Thanks. See you, Keith.'

SIXTEEN

I made my way to the jockeys' car park where I'd left the Mazda. I did a quick check to make sure it was safe – nobody lurking with intent and no damage done.

I slid into the driver's seat. It was as cold as hell. Shivering, I fired up and put the heater on.

My shoulder, unnoticed while I'd been talking to Keith Whellan, kicked in at full throttle. My shivers were not entirely due to the icy temperature and I needed to get home and soak in a hot bath. I'd engaged first gear when my mobile struck up with 'The Great Escape'.

'Hello.'

'Harry.' Annabel's voice was soft and warm. 'Are you all right? I saw your fall. Jeffrey and I were watching the racing.'

'Nothing broken, thank goodness. Are you both doing OK?'

'We are, yes. Jeffrey suggests I come over to the cottage when you get back. Would you like me to?'

Would I? By God, would I.

'What about Jeffrey? Has he somebody looking after him?'

'Yes. We've got a live-in nurse. She's a treasure. They get on very well.'

'In that case, I'd really like to see you. I could use some of your special help.'

'I'll be there. What time?'

'Better make it a good couple of hours; give me chance to drive home. That OK with you?'

'Absolutely fine. Drive carefully.'

I released the handbrake and drove out of the racecourse.

Checking in my rear-view mirror before joining the main-road traffic, I also noted, despite the pain, there was a wide smile plastered all over my face.

*   *   *

I beat my own record getting back from Wetherby. For the last half-hour of the journey, snow had been falling. To start with, a few soft, wishy-washy flakes that hit the windscreen and melted immediately. But the initial warm-up, if you could call it that, soon came to an end and a multitude of large flakes took over, clogging the wipers and building up until visibility was reduced to a couple of tiny arcs.

I noted the lack of tyre tracks in the lane leading to Harlequin Cottage and knew I didn't need to do any security checking when I pulled in through the open five-barred gate. The gravel was covered in a good inch or more of snow. And there were no unwelcome footprints advertising an uninvited caller. I crunched across and opened the back door.

First job was to turn up the central heating; the second was to make a mug of scalding tea. Then I shrugged out of my jacket, grabbed the mug and began climbing the stairs.

I'd got about halfway up when I heard a bellow behind and the soft thud of paws coming after me. Leo hurled himself at my back and cramponed his way up to my shoulder. Unfortunately, it was the one that had taken all the battering. I let out a yell and nearly dropped my tea. Bewildered by my lack of reciprocated welcome, he gave a loud hiss of frightened surprise and let go, landing on all four paws and streaking away down the landing.

I let him go – he'd come round when he was hungry – and went into the bathroom. I turned on the hot tap, added a liberal amount of muscle relaxant which foamed up invitingly, promising release of painful tension, and left the bath to fill. Taking a pull of hot tea, I stripped off my clothes. Angling in front of the mirror, I cast a quick glance at the damage.

The shoulder was a mess. The skin was broken in grazed patches and an unbelievably big bruise was spreading and darkening over half of my shoulder blade and upper arm. Adding to the fun factor, there were also four deep claw punctures that were oozing blood. Using me as a climbing frame when I returned home was a normal activity for Leo, but he'd been a little tardy in turning up tonight and I'd already shed my cushioning jacket.

I fished in the bathroom cabinet, took out a packet of seriously strong painkillers and swallowed three. Placing the tea between the taps for ease of reaching, I eased myself gingerly into the hot bubbles. It took a minute or two to become acclimatized to being boiled alive, but then the healing water began easing away the tension, loosening tight, strained muscles and tendons, and became the 'aaah . . .' factor I needed.

I sipped the rest of my tea and slid down into the bath until my battered shoulder was submerged. As painful as it was, I'd still been very lucky to escape so lightly from what could have been a nasty fall. And another great outcome was that because I'd come off Annabel would soon be here to offer her own particular brand of healing. Until I heard her car arrive, I'd simply stay put in the bath, soaking up the heat and letting the water soothe the abrasions.

I eased down a little further and closed my eyes . . .

I could hear a muted road drill. But, strangely, it seemed to be close to my left ear. I was also aware of being in the bath – and the water was getting really cold. Raising one eyelid, I took in the scene.

A few inches from my head an enormous ginger tomcat was purring for England. He lay upside down in the arms of the woman I loved – my estranged wife. No rear-view mirror in which to check, but I could feel the soppy smile spread across my face.

'I thought that might wake you.' Annabel smiled back. 'I'd forgotten what decibels he gives out when he's happy.'

'Make that two of us,' I said, 'in the happy stakes.'

'There's a pot of coffee waiting in the lounge if you're interested.' She rocked the big cat gently from side to side and his purrs rose another gear. 'And I think your bathwater's cold.'

'You're right.' I started to heave myself up, realized that along with the water getting cold, the bubbles had all but dispersed.

Diplomatically, Annabel passed over my bath towel. 'Nothing I haven't seen before.' She headed for the door. 'And, of course, with the water being cold . . .' She didn't need to finish the sentence.

I grabbed for the sponge and threw it across the bathroom at her. She skipped out of range, laughing.

I dried and dressed hastily and went downstairs. In addition to the central heating I'd upped on returning home, Annabel had also switched on my quick fix for heat when the open fire wasn't lit – the log-effect electric fire. The lounge was cosy-warm. Leo was rolling around on his back like a kitten on the carpet, delighting in warming his belly. There was a pot of coffee, two mugs and a jar of honey on a tray sitting on the side table. Annabel had also switched on the subdued wall lights. The whole effect was warm and soothing.

'Shall I pour out?'

I nodded, hunkering down beside Leo in front of the fire. I didn't tell her how good it was to have the joy of her company, even if only for an hour. And it was joy: she lit up the room, my life, just by being herself. And being here.

'What happened at that jump, then?'

I looked up from stroking Leo's soft fur and accepted a steaming mug.

'Technically, the webbing of the breastplate attached to the girths on either side, under the saddle flaps, gave way.'

She frowned. 'Wasn't the tack checked when it was put on?'

'I don't know about that because I was in the changing room. Obviously, it should have been . . .'

'Meaning?'

'Maybe it wasn't meant to hold – as in, been got at.'

'Vandalized on purpose?'

'Hmm . . . possibly.' I nodded and sipped the coffee.

She drew in a sharp breath. 'What damage did it do to *you*?'

'I landed on my left shoulder – that's buggered right now – and I got a crack on the head.'

'I take it you were checked out at the time?'

'Oh, yeah, nothing broken.'

'No blackout, concussion?'

'Nope.'

'Thank goodness.' She, too, sipped coffee.

'How's Jeffrey doing?'

'Hmm' – she swallowed some coffee – 'doing surprisingly well.'

'Would it have anything to do with giving him healing?'

She smiled and shook her head. 'I don't know, Harry. I just do the job; I'm not the boss.'

'No, suppose not.'

Since we had split up, Annabel had trained – and qualified – to become a spiritual healer, in addition to her existing career as a psychotherapist. Although she wouldn't be drawn, we both knew the effectiveness of the treatment. I was convinced that without her unselfish treatments – in person and when absent – I wouldn't have recovered as I did from my ghastly fall the previous year at Huntingdon racecourse. No way would I discount the efficacy of the treatment. It would be foolish to do so when, having been on the receiving end, my body had responded and healed very much faster than it would otherwise have done.

'Would you like some healing?'

I didn't hesitate, unlike the first time when I'd chickened out – or tried to. Thankfully, fate had then taken charge and I'd received the healing without knowing anything about it.

'Yes, please, when you've finished your coffee.'

We finished the first and poured ourselves a second mug and relaxed on the settee. Leo, predictably, lay smugly across both our laps.

'Bless him.' Annabel stroked his head. 'Doesn't forget, does he?'

'No' – I shook my head – 'he remembers the good times.' Leo always used to lie across us when we lived together.

'And they *were* good, weren't they?' She turned a soft gaze on me.

'Oh, yes, they certainly were.'

I let my arm rest around her shoulders. She didn't object, but we were both intensely aware of the line, drawn in concrete, which neither of us could cross. We honoured each other and didn't attempt to go too far. She was loyal to Jeffrey, and no way would I abuse his trust. We had a very strange threeway relationship that most people couldn't understand. It had been forged through mutual danger, pain, love and now, in Sir Jeffrey's case, necessity.

'I take it you haven't had any more trouble or threats since I handed over that letter?'

'It's worked, whatever you did, and no' – she held up a hand – 'I don't want to know anything about it. I trust your ability to handle the whole rotten situation. I've had my fill of criminals.'

'Quite right.' I squeezed her shoulder reassuringly and dropped the subject. But, inside, I was secretly gleeful at how easy it had proved to eliminate a potentially very dangerous situation.

'Anyway, shall I see if I can help your shoulder?'

'Please.'

Tipping Leo off our knees, I went and sat in a straight-backed chair. Annabel went through her preparation routine and placed her hands gently on my shoulders for a few seconds.

I closed my eyes to cut out any visual disturbance, and although I didn't feel her touch me again I knew she was working systematically on my body from a short distance away. I also knew from experience she would begin by working on the seven energy points to balance them, followed by all the joints – without touching any of them.

A feeling of extreme relaxation filled me and my body began to tingle pleasantly. I could actually feel the energy running all the way through me, down to the soles of my feet.

The area around my shoulder began to feel very warm and the tingling sensation intensified. I could, literally, *feel* myself healing. I marvelled at it and at her unselfish attitude to my bodily condition.

My race riding was the one thing that had driven her away in the first place and here she was giving me devoted healing to restore my health in order that I could return to race riding – until I came off again. And bash myself up again. It was madness, whichever way you looked at it. But it was a madness I willingly submitted to, and, I suppose, was hopelessly addicted to.

She worked on me for about twenty minutes. Until, finally, she placed her hands lightly on my shoulders.

'There. How do you feel, Harry?'

'Wonderful, darling. I feel so relaxed I could just go to sleep.'

'And your pain levels?'

'Not there. I know I had some painkillers before you came but, quite honestly, right now, I can't feel a thing. Thank you.'

She smiled. 'Now, how about I fix us some supper? I fished in the freezer at home and came up with one of my home-made salmon fish pies. I thought you'd enjoy that and, of course' – she bent over and tickled Leo's ginger ear – 'his lordship could have some as well.'

'Sounds great.'

'Have a stretch out on the settee; give your body the chance to absorb the healing. Leave me to it in the kitchen.'

I wasn't about to argue with her. I tucked a couple of squashy cushions under my neck and shoulders and sprawled contentedly.

SEVENTEEN

I made a beast of myself with the salmon pie. Leo, of course, did the same. It was sheer luxury to have a meal cooked. And Annabel was a marvellous cook, could make even a simple meal taste really special.

I insisted she sat down afterwards while I cleared up in the kitchen. I hurried it through and joined her for coffee.

'Thanks.' I dropped down next to her on the settee. 'That was a great meal.'

'My pleasure.' She accepted the mug of coffee, sniffing appreciatively. 'How's your shoulder doing?'

'Can't feel it,' I said truthfully.

'Hmm . . . see how you go tomorrow. If it's a problem, I can always send some absent healing.'

'Yes, I know, and I'm grateful.'

She flipped her hand dismissively. 'I know if I ever need help, for whatever reason, I can call on you. Works both ways, Harry; it's never a one-way street. It's called life – *and* it's tough.'

'Yes.'

'And if you're on your own, it's even tougher.'

My thoughts went to Georgia. She was on her own now. I felt somewhat guilty that I'd not yet mentioned her to Annabel. Maybe now was the time. But before I could think how to broach it, she forestalled me.

'Talking of going it alone, I want you to know, Harry, I have no claims on your life. Yes, officially, we're still married, but that apart, I've got Jeffrey. For better – or worse.'

'I—'

'And,' she continued, holding up her hand, 'it would be incredibly selfish of me to expect you to keep sitting on the fence. What I'm saying is, why not look for another woman, one who fits you – and your lifestyle?'

'What we've been through – Jeffrey, you, me – has resulted in where we are now. And there is no way back. Just like a horse race, we can only go forward. Even if we can't see where we're going.'

She nodded. 'Exactly.'

'Jeffrey's the one who drew the short straw. He's the one who is relying on us both. As to us two, like you say, officially, we're still married.'

There were words needing to be said now. Maybe they had needed to be said some time ago. But once uttered, they could not be recalled. I felt the clutch of fear deep in my guts and had to force myself to get them out. Riding over fences in the Grand National was taxing on the nerves, but I was never scared. Now, I was bloody terrified what her answer would be.

'Are you asking for a divorce, Annabel?'

She shook her head quickly. 'No. It's not something I've felt is necessary. Strange as it seems, even when I was pregnant, I didn't consider it. I married you, Harry, because I loved you. People get divorced because they've *stopped* loving each other.' She looked directly into my eyes. 'In our case, that's not true, is it?'

'No,' I said quietly. 'But if you want to marry Jeffrey, then, yes, I will give you a divorce.'

'I don't.' She studied my face. 'Are *you* trying to say you want one? Have you met someone, someone special?'

'I have met a very sweet woman . . .'

For a brief moment, I saw the pain fill her eyes before she dropped her gaze.

'But that's a long way from considering divorce. I have taken her out two or three times.'

'What's her name?'

'Georgia. She owns a florist shop in Grantham.'

'How does she feel about you race riding?'

I hesitated. I knew how important my answer would be. 'She hasn't said.'

'But she knows you're a jump jockey?'

'Yes, she knows.'

'You must tell me, Harry.' She clutched my hand. 'If you want a divorce, of course I'll agree. It's your future we're talking about here, not just mine.'

'Annabel, my darling.' I took her face between my hands and kissed her very gently on the lips. 'There is nothing, no one, that will make me want to divorce you – ever.'

'But this woman – Georgia – if you're serious about her, maybe she will expect you to.'

'If our relationship should get to that stage, and I don't know if it ever will, I expect we would simply live together, like you and Jeffrey. It's enough for you two, isn't it?'

She nodded. 'Oh, yes.'

'Then let's carry on, just as we are. We both know circumstances that we can't control have come between us. But nothing's changed – not emotionally. You're still my best friend . . . I still love you.'

'I love you, Harry. I always will; you know that.' She took a deep breath. 'But I *want* you to go on seeing Georgia. You do need some female company. OK?'

'Yes, ma'am.'

I took her in my arms and held her, felt her arms go around me, reciprocating the acknowledgement of how things still stood between us.

'It needed saying, Harry.' Her words were a little muffled against my sweater.

'Yes.'

'So,' she sighed and drew back from the circle of my arms, 'I think I should be getting back.'

We stood up. I went over and parted the curtains, took a look at the state of the weather.

'Oh . . . oh dear.'

'Bad?'

She came to stand beside me. Together we looked out on huge, swirling snowflakes and deep snow covering everything.

'You're not going anywhere tonight.'

'No,' she agreed, shaking her head, 'I can see that.'

The last time Annabel had stayed all night at the cottage, we'd been through a hellish time, were both suffering mentally and physically, and she had slept in my bed.

Tonight, we weren't in a shocked emotional state with injuries that were bleeding – tonight, we both knew without saying anything, Annabel would be sleeping in the guest room.

But not on her own. Undoubtedly, she'd have company – Leo.

Jammy sod! That cat landed on his ginger paws every time.

Snow had ceased falling at some time during the night, but at seven a.m. the temperature was well below zero. Annabel had turned on the small television in the kitchen and was watching the early-morning weather forecast as she whisked eggs in a basin.

'They say it's going to stay like this for a few days.'

'Hmm. That's what Mike was going on about last night when he rang.'

Racing was off. And I was now at a loose end, something that didn't happen very often.

'You'll be a gentleman of leisure.'

'Not what I need.'

'No, but you can't race in these conditions.'

Her words made me think about what the trainer Tally Hunter had been telling me. 'Apparently, they do over in Switzerland.'

'What, race on snow?'

'Yeah. 'Course, I think it's mostly with their homebred horses. They are used to the cold climate and the snow.'

'Do any English trainers fly horses over?'

'Yes. Not many, though.'

'Would you like to try it?'

'Me? Give over. I have enough trouble staying in the saddle when the horse under me is running on grass.'

She laughed, spooning scrambled eggs on to buttered toast.

'Looks lovely, thanks.' I took the plate she handed me. 'Don't have breakfast at home usually. This is a treat.'

'Fancied some myself, before I drive back.'

'The lane might be a bit tricky but the milkman has already been down. I should try driving in his tyre tracks.'

'Hmm . . . don't worry, I intend to. I've already had a peep outside and seen the tracks. Anyway, once I take a right on to the main road, that will have been salted and it should be clear.'

'What time did you tell Jeffrey you'd be back?'

She'd rung him when it was obviously not safe to drive home. When she'd passed the phone over so I could speak to him, he'd urged me to make sure she stayed at Harlequin Cottage overnight, until the belt of snow sweeping across the country had gone and visibility was clear again.

'She'll enjoy your company, Harry, and Leo's, of course,' he'd chuckled.

There had been no trace of anxiety in his voice at the thought of Annabel being here all night with me – just the two of us. It was this level of trust that held me safe from abusing it. It worked better than a chastity belt.

I waved her off, regretfully, at around nine o'clock. Leo, sitting in the little side window of the cottage, watched her go. His ears were flat to his head. He wasn't pleased.

'I totally agree with you, mate. You want her to stay, too, don't you? Tell you what, how about some more breakfast, eh?'

Annabel had already fed him – a total indulgence – with pilchards. It had been a large tin she'd undone, there was plenty more left.

I'd just set down his bowl on the quarries in the kitchen when the landline extension rang.

'Racing's off, then, Harry.'

For a moment, I struggled to place the voice before realizing it was Tal Hunter.

'Oh, hello, yes, the whole country. Well, maybe not the all-weather, but I should think that's down to inspections.'

'So, how about it? You've no excuse now.'

'How about what, Tally?'

'Going over to Switzerland, take in the racing over there. I was telling you all about it, remember?'

'Oh, I don't think so. Grass is my thing.'

'Don't dismiss it. The whole White Turf racing experience is not to be missed.'

'I take it you're going?'

'Too true.'

'Well, do have a great time.'

'Aw, come on, Harry . . . You're redundant at the right time. Day after tomorrow, I've got a runner – one of Lady Branshawe's, actually.'

'Oh, I get it. She put you up to it, did she?'

'Now don't be like that. She may have mentioned how impressed she was by your riding—'

'No.'

'Doesn't the thought of a couple of days away watching a racing spectacular grab you?'

'I'm not saying it wouldn't be a terrific experience – *watching* it! But I'm not actually riding.'

'Well, then, bring a friend, make it a break. It's not likely you'll get the opportunity again.' She laughed. 'Snow in both countries at the same time, plus it's fallen just as the racing's about to go off.'

Annabel's words rang in my ear. *I want you to see Georgia.* I hesitated. Georgia was into horses. It might be something she would like . . .

'What do y'say?'

'Tally, let me mull it over for a bit. When are you flying out?'

'Taking off from Birmingham airport the day after tomorrow. Could give you a lift to the airport in my car.'

'I'll think about it; there are one or two things I need to do before I say definitely, OK?'

'Uh-huh, but if you're worried about getting a seat on the plane, I can easily look it up on the computer and book you one.'

'If I do go, you'll need to book two.'

'Right. Wait to hear from you. Bye.'

She rang off and left me trying to get my head around the offer. Firstly, I'd need to ring Georgia, or maybe it might be better to simply motor over to Grantham. Surprise her at The Trug Basket. The added advantage of surprise might make her say yes. I caught myself up. Was I seriously thinking of taking this opportunity? With a thrill of anticipation, I realized the answer was yes.

It would provide us with space away from our home ground to see how we got on. Holidays were notorious for either cementing friendships or pointing up the differences and breaking ties.

However, it wasn't simply following through on what Annabel had said; there was the unfinished business of John Dunston's plea in his letter. My conversation with Nathaniel Willoughby had reinforced the possible connection with Switzerland when he had told me about Jackson Fellows. And the further question that it might also involve Mike's late wife, Monica.

At that point, I suddenly remembered. I had the disposable camera that Pen had found. Photographs that Monica had taken while on holiday in Switzerland. So far, the camera was still sitting in the dash of my Mazda. I'd meant to take it into a chemist, get it developed. I'd forgotten.

I made a hasty decision. I'd drive over to Grantham and drop off the camera for fast developing before going to see Georgia.

With luck, the film could be picked up on my way home. It would be very interesting to see just what shots Monica had taken. Especially if they were shots of individual people. According to what Jackson Fellows had told Nathaniel, they were incriminating.

And it would be even more interesting to see what Georgia thought about going abroad with me.

EIGHTEEN

'**D**'you know, you're as bad as that cat, always landing on your feet – well, in Leo's case, paws. I don't know how you do it. Wish I did.' Mike shook his head in mock disbelief. 'Taking off to fly to another country at a moment's notice, getting waited on in a hotel – no work to do. *And* with a beautiful woman to hold your hand' – he grinned slyly – 'or anything else.'

'Mike . . .' Pen said warningly. 'Take no notice of him, Harry.'

'Pulling your leg, Harry,' he said hastily. 'Of course, I'll feed the main man while you're away. And, by the way, I'm very pleased for you. Georgia decided she'd like to go. What you need – a new woman.'

'That's what Annabel told me.'

'Did she? Well, she's right. You go and have a good time.'

'Appreciate it, Mike.'

I'd called in at the stables on my way back from Grantham. It had been ridiculously easy to persuade Georgia that she couldn't possibly pass up the chance to see the snow racing.

'Are you sure you want *me* to come with you?'

'Yes, I am sure.'

'I'd really love to watch those races. It sounds brilliant.'

Her enthusiasm acted on me like an accelerant on a pile of smouldering logs, and suddenly I found myself burning with anticipation and relishing the chance to go to Switzerland.

'Is there anything else you need doing, Harry?' Pen asked as she thrust a mug of tea in my hand.

'No. As long as Leo's OK, I guess that's it. If there is any emergency, you can always ring my mobile. I'll also give you the number of the hotel, when I get it sorted.'

'Take plenty of photographs to show us, Harry.' As soon as

she'd said the words, Pen's face betrayed what she was thinking. I needed to get her off the hook before Mike noticed anything wrong.

'Don't worry about any snapshots, Pen. I'll make sure of them.'

It felt devious, deceitful, to be talking subtext here with Mike standing in the room, smiling at us. But there was no chance to tell her what progress I'd made with developing the photographs in Monica's camera. At least now she would know I hadn't forgotten about them.

And until I'd had a chance to unwrap the package I'd collected from the chemist, had a good look through and decided if they were hot or not, it was best to say nothing further.

No fresh tyre tracks indented the snow in the lane leading to Harlequin Cottage. I drove confidently through the open gate and crunched gently to a stop by the back door. Whatever the advantages of this weather, the best one was the sense of security it gave me on arriving home. No need to check if any undesirables were staked out ready to jump me. I knew there weren't any. Apart from my own footprints – and Leo's paw prints – the snow lay pristine and utterly beautiful in its smooth perfection.

And if it looked this good in my own garden in England, what would it look like over in Switzerland?

St Moritz was the ultimate venue. Frequented by royalty, the wealthy and assorted film stars – it was alleged Kate Moss and George Clooney had been spotted recently – magnet-like, it attracted the famous and successful too, like the effervescent flat jockey Frankie Dettori. He had certainly raced on the frozen lake. All those fabulous winter sports – not least, the fearsome Cresta Run. With Piz Nair towering impressively above the town and lake, all cloaked in white glory, it was going to be some experience.

With a thrill of expectation, I thought about Georgia. It was high time I broke my duck and shared a bed with a beautiful woman again.

I shoved the kettle on to the Rayburn hotplate and, while it came to the boil, slipped upstairs and gathered up several shirts, sufficient underwear and socks, plus – an afterthought – my silk pyjamas, returning to the kitchen to toss them into the washer.

Going through to the office with a scalding mug of tea, I

took the package of photographs from my pocket and sat down at the desk. Picking up the heavy, silver paper knife, I slit open the wrapping. Upending the folder from inside, I shook out the contents. They slithered all over the leather desktop – twenty-odd photos.

Taking a gulp of tea, I sat the mug down on a coaster and nudged the photographs apart, placing them face up. Monica had been no Lord Lichfield. Two or three were useless shots, ruined by too much light. I examined the rest one by one.

Several were shots of Clara, Mousey's late wife, who had accompanied Monica on holiday. I looked at them and felt a pang of sadness. She looked so happy, carefree. The pair of them did. Obviously, they'd cajoled some other holidaymaker into taking several shots of them together. Both Clara and Monica were grinning cheekily at the camera. In one Monica was waving a ski pole, either having successfully returned from a ski or about to head off down one of the slopes. The overall impression was that they were having a great time.

But for me, the person seeing these photographs for the first time, the knowledge that both women would be seriously injured – in Monica's case, dead – so soon after was gutting in the extreme.

I stood up, took my mug of tea for a walk around the room and sank the contents.

Then I bent over the desk and looked at the rest of the snaps. Most of them were of the spectacular landscape, Alps in the background, plus hotels, shops and ski-lift. Monica had tried to have a foreground subject to give perspective, usually people. I pondered over what threat could be contained in these innocent-looking holiday shots.

Two or three group snaps showed people clustered around outside tables, drinks in hand, smiles abounding. I didn't recognize anyone. But just one picture, showing two men standing beside some snow-laden trees, tweaked my antennae. Something about one of the figures seemed vaguely familiar. Not facially – they were both wearing dark glasses – but the stance of the body, undoubtedly aggressive, had me interested. I studied it closely for several minutes, but nothing enlightening came to mind.

Beginning at the first picture, I worked my way through them again. Nothing. However, concentrating on the pair of figures again, I felt a prickle at the back of my neck. Exactly what it signified,

I'd no idea. I couldn't recognize either of the men, but the feeling persisted, niggling at the edge of my mind, that there was definitely something familiar about one of them. It was bloody frustrating but trying to force recognition wasn't going to work.

Finally, in exasperation, I scooped them up and slid the whole lot back into the folder. They could keep until I returned from Switzerland. Maybe, by then, my subconscious would have come up with the answer. Since I'd been virtually kneecapped into chasing killers, I'd come to rely quite a lot on my sixth sense, intuition . . . whatever.

The landline on the desk rang. It was Tal Hunter.

'Everything OK, Harry?'

'It surely is, Tal.'

'And?'

She didn't need to ask if there'd be two tickets needed on the aeroplane: the cheeky lift to her tone said it for her.

'Yes . . . two needed.'

She giggled. 'Don't forget passports. You'll need them, have to go through passport control at Heathrow' – then dropped her bomb-shell – 'even though we're going in Lady Branshawe's private jet.'

'*What?*'

'Pick you up in my car around nine a.m. tomorrow morning – that all right?'

'Doesn't sound like I have a choice.'

'Now, come on, Harry. These offers don't come along very often. Think how impressed your lady friend's going to be.'

'How come you didn't tell me straight off about the travel arrangements?'

'Not down to me. What's the trainers' mantra?'

'Keep the owners sweet.'

'Exactly.'

I could practically hear the smile on her face. 'Mike says I'm devious. I reckon you're way out in front.'

She was openly laughing now. 'See you, Harry.'

I'd telephoned Georgia immediately. Arranged to collect her from Plungar at eight a.m.

'You see,' I said, as we drew up at the cottage in plenty of time to be picked up, 'far better than you driving yourself here and having to leave your car outside in the snow.'

Georgia stepped out carefully on to the snow-packed gravel while I lugged her suitcase from the boot of the Mazda.

'Oh, look . . . is that Leo?' She pointed towards the back door where a large ginger cat was sitting on the doorstep.

He was sizing her up. I could almost read what he was thinking. *Not Annabel – so who?*

'Yep. The village stud.'

'What can you expect if you don't have him neutered.'

'Shhh . . .' I said. 'I'll be mugged by all the queens.'

'Idiot.' She laughed. And walked across to Leo, held out a hand for his inspection. With much whisker-twitching, he sniffed delicately.

'Will I do?' she asked.

Leo stood up unhurriedly, prowled over the snow and launched himself at me. Reaching my shoulder, he bashed his head against my face and bellowed a greeting.

'Does he always do that?'

'Pretty much,' I said. I walked up to the kitchen door and opened it.

'He must weigh a ton, he's massive.'

'Can't argue with that.' I stood to the side and gestured her into the kitchen. 'He's not over-friendly with strangers. Soft as melting ice cream with Annabel, of course.'

'His mistress,' she agreed.

We stood there, the echo of her words lingering. I broke the suddenly charged atmosphere. 'Just get the brute fed. Tal will be here in a few minutes.'

'Point me to the bathroom. It's a good drive to Birmingham.'

'Sure,' I nodded, 'upstairs, first right. Oh, and by the way, it's a good idea because we're going right down to Heathrow.'

'But I thought you said . . .' She hesitated, a tiny frown wrinkling her forehead.

I nodded again. 'I did. But Tal's bowed to the wishes of Lady Branshawe. Apparently, we're going over to St Moritz in her private jet.'

Tal would have been gratified with Georgia's reaction to that bit of news. Her mouth opened in an 'O' of surprise.

'My word! I'm very impressed.'

I grinned. 'Tally said you would be.'

'She was so right.'

'Still glad you agreed to come on the trip?'

'Are you joking, Harry Radcliffe? It's a fairy tale that's getting better all the time.'

I put Leo's dish down on the floor and he took a dive off my shoulder, applied himself to the serious business of eating his breakfast and promptly ignored us.

'I sincerely hope you enjoy everything.'

She reached out, took my face between her hands. 'I'm *sure* I shall. Thank you again for asking me, Harry.'

Then she gave me a very quick kiss before turning and heading upstairs.

A few minutes later, the horseshoe knocker sounded a loud bang, bang, bang on the back door.

'Ready?' I asked Georgia.

With eyes sparkling with excitement, she nodded emphatically.

I opened the door. Tally, wearing a furry hat and her St Moritz coat, smiled broadly.

'Do introduce me, Harry.'

'I'm Georgia. Hello. You're Tally Hunter, aren't you? And yes, you were spot on: I'm *very* impressed.'

'You're happy with the new arrangement?'

'Absolutely.'

It was quite clear. Georgia was fizzing with barely held-in excitement. Tal laughed and gave her a hug.

'I can see you're going to be good for our Harry.'

NINETEEN

Aboard the private jet, seated in white leather facing seats, comfortable as armchairs, we were all buckled up, prepared for arrival in Switzerland.

'Of course,' Lady Branshawe said, leaning towards us, 'it all begins with a party this evening.'

Even as she spoke, the aircraft began its descent through an unbelievably blue sky to Samedan, the airport in Engadin. We had covered the distance between England and Switzerland in a staggering one hour and fifty minutes – a swift and creamy-smooth flight.

'I told Harry it's a fairy tale that keeps getting better,' said Georgia, 'and I wasn't wrong.'

'Well,' I said, 'flying in by private jet certainly qualifies. I'm not saying it hasn't been a fabulous way of flying, but a commercial airline could have delivered us safely, and much less costly, I'm sure.'

'Oh, Harry,' Lady Branshawe said, laughing, 'it's only money. And the beauty of money is that it's meant to be enjoyed. Just tell me you've all enjoyed your flight.'

'Oh, absolutely,' Tally said.

'We have – it's been sheer luxury,' Georgia agreed.

'I think,' I said, 'we'll all remember this trip years into the future.'

'Well, there you are, then, Harry – totally worthwhile. Sometimes happiness *can* be bought.'

'And we'll be even happier if we have a winner.'

Lady Branshawe had entered two horses. Tally had earlier supervised their journey by horse transporter through the Channel Tunnel – a distance of just under eight hundred miles – with two stable lads in attendance. They'd be safely rugged up and ensconced in the racecourse stables now. I hoped they wouldn't be too unsettled by the thinner air and, of course, the drop in temperature. Even though England was currently experiencing sub-zero readings and snow, over here in St Moritz it would be very much colder. Maybe going down to as low as minus twenty degrees overnight and into the early hours of the morning.

Some horses didn't acclimatize – it was certainly a factor that couldn't be foreseen – but most horses adjusted very well and turned in fine racing performances on the frozen lake.

The temperature had to be low to allow the requisite sixty-centimetre depth of ice to form on the lake before it would be decreed safe for the enormous weight of all the marquees, equipment, people and, of course, the horses themselves, thundering along at thirty plus miles an hour.

I drew my attention back to the present. We were coming in to land. Samedan Airport was about five kilometres from St Moritz. However, Lady Branshawe had, once again, put her generous hand in her pocket and informed us, as we flew in over the glistening white Alps, that a helicopter awaited us to complete our journey.

At that moment, I'd glanced quickly at Georgia's face. I'd had to smother a laugh because it was clear from the way her chin began to drop that she'd struggled, successfully this time, to prevent her lips forming that 'O' of delighted surprise. But her hand had found mine and given a little squeeze of excitement. I squeezed back. She'd turned her head and smiled into my face before silently mouthing 'Thank you'. What she didn't realize was that it was a pleasure to watch her almost childlike delight at everything that was unfolding.

It increased my own enjoyment and my thoughts flicked quickly to Annabel. Without her prompting, I doubted whether I would have agreed to come on this trip. How tonight would pan out, I didn't want to consider right now. Georgia's acceptance of my invitation to St Moritz in no way compromised her regarding our sleeping arrangements.

A picture of the pub manager's face at the Dirty Duck halted any further thoughts in that direction. There had definitely been an attachment – albeit, maybe only on his side – when I'd taken Georgia out for a meal there. Her attitude to him had been totally relaxed – friendly, but nothing more.

One thing was for sure: no way was I going to put pressure on her. We both needed to find our way through our own particular emotional minefield. But for now, looking at the happy expectancy on her face, I was content to let things happen in the right way – unforced, naturally.

The helicopter was a superb model, decked out inside in cream with navy seats. With everybody wearing the regulation ear-protectors, it lifted off for the ten-minute flight, swooping over a winter landscape that was totally wonderful. The Alps, imposing when seen from the jet, were suddenly soaring above us, a different perspective, a stupendous backdrop to St Moritz, with the effect of effortlessly raising blood pressure with their regal magnificence.

'Pinch me, Harry,' Georgia whispered. 'I must be dreaming.'

I obligingly gave her hand a squeeze.

Lady Branshawe had caught the whisper, however, and leaned forward, smiling. 'I think you'll find it's very real.'

'Too true,' Tally agreed.

She had been here before, so the stunning impact that was

working its magic on Georgia was, for her, somewhat diluted. But it was still high-proof for all of us.

The helicopter circled around the lake, giving a marvellous overview, blades whipping around in a sudden flurry of snowflakes, before very gently descending and landing without a bump.

We all breathed out deeply, none of us aware that we'd been holding our breath with the wonder of the flight so skilfully executed by our pilot.

Lady Branshawe had informed me during the flight that we were all staying at Koselig Hotel, one of the acknowledged premier hotels in St Moritz. I'd gulped when she'd said it. Heaven knows how she'd managed to arrange for us to be accommodated at such short notice. I didn't dig. It was enough that we were so superbly catered for.

But my opinion of Lady Branshawe rose sharply. If she carried clout like that, I definitely needed to increase my respect. Of course, the simplest reason could be that she was fabulously rich, but I suspected it had more to do with her personal standing as a member of the aristocracy.

The taxi deposited us at the entrance of the huge hotel and we were ushered in by a concierge smartly dressed in maroon and white, our luggage discreetly whisked away to be put in our rooms, and we were ushered across and signed in at reception.

'Welcome to Koselig Hotel, Lady Branshawe,' said a smiling young woman in perfect English, although she was undoubtedly Swiss. She handed over our keys. 'Do enjoy your stay.'

Although Tally and Lady Branshawe had adjacent rooms on the first floor on the south side of the hotel overlooking the lake, my own double room was on the second floor, facing north, as was Georgia's. I wasn't about to grumble in any way. Our view was one of Piz Nair. When I thought about how I so nearly hadn't taken up Tally's offer, my stomach lurched. I'd been a complete idiot to even contemplate not coming. I took my key and we agreed to split up for now and meet in the restaurant for refreshments in an hour.

Tally and Lady Branshawe stepped out of the lift on the first floor, leaving it to travel on upwards to the second floor where our rooms were. Georgia followed me along the thickly carpeted corridor to Rooms 203 and 204. I opened the door to my own room, 203, and ushered her in first. She caught her breath. The

room was decorated in muted shades of gold and cream. Only one
word could describe it: palatial. And if *our* rooms were as grand
as this, what on earth was Lady Branshawe's like? And, in addition, she had access to a balcony overlooking the racecourse. I
slipped off my jacket and turned to Georgia.

'Well?'

She shrugged her shoulders, spread her arms wide. 'I'm definitely dreaming.'

'I think your room is a single. Are you OK with that?'

'Harry, we could have been spending the night down in the
stables on straw. Lady Branshawe's worked miracles to get us
these lovely rooms.'

'Even so—'

She took a couple of steps forward and gripped my upper arms,
giving me a tiny shake. 'Shush . . .' Then kissed me lightly on
the lips. 'One step at a time, I think. OK?'

With my eyes locked on to hers, I nodded. 'Tiptoe, if you need to.'

She grinned. 'What I need . . . is a cup of coffee, with some
lovely Swiss cream poured in.'

'Ha, yes, world-renowned, isn't it, the cream? And don't
leave out the cheese – one of the things the Swiss do best.'

'Hmm' – she opened her eyes very wide – 'but don't forget the
cuckoo clocks.'

We both collapsed with laughter on to the double bed. I risked
a kiss, lifting her long hair with both my hands. Her response was
immediate . . . before she drew back swiftly. 'Coffee, Harry.'

I stood up. 'I'll join you.'

Coffee downed, clothes unpacked and hung up, we returned
downstairs to the lounge. Lady Branshawe and Tally had just seen
off some refreshments and were suitably revived and energized.
We all agreed that before the evening celebrations began, we should
take advantage of the chance to see the centre of St Moritz itself,
up close and personal.

Accordingly, we spent an enjoyable couple of hours walking
around, exploring the many sights of St Moritz. There were delightful
cafés selling tempting arrays of exquisitely made cakes and delicacies. With difficulty, we resisted the lure of calories.

Instead, we turned our attention to the shops: upmarket ones
that boasted names such as Fabergé and Cartier, and many shops

selling assorted tourists' souvenirs – cowbells, china jugs emblazoned with the flag of Switzerland – and, of course, a preponderance of clocks, most of them sporting white enamel cases and faces. One shop that particularly intrigued Georgia sold only cuckoo clocks, all sizes, all prices – mostly very expensive prices.

We wandered around like mesmerized kids looking in the windows. And in a totally white world, it was amazing to see the roads and pavements completely free of snow and actually glistening. The Swiss had perfected living with freedom of mobility in an environment that could have seemed hostile. If England experienced this degree of snowfall, it would have completely seized up travel. One key factor for achieving this smooth efficiency of movement of transport and pedestrians was down to the snow-ploughs and the mini-snowploughs used on the pavements. Instead of being poleaxed by nature's generous dumping of snow, the Swiss had turned it to their own advantage, and tourism and winter sports were big business.

What struck me most was the purity of the air. There was a crispness and exhilaration in breathing in such crystal oxygen. And it wasn't just the experience of such a rarefied atmosphere: there was a sense of order and cleanliness everywhere.

Everything was done in an efficient fashion; the streets were free from any litter whatsoever and no graffiti shamed any of the walls or buildings. The whole town was pin-sharp and pristine – and bathed in sunshine.

'It's amazing,' Georgia said, putting into words what I was thinking.

'Everywhere is *so* clean, so beautifully laid out. It really is breathtaking, isn't it?'

Lady Branshawe agreed.

'But you must agree,' Tally said, 'that back home when we have a substantial snowfall, everything suddenly becomes beautiful, all the dirty imperfections are painted out.'

She was right. But here in Switzerland it was all somehow so much more glamorous.

We had completed our walk along the main street, past the variety of shops, and were almost back at the lake now.

I would have liked to go and look round the stables, but if it was subject to the same rules we had operating in England, that wasn't going to be possible without a pass.

'Has Sam contacted you yet, Tally?'

Sam Smith was Tally's travelling head lad. Keeping him company on the journey over was Brian Dorset, one of Mousey's stable lads. They would be billeted in the lads' quarters.

'Hmm . . . yes. I spoke to him earlier while Lady Branshawe and I were having coffee. Both horses are fine, settled into their stables and eating their heads off.'

'Sounds about right.' I grinned. 'Any chance of getting clearance to have a look round?'

'I did intend to go round later, probably before the party. See what I can do.'

'Thanks, Tally.'

Our wandering footsteps had brought us to the frozen lake. All the marquees were spread out, offering a wide variety of food and drinks for the delectation of the racegoers. Bathed in sunshine, the shimmering bright colours of the little village, enclosed by the edge of the lake, were an amazing sight. All manner of tantalizing smells drifted on the keen air as we meandered between the different tents.

'Mmm . . .' Georgia lifted her face and sniffed like a hound on the trail. 'Something smells very tempting.'

'And what would that be?' Lady Branshawe asked.

'Hot chocolate, Swiss style, at a guess.'

All three women reacted like Pavlov's dogs.

'Oh, yes,' Tally agreed, 'I'm definitely up for one of those.'

'And me,' Lady Branshawe and Georgia chorused in unison.

Laughing, they dragged me into a sumptuously equipped marquee that had a carpeted floor – amazing to think that underneath was sheer ice – chairs and tables and a fabulous display of beverages.

'My treat,' Georgia said. At the head of our group, she went up to the assistant. 'Harry? Shall I order four?'

'Oh, no.' I held up a hand firmly. 'One of those will set my weight-watching back for a month. No, thanks. I'll settle for a black coffee.'

We watched as the girl filled three elegant mugs with hot chocolate topped with sweetened whipped cream and a million calories, and poured one black coffee.

'No cream?' Lady Branshawe said incredulously. 'We're in the land of cream.'

'No cream,' I said.

'You don't know what you're turning down,' Tally taunted, reaching for the tray to assist Georgia.

It certainly looked good, but a strong coffee would do me fine. It had been a chilly trip into the town.

The women added sugar to their drinks and took a first sip.

'Oh, my word' – Lady Branshawe closed her eyes briefly – 'that is the very best hot chocolate I have *ever* tasted.'

I looked enquiringly at the other two. They appeared to have gone to a heavenly place themselves.

'Definitely worth flying over for.' Tally dabbed the corner of her mouth. 'You can't get hot chocolate like this anywhere else in the world. Not to be missed.'

'And you, Georgia?'

She had just taken a further sip and was savouring the drink, also with eyes closed. 'Oh, yes, just perfect. I can feel it going right down to my toes and warming them up.'

I shook my head at them, laughing. 'You're all easily satisfied.'

My own coffee was excellent.

We relaxed in the warmth and comfort, enjoying ourselves, looking forward to the evening party and the next day's racing.

Until a voice behind me instantly dispelled the 'feel-good' mood.

'They do say, chocolate is a lady's substitute for . . . something else pleasurable.'

I recognized the voice, hoped to goodness I was wrong, but knew I wasn't. In every garden of Eden, it seemed, there was a serpent.

I turned and met the mocking eyes of Rawlson.

TWENTY

Lady Branshawe's lips had drawn tightly together.

I threw Rawlson a 'back off' look that he ignored. His whole attitude was one of self-importance as he stood there, smirking.

Tally intervened, Lady Branshawe's disapproval not having gone unnoticed; she called him to order. 'Yes, Duncan, as you say, we are ladies. I suggest you save that sort of comment for the weighing room or the stables, OK?'

'Certainly,' Rawlson smirked. 'You're the boss.'

There was an uncomfortable silence that stretched. The ease and enjoyment of only a few moments ago had totally disappeared. I felt my anger start to rise. Lady Branshawe had paid out a hefty sum to get us over here and, on top of that, footed the accommodation costs. She didn't deserve to be irritated by Duncan Rawlson and his big mouth. But no one else seemed about to speak, so I needed to kickstart the conversation. In the flurry of attending to necessary arrangements before coming to Switzerland, I'd been very remiss and not checked up on the racing details.

'You're here to ride, I take it?'

'Got it in one.' His smirk was pure Cheshire cat. 'And, I take it, you're not.'

'Harry is here as my guest,' Lady Branshawe said imperiously, 'not as my employee.'

The smirk abruptly left Rawlson's face and he glared daggers at me.

Georgia, trying to defuse the tension, said generously, 'I hope you win tomorrow.'

He swung round and stared at her, no longer glaring, but appraising.

'You're Radcliffe's girlfriend, yes?'

Georgia, seeing his interest rising almost to a leer, reddened and nodded.

'Very nice.' He peeled his gaze away. Then sneered at me. 'You've got taste, I'll give you that. Still, when you get back with your wife – and you can't deny you want to – I'll be here to step in.'

At his words, the colour drained from Georgia's face, leaving her white and strained.

'I think you'd better leave, Duncan.' Tally had stood up, emphasizing her authority. 'I'll speak to you tomorrow, before you race.'

He inclined his head. 'Whatever.'

There was a distinct lightening of the atmosphere as we watched him walk away through the marquee entrance.

'Sorry about that, Georgia.' I reached for her hand. 'Take no notice. He's just being vindictive. It's nothing personal against you. It's me he's gunning for.'

She smiled wryly. 'Let's hope he rides a winner. That will massage his ego.'

'We're all hoping for a winner,' Lady Branshawe said. She leaned forward towards Georgia and added, 'What I said in the plane on the way here is what really matters. The most important thing is to enjoy the experience.'

'And I'm sure all of us have,' Tally said. 'So far we've had a wonderful time and the racing tomorrow will be totally different to anything you've seen before. It will blow you away. Please excuse the jockey's mean-spiritedness.' She turned to me. 'It's really only jealousy.'

'Don't apologize for him, Tally. He's a grown man. If he chooses to act like an idiot, that's his affair.'

We opted for a further round of drinks and settled back, people-watching and simply soaking up the happy, relaxed atmosphere. A beautiful piece of piano playing – Chopin – had just begun. It was the perfect build-up to the evening's party.

When the piece ended, Tally excused herself and took Lady Branshawe to see their two horses at evening stables. Georgia said she'd prefer to see the special racing preparations being carried out on the following morning. I wouldn't have minded doing both stable visits, but it would be churlish to leave Georgia by herself.

I'd left my mobile switched on after I'd rung Mike to let him know the name and telephone number of the hotel, so I wasn't expecting a call but the phone rang just as we'd said goodbye to the other two. The strains of 'The Great Escape' contrasted sharply with the classical piece we'd just heard. It was Nathaniel Willoughby, the horse artist.

'Harry, how're you doing?'

'Doing great. You were quite right: it's a fabulous place.'

'Glad you're having a good time. But the reason I've rung is that I've just been scrolling down the pictures on my phone and I've found one I think you'd find interesting.'

I looked across the table at Georgia. I knew I needed to choose my words carefully. No way did I want to involve her.

'What's the subject?'

'It's one that somebody took when I was over in Switzerland before and it shows me with that er . . . that certain person I was telling you about. You remember, the broken fingers . . .?'

'Ha, yes.' I did remember. It was one of the reasons I'd decided
to come here. 'Could you send it to my phone, Nathaniel?'

'Yes, I'll do it now, OK?'

'Thanks.'

Georgia, sitting opposite me, was trying not to listen. I slid the
phone back inside my jacket pocket. I'd look at it in private later.
The photo was going to prove invaluable in trying to spot Jackson
Fellows. No point in looking for someone with two bandaged
fingers; by now they would be completely healed. My best chance
would be to study the photo and fix his face in my mind and see
if I could find him during the racing tomorrow.

Nathaniel had said that Jackson came to watch the snow racing
every year. No doubt he'd be one of the many pressed up to the
barriers at the side of the lake tomorrow. But thinking of the
thousands who would be doing just that, my optimism took a hit.
I was going to need a big helping of luck.

Earlier, having gone to our separate rooms to freshen up and
change for the evening's entertainment, we were now dressed in
our best and ready to party. Leaving the hotel at around seven
o'clock, we came outside on to the frozen lake.

There was a band playing some popular music in the massive
marquee and an area of the polished floor had been cleared to
accommodate dancing. Chandeliers and spinning, glittering globes
hung from the roof lighting in the interior while, outside, darkness
had fallen and the temperature had dipped steeply.

However, inside the marquee we were kept comfortably warm
by hot-air fan heaters. We were surrounded on all sides – and
underneath – by temperatures well below zero. Yet we were
unaware of the coldness. It was truly amazing, a successful feat
on the part of the management. It was also a good job, given the
off-the-shoulder Grecian dress Georgia had chosen to wear.

We'd managed to stake a claim for a table for four and proceeded
to load our plates from the tempting buffet laid out. It included all
the normal types of cooked meats, fish and, of course, cheeses, plus
roasted venison and German sausages . . . the smells were delicious,
the choice endless. Whatever your preference or dietary needs, it
was catered for – in abundance and variety. We were being spoilt.

'Can you indulge?' asked Georgia, teasing, a twinkle in her
eye.

'Oh, I'm sure he can.' Lady Branshawe popped an elaborate concoction of hot runny cheese into her mouth. 'You can't ride right now, can you, Harry, so why not indulge yourself?'

'Yes, go on, Harry, make a beast of yourself for once.'

I faced the three females, the sisterhood all ganging up on me, smiling gleefully. 'Whoa, I'm outnumbered here.'

No sooner had I said it than a tap on my shoulder gave a lie to my words.

'Hello, everyone.' Clive Unwin, the trainer from Leicestershire, part of a group of four men, had arrived behind me.

'Hello, Clive. Thought you might be here,' Tally said.

'Oh yes, and looking forward to seeing the racing, the same as you. I think we all know each other, but won't you introduce your young friend?' He beamed at Georgia. 'Of course, I know Lady Branshawe. And everybody knows Harry,' he said, laughing.

I did the honours and introduced Georgia to the four men: in addition to Clive Unwin, there was Edward Frame, a businessman from Lincolnshire, whom I'd first met at North Shore Hotel at Skegness in what had started out as a celebration but degenerated into horrific circumstances; Nigel Garton, Victor Maudsley's son-in-law; and, rather unexpectedly, Philip Caxton, the solicitor from York.

'We're part of the syndicate,' explained Edward. He named one of the horses that would be running tomorrow.

'I didn't know you were interested in horseracing,' I said to Caxton. I'd not seen him since the funeral business.

'Oh, yes, have been for years. Never owned one outright, though, you understand,' he said. 'I expect I own half a leg.' He laughed. His involvement in racing probably explained why Dunston had chosen him when looking for a suitable solicitor. 'Seemed a number of us chose this year to come over and watch.'

Unwin took over the reins of the conversation. 'Philip Caxton's my solicitor, actually. I engaged him straight off the ark.' He bellowed with laughter. 'These three chaps are part of the "Win or Bust" syndicate – twelve in it altogether, been going for years. Obviously, some come and go, but this trio all keep going, thank God. However, this is the first year we've had a horse that's running on snow. So, here we are!' He rubbed his hands together with exuberant anticipation.

'And we're hyped as hell,' Edward agreed.

'What about you, Mr Garton?'

'Oh, do call me Nigel, Harry,' he said, with the so-smooth 'I'm your best friend' approach of the vote-seeking politician. 'As I'm sure you know, my father-in-law was a trainer before he retired, so it's rubbed off, I guess.'

I certainly did remember Victor Maudsley – with mixed feelings. I'd ridden for him many times, years ago, when Victor had been actively training. But after his retirement from racing, our paths had crossed in unbelievable ways. Ways that were prompted by my being asked to ghostwrite the biography of his wife, Elspeth, who had taken over the running of Unicorn stables.

I wanted to forget about that time in my life – a very bad time, which had all ended in tears . . . and death.

Nigel was married to Paula, Victor's only daughter.

'You're an MP, I believe?'

'That's correct, Lady Branshawe, but a junior one.'

'I'm sure that's only for now. Head for the top. Even if you don't actually hit the moon, you're sure to end up on a star.'

'Very kind of you to say so.' Garton smirked at her words.

But it was true: he had ambitions for the top, had a thrusting personality. The phrase 'win or bust' could also be applied to his approach to life and other people.

But seeing the four men together, disparate in their choice of careers, yet united in their interest, it proved the point that racing did indeed hold an attraction for people from all social strata.

'Do let me get you all a drink,' Nigel urged, beaming round at us.

I cynically thought he no doubt had an eye on possible future votes. I knew he spent a good deal of time down in London while his wife, Paula, and their three exuberant sons – hell-on-wheels on skateboards – lived in Lincolnshire.

It was a situation I myself couldn't envisage. If I could still claim Annabel as my wife – which obviously I couldn't – I wouldn't want to spend three-quarters of my life living apart from her. I did that now – and found it hell.

'How did you travel over?' Edward asked, accepting his beer.

'We caught a plane to Zurich and then came on by train.'

'I coerced them into flying with me,' Lady Branshawe said, laughing. 'All my fault, I'm afraid.'

'No point in having empty seats, I suppose,' Caxton said. But I caught the barely concealed touch of envy in his expression.

'Lady Branshawe was very generous in asking us,' Tally put in.

But Lady Branshawe waved away her words. 'Nothing is ever a free ride. I had the pleasure of good company – and am still enjoying it.'

''Course, we sent the horse overland by transporter,' said Clive.

'Did you get to see your horses, Tally? Have they settled in?' asked Georgia, sipping her wine.

'They have, plated up, rugged up and eating up. You and Harry could have come with us. It seems very relaxed – no rigid rules.'

Tally turned to me. 'You must both come tomorrow.'

'We will.'

'I particularly want to see the special racing plates,' Georgia said.

The drinks and conversation continued to flow on racing matters, and every now and again, I cast an eye around the marquee looking for the face that matched the one in the photograph Nathaniel had sent me. But as the band finally finished playing at the end of a convivial enjoyable evening, and the party drew to a close, I was no further forward in finding him.

'Brrrr . . .' Georgia gave a little shiver and rubbed her hand up and down her bare shoulder. 'Getting cold suddenly.'

And it was.

Tally laughed. 'I remember what happens. Don't forget, I've been here before.'

'What happens?' Lady Branshawe queried.

'It's a slight hint. They turn off the heating. Meaning it's about time the guests trotted off. Bearing in mind that we're actually sitting on top of sixty centimetres of solid ice, it would be impossible to stay here without some warmth.'

'Better than calling time,' Edward chortled, as we all stood up to leave. 'You're quite right, Georgia, it is getting cold.' He looked pointedly at her flimsy dress. 'And I've got a jacket on . . .'

I slid Georgia's stole around her bare shoulders and we all walked out over the ice back to the welcome warmth of our respective hotels.

We said goodnight to Tally and Lady Branshawe as the lift stopped at the first floor inside the Koselig Hotel. They stepped out and walked away.

Now it just left the two of us. The lift rose to the second floor. Without speaking, we stepped out and walked down the thick carpet to number 203. Georgia stopped, turned to face me.

'Coming in?' I invited, saying the words lightly, leaving the decision entirely to her.

She was standing very close. Her perfume drifted in the warm air, filling my nostrils, a delightful exotic musk. The warmth and the perfume together were acting as an aphrodisiac. I hadn't shared a bed with a woman for a long time – far too long. I reached out and placed my palm against her cheek.

'I'd like you to.'

'Would you, Harry?' She stared into my eyes.

'Yes. You know I would.'

She continued to stare, her questioning gaze penetrating deep inside me.

'But you would much rather it was Annabel.'

It wasn't a question.

'Georgia—'

'No, Harry. What that man said – it was *true*, wasn't it?'

I let my hand drop away from her soft cheek.

'Georgia, Annabel's not here. You are.'

As soon as I said the words, I knew they were wrong, clumsy, cruel. And I hadn't meant it to sound so insensitive.

She flinched, drew away. 'I'd prefer to sleep in my own room – if you don't mind.'

'I do mind. I'd really like to spend the night with you, Georgia.'

'Hmm . . .' She smiled thinly. 'But I'm not going to, Harry. I'll see you in the morning.'

Before I could reply, she'd taken a few steps further down the corridor, opened door number 204 and disappeared inside. I watched the door close behind her and cursed myself for being a crass, hurtful prat.

And the words I'd said to Tally earlier now came back to taunt me.

Rawlson wasn't the only idiot around here.

TWENTY-ONE

I f you arrived with your eyes closed, you would still know, straight away, there were horses here. Just inside the racecourse stables – surprisingly, they were located in an area that was difficult to find – I briefly closed my eyes, took a deep breath. The smell was one of my favourites, had been since childhood. It was like coming home: the comforting, familiar smell of warm horse-flesh, exacerbated by the small, enclosed space within the stables.

Outside, the temperature was reading minus ten degrees; it was a cold one today and smells seemed reduced.

But inside, near the horses, which were powerhouses of warm energy, the smell was heightened. Mixing with the inevitable ammonia, it was pungent.

Apart from the distinctive smell, the stables were also filled with conversation and noise. Horses whinnied and struck out, catching the sides of their boxes; head collars and bridles were shaken and rattled. And overall the urgent pounding of the farrier's hammer added to the build-up of the tension in the air and excited anticipation. It was a bustling, busy place.

'You're doing your "Bisto Kid" thing again, Harry,' Tally teased, as she threaded her way between the farrier and a number of stable lads and proud owners.

'Guess I'm an addict.'

'A horse nut,' Lady Branshawe quipped, keeping a straight face.

'Pity we haven't got any to offer them,' said Georgia.

I followed the three women down the central concrete walkway between the boxes. Lady Branshawe's horses were at the far end in two facing boxes. They both swung quarters over and came up to put inquiring heads over the half-doors. As we approached, they whickered softly. Georgia clicked to them and pulled their ears gently.

'You're going to win for me, aren't you, my lovelies?' Lady Branshawe took off her glove and stroked the white blaze running down the bay's face. The big softie allowed his long-lashed eyelids to close gently over intelligent eyes.

Tally and I exchanged glances. There was a subtle difference in the way the two women reacted to the big animals and how we did. For us, we respected and had affection – and sometimes, if we didn't watch it, deep affection – for the horses. But to us, they weren't pets. Horses were an essential part of our working life; without slightly distancing our emotions, it wouldn't be possible to operate.

Racing was a tough business. Always, at the start of a race, you would set off on a sound eager horse, but if disaster struck partway down the course, you could find yourself ending the race alone. It was a gutting experience to lose a horse, but it happened. Allow too much emotion, and you were done for. So it was like a personal insurance – a damn fine tightrope you tried to walk. And I'd be the first to admit, seeing those screens go round a faller gave me a sock in the solar plexus every time. And sometimes, just sometimes, if it was fatal, I cried.

However, it was the stable lads whose emotions took the worst hit. A good stable lad loved his horse, really loved it. Lived, ate, slept and breathed his horse – or, in actual fact, his four, even five horses these days. 'Do your two' had been the norm years ago, before life speeded up. But the struggle to find enough stable staff, coupled with the struggle to find sufficient finances, had killed that off. Now it was how many could a lad cope with? And the number started with four, which was a tough life – usually a young person's life – not a pace an older worker could keep up. And for a stable lad to take his horse to the racecourse, full of hope for winning the 'best turned-out' prize or, even better, a placing or – if God was in his heaven – a winner, only to see that horse come down and not get up again, it practically killed him off, too.

And that nail would be knocked in ever harder with every turn of the empty horsebox wheels, all the way back home, where he would then be faced with looking at an empty stable.

A farrier emerged from the next box to Tally's, heavily muscled and wearing a stout leather apron. Despite the coldness outside, his red face was bathed in sweat. We gathered around the open door to watch. He proceeded to remove a loose shoe from the hoof before replacing it with the special snow-racing one. These shoes were made with three deep bars, one to the front and one each at the sides. The farrier looked sideways and up, smiling at Georgia's keenly eager face, answering her queries, pleased to be the recipient of her interest. He pointed to the edges of the three bars.

'Very sharp – need to get a grip, see? But they can be dangerous. A horse can strike and cut himself, or another, with these plates.'

'But you couldn't race a horse here without them, could you?'

'No,' he agreed. 'Watch the races and you will see they're necessary.'

He finished lightly paring the hoof and hammered the last plate into place.

I took a quick glance at my watch. It was already ten fifteen. The first race was due off at eleven forty-five.

'It's fascinating, isn't it? But do you think we should get back and have some coffee?' Lady Branshawe asked.

'Would you like coffee, Georgia?' I asked.

'Oh, yes, please. It's been great watching the race preparations. Can't wait to see the actual racing.'

'Me, too.' I smiled at her.

No mention had been made at all about how things stood between us since last night. I'd enquired if she was all right when we met for breakfast in the dining room, and she'd been her usual relaxed self, no sign of being uptight. I hadn't pushed it. When she was ready to talk, I'd be waiting to listen. Until then, I was just relieved there was no awkwardness between us.

We made our way back in the brilliant sunshine to the lake and went into a marquee for coffee – and, for the girls, some very naughty nibbles. The very decent breakfast I'd downed would last me for quite a while.

In some ways, it was like a normal racecourse here – crowds flooding in, expectant, happy, keen to watch the racing. But here the similarity ended. It was in no way like an English racecourse! The backdrop of the Alps, starkly white, the crowds, a good percentage wearing furs, all wearing dark glasses to counteract the glare of sunshine reflected off the dazzling snow, and the overriding atmosphere of wealth. Not just wealth – fabulous wealth!

I reminded myself that this was the playground of the privileged rich. However, intertwined in the beautiful tapestry of humankind displaying goodwill to each other, there were also the local people and visiting tourists.

But for each and every person – *however much* their wallet held – their base line was enjoyment.

* * *

As the clock ticked on to eleven thirty, the buzz of expectant energy in the air increased the tension until the charged electricity was almost tangible.

And the weather couldn't have been better – brilliant, warm sunshine. It reflected off the stands of BMW cars, waxed, polished and gleaming. A light breeze fluttered the flags and insignia-printed banners. The sponsors were BMW.

The starting stalls, painted in bright yellow and green, were drawn on to the ice by four-by-four vehicles and set in place on the ice at the start of the race.

It was a strange feeling, standing behind the firm wooden and plastic barriers, watching the preparations going on and the horses and jockeys circling round prior to loading up. It felt wrong and I experienced a pull to get myself down among them. Being a spectator didn't do it for me.

Georgia was watching me. 'Wish you could be in one of those saddles?'

I nodded. 'Yes. But it takes an experienced jockey to race in these conditions. I'd be hopeless.'

'Oh, I don't think "hopeless" is the right word. But I have to admit it looks very testing, if not downright dangerous. And what about the skijoring?'

'One of the most dangerous sports in the world, I believe.'

'I can believe it. Racing on grass is risky, but racing at that speed on top of slippery ice and snow, well . . .'

'I've heard it mentioned that securing a good position before the first bend is key to doing well in the race. Still, I suppose all the other jockeys are going to be going for it, too. Could end up a real scrum.'

'I have to trust the skill of Gerard Faulkes. Tally says he's ridden on snow before, so it's not an unknown experience for him,' Lady Branshawe said. 'And he was successful, too.'

'It would be great if he wins today,' I said.

And I hoped he would. Lady Branshawe was just the sort of owner that trainers – and jockeys – hope will use their services. Despite her wealth and position, there was no side to her whatsoever. Indeed, I'd pointed out to her she was quite entitled to share the marquee designated for VIPs, but, with a wide smile, she'd shaken her head.

'Thank you, Harry, but I'd *much* rather be right here with all of you.' She waved an arm out towards the lake. 'What you could call "up close and personal". Tally says the kickback from the hooves causes quite a mini-snowstorm. I might even feel the snow. You know, like walking by the side of the sea, feeling the spray on your face. It's all part of the pleasure.'

'I don't know if the jockeys would agree with you. They have to wear plastic ski masks to race in because it's not just snow but ice as well that gets balled up and hurled at them by the hooves. At the speed they race, it could cut their faces if they weren't wearing any protection.'

She nodded. 'I'm sure, Harry. And, of course, they're all very brave to be riding.'

'Brave or foolhardy,' said Tally, joining us and picking up the conversation.

'If they thought too hard about the risks, they wouldn't do it,' Georgia said.

I cast a glance at the time. Almost eleven forty-five. The first race was about to start.

'You happy to watch from here, Lady Branshawe?'

'Oh, yes, Tally. I was just explaining to Harry that when we stand by the barriers, it's somehow more thrilling.'

Over the loudspeakers we were informed that the horses had now all been loaded into the stalls and, moments later, 'They're off!'

Lady Branshawe's choice of the word 'thrilling' was certainly appropriate. As the stalls opened, the eight runners burst forward on to the ice. What appeared to be a white cloud rose up and enveloped the horses. And with hooves crashing on the crusty snow-topped ice, they raced towards us, bringing the snow cloud with them. At that distance, it looked like a toy – a globe that, when shaken, caused a snowstorm within to whirl upwards and circle around in one enclosed space. But this was no toy. This was real, almost frighteningly alive, and coming straight down the lake heading towards the winning post.

As they drew closer, what struck me the most was their leg action. Perhaps caused by the different racing plates, it was high, almost a prancing action, particularly with their forelegs. But it was like looking through a cloud of white smoke.

However, as they swept up the course to draw level with us, their lower legs were practically hidden by a blur of white. The horses appeared to be racing through a blizzard of snow, albeit a snowstorm that rose up rather than came down from the sky before it fell in a lingering white haze behind them. Without the goggles, the jockeys could have been blinded by the whirling and swirling snow and ice. It was magnificent and scary at the same time.

In awe, we stood watching, speechless, the spectacular action taking place in front of us casting a spell that held us almost breathless. The white cloud followed the horses down to the winning post. And as the horses galloped past, the crowd erupted with whoops, cheers and excited laughter.

And suddenly we were whooping along with the other racegoers. The noise was so loud that it almost wiped out the speaker announcing that number seven, Dark Dream, had come first – Lady Branshawe's horse! And then we were all hugging each other and laughing, sharing her success.

'Oh, that was magnificent,' she managed to say joyfully through choking emotion. 'Absolutely superb.'

And so it was – an experience that couldn't be described adequately.

'Wow.' Georgia's eyes were starry with excitement. 'Thank you *so* much, Lady Branshawe, for letting me come to witness *that.*'

'I told you, didn't I?' Tally said, laughing with delight, 'I knew it would blow you away. It's a totally unique racing venue. What did you think, Harry?'

The women all turned to me, faces alight with joy, all as high as kites in a strong wind in the aftermath of seeing our horse win.

I shook my head. 'If someone back home asked you to put it into words, you couldn't. You have to witness it yourself.'

'You were all watching it for the very first time. That's why it made such an impact.'

'I'm certainly very glad I changed my mind about coming, or' – I wagged an admonishing finger at her – 'had it changed for me.'

Tally laughed, 'You'll all be dining out on the story for months.'

TWENTY-TWO

Despite Tally's warning that the first time of witnessing was not repeated in quite the same way again, I didn't agree. Each subsequent race still filled us with awe and held us riveted against the barriers as the horses powered past, bathed in their ball of flying snow.

However, the skijoring race was an eye-opener – an incredible feat of athleticism and courage on the part of the jockeys. This time, they weren't seated astride the horses but had their boots locked into skis that ran along the surface of the ice and snow. Long reins trailed back behind the horses and the jockeys used these to balance as they skied, weaving from side to side, trying to stay upright, while being pulled along at a seriously frightening speed.

A flapping, narrow sheet of fabric was used as encouragement, lifting and dipping behind the horses' rear legs. If the risk factor in traditional riding was hair-raising under these icy conditions, then the skijoring was sharply terrifying. With little control, the jockeys flapped encouragement to the prancing, whinnying horses and set blistering speeds along the frozen lake.

The watching crowd roared their appreciation at the sheer bravado and nerve of the participants. The eager yells of the jockeys, coupled with the harsh hiss of around ten pairs of skis, added to the noise and excitement levels. It was a spectacular sight, enhanced by being such an incredibly dangerous sport.

Rawlson was one of the jockeys. And this was his first time skijoring.

Georgia watched with eyes wide with apprehension, hand over her mouth.

'Don't worry,' I whispered. 'The devil looks after his own.'

'It's more scary than the Cresta Run.'

'Hmm . . . you need a deal of nerve.'

'Not for you, Harry?' Tally asked mischievously.

I shook my head. 'No, ma'am. No way.'

'My word, I should say not.' Lady Branshawe was gripping the top of the barrier tightly.

'Gerard's doing well,' Tally said.

Faulkes, an experienced jockey, was also strutting his stuff. He was taking part for another trainer.

'He won one before, didn't you say?'

'Yes, he did.'

We watched, mesmerized, as the skiers and horses drew level. It made my own efforts on an English racecourse look like strolling down a country lane. I might not like Rawlson, but at that moment I found I had a grudging respect for him. Both men warranted a gesture of appreciation for their bravery in taking part, whether they won or not.

The horses swept past, throwing up balls of snow and ice that left the desperately striving skiers behind them caked in glistening white. The sight held the racegoers in fascinated suspense. And then, quite suddenly, the horses reached the winning post and it was over. The applause and cheering that rang out would have shamed a crowd at a cup final.

'Oh, my goodness,' Lady Branshawe said, shaking her head, 'that is one of the most amazing things I've ever seen.'

We were all in agreement.

But while the women were lit up, busy relishing, reliving every minute and giving a personal take on it, I stood beside them, smiling, nodding agreement at the comments – and shamelessly using the cover of our little group to scan the crowds.

I'd been doing a quick recce most of the afternoon, except when the action on the racecourse demanded fullest attention. And as I now panned my gaze around the ardent racegoers, I knew with depressing certainty that Jackson Fellows wasn't here.

Yet, even as I silently cursed his absence, I wondered if it was significant. I decided it had to be. Nathaniel Willoughby had said Jackson came every year, but just this one time he'd seen fit to stay away. Why?

It was a question that I knew I'd be asking myself all the way back to England. If I could work it out, the answer could prove enlightening. Because there had to be a sound reason he'd ducked it this year.

*   *   *

Most of the very best parties I'd attended had been given by Barbara Maguire, a trainer from Leicestershire, a good friend and a very present help in dangerous times. But even Barbara's parties would have found this evening's one a challenge. It was held in the Barouche Bar, in the middle of St Moritz, a fabulous setting, which supplied every need in catering and alcohol – and stayed open until four o'clock in the morning. Well, I was told that the next day.

Georgia had declared it time for bed at around two a.m. I'd been a hundred per cent in accordance. Rendered considerably uninhibited but not quite plastered, the pair of us had returned through the black, star-spangled night and walked up the steps into the warmth of the foyer of the Koselig Hotel.

'Must you leave?' Lady Branshawe had swayed gracefully against me as I'd taken our leave. 'Tally and I are staying to the end.'

I'd cast a glance around at the joy-filled crowd raising the roof along with their drinks, the uproariously laughing females who had commandeered the tabletops for dancing, and nodded.

'See you on the other side, in the morning.'

'Have a good night,' Tally said, and winked lasciviously at us.

Georgia, already flushed from alcohol and having danced me around the floor most of the night, turned a deeper shade of pink.

Now, closeted close together in the hotel lift on the way to the second floor, she leaned against me.

'That was some party.'

'Some party,' she agreed, nodding and wobbling.

'I think coffee's called for.'

'I *think*,' she said solemnly, with distinct care, 'I'm pished.' And giggled.

I put an arm around her for additional support. 'I think you could be right.'

We fell out of the lift at the second floor, both of us laughing helplessly and stumbled along to room 203.

'Are you coming in?'

Our eyes met, locked – those same words I'd spoken last night.

'Since *I'm here*' – she emphasized the words – 'I will.'

'You sure?'

'I'd like to.'

'I'd like you to, as well.'

I turned the key and let us in.

Suddenly, there was no urgency. We sat on the plush two-seater settee, sipped coffee, came down from the overheated mood of the party, and talked. And talked: Georgia about her man, the serving soldier in Afghanistan; me about Annabel.

When the talking stopped, we slid between cool white sheets, reached out for each other and held on tightly. It felt good, a warm body and a beating heart held close against my own. I'd forgotten the solace it could bring. I drank it in, drowned in the moment.

'I need some comfort, Harry.' Georgia nuzzled her face between my chin and shoulder.

I didn't reply, simply nodded and began kissing her face very gently, very slowly, beginning with her closed eyelids and finding my way down her softly rounded cheeks to her waiting lips. The rest should have followed on naturally – but didn't.

By the time I remembered that drinking quantities of alcohol didn't do lovemaking any favours, I also realized by the slackening of tension in Georgia's body and her slower breathing that she'd fallen fast asleep in my arms. As I willingly succumbed and followed her example, my last thought was that she had saved me from the ultimate in humiliating embarrassment.

But at seven o'clock the next morning, we awoke together as the muted alarm clock went off. And this time I wasn't feeling in the least embarrassed. The last woman I'd made love to had been Annabel, a long time ago – far too long.

Georgia was still sleepy as I stroked her silky smooth skin, kissed her nipples, felt them harden into desire as she came fully awake. I ran my lips softly down her neck, smelled the echo of perfume still clinging to her. Cupped her cheeks with both hands and kissed her warm, waiting lips. She returned my kisses, increasingly hungrily. Then, as her seeking hands traced their way down my chest, my belly, and found my pulsing hardness, she caught her breath in a gasp of desire.

The heat of our need and passion turned into a conflagration that melted away the material world outside. Nothing else existed; it was just the two of us – as one – in our own unique universe. Our lovemaking was urgent, passionate, yet tender. I honoured her rhythm, lasting until the sensation was totally beyond control, and climaxed with her. The exquisite relief was as needed as snow on a ski-slope, but as my heart rate steadied, I felt Georgia's body begin to move jerkily, awkwardly beneath me.

Raising myself, I looked down at her. Her eyes were squeezed tightly shut, face flushed and lightly dewed. Then the tears she was struggling so hard to contain overflowed, flooding down her cheeks.

'I'm so, so sorry,' she sobbed, rolling her head from side to side.

'For what?' I ran a finger across her cheek, displacing the flow of tears. 'What's the matter?'

She just shook her head helplessly. I eased away from her and got out of bed.

'Would a cup of tea help?'

She choked and sobbed, laughter and tears battling it out. 'England's answer,' she managed to say.

I bent and kissed her wet cheek. 'Lie still; I'll make us both some.'

I flicked on the kettle before going over to the window. I drew back the heavy drapes. The early-morning view of the glistening white Alps was glorious – it was a beautiful day. Sunshine bounced off the snowy peaks and poured into the room.

When I returned to bed with two steaming mugs, Georgia had collected herself and was sitting propped up against the pillows.

'Thanks.' She took the tea I offered.

For two or three minutes we sat in bed and sipped in silence. But it wasn't a comfortable silence. As tension crept in and the silence stretched, Georgia placed a hand on my arm.

'I have to tell you, Harry.' She buried her face over the drink. 'I *must*. And I'm so very sorry.'

'Don't be. I know what you're going to say.'

She shook her head. 'How can you?'

'You're sorry because at a . . . shall we say, crucial moment – or maybe even before – you imagined it was your soldier . . . not me, loving you. And now you're feeling guilty.'

'Oh my God, yes!' She stared wide-eyed at me. 'I *did*. And it's so disrespectful to you.'

I put a hand out and smoothed back a stray lock of hair from her damp forehead. 'Let it go; it doesn't matter.'

I watched her hand shake as she took a big gulp of tea.

'It does matter; believe me, it does,' she said, her voice barely a whisper. Hastily draining the rest of her drink, Georgia pushed back the duvet and climbed out. She stood at the end of the bed, naked and beautiful. 'Do you understand what I'm saying, Harry? It matters very much – *to me.*'

I watched her disappear into the bathroom and close the door. She was a brave woman – much braver than I was. She was absolutely right. To her, it wasn't something she could dismiss lightly. As she'd said, she needed comforting. Of course she did: she was still grieving for that incredibly brave soldier who had gone to Afghanistan to fight for his country. He had stepped on a concealed IED, been blown to pieces, and never came home.

I moodily drank my own tea. Was it for her sake, or my own, that I'd not confessed? The reason I'd known what she was sobbing for was because in those fierce flames of passion, deep inside me, I'd been crying out for Annabel. And I should have come clean, admitted it – but didn't.

God, I was a spineless bastard.

TWENTY-THREE

Some fifty-odd hours ago, we'd started out from Nottinghamshire. Now, we were high above the tableau of white peaks in Switzerland and climbing in the vast blue sky.

I cast a brief glance at Georgia sitting beside me, but her attention was focused on the view far below. Leaving St Moritz for Samedan Airport the conventional way this time, by limousine, had given us a drive of around five miles and afforded a totally different up-close view of the countryside. It confirmed all our earlier impressions – Switzerland was spectacular. The pride the Swiss people had in presenting their country in all its perfection to visitors was as crystal clear as the air we were flying through.

I leaned closer to Georgia. 'Not a visit to have missed.'

Without taking her gaze away from the scene through the window, she nodded. 'I'm so very glad I came.'

'Truly?' I felt the need to ask. Although she had been perfectly pleasant and sociable since we'd awoken this morning, there was a reticence about her. I sensed she'd stepped away emotionally and put space between us.

'Oh, yes, I've enjoyed it hugely.'

Across from us, Lady Branshawe, without obviously listening in to our conversation, had heard Georgia's comment. She beamed at us.

I sat back in my seat. There was so much I wanted to ask Georgia, but in the restricted space of the aircraft, it wasn't possible to have a private conversation.

And what I wanted to ask was most definitely private.

'Such a pity we couldn't all have stayed for a little longer,' Lady Branshawe said. 'However, I'm expected at a dinner in London tonight, so I regret it isn't possible.'

'Not just as a guest, but guest of honour, yes?' Tally said.

Lady Branshawe cast her eyes down modestly. 'Well, yes . . . but there are other guests, too. I believe Mr Harper, our speaker, is a barrister – a man of wide experience and standing. And afterwards there will also be a piano recital by a Mr Jackson Fellows.'

'I'm sure it will be an excellent evening.' Tally nodded.

'Could I ask what charity it is?'

'Of course, my dear. It's a charity devoted to the welfare of adopted babies and children. I've been patron for many years.'

'A commendable cause.' I forced myself to contribute to the conversation.

However, inside, I was reeling at Lady Branshawe's words. Small wonder I'd not managed to catch a glimpse of Jackson Fellows at the racecourse. No doubt he was busy in London practising for this evening's performance.

'I find people are so generous towards the charity. It seems to resonate on a deep level.'

'Possibly because babies are completely helpless and need to be looked after. Maybe it brings out the protective instinct.'

'I'm sure you're right, Georgia. Anyway, since both Mr Harper and Mr Fellows are giving their services free, I've invited them to a party I shall be giving at home tomorrow night.'

Home was Hempton Hall. According to Tally, it was a non-crumbling pile, renovated and restored to the highest standard by Lady Branshawe's late husband, Lord Rudolph Branshawe.

She hesitated, then added, 'Are either of you doing anything tomorrow?'

Georgia shook her head.

'Not that I know about,' I said.

'Then, what about joining us? Tally's coming as well.'

'I certainly am.'

It was base of me, but the chance to meet Fellows was a gem, not to be turned down. 'I'd like to very much.'

'What about you, Georgia?' Tally asked. 'Do come.'

'Hmm, yes, I'd love to. It's not just other people who are generous, Lady Branshawe; thank you.'

'You will all be doing me a favour. I simply love company. The hall's a big place, meant for lots of people.'

And she'd done me a favour without knowing it. Her offer would neatly tie up one of my loose ends, if I could find an opening at the party to chat with Fellows. But it would also depend on how much he was prepared to reveal. That just left me with the tricky problem of sorting out where I stood – or didn't – with Georgia.

Conversation turned to horseracing and moved on.

England was still snow-bound. Racing, obviously, was still off.

Harlequin Cottage was sitting regally on an unbroken white carpet. It must have snowed quite recently – no cat prints violated the pristine surface.

'Sure you won't come in for a drink, Georgia?'

'Better get back, if you don't mind.'

We were standing in the snow outside the kitchen door. We'd just waved an enthusiastic goodbye and many thanks to Tally and Lady Branshawe as their Range Rover turned out of the gate, headed for Leicestershire, and now it left just the two of us. However, it seemed that it wasn't simply the snow that was cold.

I loaded her case into my car boot and she climbed into the passenger seat. Sliding in behind the wheel, I switched on the Mazda and, turning the car heater to max, followed Tally's example and drove out of the gate into the snowy lane. The main A52 was mercifully well gritted and progress was fast until we had to leave it at the Granby turn-off. Then it was back to skiddy, narrow lanes with snow banked up high at the sides of the hedges.

I broke the silence that had lasted since we set out. 'Are you opening the flower shop tomorrow?'

'Oh, yes, I've lots of orders to fill.'

'Uh-huh.'

'You? What will you be doing? Not racing, obviously.'

'No, but I'll probably be working at Mike's stables, among other things.'

'Hmm.'

And that was the sum of our conversation – surface stuff, polite. We could have been strangers. Amazing to think we had spent the previous night sharing a bed, sharing love.

Reaching her parents' house, I swung in at the open gate and she hurried to open the front door.

'I'll call you, then, tomorrow evening, when I get back to the cottage,' I said, hefting her suitcase from the boot and carrying it up the steps.

'Text me, Harry.'

It was an arm's-length job. How many degrees of frost unknown, but I certainly wasn't going to push it.

'OK.'

She took the case from my hand without inviting me in. 'Thanks for everything, Harry.'

I stepped back and only just escaped the door as she shut it swiftly behind her.

It was a dismal anticlimax to a fabulous trip.

When I got back to Harlequin Cottage, the first thing I noticed was a line of pawprints marring the surface of the snow. An enormous ginger cat was sitting on the doorstep. He could have gained access through the cat-flap but had chosen to wait out in the snow for my arrival. His radar, as usual, was in full working order. He knew I was coming home.

As I drew up and cut the engine, Leo stood up and gave an exaggerated stretch and a yawn. I walked to within four feet and he leaped up, hooking claws in my jacket and hoisting himself on to my shoulder. His purrs reverberated so deeply that it was a wonder he didn't shake himself loose.

'At least someone's pleased to see me.'

He bashed his head against my cheek in agreement.

I opened up and sighed with pleasure at getting home: a warm cosy kitchen, a kettle soon to boil for some tea, plus a purring cat – perfect. Well, nearly. If Annabel had been here to welcome me home, it would have been. And at that point, I knew Georgia was probably right in keeping her distance. We seemed great as friends, someone to go out with, share a meal – but share our lives? As she'd said, we had taken some comfort in the snowy night and simply shored each other up. It was best to leave the situation as it was. Things might develop – or not. I shook my head to clear the thoughts.

I took a mug of tea to the lounge and dialled Annabel's telephone number.

'Hello, I'm back, cat-sitting again.'

'Harry, did you have a good time?'

'Marvellous. It was definitely a once-in-a-lifetime job.'

'What was the snow racing like?'

'Pretty much indescribable.'

'That good?'

'Yes.'

'Were you tempted?'

I laughed. 'No, very happy to remain a spectator.'

'And Georgia? Did she enjoy herself?'

I hesitated. I didn't feel guilty for sharing a bed with her, but I did feel uncomfortable about Annabel knowing. It felt as if I was being unfaithful, which was rubbish since we lived apart. And, in any case, Annabel slept each night with Jeffrey. But the cold truth was they wouldn't make love, couldn't, not with the severity of his injuries. Might never make love again.

What a sad mess life was.

'I think she did.'

'Only think? Come on, Harry . . .'

'She was certainly thrilled going over by private jet. So was I, come to that. And the actual racing was an experience I doubt she'll ever forget.'

'What about the hotel – was it very plush?'

'Oh, indeed, yes. The word for it was palatial. And the food was truly excellent.'

'But? I do sense a but, Harry.'

'Let's just say, I think Georgia was disappointed in me.'

'Tch, then she's a silly girl.' Her annoyance was coming down the phone line in a big wave.

'Like everybody's life, Annabel, her situation's complicated.'

'Hmm . . .'

I could tell she was not placated. 'She's been through a tough time. I think, emotionally, she needs time to work through it. Maybe I was expecting too much of her.'

'And I think you are making excuses for her.'

'Can we drop the subject, please?'

'Are you seeing each other again?'

'Well, yes, but just not as a couple. We've both been invited to a party at Lady Branshawe's tomorrow night. It's a thank-you spinoff from a bunfight that's happening in London right now – a charity do. She's patron of Childhood, a children's adoption charity.'

'Really? That's interesting.'

'Worthwhile, certainly. Anyway, I'm driving Georgia over to Hempton Hall.'

'Well, maybe she will have had time to realize how lucky she was to go to Switzerland. And appreciate the enjoyable times. Anyway, I hope the evening goes well for you both.'

'You're a lovely woman, Annabel. Thank you. Yes, I hope it goes off all right, too. It's not Georgia's fault everything didn't run smoothly. I know she's had a lot of hurt recently.'

'She's not by herself – we've all experienced a lot of hurt.'

'I can't argue with that. But life continually keeps throwing stuff at us. We can try ducking, of course, but it doesn't do any good.'

'I wouldn't say so, Harry. I think you did a super job of ducking when you sorted out the threat to Jeffrey.'

'Everything still OK, then?'

'Not heard another squeak, thank goodness.'

'Seems we've deflected the boss-man, then, whoever he is.'

'Yes. I guess you can rest easy now. Relax a little; enjoy yourself, until the snow lets up.'

'Sounds pretty good.'

'All right, then, darling. Speak to you again soon.'

'Bye, Annabel.'

I replaced the receiver. It was good advice, but then she didn't know the details about John Dunston being murdered.

I sighed, opened the desk drawer and took out the folder of photographs Pen had found in Mike's loft. I didn't bother with the majority, but took out the one photo that showed two men standing under a snow-laden tree. I didn't recognize either of them. I flicked open my mobile and scrolled down to the photo Nathaniel Willoughby, the horse artist, had sent me, spread my thumb and forefinger wide and enlarged the image. Then placed the mobile next to the original photo.

In the top drawer of the desk was a magnifying glass. I took it out and positioned it over Nathaniel's photo. The picture sprang into fierce focus. It showed a man, late twenties, dark hair, medium build. Not a forceful character, I guessed. There was a slackness about his face, the weak line of his jaw – a follower rather than a leader.

I contrasted it with the second photograph. With the help of the magnifying glass, I could see it was definitely the same man, although he was now wearing dark glasses.

So that just left the man talking to him. A man who was also wearing dark glasses that disguised his face. But this man was of a different cut. There was an aggressiveness in the way he was standing . . . jaw lifted, shoulders squared. He looked about ten years older, maybe more. I held the glass steady and studied what I could see of his face. He was somehow familiar, although I couldn't place him.

I knew I had seen this man before. It would have been in a different setting, of course, but take people out of their normal environment and very often you didn't recognize them.

The feeling of surety in my gut caused an itch of frustration at my brain's tardy computing in not coming up with the name. But past experience had shown me many times before that pushing yielded nil results. The better way was simply to imprint the facts or images in my mind – and let go. It wasn't magic, but it was crucial to have complete faith that the answer would come. At some point, that eureka moment would fire in my brain, usually when I was least prepared for it. And when it did occur, it vindicated the trust I'd placed in my subconscious and was very sweet.

TWENTY-FOUR

The ringing of the landline telephone broke into my introspection.

'Harry. Wasn't sure if you'd be back yet from St Moritz.'

It was Victor Maudsley, the former racehorse trainer. I'd ridden for him years ago before he retired to the east coast near Skegness.

I'd visited him several times. The house was beautiful, with gardens that reached right down to the beach and within walking distance of the golf course. We also shared an unorthodox history, a past that linked us emotionally on more than one level. Links that could never be severed, that I'd known nothing about until this last year. And I was now thirty-five.

'Hello, Victor. Yes, came back in style – and with speed.'

'Courtesy of Lady Branshawe?'

'That's right.'

'Hmm, Mike told me when I rang him.'

'So, what can I do for you, Victor?'

He hesitated. 'Can't really discuss this over the phone.'

'Oh, that sort of problem.'

'You got it. But I do want to see you, Harry. Get your take on the situation. With this atrocious weather and racing being off . . .'

'You thought I'd have some free time?'

'Exactly. What I suggest is, if you're agreeable, how about driving over to North Shore tomorrow? Obviously, like racing, the golf's off, but I could stand you a decent meal at the hotel. And I can ask you . . . what I need to ask.'

'As you say, there's no racing so, yes, I'm OK to meet you for lunch.'

'Around twelve?'

'Yes, fine.'

'Tell you what, Harry. Park up on my drive. We can walk up the beach to North Shore Hotel. Then after lunch, we can have a drink at mine.'

'Will do, Victor. A blast of sea air would be nice. See you at twelve, tomorrow.'

'Blast is definitely the right word in this weather.'

I replaced the receiver, sat back in the chair and thought about the conversation. Once before, I'd been asked to do a similar thing – also by a retired trainer, Mousey Brown. His revelation over lunch in a Yorkshire pub had completely blown me away.

I was sure Victor's forthcoming chat wasn't going to reveal anything quite so personal. That it would be a sensitive subject was for sure. But if it was simply, as he put it, for 'my take', that was fair enough. I'd certainly help him if I could.

However, I hoped like hell it wasn't something Victor wanted me to do that would cause me to have to don my second hat – the deerstalker I'd acquired through necessity, not desire – and investigate somebody.

The timing worked a treat. Just after ten the next morning, I drove into Mike's stable yard. His monster of a four-by-four was missing. The second lot would be up on the gallops and he would be noting the horses' individual performances. Pen would most likely be by herself.

I locked the Mazda and knocked on the kitchen door.

'Come in,' Pen called out.

I found her, gloved hands covered in soapy bubbles, squaring up the breakfast dishes.

'You've just missed Mike.'

'Yes, thank goodness.'

Her eyebrows raised.

'I've brought you those photographs I had developed before I went to Switzerland.'

'Ah' – she nodded – 'and did they prove interesting?'

I laid them down on the kitchen table. 'Not really. There was just one that might be.' I picked it up and held it out in front of her.

'Two men – in the snow.' She carried on washing up and shook her head. 'I don't think that's interesting.'

'It's a piece of the jigsaw, Pen. This case is exactly that – a jigsaw. I look on the bits of information I gather up as pieces of the picture. Get enough pieces and that's it: case solved.'

'Hmm . . .' She stared at me. 'You know what, Harry?'

'What?'

'You're beginning to talk like a private eye.'

It was my turn to stare at her.

'You've just called it a case.'

'Slip of the tongue,' I said hastily. 'I was just trying to describe how I see it.'

'Hmm.'

I ploughed on. 'Anyway, I'll leave these photos with you, but I'd like to keep this one if you don't mind.'

'Of course I don't mind.' She reached for a tea towel, dried her hands and collected up the rest of the snaps. 'It's a bit of your jigsaw. And you certainly need all your bits.' She was grinning, taking the Mick.

'Give over.'

She relented. 'Tell me how your trip went. Was it all good, or like the curate's egg?'

'On a general level, yes, it was extremely good. On the strictly personal, I'd have to say more of the vestment and yolk.'

'Oh dear. Do you want to tell me?'

'I promise, if I need to, yours will be the first shoulder to get wet, Pen. But right now' – I slid the single photograph into my pocket and opened the kitchen door – 'I've got a date with Victor in Skegness. Not a hot date, because I believe right now there's a good layer of snow on the beach.'

'Lovely crisp salt air. What could be nicer?' She smiled. 'Take care of yourself, Harry. Bye.'

There was minimal traffic on the A52 from Grantham leading to the Skegness roundabout. Not surprising really; kids would have to scrape off the snow before they could make sandcastles. Come summer, it would be a different matter.

I made good time before turning sharp right on to the A158 Burgh-le-Marsh Road and drove the seven miles down the wide, straight road into Skegness. I passed the local landmark, the Ship pub, and began weaving my way through the side roads leading to St Andrew's Drive.

The gate leading to Saddler's Rest was wide open. Victor's white Range Rover was parked halfway up the long drive. I swung in and parked behind it. Pen had called it crisp salt air. She should have said freezing salt air. The cold scoured my face the second I climbed out of the car. Switzerland had been cold, extremely cold, but somehow the cold in England had a bone-chilling, raw quality about it. I hastened up the slope of the drive and was about to reach for the knocker when Victor opened the door.

'Harry, good to see you, lad. Come on in.'

'Glad to, Victor. Brrr . . . it's brass-monkey weather out there.'

'I've got coffee on. Will you have one before we brave the beach approach to the hotel?'

'Yes, please.'

An open fire was burning in the inglenook in the lounge, and I took fullest advantage of it while Victor was fixing the drinks. Around the walls hung oil paintings of some of the famous horses he had trained. It was clear a gifted artist had painted them. Some were on the flat at prestigious courses – Goodwood, Newmarket,

Ascot – with jockey silks bright above summer green grass, while others were caught in action going over fences in winter, mud up to the hocks. The horses were totally alive, joyous in their racing.

I looked closely in the bottom corner of several. It confirmed what I'd thought – they were the work of Nathaniel Willoughby. I had expected it, yet, given the history between Nathaniel and Victor's wife, Elspeth Maudsley, it was surprising. Victor must be viewing the paintings as an investment.

At the far end of the lounge, through French doors, there was a magnificent view right out to sea. Even indoors, I could hear the endless boom of the breakers.

At the end of the long garden was a tall, wrought-iron gate with deterrent spikes along the top. It gave access on to the narrow stone-topped pathway running along the edge of the beach all the way from Skegness to Winthorpe, about a couple of miles north. We'd shortly be walking along it, taking in the sea air, on the way up to North Shore Hotel, without struggling in the deep sand along the beach. However, above the high-tide mark, the sand was not only deep where the savage winter gales had blown it into drifts, but also topped with a thick crust of snow. We'd be well ready for a hot meal in the hotel.

'Here you are. Wrap yourself around this.'

Victor crossed the room and handed me a steaming mug of coffee that smelled delicious.

'Cheers, Victor.'

We sat in deep, maroon leather armchairs before the blazing fire and sipped the scalding coffee. It tasted even better than it smelled. I reminded myself that before his retirement as a racehorse trainer, Victor had 'held the reins' of a stable that accommodated upwards of 120 horses. His income must have been sizeable. The whole house, setting and internal furnishings – plus top-quality coffee – said wealth. Maybe not in the same bracket as Lady Branshawe but doing very nicely all the same.

'Lovely coffee, thanks.' I drained my mug and put it down on a convenient coaster. 'So, did you want to have a chat before we go up to North Shore?'

'No, oh no, not just yet, Harry. Let's enjoy our walk, which will no doubt be stimulating' – he laughed – 'and then have a good tuck-in before we talk business.'

At the word 'business', my shoulders involuntarily tensed and drew up. He'd said he wanted my take on a situation. Now I was here, on his patch, I realized he was going to capitalize on that and overrule any objections.

'Now, just a second—'

'No, Harry. I asked you over and I insist we enjoy ourselves first before we dig into the muck heap.'

Now my shoulders were no longer drawing up; they had dropped – along with my spirits. I should have known this wasn't going to turn into a fun day out.

Victor had said the walk would be stimulating. It was the right word. We arrived at the junction of the stone path and the gravel car park to North Shore Hotel fully stimulated, freezing cold and with the overriding desire to escape inside, away from the bitter salty wind. As we stepped into the welcome warmth, the heavy glass door sighed closed behind us. We echoed it.

'If that hasn't sharpened your appetite, lad, nothing will.' Victor led the way down the long-carpeted reception hall into the bar and restaurant. The air was redolent with the tantalizing smell of food cooking. Placing our order at the bar, Victor insisted on paying. 'I've dragged you here and it's my treat.' We carried our beers down the four centre steps into the long conservatory that acted as a daytime restaurant, giving panoramic views over the eighteen-hole golf course and down to the sea.

I took a long pull of my beer. 'Best place ever to eat.'

If the weather hadn't been so inclement, the course would have been studded with brightly clad golfers, blue golf buggies buzzing around and, with the first and eighteenth greens in full view, an active ongoing floorshow.

'I do so agree, and having company adds to the pleasure.'

Our table was next to a hot radiator and, thawing out now, our battle up the beach path through the snow to get here was a minor achievement to relish.

'However,' Victor continued, 'I reckon the civilized way along St Andrew's Drive is favourite to get us back to Saddler's Rest.'

I nodded. It would certainly be quicker, and it would speed up the moment Victor enlightened me about his problem.

But even as I agreed with him, I was also wondering about another little problem. Just why, a few seconds after we had stepped round the corner off the beach path into full view of the hotel, had two men in a black Beamer swiftly exited the car park? Even as the motor screamed away down the road towards the junction with Roman Bank, the main road into Skegness, I'd mentally noted the number of the registration plate. Since I'd been caught up in this bloody silly game of catching killers, noting data – like car numbers – had become a habit. I hadn't recognized the vehicle, but I knew the driver. More importantly, I would very much like to know just who his passenger was.

The man was wearing black glasses – and had a vaguely familiar, distinctive jut to his chin.

Our food arrived: roast pork for Victor, turkey for me, plus a generous selection of vegetables. We did justice to it all.

Victor sat back, obviously replete, and dabbed his mouth with a napkin.

'That was excellent – as usual. Yours, Harry?'

'Oh, yes, a great meal. Thank you.'

He flipped a dismissive hand. 'You're most welcome.' Then shot a look at me. 'I'd like you to promise me something, Harry.'

I put the last forkful of turkey into my mouth – and shook my head. He waited until I'd finished masticating the food.

'It's not for me—'

'I'm not promising anything, Victor. Sorry. Especially' – I tried a weak joke to soften my refusal – 'when you've forked out for the food, but the answer's no.'

He dabbed his mouth again, screwed up the paper napkin and dropped it on to his empty plate.

'It involves the grandchildren.'

I swallowed. As a lead-in to a spot of emotional blackmail, it probably couldn't be bettered.

'Victor, I've got a situation right now that could get nasty. I don't want another one.'

'If you don't help me, Harry, I've no idea where else to turn.'

'Why me?' Those words had echoed down the ages – and still no reply.

'You don't need to ask, do you?'

'Look, is someone's life at stake – any of the grandchildren?'

'No.'

I breathed a sigh of relief. 'Then I'll help you sort out whatever the problem is, but it's still your problem. OK?'

He pushed back from the table, then leaned over and said in a low voice, 'Even if it's going to bankrupt me? You'd sit back, let that happen, would you?'

I didn't know how to answer him. My thoughts skittered, ironic-ally, to the many paintings hanging on the walls inside his house – and all the money invested in them. Original Willoughbys, they were appreciating year on year. Victor led a quiet, parsimonious life. Bankruptcy surely wasn't possible.

His face set firm, lips a thin line, he led the way back up the steps, through the bar and out of the hotel. We didn't speak again on the walk back to Saddler's Rest.

He showed me into the lounge, motioned me to one of the two armchairs by the fire. Poured us both a whisky. He took a gulp from the chunky glass and stared at me.

'The problem is Nigel,' he said abruptly. 'My bloody son-in-law.'

TWENTY-FIVE

I stared back at him.

Victor's son-in-law was Nigel Garton, MP. He was Paula's husband, father of her three children, Victor's grandsons. The man, full of charm and bonhomie, who'd bought me a drink in the marquee in St Moritz.

I followed Victor's example and took a sip of my whisky. 'OK. I'm listening. Let's hear it.'

'I've had Paula here, sobbing away. Poor lass, I couldn't pacify her. She's worried to death about him.'

'What's he been up to?'

'Now that's the point. Oh, he's definitely playing an away game, but just what, Paula doesn't know.'

'You talking about another woman? Is he having an affair?'

'No. I asked her that straight away. It's something dicey to do with money. A lot of money. She says it's flowing out of the bank account. If I had to guess, I'd say he's gambling.'

'Is it going out at the same rate, same time frame?'

'No. Well, not the same rate. As to the time frame – well, yes, I suppose it is. Seems to be weekly from what she tells me. Any ideas, Harry?'

'If it's not the same amount each time, it's unlikely he's being blackmailed.'

'Good God! I'd not even considered that.'

'And I don't think it is. But you could be right about gambling. Does he go online, do you think?'

'Oh, no, no. Nothing like that.'

'How can you be sure?'

'Because of what Paula told me. That's how she's found out, see.'

'Sorry, but I'm struggling here. What has she found out?'

'Apparently, he comes home every weekend, yes?'

'Yes.'

'And he takes Paula and the boys out on Saturdays – during the day, of course. Then in the evening, they generally go out together for a meal. They have a babysitter in to look after the kids. Well, when our Paula's had them on her own all week while he's down in London, she needs a break from them.'

I could well believe it. They were little hellions. I felt sorry for the babysitter.

'Anyway, he seems to think he's done his duty by Sunday teatime and takes himself off. Says he's going to visit his mum and dad. They live near Doncaster. Paula's quite happy about that. She doesn't get on with his mother, so if Nigel wants to go on his own, that's fine by her.'

'Seems innocent enough.'

'Hmm . . . except since Paula's found out about the bank balance going down, she's got suspicious. I think she did reckon he'd got another woman – was spending out on her, you know.'

I nodded.

'Since she couldn't ask him straight out, she thought up this plan to try to find out.'

'Yes?'

'She made a note of the mileage on the car before he left on a Sunday and then again when he'd got back in the evening.'

'What did she discover?'

'It was the same mileage every time. But it wasn't the right mileage for simply visiting his parents. He did call to see them – that's true enough because sometimes he came back with a present for the kids from their grandparents. But the mileage didn't add up. It was a hell of a lot more.'

'Hmm . . . well, short of tailing him next Sunday, there's not a lot to go on.'

'That was my reasoning as well.'

'And you're going to?'

'I'd rather hoped you'd take it on, Harry, and I would pay you.'

'Talking of pay, why on earth did you say you could go bankrupt?'

'If Nigel's not stopped, whatever it is he's doing, I know where it will end. I'll have to bail him out.'

'I think that's a bit extreme.'

'Oh, no, it's not.' Tension heightened the tone of his voice. 'We're not talking pennies here, Harry. Paula came to ask me for a loan. Tch, I ask you, a loan – silly girl. Seems she had been on a spending spree – some fresh furnishings for the house or some such. Found there wasn't sufficient to cover it. She had no idea things were that bad.'

'Well, she's not going on a spree every week, is she?'

'Maybe not, but there's a hell of a mortgage payment to be met every month.'

'Has she talked to him about it?'

'Seems so. But you know what Nigel's like . . . I mean, he's a politician, for God's sake. Lying seems to be a requisite on the CV.' Victor shook his head worriedly. 'And that's not all. Paula was sending a couple of his suits to the dry cleaners a few days ago. She went through all the pockets, didn't she – found an IOU for ten grand. It had the one word written through it – "Thanks".'

'Which explains the sudden drop at the bank, I suppose.'

'I'm afraid so.'

'Well, if he's that deeply into gambling, he's not going to stop. It's like being an alcoholic – he can't stop.'

'That's exactly what I'm afraid of, Harry.'

'He was over there in St Moritz. Seems he's part of a syndicate. And that's not a cheap pastime. There will be steep racing bills payable.'

'I know. He's with Clive Unwin.'

He downed the remains of his drink and poured another, gesturing with the whisky bottle towards my own glass. I waved it away.

'Uh-huh, I've got to drive home.'

He nodded morosely. 'What am I going to do? I feel I have to support Paula, naturally. And I will. She's my daughter, for God's sake. But I don't want Nigel's gambling debts hanging round my neck. Oh, I know, I'm not short of a bob or two, but even so, money's harder to bring in than to send out. Interest rates have been flat to the boards for a long time now.' He shrugged his shoulders. 'And who knows where this situation will lead.'

I could see his point. Paying out for your own excesses was one thing, but finding yourself responsible for meeting an unknown amount of debt – one that was ongoing – for somebody else was definitely not on. I wouldn't want to find myself in this situation. It was far from pleasant.

OK, I'd been over a barrel paying nursing-home fees for my severely disabled half-sister for years. It was a straitjacket that exerted a hot-rod prod forcing you to work hard to bring in the necessary monies. The need to bring in the money had been a ceaseless nag of worry. In my own case, I was relatively young, fit and capable of working hard. But Victor was an elderly retired man. I empathized with him. It was an ugly position in which to find yourself.

'Look, how about I do a tailing job next Sunday, find out where Nigel's going? Will that help?'

'It certainly will.' His eyes lit up with hope.

'One condition – you don't pay me, OK?'

'I can't expect you to do it for nothing. No, no, I *must* pay you.'

I held up an index finger. 'Expenses, diesel costs only; otherwise it's no go.'

Hearing the finality in my voice, he nodded reluctantly. 'OK, whatever you say, Harry. I'm in no position to call the shots in all this mess.'

'One thing: did Paula keep the IOU?'

'She gave it to me. It's in the top drawer of my desk. I'll get it.'

I finished the last of my whisky, leaned my head back against the plump soft headrest of the armchair, closed my eyes. Asking for expenses was merely a sop to Victor's self-respect. I certainly didn't want paying to help the man – if, indeed, tailing Nigel was going to help. Even if I found out where his destination lay, it still wasn't going to stop his gambling. But as I mulled it over, something else came to mind.

He wouldn't be gambling by himself. For that amount of money, there was bound to be three or four men involved – could well be more. That old adage 'knowledge is power' might prove to be true. If I could give Victor the names of Nigel's cronies, he might find a way to put pressure on Nigel.

'Here you are.' Victor returned holding out the slip of paper. 'What are you going to do with it?'

'No idea, yet.' I took it from him.

'Keep it. If Nigel finds it's missing, Paula will have to smuggle it back into their house. If not, do whatever you have to do.'

I heaved myself up regretfully from the comfortable depths of the armchair. 'Best be going, Victor. Could you have a word with Paula? Ask her to tell us what time Nigel usually leaves on the Sunday and what road he takes after leaving their place. Also, I want to know what car he will be driving, the colour and the number on the registration plate. I need to be in place well before he leaves so it doesn't raise any suspicions.'

He nodded. 'I'll certainly do that, Harry. Give you a ring when I find out.'

I crunched my way carefully back down the slope of his driveway and, with the Mazda's heater on full blast, headed away from the coast back home to the Midlands.

It was edging towards evening when I got back. Pointless to think of going over to Mike's stables now. Evening stables would be half over. Far better if I applied myself to writing my weekly column for the newspaper – get it done and out of the way. I routinely procrastinated, sweated, swore and wished myself anywhere but seated at the computer. But in the past I'd been grateful for the regular money coming in. It had been much needed to pay nursing-home fees. Thinking about it, I realized that Annabel now was in the same situation of having to fund nursing care for Sir Jeffrey. Life was a bitch.

However, the first thing needed was to feed Leo. At the sound of the engine, I'd seen the curtain at the little side window in the lounge sway to one side and had spotted his ginger head peering round. He was only a cat – only! – but how welcome was the sight of him watching for me coming home. Knowing the cottage wouldn't be empty and the welcome would be warm when I walked in made all the difference in the world.

Column written, both of us fed and with a mug of scalding tea to hand, I switched on the table lamp in the lounge. Taking the slip of paper Victor had given me, I held it close to the light and scrutinized it. The paper itself was substantial – thick, with a very smooth finish. I tilted it up to let the light shine through it. There was an almost indistinguishable watermark. So, not just a scrap of paper.

It had been torn from a sheet, maybe even a pad, of expensive paper. Given the amount owing written upon it, that it was quality paper came as no surprise. It immediately gave a clue to the person who had written upon it. Someone with a sizeable bank balance who extended his expensive purchases to include even something as basic as paper to reflect his own personality. An egotist, probably – a well-dressed, self-assured man for whom nothing but the best would do. And the one word written diagonally across the sum – *Thanks* – was written with an assured hand. A professional man, certainly.

TWENTY-SIX

I didn't get to meet Georgia's parents – in itself a fair indication of the way the wind was blowing. I parked up on the drive at exactly seven o'clock – the striking of the village church clock confirmed my timekeeping. But before I'd even had time to switch off the engine, Georgia slipped out of the front door, closed it quickly behind her and slid into the passenger seat.

Her winter coat parted and displayed a full-length black-and-white dress. The split down the side exposed a deliciously tantalizing length of slim thigh. Memories of our night together flicked through my mind, but her choice of footwear effectively earthed my thoughts. Incongruously, she was wearing a pair of much-used battered wellies.

'I did hose them down after doing the stables,' she commented dryly, noting my down-swept glance. 'I don't think they smell.'

'Actually, I was about to say your perfume's lovely. Not the slightest hint of horse.'

She shot me a swift smile. 'Thanks.' She reached into a bag, partly withdrew a strappy sandal – 'See, house-trained' – before letting it slide back inside. 'So . . . which way are we going?'

'Is that a logistical question – or merely a loaded one?'

'Shall we just set off, see where the road takes us?'

I engaged first gear and pointed through the windscreen. 'Well, it definitely won't be the scenic route tonight.'

Stray flakes of snow, no doubt harbingers of a whole lot more, were beginning to float down.

The snow continued to fall lightly all the way, but it stayed in first gear and didn't add any depth to the already lying snow. I knew the direction and roughly whereabouts Lady Branshawe's place was, but the satnav was useful for the last two or three miles.

The drive itself was a long one, marked by just two well-worn furrows from the many vehicles that had obviously preceded us. A swing to the left at the last minute brought Hempton Hall into view. It was as imposing as I'd expected: a Georgian mansion with sweeping steps leading to the heavy oak door, flanked by two enormous grooved pillars.

I reached for the circular iron ring and gave it a hefty tug. The ensuing loud peeling could have stood in for a bell in the local church tower.

'Now that's some doorbell,' murmured Georgia.

The echoes were still dying away when a man in full butler fig opened the door and graciously asked us in. He relieved us of coats and, in Georgia's case, wellingtons, before showing us into the main reception room. All the great and the good seemed to be here; the room was packed.

Lady Branshawe came forward, smiling widely. 'Georgia, Harry, so good of you to come. Now, do help yourselves to a drink . . .' A waitress had been hovering just behind her and now stepped forward and proffered a tray of filled flutes. 'Is it still trying to snow out there?'

Georgia nodded. 'But it's only a dusting.'

Lady Branshawe laughed. 'That's good.' She waved a hand towards the throng of people in the room. 'I'd have a problem bedding down all my guests if it snows heavily.'

'The hall's quite isolated, isn't it? I was glad of the satnav.'

'It is rather remote,' she agreed. 'But it probably fools the burglars. They give up looking for us long before they get here.'

While she was talking, she was discreetly ushering us in the direction of the huge inglenook fireplace. Filled with a four-foot-wide basket crammed with flaming logs, it threw out a massive blast of heat and effectively counteracted any amount of snowfall. But it wasn't simply her wish to warm us after the journey. Leaning against the wall alcove to the side of the inglenook was a tall man, hair brushed back from a wide, intelligent forehead and a paunch that said life had supplied all his needs – mostly edible, but also no doubt washed down by the finest alcohol.

He had noted our progress across the crowded room and unhitched himself with a smile.

'Ha, good evening.' He nodded affably to Georgia. 'And you are my daughter's talented new jockey, eh?'

I nodded.

'Daddy, may I introduce the famous Harry Radcliffe and his friend, Georgia.' She turned to us, 'My father, the Earl of Deymouth.' Hands were shaken all round.

'No racing in this weather, though?'

'No, sir, we've been firmly grounded.'

'I did offer him a chance in St Moritz, but he turned it down.'

He guffawed. 'I don't blame him. He doesn't look like a man to take unnecessary chances.'

I lifted the glass to my lips to conceal a smile. If he knew some of the chances I'd been forced to take, he wouldn't make such a glib comment.

'Oh, Aunt Daphne,' Lady Branshawe welcomed a well-preserved woman who had fetched up at the side of us. 'My father's younger sister . . . Daphne Brown.' She waved a hand. 'This is Georgia, and this is Harry Radcliffe, the Champion Jockey.'

'So pleased to meet you,' purred Daphne. 'We do have race-horses, but not up here in the north.' She gave an elegant little shudder. 'Too bleak. No, we're down in Berkshire – Lambourn, actually.'

'The valley of the racehorse,' said Georgia.

Daphne beamed a radiant smile at her. 'Sooo . . . you're into racing, as well?'

'No.' Georgia wrinkled her nose. 'But it rubs off, having horses and being around racing people.'

'You own racehorses?'

'Goodness, no. I run a flower shop – which doesn't run to owning a racehorse. I've simply taken in a couple of needy ones from Bransby.'

'Ah . . . yes.' Daphne scrutinized her. 'I have heard of them. A horse rescue charity.'

'That's right.'

'And have you perhaps heard of Elaine Brown?'

'Not sure, but I knew an Elaine at university.'

'Elaine is Daphne's daughter, my cousin,' said Lady Branshawe. 'And also a supporter of Bransby Rescue Centre.'

'I see.' Georgia smiled at Daphne. 'They do need all the support they can get.'

'Unfortunately, all charities do,' said the Earl. 'However, we are fortunate to have Mr Jackson Fellows playing for us tonight. So very kind after he gave his services freely last night as well in London.'

'How did it go, sir?' I enquired.

'Marvellously well, thank you, Harry. We raised a really substantial sum to swell our fundraising. But you and your lady friend don't seem to have taken advantage of the buffet . . .' He cupped Georgia's elbow. 'Come along. After that cold journey, I'm sure you could do with some sustenance, my dear.'

Georgia managed to give me a swift sweeping glance before allowing herself to be escorted to the far end of the room. Taking my cue, I followed them to where a snowy-white linen-covered table was seriously in danger of collapsing under the weight of an array of food that would have fed an army.

We loaded plates, although my own choice of delicacies, well spaced out, paid only lip service to that impression. As we turned away from the magnificent spread, looking for a couple of seats, I heard a familiar voice.

'Harry, over here – do join us.' And I saw Tally beckoning us. She was with Jim Crack and a couple of other people – strangers – at a table for six in an alcove near one of the windows.

'Shall we?' I queried.

Georgia nodded, whispering, 'Do introduce me. I've no idea who the others are.'

'I'm with you there – well, as regards two of them.'

But Tally took the reins. 'Mr and Mrs Webley, Ernest and Portia. Harry Radcliffe and Georgia.'

We shook hands.

I turned to Georgia, 'Obviously, Tally you already know, and this is Jim Crack, also a trainer and an old friend.'

'Hello.'

We sat down at the table.

'I gather you had a good trip over to Switzerland.' Jim beamed at Georgia.

She responded by blushing. 'Yes, indeed we did. So glad not to have missed it.'

'Unfortunately, I did, this year.' A voice over my shoulder had everybody looking up.

'Hello, Jackson. Do join us,' Tally said.

He was astonishingly like his photograph – the photograph I'd received from Nathaniel Willoughby. The photo I'd carried around at the St Moritz racecourse while desperately trying to locate him among the crowds. Jackson Fellows, the pianist.

'Would love to.' He spread his hands – sensitive, long-fingered hands. 'But I'm needed at the piano in a couple of minutes.'

'We're all looking forward to hearing you,' Ernest Webley said. 'It was a real treat listening to you play in London.'

'So kind. Let's hope I don't disappoint tonight.'

'Neither Georgia nor I have heard you play before,' I said, 'so it's a first for us.'

'Pressure, the pressure,' he said, dramatically sweeping a hand across his forehead.

'A shame you missed out on the snow racing.' I dropped in the bait.

'Yes' – Georgia innocently carried on my line of thinking and I could have blessed her for it – 'it was stupendous. But if you normally go, why not this year?'

Maybe I imagined it, but his jaw seemed to tighten slightly. Georgia's smile, however, softened the directness in the question. Probably, I wouldn't have got away with asking, but, like the majority of males she came into contact with, he seemed pleased by her attention.

'I so hate to let people down. Duty before pleasure, you know. I was playing these two venues back to back and I needed to spend time at the keyboard, practising.' His reply came out swiftly, pat, almost rehearsed.

She smiled. 'I understand.'

And I understood that his no-show at the races was not solely due to his scheduled performances.

If I had my doubts, they were dispelled as I watched the muscles in his face relax as he walked away. The look of relief was clear as he made his way over to the piano. I doubted that any of the others at our table would have noticed anything, as they weren't looking, but I was, with my chair angled just right – and I had a good view.

Georgia had used the word 'stupendous'. And it was certainly the word to describe the music flowing from beneath Jackson's fingers as they stroked, glided and firmly claimed the piano keys.

The buzz of chatter in the room died instantly and we were all held by the passion and feeling in the music.

He began the recital by playing a rendering of Scott Joplin's popular and vivacious 'The Entertainer', before becoming serious with Beethoven's 'Moonlight' Sonata and moving effortlessly to 'Fur Elise', followed by Einaudi's 'Le Onde' – The Waves. We were all swept away by his expertise.

'And to finish,' Jackson said, as the music trickled away, 'one of my personal favourites. OK, now I know that can't be rain coming down outside – it's white – but I'm sure you can all use your imagination.'

And he proceeded to take our breath away with Chopin's 'Raindrop' Prelude.

The storm of clapping that followed was deafening. And I could well understand Nathaniel Willoughby's appreciation of Jackson's talent. And his disappointment when, with two fingers broken on his left hand, Jackson had been forced to forgo his performance in Switzerland. But those fingers were well healed now and doing a truly wonderful job.

The questions that needed answering were who had broken Jackson's fingers? And how the hell was I going to find that out? Followed by why were they broken? Was it something he'd done, or not done – maybe something he knew? But having listened to his playing, those two deliberately broken fingers took on a deeper significance that smacked at vindictiveness aimed at Jackson's wonderful talent. Had they not healed correctly – and that must have been a possibility – the loss of his gift would have deprived a lot of people of a lot of pleasure. Yes, there was a very sour and spiteful feel behind the attack, almost as though the person was deeply jealous of Jackson himself. It was a further piece of the jigsaw.

I mentally stored it away in the box – as yet without an illustration on top – with all the other pieces. One day, without doubt, I'd have enough to join up and I'd see the complete picture.

And as had happened in the past, sometimes I didn't need all the pieces. Given a fair proportion, I would mull over what I had and my sixth sense would take a wild leap, giving me the answer.

Right now, though, there was nothing esoteric about my hands. They were aching from all the exuberant clapping which lasted until Jackson, acknowledging the appreciation of his audience, ran *his* hands once more over the keys and treated us to Chopin's 'Nocturne in E flat'.

TWENTY-SEVEN

'I know I said I was glad not to miss the Switzerland trip, but how wonderful was that?' Georgia sighed, her face glowing with pleasure.

'Couldn't agree more,' I said. 'I'd no idea he could play like that.' I'd certainly had reservations before coming tonight, wondering how it would pan out, but, like Georgia, I was very pleased not to have missed that performance.

Tally and the others at our table nodded agreement. 'It was marvellous.'

I caught the waitress on her way past our table, took two flutes of champagne from the tray and handed one to Georgia. 'We'll drink to a lovely evening, shall we?'

'Why not.'

Holding eye contact, we took a sip of our drinks. However she wanted to play it was fine by me. Without commitment or expectations, it felt easy and comfortable again between us.

On the periphery of my vision, I noted Jackson finally managing to withdraw from a tight circle of admirers and head for the door.

'Would you excuse me? Must go to the gents,' I said, setting down my glass.

Without hurrying, I followed him from the main lounge and out into the hall, and although by now he'd disappeared, I was pretty sure he was headed for the cloakroom to grab a few minutes' peace and relief. His adrenaline levels needed a chance to lower. Unfortunately, I was about to push them back up.

Opening the door, I went in. Like the rest of the hall, it was perfectly equipped to cater for parties, with a run of three separate toilets and a line of hand basins set in a long mirror-backed vanity unit. I swished hot water into one of the hand basins and kept an eye on the mirror, all the time praying that no one else would feel the need to take a comfort break right now. They didn't. But a toilet flushed and Jackson Fellows was reflected in the mirror in front of me.

Our eyes met.

'That was some performance,' I said, and meant it.

'Glad you enjoyed it.' He washed his hands in the next basin and ran wet hands through his long hair. It was black and lush. He could have doubled for a young Ian McShane. I was sure he had no trouble attracting the girls.

There was no easy way to open the conversation. I jumped in.

'Sorry you have a problem.'

His eyes flicked sideways in the mirror. 'No idea what you're getting at. I don't have a problem.'

'Hmm. I'm just really happy for you that those two fingers mended perfectly.'

He gave himself away by glancing quickly down to his left hand.

'Oh, oh yes, those. Had an accident. Caught them in the car door.'

'Really . . .' I nodded slowly. 'Not what I heard.' I reached into my pocket and drew out the photograph taken in St Moritz. Holding it out to him, I said, 'Come on, Jackson, you do have a problem – admit it.'

'Where did you get this?' His face drained of colour.

'Has it anything to do with your fingers getting broken?'

'Nothing to do with you.'

'No? When three people have lost their lives? Five, if you count the men who died in prison.'

'It wasn't me. I'm not responsible.'

'So, who is?'

'It was an accident. Those two women . . . they went over a glacier . . . nobody's fault.'

'And was it also an accident John Dunston went over Flamborough Head?'

His face screwed up in pain. 'The newspapers said it was suicide. It was, wasn't it?'

He very much wanted to be reassured. His dismay was genuine, and at that moment I believed him innocent of the crime of John's murder.

I slowly shook my head. 'No.'

Taking a deep shaky breath, he gripped the edge of the hand basin. 'None of it's my fault. I just want to put the past behind me.'

'Seems you are involved. And you are being blackmailed, aren't you?'

His grip on the basin tightened, fingers whitening. 'I just want to be left alone, play my piano . . .'

'Tell me,' I urged. 'Maybe I could help.'

'Why should I?'

'Your fingers might not heal so well the next time.'

He caught his breath and his face, already very pale, whitened even more. 'I *must* play. Music's my life. But you see' – his voice took on a desperate tone – 'there's no money in it – not for a solo pianist. Not yet, not until I can build up my reputation. Oh, in an orchestra maybe, but that's not what I want.'

'In the meantime, someone's putting a squeeze on you.'

For a long minute, he stared at me in the mirror, then gave a nod. 'OK, yes, I am being blackmailed. But I'm not telling you who – or the reason.'

'Why not? Why protect him?'

'I'm not. I'm protecting other people.'

'I'd say you need to protect yourself, wouldn't you? Rule number one, when you're looking out for someone, look after yourself first. Because if you don't, and you go down the pan, they're going to go down, too.'

'I'm just trying—'

'To juggle all the balls, hope none will fall, and the situation will go away?'

He continued to stare at me. Until, finally, he dropped his gaze and let go of the hand basin. 'Yeah, something like that.'

'But it's not going to happen, is it?'

'No . . . I realize that. I'm on borrowed time. So is he, right now.'

'He?'

Jackson stabbed a forefinger at the other man in the photograph. '*Him!*'

'Was he the person who broke your fingers?'

'Yeah.'

'Was it simply a warning – or something more?'

'Both. A taster of what's to come if I don't give him what he wants.'

'Which is?'

'Look, I said I wasn't telling you – and I'm not.'

'Right. And when this man contacts you again, you're going to give him what he's after, are you?'

'It's his anyway.'

'What is?'

'It's not going to help you.'

'Then tell me.'

'Essential paperwork.'

A picture flicked through my mind of the IOU Paula had found in Nigel's pocket that she had handed to Victor.

'You mean . . . like a gambling debt?'

'I didn't say that. I'm not answering any more questions, OK?'

'Fine. But if you want to keep on playing, I'd advise you to get hold of it smartly.'

'I *can't*, damn it. It's tricky.'

Two men, laughing and talking and obviously well tanked-up, burst in through the cloakroom door and put paid to my opportunity to find out anything else. Jackson seized his chance and bolted out, probably to return to the main lounge.

Quickly sliding a comb from my pocket, I made a show of combing my hair. I certainly wasn't going to follow Jackson back to the party. The less Jackson and I were seen together in public the better. He was in a dicey and dangerous situation – that much was clear. If our names became linked, given my growing reputation – albeit unwanted – as a successful detective, it could only escalate the outcome.

And from what Jackson had revealed, it was an outcome that involved extreme violence.

'Thanks for a really great evening.' Georgia leaned across and planted a kiss on my cheek. I waited, wondering, but she said no more, just opened the Mazda's passenger door. Carefully planting the battered yet waterproof wellies in the snow on her drive, she got out of the car. 'I'll give you a ring, shall I, Harry?'

I nodded. 'Anytime you're free. Me – well, I'm pretty much unemployed right now.'

'I'm sure you'll find something to occupy yourself.' She came round to the driver's side, bent down and kissed me on the lips. 'Goodnight.'

I waited, watched until she'd safely made it up the snowy slope and opened the front door, then put the Mazda into reverse, turned in the drive and drove home.

The temperature was falling steadily and was well below zero when I swung in on to the gravel outside the kitchen door.

Indoors, however, the Rayburn was doing a sterling job and the cottage was toasty warm.

I shoved the kettle on the hob and reached for a mug. The next second a large ginger bolster of a cat had landed on my shoulder. Leo, having spent the evening curled up in his basket above the heat source – he wasn't daft – had launched himself at me and was now looking for company.

'Too cold for it tonight, eh?' I scrubbed my knuckles along his chin. He kneaded claws into my shoulder and produced a purr rivalling a road drill. 'I dare say all your lady friends are tucked up nice and warm as well.'

I made tea and took it through to the lounge, Leo still riding high on my shoulder. Flicking on the electric fire, I stretched out on the sofa and watched the orange and red flames, allowing the mesmeric flickering to soothe and unwind any knots of tension. With the combination of a warm room, a mug of tea and a purring cat, total relaxation was a given.

And when I achieved this level of relaxation, solutions to impenetrable problems seemed to occur spontaneously – but only when I was in possession of sufficient pieces of the jigsaw. Pleasant though this reverie was, no ideas presented themselves. I gave it an hour but I was no further forward.

Giving up on the softly-softly approach, I fetched a notebook and pen and made notes on my conversation with Fellows. A fair bet would be that the paperwork was in regard to a gambling bet; Fellows' choice of words upheld that theory. So that said, the man in the photograph was probably a member of the group to which Nigel had attached himself. That thought led me straight to the promise I'd made to Victor: on Sunday evening, I was going to have to leave the cosy cottage and go on surveillance. And it could be difficult. If the weather held, the roads would be unpleasant, particularly any country lanes, and the main worry would be the lack of cars on the road.

People tended to go to ground at night, especially on a Sunday and even more so when it was this cold. I'd certainly run a high risk of being spotted unless I could tuck in two or three cars back from Nigel's car. But as yet, I had not received any instructions from Victor detailing just what type of car Nigel drove or the starting point. The one thing I did know was I would need to fill up the Mazda before attempting to trail him because it was going to be a fair distance there and back.

So, that took care of keeping me occupied, as Georgia had commented, on Sunday.

I'd heard nothing from Annabel, which was reassuring. No further repercussions from the letter John Dunston had entrusted to me. And I could only hope that my deflection of the hostility deriving from it would continue to hold off any further threats to Sir Jeffrey.

In the meantime, there was still one other thing I needed to do – and I'd been putting it off, telling myself not to open a further can of worms, yet knowing it must be done. I could get away with not doing it tonight – too cold, too dark, too late. The excuses flowed – all legitimate. However, come the morning, there would be no excuse. Of course, it would depend on what I found, but I was willing to bet Harlequin Cottage on the outcome being explosive.

My gut feeling told me it was going to act as a catalyst, one that, while stretching away with its roots buried in the past, was also reaching forward, affecting the present.

I locked up, went to bed and set my alarm for six a.m. Nobody would be around at that early hour. The cottage was situated down a remote country lane, the nearest neighbour a good half-a-mile away. The only people to come past on a weekday were likely to be the milkman, due around seven o'clock, the postman – and I was lucky if he arrived by nine – or maybe a stray tractor from the nearest farm any time in between, but at six o'clock on a Sunday – no one.

Climbing into bed, I switched off the light and gave myself permission not to think about tomorrow or what unpleasant, undoubtedly dangerous discovery I would make. Tomorrow, very definitely, fell into the category of 'sufficient unto the day'.

TWENTY-EIGHT

'd slapped off the alarm, dragged on several layers of clothes and gone downstairs to the kitchen. Leo opened one eye, just a slit, to make sure it was me and to make absolutely sure there was no food forthcoming right now, before tucking round into an even tighter ball, tail wrapped fox-like around his nose.

I shook my head at him. 'You lucky tom. Next time, I'm coming back as a cat,' I told him, and added, 'with a besotted owner, of course, to provide creature comforts like grub, warmth and fuss.'

The ears twitched, taking it all in, but he decided it wasn't worth lifting an eyelid for another look.

I shrugged into a thick parka, found flashlight and gloves, then followed Georgia's example from last night and put on wellies.

Outside, the night, still as dark as the grave, was not a place to linger. The wind was high and howling. It carried tiny, hard-packed balls of frozen snow that smashed against my cheeks, making my nose and eyes run with the extreme cold.

I did a shuffling trot – anything faster and I'd risk finding myself flat on my back – across the yard to the brick outhouses.

Snow had piled up against the heavy old wooden door and I had to drag it open, fighting against the wind that threatened to slam it shut again. Once inside, I gave up the hopeless struggle to close it from the inside and let the wind have a field day batting it back and forth. I went over to the workbench and dropped on to my knees, feeling underneath for the sack of cat litter. Gripping it by the top corner, I dragged it free and out into the middle of the floor. The granules had, of course, done the job I'd expected and shifted around the package, but the action of moving the bag free of the bench had caused the package to slip further. And reaching down only allowed more and more granules to do their own thing.

I ended up with my arm rammed inside the bag as far as my armpit, scrabbling about to get a grip on the paper surrounding the package. A good deal of the litter ended up on the cobbled floor of the outhouse, but it could stay there. At six o'clock in the morning, in brass-monkey weather, no way was I going to linger sweeping it all up.

Renewing my fight with the wind, I secured the door and slipped and slid back to the warmth of the cottage. How true it was that you couldn't appreciate the sun if you hadn't experienced a downpour of rain – I gasped my way back into the kitchen and thankfully shut out the darkness and the snow.

Despite wearing gloves, my fingers were numb as I fumbled and struggled to fill up the kettle and get it on to the Rayburn hob. There was no reaction at all from Leo – head down, dreaming deeply, he'd gone to cat land.

Clutching a reviving mug of tea, I made a mental note that if I had to go out today, I must make sure I set the boiler to provide daylong heat for him. Well, if Annabel was still living here, that's what she'd do – she's a complete softie as regards Leo. However, since Annabel's busy looking out for Jeffrey, all Leo's got now is me to look out for him. I couldn't let him down.

I leaned, shivering, against the Rayburn and drank the tea. Then, having thawed out a bit, I made a second mug and took that and the package through to the office. In appearance, it was like a shoebox, but not really oblong – more of a square. I found a small pair of scissors and set about cutting off the brown paper wrapping. It had been securely bound by sticky tape and resisted being ripped off. But after a couple of minutes, the tape gave up the struggle against cold steel and came apart.

Beneath the brown paper wrapping was a sturdy cardboard box, also securely sealed with parcel tape. I tried giving it a shake but whatever was inside must have been wedged tightly and it gave me no clue whatsoever. My thoughts scrambled around as to what I might release once I'd got it opened. Something lethal? A bomb? Not ticking. A poisonous spider? Not likely. Besides – I brought a halt to my fancies – John Dunston had specifically left it for me, and that had been conditional upon my attendance at his funeral. He had been testing my feelings out for a certain level of respect – loyalty perhaps; he wasn't intending to harm me. In fact, from the tone of his letter, he'd been asking for my help in bringing his murderer to justice. No, there was nothing harmful inside the box.

I cut away the restraining tape and opened the box. As I'd expected, whatever it was had been wrapped up tightly before being placed inside. All I could see so far was what looked like some sort of absorbent material . . . terry towelling? It was predominantly white but easing it out of the box with the end of my biro, I could see there was a stripe of colour running through it – blue. Seeing that colour emerging set bells ringing in my mind. I'd been told about this – a good while back – before the St Moritz trip – and now, here it was lying on my desk. It belonged to Keith Whellan, Mousey Brown's horsebox driver.

I took a deep breath and pulled out the rest of the material.

There was something hard and solid in the middle, and as I let the towelling fall away, I could see streaks of dried blood and a heavy glass ashtray.

Caution sent me to the kitchen and I returned with a pair of rubber gloves. Lifting the ashtray from the nest of towelling, I could also see that around the base was a crust of dried blood. Ripping a sheet of A4 from the printer, I placed the ashtray down on it. Hooking my foot around the leg of my chair, I pulled it out, sat down and studied the unlikely object. If I'd been offered a million pounds – and a million chances – I could never have guessed what the box contained.

The more I stared at it, the more peculiar the whole situation appeared. Why had John gone to the trouble of sealing it inside the box and leaving those precise instructions with the solicitor? Obviously, he'd needed to be certain of my commitment to find the killer; that much was clear. But an ashtray? He'd said it was proof – a clue, then – to the killer's identity. The crust of blood on the bottom edge was old, dried on and iron-hard. To remove it would take either a long soak in hot water or even scraping off with a knife.

The sorry tale it told was that the blood would most likely have come from a wound on the victim. OK, it was the most rational conclusion. But, if so, that simply raised two further questions. Who was that victim and who was the killer? And I had no answer at all to either question.

Stripping off my rubber gloves, I left the bloodied ashtray sitting on my desk and went upstairs to have a bath and a shave. Later still, having distractedly scrambled a couple of eggs and washed them down with a coffee, my mind churning over the puzzle, I went back into the office. Although I'd mulled over the whole business from several angles, I was still at a complete loss.

Staring moodily at the ashtray, I changed tack in my approach. John would not have gone to all this trouble if he'd not been sure I could fathom out the truth behind it. So, I put myself in his shoes. What had he thought as he parcelled it up so securely? I'd always thought the roots of this went down deep. Did the ashtray have any connection to an old case that had a bearing on a death? Possibly a case I'd solved in the past? I was sure John had been killed because he knew too much or had witnessed something damning.

I scrutinized the ashtray for a long time, thinking through the previous three cases. They were linked – I was sure they were – in a *danse macabre*. Like a bizarre game of deadly dominoes. As each victim fell dead, so the next one followed. Mirroring real life, one action led inexorably on to the next. And just as no one lives in an isolated vacuum, the actions all involved other people: families, friends, enemies.

If I was on the right track, what was needed was an appraisal of any ashtrays I had seen, at any time, during any one of those previous cases.

The door pushed open a fraction and a huge ginger head slid round, green eyes wide, accusing, their message clear, accompanied by a strident eardrum-blasting bellow, the sort only a cat of Leo's size could produce: the expected breakfast had not been handed out.

I dutifully got up. 'Sorry, mate. I forgot.'

He was definitely not about to forgive me. The disgusted look in his emerald eyes conveyed what he thought of me.

However, seeing that he had my full attention, he stalked off in front, tail pointing to the ceiling, and took up a position next to his empty dish in the kitchen. I tipped in some cat food and refilled his water bowl. Then poured a further coffee, hoping it might aid my brain cells. I made it black and very strong and added a spoonful of honey for good measure before returning to my desk.

OK, if my deductions were right, I needed to cast back and analyse the first time I'd been roped in – chained with a steel hawser, more like – to a deadly situation from which I could not simply walk away. At the heart of it was the proposed danger to my disabled half-sister, Silvie. Nothing like the threat of danger to your family to ensure that when your strings were pulled, you jumped to the correct height – whatever height that might escalate to in the end.

So, whose house had I been inside when I'd seen an ashtray? None of my friends smoked. But it must have been a private house. The smoking ban had been introduced and vigorously enforced in all public houses and restaurants. Realizing that fact was cheering. It eliminated a great number of possibilities.

I couldn't remember any of my racing colleagues who smoked. When it came to race riding, fitness was everything – we all needed every gasp of breath going when it came to riding a finish. And upon that thought another quickly followed. Smoking was banned, of course, at Silvie's nursing home. Lung infections were bad news. They could prove fatal.

My own movements at that time had been curtailed. I was getting over a bad fall and, apart from doing loads of physio work, was supposed to be resting. I hadn't gone to many places or travelled very far. The flower shop, prior to visiting Silvie, and the solicitor's office was about it. I'd never seen Janine smoking even before the ban when I'd called into the shop to buy freesias – always white ones – for Silvie. And certainly in the solicitor Nigel Broadbent's office, there had been no sign of an ashtray.

One place I had frequented, however, had been the home of the soon-to-be-retired racehorse trainer, Elspeth Maudsley. Had there been any ashtrays in her lounge when we'd sat down with coffee and discussed my writing her memoirs? The short answer was no, there hadn't been. Elspeth was a non-smoker.

But . . . her son was a smoker.

On the evening of the birthday party for Chloe, her daughter-in-law, Elspeth had drawn me aside into the office. There had been a telephone call for me from Aunt Rachel. I knew for sure there had been an ashtray on the desk. And a half-smoked, stubbed-out cigarette adorning it. Oh, yes, I could remember that clearly.

Elspeth had wrinkled her nose. 'I'm sorry about the smell,' she'd said, 'I do apologize.' She'd left the office, closing the door behind her to give me some privacy. Taking advantage of her absence, I'd picked up that cigarette butt and put it into my pocket – it had been evidence. The scene came into my mind with remarkable clarity, as if I was actually looking down at that ashtray, picking up the stub.

Only one thing wrong – the ashtray wasn't the same one.

TWENTY-NINE

The Leicester races murder. That had been the title by which people referred to the first case. They still did. Mentally, I drew a red line underneath. No, I hadn't seen the bloodied ashtray at any time during that horrible affair.

So, the second time I'd been dragged into investigating a murder – this time at North Shore Hotel and golf course where Mike and I had been guests at a wedding – would need checking out. Obviously, since there were no ashtrays in the hotel itself, that venue could be ruled out for a start.

I sat and mulled over various other places, but apart from race-courses, they'd been mainly pubs so the answer was the same. It had to have been a private house or establishment. But whom had I visited?

I thrashed away at the problem for a couple of hours and came up with nothing. What I needed was a second person, someone who knew me well and could look at it in a different way. Only one person fitted that – Mike. He'd always been my main man in a crisis, a lifesaver more than once. Maybe his take on this would help.

I reached for my mobile and sent him a text. A couple of minutes later his reply bleeped back. *Yes, come over. Hot grub in 1 hr.* I grinned. Good old Mike: just what I needed in this atrocious weather.

Pen opened the door. She was wearing a scarlet apron. The sight of her lifted me from the mud I was wallowing in. Solitary living was fine, up to a point, but there came a moment when friends were a blessing.

'Something smells good. And you look good enough to eat.'

She laughed, lifting her cheek for a kiss. 'You're most welcome, Harry. Go straight through; Mike's in the kitchen.'

He was sprawled out in a chair, feet up on another, with the *Racing Post* spread out on top of his thighs.

'Hi. How did your bash at Lady B's go off, then? Any little nuggets get dropped?'

'It was productive, yes.'

'Never mind all the sleuthing,' Pen said, following me into the kitchen. 'Tell me about Georgia. Did she wear a nice dress?'

'What Pen really means, Harry, is did you two—'

'Mike! That's enough.'

He grinned, unabashed, and thrust the *Racing Post* supplement into my hand. 'Saved you this from Sunday as you were in Switzerland. In case you didn't see it, there's an interesting article on a stable visit up at Mousey's.'

Obediently, I sank down in a chair and began reading, savouring the delicious smell of roasting pork, the heat from the Aga and the warmth of their friendship. I pushed away all problems and totally relaxed. Sunny, Pen's old yellow Labrador bitch, pottered over from her basket and slumped down across my feet. I reached down and fondled the soft ears. This was the real world, my world – the only one that mattered. And it felt good.

OK, living it up in St Moritz had been great, but it was unreal and transitory against the pleasures of home and the company of long-standing friends. And there was only so much ice and snow you could take. Here, in England, in a few days, the thaw would have set in and I'd be back in the saddle racing; over there, they would still be trapped in their winter wonderland for weeks.

After lunch – apple sauce to complement the roast pork and three choices of vegetables, plus roast potatoes – most regretfully, I introduced the subject of ashtrays.

'I need to try to retrace my movements during the time of that second *case*.' I gave emphasis to the word.

'I told you, didn't I? You've started talking like a private eye.'

'Sorry, Pen. I'm *not* a private eye. I don't get paid to chase down killers. But I don't know how to refer to it really.'

'How about the golf course murder, eh?' Mike said. 'It's what everybody else calls it.'

I was forced to agree. 'What I need to remember is where I've seen something before . . .' I hesitated. 'Don't laugh . . . actually, it's an ashtray.'

'Of all the things you might have said . . .' Pen shook her head. 'You could have put money on our never guessing.'

'I'll say.' Mike looked bewildered. 'How can we help?'

'Remind me, Mike, of the places we went to – probably private dwellings.'

'Yes, you wouldn't have found ashtrays in pubs, would you? Not with the smoking ban.'

'True enough, Pen.'

Mike laughed. 'Face it, Harry: it was mostly pubs we frequented.'

I nodded. 'But I'm sure there *were* others – must have been.'

'Well, for a start, Barbara Maguire threw a party at her place. You took Chloe.'

'So I did. D'y'know, I'd totally forgotten.' I ran the scenario through my mind before shaking my head. 'Pity. It could have been the answer, but no.'

'And don't forget, you visited Alice's husband, Darren Goode, in Nottingham Prison.'

We all grimaced together.

'Nice try, Mike. Not good enough.'

'I remember something you once said, Harry.' Pen screwed up her forehead. 'It was to do with that criminal who'd been released after doing time for GBH. What was his name now? Jake?'

'Yes, that's right. Jake Smith.'

'You visited a relation of his, I think. Would it have been his father?'

'Dead right. Thanks. I went over to Newark, spoke to his dad, Fred. The house was a tip, smelled to the rafters of booze, fags, urine, and anything else you could imagine.'

'Sounds revolting.'

'Hmm, it was.'

'Wait a minute,' Mike said. 'You mentioned fags. Did you happen to notice if there were any ashtrays around?'

I pictured the interior as I'd walked up to the dirty front door and let my mind's eye travel around as Fred showed me through to the living room. I'd been aware that on top of the sticky old carpet it was crowded with furniture, and every surface was cluttered with accumulated junk, littered with empty beer cans and crumpled newspapers. It had not been a room to linger in.

I forced myself to concentrate on the most likely place to stand an ashtray. The coffee table had been ringed and ruined by numerous mugs and glasses, but on the corner nearest Fred's battered armchair there had been an ashtray. I closed my eyes and concentrated. What had it looked like? My interest that day had been cursory to say the least. But I had noticed it was overflowing with cigarette butts. On that basis, it must have been a large one.

My subconscious came up trumps and provided me with an image. It had been a deep, heavy ashtray and around the edge of the pottery was a picture of Robin Hood in green and red. I nodded, satisfied.

'Yes. I *did* see one, Mike.'

'But?'

'It's not the right one.'

We gave a collective groan.

Pen rallied first. 'But we're getting closer. Even if it's only to eliminate one.'

'Might be easier to think of who you know that smokes.'

'That's another way of looking at it, Mike.'

'Who might have offered you a cigarette? Like a casual acquaintance who didn't know you're a non-smoker?'

'I've just remembered someone,' Pen said excitedly, 'and you went to interview him.'

'Who?'

'Benson McCavity. You went over to Grantham to check on Benson, at his garage.'

'Yes, I remember. He made tea for us in Union Jack mugs. But he didn't offer me a cigarette and I didn't see any ashtrays.'

'Right . . .' Mike pulled a wry face. 'So where does that leave us?'

'I don't know—' I began and then, quite suddenly, I remembered another house. I'd gone there because I'd been beaten up, left for dead. And I'd seriously wanted to know the would-be assassin's name. Only one person would be able to tell me – the prostitute, Alice. If she didn't know, then no one would. So I'd gone visiting.

Alice had shown me into her living room. Apart from the three-piece suite, there had been a coffee table. And on that table had been an ashtray. Made of heavy clear glass, it was identical to the one wrapped in the terry towelling – or had been, before the crusted blood. When I'd seen Alice's ashtray the first time, it was simply clear glass, no blood on it. But then Alice had still been alive. Even as the thought went through my mind, my next one gave me a physical jolt. It was more than probable – it was almost a certainty – that the ashtray had been used to kill her. The dried and encrusted blood around the base was Alice's blood.

Lost in dark thoughts, I gradually became aware that the other two were sitting watching me curiously.

'What have you remembered, Harry?'

I looked up at Pen. 'Exactly where I saw the ashtray. But . . . more importantly,' I said slowly, 'the victim's name.'

'Which is?' Mike prompted.

'I'm pretty sure the ashtray was used to kill Alice Goode.'

'The prostitute?' Pen said, her eyes fixed on my face.

I nodded. 'I saw it on her coffee table, the afternoon I drove over to Newark to ask her if she knew who it was that had beaten me up—'

'Oh, yes,' Mike interrupted, 'and she told you it couldn't have been Jake Smith. He'd have finished the job.'

'Too true.'

'But then you cracked the golf course murder.'

'Yes, but Alice was murdered very soon afterwards.'

An unwanted image came into my mind of Alice lying on the floor, her skull smashed and bloodied. The attack had been frenzied. But, as far as I knew, the police hadn't found the murder weapon. It was certainly never reported.

'I'd only just got out of hospital, if you remember, when I discovered Alice – and finding a body was the last thing on God's earth I needed. Normality and peace were what I had in mind – you know, time to heal?'

They nodded.

'You've had precious little peace this last year, Harry.'

'Tell me about it, Pen.'

'I thought it was all cut and dried about Alice's death,' Mike said. 'Case closed.'

'So did I,' I said gloomily. 'But somehow it's tied in with this latest murder.'

'John Dunston being thrown over Flamborough Head?'

'Yes. Apart from that letter I received at his funeral, there was this other thing – a small package left at the solicitor's office up in York. I went up to collect it.'

'The day you took your car so you could drive straight to Leicester races.'

'Yes. Well, when I finally got to open the package, inside was this bloodied ashtray wrapped up in a bit of terry towelling. John had said in the letter that it was the only bit of evidence regarding his death.'

Mike nodded slowly. 'So there had to have been someone else

involved with Alice's death, and this person murdered Dunston. He was silenced because – and before – he could point the finger.'

'That's how I see it, Mike.'

'But why didn't Dunston just tell you who it was?' Pen put in.

'Because I suspect he was trying to protect someone else. John was a generous man; he gave me the option of either going ahead and clearing his name – seeing justice done – or backing off.'

'Harry, faced with doing the right thing, no matter how bloody dangerous, or backing off . . . *come on.* You have never backed off.'

'You wanted me to, though, Mike. You told me to give the blasted letter back and have done with it.'

'And I knew damned well you wouldn't.'

'Hmm,' Pen shook her head disapprovingly, looking from one to the other. 'Leopards and spots. You're as bad as each other.'

Mike smiled and reached for her hand. 'Would you have us any other way, my sweet?'

THIRTY

As we talked, the afternoon had drifted unnoticed through dusk into early evening, and by the time I arrived home at the cottage it was quite dark. The light outside the kitchen door came on announcing my arrival. The golden gleam hit the ice-white snow and reflected upwards again. It was very still; no breeze disturbed the air of watchful waiting which hung about the cottage.

I locked the vehicle and made my way round to the brick outbuildings. Although wide open and battered by the earlier gale-force winds, the door to the first one was still intact, hinges holding. I checked that Leo wasn't sheltering inside, then closed it securely. There was no need to replace the package in the bag of cat litter – its secret was a secret no more. I had found the answer to the first of my questions – the victim's name. But sorting out the backstory had inevitably thrown up the crucial second question: *who* was the murderer? That it was someone I knew was a given – had to be. But just who was it? If John hadn't been sure I could find out, he'd never have gone to all the trouble of leading me on in this way. But he'd also been covering his tracks, thus preventing harm to anyone else – except me. Probably why he'd given me an option.

I stamped off the clinging snow at the doorstep and went through into the welcome warmth of the kitchen.

'Hi, you lazy bugger.'

Leo languidly stretched out a long, ginger back leg over the edge of his basket, opened his eyes and almost swallowed himself in a gigantic yawn. He didn't appear to have shifted an inch all day. But now, since I'd finally deigned to come home, he launched all eight kilograms of body weight and dug grappling irons firmly into my shoulder. It was a good job I still had my coat on.

'Food, right? That what you want?'

I carried him into the pantry and took down a tin of pilchards from the shelf. Well, since I'd been fed magnificently at Mike's stables, it seemed only fair. His purr, when I took off the lid, practically rattled the pantiles on the roof.

Cordial relations established, I took a mug of strong tea into the lounge. Picking up my folder of notes, I settled on the settee to write up my latest piece of the jigsaw. It wasn't a picture, but sometimes words were equally good. Sometimes they were better. Words allowed the subconscious to form its own imaginative illustration.

The ashtray still sat where I'd left it on top of the pristine sheet of A4 on my desk. Pity it couldn't speak, tell me what I needed to know: the man's name. And, taking into account the strength involved in dispatching John, yes, it had to be a man. But now that I knew this bastard had been the same one who had also murdered Alice, my resolve to track down the killer was absolute.

However, before I began to write today's input, I decided to reread all my notes from when I attended John Dunston's funeral. Because I'd now discovered Alice was the first victim, it coloured my perceptions somewhat differently. I had to ask myself a big question: did John know that the man who was gunning for him had been the same one who had killed Alice? It seemed very likely. And if John knew, it wasn't too far-fetched that Keith Whellan, his friend and ally, might also be aware of it. Keith had promised to help in any way he could.

As Mike had said, as far as the police were concerned, the case was closed. Without any convincing new evidence, they wouldn't be interested. Far better to let the mud rest at the bottom of the pond than stir it up. Since then, though, John had met his death . . . The police had written it off as suicide. That wasn't good enough for me. It left an ongoing dirty smear against John's character – and let a murderer go free. But the only evidence I had was the encrusted blood that could, possibly, be checked against data on Alice's file. Likewise, if the police were to check for fingerprints, they might find some – or then again, not. That was their field of expertise.

As for me, there was nothing I could do. Except keep on digging and hope to uncover something useful. It was amazing I'd come this far on only the slenderest of leads. And yet again, it seemed I was the only person who could do anything about the situation, however much I kicked against it.

The ashtray had been found in the horsebox. Why? Obviously, to conceal it. I thought around the question. There was also another possibility. Perhaps the killer had meant it to be found. It could then direct suspicion towards John. If the bastard was trying to implicate John in Alice's death, then it was only a short jump for anyone to assume his suicide was also prompted by a case of guilt, as well as grief over his son's death. The more I thought about the scenario, the more it stacked up: with John dead, it was the end of the trail.

Which left me where? Trying to find a loose end so I could unravel the truth. I supped tea and read on, finished the notes, then mentally added all the information I'd discovered today.

Having fed all the facts into the most complex and superior computer ever devised, the brain, I leant back against the settee cushions, closed my eyes and let my thoughts drift. Leo picked up on my relaxed mood and stretched out on my chest, kneading with half-sheathed claws and purring gently, hypnotically. He was, without doubt, triple A at stress busting. I let my hand glide over his warm silky fur, let go completely and gave my subconscious mind every chance to come up with answers. Nature gleefully took charge and we both fell into a deep, restorative sleep. Must have done. Two hours had past when I next opened my eyes.

Regretfully, there was no lightning flash of illumination, but I did end up with two possible leads – two men I definitely needed to check out. One advantage to being snowed off from the race-courses was that it gave me the necessary time to follow through with this investigation.

So in the morning, I decided, I'd go and interview the man driving the black Beamer. He'd driven away from the car park at North Shore Hotel just as Victor and I arrived. And I would ask him straight out the name of the man who had been sitting beside him, the one with the jutting chin. I already had an idea who it was. For the sake of the man's family, I hoped I was wrong.

The second man I had to see, of course, was Keith Whellan. He'd been the only person privy to John's private thoughts. But it was also odds-on he wouldn't know who the man was. A dead end in that case.

I fished out my mobile, checked and tapped in the number for the first of my leads. 'Hi, Edward. Harry Radcliffe. Any chance you're free tomorrow morning? I really need to speak to you.' Edward Frame, who lived in a massive barn conversion over near Wilsford, was free. 'All morning. Come for coffee.'

'Will do,' I replied. I remembered he served the world's best coffee.

The snow was banked up thickly along the hedgerows alongside lanes just passable at little more than a crawl. I'd found the journey from Nottinghamshire comparatively easy – the council gritters had done a great job overnight – but rural Lincolnshire was definitely out-in-the-sticks country.

Edward, no doubt, had had plenty of time to see my car approaching down his long drive, and before I'd even turned off the engine, he'd opened the iron-studded oak front door.

'Come in, Harry. This weather's best appreciated looking at it through the triple glazing.'

'Morning, Edward.'

Heat wrapped itself around me as he showed me through into the magnificent lounge, complete with blazing log-burner. Edward was a man who liked his comforts – in all departments. The last time I'd visited, he'd been upset about Alice's death. He'd told me that he sometimes booked Alice for the whole weekend. She had been mightily impressed by this palatial place and called it Buckingham Palace. Edward said she'd loved coming here. Not for a moment did I think he'd had any part in her murder, but I hoped he'd come clean about the identity of the man he'd been chauffeuring away from North Shore Hotel.

'Coffee is perking. Just go and pour out. Make yourself comfortable.'

'Same coffee as last time?'

'Of course. Only the best.'

'Great.'

He chuckled and left me to find a seat. Two dark-green leather armchairs had been drawn up before the fire. In front was an oak coffee table strewn with some papers and envelopes. Within a couple of minutes, Edward reappeared with a tray and I was instantly reminded of that previous visit I'd made. The smell of the coffee was the same – and it was wonderful.

'Just push those letters aside, Harry, so I can put the tray down.'

I bent over and slid the papers to one side. The top one had been handwritten, something that was getting to be a rarity nowadays. From my present position, now only inches away, just one word caught my eye: *Thanks.*

'You take honey in coffee, don't you, Harry?'

Edward's query stopped me from making a prat of myself. While inside, nonverbally, I was yelling 'Yes!' with delight, wishing I could punch air, I just managed to tone down the volume into a verbal 'Yes' of agreement. A near thing. I was sure Edward hadn't noticed. He was busy unscrewing the lid off the jar of honey. Taking advantage, I skimmed a glance over the signature on the letter before lifting my gaze in time to receive the mug he was holding out.

'Well worth the journey to get here, Edward. Thanks.'

For a split second there, I'd thought the journey had been worth it just to read those words and I'd been trying to conceal my delight; now I was trying to conceal disappointment.

'So, what brings you to snowy Lincolnshire?'

'I need to ask you something.'

'OK. Ask away. Oh, by the way, did my bit of information last time prove useful? You know – Jim Matthews, the saddler at Bingham.'

'It surely did. I went over to see him.'

'And he helped?'

'Oh, yes,' I laughed. 'Well, eventually. He told me everything

he knew and it helped me to piece together other bits of information. Thanks again for helping me out on that.'

He flipped a dismissive hand. 'Don't need thanking. Just glad
to help.'

'Can I ask you what could be a tricky question right now?'

'Sure.'

'I saw you driving away from North Shore Hotel in a black
BMW a few days ago. Around lunchtime, actually. There was
another man sitting in the passenger seat. Who was he?'

He lifted his coffee and took a sip. 'Can I ask why you want
to know?'

'It's just one question in among a whole heap of questions I
need to find answers to.'

'Hmm . . . in other words, you aren't going to tell me why.'

I studied my coffee and waited.

At John Dunston's funeral there had been upwards of forty
people. Theoretically, it could have been any one of them – had
to have been. But there was one name going around in my brain,
and I so sincerely hoped I was wrong.

He sighed heavily. 'It's no big deal. We'd been for a meal,
talked a bit of business, as you do.'

'His name, Edward?'

'I've a feeling you already know.'

'Humour me.'

He smiled wryly. 'All three of us will probably end up doing
business together.'

'Unlikely, I would say.' I took a gulp of coffee. My heart began
to race and it wasn't due to the caffeine. He was right: I did know
who he was talking about. But I still needed him to tell me.

'He came here one Saturday. It was one of the weekends when
I'd asked Alice to stay, actually. She was quite taken with him.
As I recall, they ended up talking racing. Alice said something
along the lines of "like father, like son" . . .' He stopped and
narrowed his eyes, staring hard at me. 'I don't know what he's
done, and I don't really want to know. The very fact you're here,
asking about him, says everything – without words. Don't forget,
Harry – as if you could! – I've seen you on a man's trail before.'

Edward Frame was in my debt forever, as he saw it. Fate –
whatever – had drawn us together in the most terrible circumstances
that linked us for ever. He'd lost family and I'd brought him justice.

So I waited. I knew he would tell me.

'I'd not heard anything detrimental,' he continued. 'Anyway, I took him for a meal and a celebratory drink at North Shore Hotel; we were finalizing details. I've already gone ahead, committed myself. The man who was in the passenger seat is going to train a horse for me. His name's Patrick Brown.'

THIRTY-ONE

Patrick Brown – Mousey's elder son.

My immediate feeling was sadness for Mousey. He'd given up training himself – been forced to – and had handed over the business and stables to Patrick, trusting him to run the show. OK, if he couldn't do the job himself, at least he could still live the racing life, albeit vicariously. But if Patrick was convicted and sent down, it would be the end of Mousey's world, the stables, maybe even his home – indeed, his whole way of life. And, of course, there was Jackie, Patrick's wife. A lovely girl like her didn't deserve such a devastating blow.

I thought back to when I'd gone to visit Mousey. One phrase he'd used was somewhat telling. It was, according to Edward, the same as used by Alice – 'Like father, like son . . .' I've no doubt he thought Alice was referring to both men as racing trainers. But I saw a connection that Edward wasn't in a position to see.

At the time, I hadn't really registered what Mousey meant. I doubt if he would have explained if I'd asked him. It had been more a case of his thinking aloud, rather than wanting to tell me. But, with hindsight, those words took on a deeper, darker meaning. Mousey had definitely been referring to his own association with Alice – his confession later proved it – but those words seemed to indicate that he suspected his son was also using Alice as a prostitute.

And all the time, Clara, Mousey's wife and Patrick's mother, was lying in bed, slowly dying. The thought made me feel sick to my stomach.

'Is that the man you thought it was?' Edward's query jerked me back from my unpleasant memories.

'I'm very much afraid so.'

'Is he a wrong-un? Am I a fool to be doing business with him? Where does it leave us, Harry?'

'Yes, I'm pretty sure he is, to your first question. As to the second, that's entirely up to you. I can't advise you what to do. And where it leaves either of us . . .' I spread my hands. 'You play the cards as they fall.'

'What exactly has this man done?'

'Now, that's the question. I've no proof.'

'OK, what do you suspect he's done?'

'Killed two people.'

'My God!' Edward's jaw dropped.

'I can't prove it. Not yet. I'm asking you to keep quiet about all this. If he suspects I'm after him, he'll be covering his tracks.'

'But you're in a damn dangerous position, Harry. Hey' – he grabbed my arm – 'now you've told me, does that mean I'm in danger, too?'

'Not if you keep quiet. Who's to know what we've been talking about this morning? Nobody.'

He nodded slowly, recovering his composure. 'Don't worry; I'll keep schtum, all right.'

'Good.'

'Those two people who died – who were they?'

'You don't want to know, Edward, believe me.'

'Does that mean I knew them?'

'Not sure about the second one, but, yes, you knew the first person.'

'Will you tell me, if you get proof and he's convicted, put away?'

'Yes.'

'I'm not going to insult you by asking what happens if you can't find the proof—'

'I'll find it.'

He nodded. 'What do you want me to do?'

'Carry on as normal.'

'That's a tough one, in the face of telling me your suspicions.'

'When are you meeting him again?'

'I'm being shown round his stables up north tomorrow.'

'Right. Now, if I draft a few questions, do you think you could have a try at dropping them into your conversation? Make it natural. If it would seem obvious, don't ask them, OK?'

'I'll do my best, Harry.'

'Thanks. I'll ring you later today when I've thought them out.'

Edward got to his feet. 'I think we both need another cup of coffee – with a stiffener in it.'

'I'm up for that. Sounds just what we need.'

When I left him a short while afterwards, he was in a very chastened mood. His immediate reaction, I knew, was to sever his involvement and business connection with Patrick, but I needed a mole on the inside. It was a fortuitous set of circumstances, and although it could completely collapse without any further leads or information forthcoming, I had a gut feeling that Edward was astute enough to go for the gap if he saw any chance of learning something useful for me.

Carefully negotiating the country lanes back to Wilsford, I'd just passed The Crown pub halfway down the main street when 'The Great Escape' sounded from my mobile.

Drawing up at the kerbside, I answered it.

'Hi, Harry. Is it OK to speak right now?'

'Yes, sure, Georgia. How are you? Blooming, I hope.'

'Fine.' She laughed. 'I've got some news for you Harry. Whereabouts are you? Any chance of a quick half-hour lunch in the Singing Kettle?'

'Every chance. I'm just about to leave Wilsford. Half an hour do you?'

'Great. Yes, I'll lock up and go round to the café now. Shall I order the same as last time?'

'Do for me. See you, bye.'

There was a fresh pot of tea waiting – as well as Georgia – when I walked into the café. She smiled, wiggled her fingers, when she saw me. 'Smelled the tea, obviously.'

'Dead right.'

I slid into the chair opposite her. She looked good, make-up carefully applied, perfume recently sprayed. I covered her hand with my own as she reached for the teapot handle. 'It's really great to see you.'

'Likewise. But may I pour out? I do like tea hot and I know you do.'

I grinned and let go of her.

The café filled up around us as we drank tea, nibbled toasties with salad and chatted.

'So,' I said, draining my second cup, 'you haven't told me yet this news you promised.'

'Hmm,' she nodded, swallowing her last mouthful, 'I had a telephone call. It was from Elaine Brown . . . you remember, at Lady Branshawe's party? Her mother, Daphne, was telling us about her daughter. Elaine is Lady Branshawe's cousin. Well, Daphne told Elaine, who rang me to suggest a girls' night out . . . you know, catch-up job and all that.'

'You were at university with her, weren't you?'

'Yes.'

'Are you going to this bunfight?'

'Tonight, yes. Apparently, Juliet, who was also at university with us, had contacted Elaine a few days before that party and they'd arranged to meet this evening. When Daphne told Elaine she'd seen me at Lady B's party, both girls wanted to meet me again.'

'Always good to meet up with people.'

'Yes, but wait, Harry. That's not all. The pianist, Jackson Fellows, was Juliet's boyfriend. I'd forgotten about that. Elaine said she and Ian made up a foursome with them sometimes at university.'

'Ian?'

'Ian Brown, her boyfriend at the time.'

A familiar little prickle ran down the back of my neck.

'And did you take *your* boyfriend to those orgies?'

Georgia giggled. 'No. I was a bit of a swot – a lot of a swot. Driven by the need to achieve. Do you know what I mean, Harry?'

'Oh, yes – do I!'

She laughed. 'It did leave me out on a limb at times, but the fear of failing my exams – not to mention losing the chance to run my own florists – well, that plus a very strict Christian upbringing proved a very efficient chastity belt. Although, talking about religion as a bit of a stopper, I've just remembered that Juliet and Jackson are both Roman Catholics. So that theory doesn't hold water.'

'Unlike the font,' I quipped. 'Still, the late teens are a very intense emotional stage.'

'I suppose I was lucky really to keep Elaine as a friend. Looking back, I must have been a drag. But we got on so well, liked the same things – horses for a start. One of the reasons she fancied Ian was because he was into horses. In fact, he only did about eighteen months and then chucked it in. He's a jockey, too – flat racing, I think.'

I didn't just think: I *knew*. But I didn't interrupt her. This conversation was proving far too interesting.

Georgia mused on. 'Can't think why I haven't been in touch with her for so long, except, of course, I've ploughed most of my energies into The Trug Basket. Well, ever since Peter's death.' A shadow of loss flickered across her face.

'Anyway, you'll get to see her and this Juliet tonight. You can catch up on all the gossip.'

'Ah, yes . . . now that does remind me.' She took a deep breath. 'Don't know whether I should snitch and tell you, Harry.' She looked sideways under her long lashes at me, weighing up whether or not she should.

'Go on: rival a canary.'

'What?'

'Sing out the secret. Policemen love canaries.'

'You're not a policeman.'

'Well, no, I suppose not.'

She made up her mind. 'These days it wouldn't matter much – nobody bothers, do they?'

'About what?'

'Abortion.'

I stared at her. 'I wouldn't say people don't care. After all, it's still taking a life, isn't it? Just who are you talking about, Georgia?'

'Juliet. But please don't ever mention it, Harry. At the time, we all closed ranks. Jackson was absolutely terrified it would come out.'

'Do I take it Jackson was the father of this aborted baby?'

'Yes.' She bit her lip. 'I don't think I should have told you.'

'It was a long time ago,' I soothed her, while at the same time, the jigsaw pieces were clicking into place in my brain.

''Course, poor Jackson didn't have a clue what to do. He's not very worldly. All he really cared about was playing the piano.'

'The way he plays, I can understand his passion.'

'Yes. I didn't know he was that good.'

'So, he left it all to Juliet, did he?'

'Oh, no. The only one of us who was clued up about that sort of thing was Ian. He arranged everything.'

'But it would have cost a lot. Where did a student get that sort of money?'

'Oh, the paying part was easy enough. Ian begged it off his brother – said he earned good money, so I suppose he could afford it.'

'Hmm . . .' I agreed, nodding. 'I expect he could.'

'Anyway, it was all done very discreetly.'

'Well, I promise you I won't spread it around.' I very nearly said I wouldn't tell anyone – but that would certainly have been lying. 'Now, how about another pot of tea?'

She cast a glance up at the café clock above the counter. 'I would love to, Harry, but I'm afraid I have to get back to work.'

'Never mind, I'll give you a ring, if I may – arrange another time.'

'Yes,' she smiled, 'you may.'

We walked back the few yards to The Trug Basket and I gave her a kiss. 'Have a great time this evening. Take care, and let me know how it goes.'

'I'm really looking forward to seeing them. Sad, isn't it?' She giggled. 'I feel like I'm regressing back into a teenager.'

'Temper the feeling with the wisdom of your advanced years and you'll enjoy it even more.'

'You're a lovely man, Harry.' She stood on tiptoe and kissed me goodbye.

Then she stepped into the warmth of the shop, leaving me outside in the snow.

THIRTY-TWO

The next morning, early, I drove away from the cottage and headed north. I suppose I could have telephoned, warned him I was on my way, but maybe it was simply better to take full advantage of the element of surprise.

The further north I drove, the deeper the snow became. Not on the main roads – they'd benefited from a zealous council's gritting procedure – but the fields beyond the roads swept away like plump white quilts, while the low-lying hedges struggled to maintain their boundaries, and in parts where even lower stonewalling had taken over, they had lost their fight almost entirely. When snow fell in Yorkshire, it certainly fell.

The leaden sky pressed down and wasn't promising to yield and let the sun though any time soon. Rather, it seemed likely that more snowflakes could very soon tumble down to join the billions already blurring outlines and obscuring everything they touched.

The sun wasn't the only thing not working today; racing was also laid off. Which meant, of course, that there'd be no call for horseboxes and, likewise, no drivers. Keith Whellan would certainly not be working today. It was odds-on he was simply holed up at his cottage. It was a bet I was prepared to take. I needed to ask him some questions.

Last night, I'd spent some time thinking about what questions I needed Edward to put to Patrick Brown. But the big question, as far as I was concerned, was had John Dunston known who had killed Alice? And following on from that, had he known the bloodied ashtray belonged to her? Was that why he'd sent it to me? He'd written in the letter that it was the only bit of proof he had, but on its own it was useless. I needed to find some answers.

I motored on while the sky grew more and more lowering, and when I finally reached Whellan's tiny cottage, the windscreen of the Mazda was covered with flecks of snow, forerunners, no doubt, of the next heavy fall. Locking the car, I walked up to the front door and, since there was no bell, gave it a good knock. A dog barked somewhere – not a yap, a real depth-charge deep bark. Otherwise, nothing stirred. I knocked some more and then again, and was eventually rewarded by a man's voice yelling at me to stop making such a bloody racket, he was coming . . . 'Coming, all right?'

I leaned against the rough stone wall and waited. Keith Whellan yanked open the door and stuck his head out. His scowl faded.

'Thought it must be the bloody bailiffs.'

'Expecting them, are you?'

'You never know,' he said darkly. 'Come on in out of this lot.' He waved a hand at the dancing white stuff. Pushing up behind him was an enormous black Newfoundland dog.

I gladly closed the door behind me and followed him into the minuscule kitchen. The big animal followed me.

'Hi, big fella.' I bent over and rubbed the dog's thickly furred ears.

'Name's Tugboat – Tug usually, unless he's being wicked.'

'You, wicked? Don't believe it.' I rubbed away at his ears and the soppy animal slobbered all over my face.

'Can I get you a coffee? Going to have one myself . . . now I've got up.' Keith grinned a little shamedfacedly. 'Should never have had that spare telly installed in the bedroom. More seductive than a warm woman.'

As he was talking, he busied himself making the drinks.

'Sorry I disturbed you.'

'Nah. Glad of a bit of company, actually. I was getting used to having John dossing here. Now he's gone . . .'

'It's about John that I've come.'

'Hmm . . .' He handed me a mug. 'I thought it might be. Come on through.'

He led the way into a twelve-feet-square sitting room and snapped on the coal-effect gas fire. It was a meagre enough source of heat for the conditions outside, but with the low ceiling and small dimensions, it might, eventually, hold its own. Right now, it was Baltic. I could well understand that, with no work on, the attraction of staying tucked up in bed was not indulgence, it was survival. I sipped my drink and kept my coat on. The dog commandeered the first four feet of floor space in front of the fire and immediately began to snore.

'Snowed-up down your end?'

'Pretty much. Not so bad, though.'

He nodded. 'It's going to take some shifting. Not good on the work front.'

'No,' I agreed.

'Still, it might cool Rawlson off.'

'How do you mean?'

'No racing, so you won't be nicking his rides. And he can't afford to miss rides. Word is he needs the money, got himself dug in deep with gambling. Cards are a fool's game.'

I filed away the gem of information.

'I never nicked the rides to begin with. Lady Branshawe told Patrick she wanted me aboard.'

'Hmm. Well, Rawlson doesn't see it like that, does he?'

'His problem, not mine.'

'So what *is* your problem?'

'Did John ever say anything about that woman who was murdered? Alice Goode.'

'A prossie, she was.'

'Yes.'

'John wasn't into a bit extra, know what I mean? Not before Lilly's death, nor afterwards.'

I shook my head. 'No. I didn't mean that. What I'm trying to find out is whether John told you anything that might have linked the man he knew was after him with that woman's murder?'

Keith shivered and hutched his chair a bit closer to the fire. The dog never moved.

'I dunno, Harry. I reckon none of this kicked off until that afternoon when the horsebox broke down at Southwell.'

'That was the day Alice died.'

'Oh.'

'Talk me through it, Keith.'

'Well, I drove our box down for Mousey, and John drove Robson's horsebox.'

'You didn't share one?'

'No.'

'OK. Carry on.'

'Trouble was the horsebox broke down after we got there. Patrick told John to load Robson's horse into his box and left me waiting for the mechanic to come and fix it. Robson agreed it.'

'So where does Patrick fit in? Did he go back up north in the horsebox?'

'No. Patrick didn't come down with the box. Dunno why. We'd only the one horse. He drove down himself in his car.'

'And, presumably, drove home in his car?'

'Yes.'

'What about the jockey? Who was it?'

'Rawlson.'

'How did he get down and back?'

'Far as I know, he was in Patrick's car, with him.'

'And you didn't notice the smear of blood near the dashboard until you came back from the gents?'

'That's right. It was all a bit of a scramble when we found the horsebox had broken down. Patrick told me to hurry up and take a slash before they drove away because I might not get the chance again. I had to stay behind and wait for the mechanic, and it might take some time. He told Rawlson to go an' all.'

'What were his exact words, can you remember?'

'Yeah, he just said, "Rawlson, you go with him as well."'

'Right,' I said, and hoped I'd kept the note of satisfaction out of my voice. It wasn't good enough evidence for the police, but it was good enough for me.

'When you went to the gents', did you lock the horsebox?'

'Nah, wasn't going anywhere, was it?'

'So anybody wanting to get in could have?'

'Yeah, they could.'

'Apart from you, who else has a key?'

'There's two keys, mine and . . . Patrick's. Hey, wait a minute, do you think Patrick sent me to the bogs on purpose?'

'I do, yes.'

'Why?'

'John found something . . .' I dropped a hand into my coat pocket and took out a plastic bag containing the piece of blood-stained terry towelling. I passed it to him. 'Look familiar?'

Wrinkling his face in distaste, he reached out and held it, dangling, between finger and thumb. 'It's my bit of rag for wiping the windscreen.'

'You sure?'

'Oh, yeah, I'm sure. Except the last time I used it, there wasn't any blood.' He handed the bag back. 'How did you get hold of it?'

'John left it for me, with the solicitor.'

He nodded slowly. 'Yeah. Me, too.'

'Eh?'

'I got a letter . . .' He went out of the room for a minute or two and returned with an envelope. 'Here.' He handed it to me.

I took out the single sheet of headed paper. It was short, just one paragraph. John had left his meagre savings to Keith – plus one other bequest. The letter asked him to collect the cheque and bequest from the solicitor's offices.

'There weren't much – 'bout four hundred quid.' He shook his head. 'Surprised he had that much left after paying out like he did for Lilly's carers and her funeral costs, o'course.'

'Hmm, dying doesn't come cheap.'

He put a hand in his pocket and drew out a shiny round object. 'And this. The solicitors called it a "bequest". Stupid bloody word. It's just a present, something to keep, to remember him by.'

He gave it to me. On one side was his name, Keith Whellan, and a phone number. I turned it over. On the other side of the silver-plated disc was just one word: Tugboat.

'Haven't got round to fixing it to his collar yet.' He affectionately nudged the ten stone plus of sleeping dog with his foot. Tugboat gave a deeper snore but didn't stir.

'Hold on, there's something else you need to see.' Keith leaned forward and reached for a piece of paper filed under a candlestick on the mantelpiece. 'John wrote it. It was folded inside the package with the dog's name disc. I'm sure nobody else has seen it. He'd make bloody sure of that.'

I read the message.

If H takes the bait – God bless him if he does – tell him I saw that murdering bastard hiding it when I came back from the gents. He didn't see me. It's evidence of some sort, so I nicked it. Maybe H could sniff it out. That's all you need to know. Keep safe, mate. John.

'Obviously, he saw whatever it was being hidden that day. He was coming back from the gents' just as Rawlson and me were going over there. I didn't see him again to speak to because he was in the driving seat about to drive off when I got back.'

A rise of excitement brought up the hairs on the back of my neck and, struggling to conceal my elation, I put the piece of paper down on the table beside my chair. Keith stared at me.

'Well? Are you going to tell me what it was John nicked?'

Relief at his question was sweet: he hadn't noticed. 'Safer if you don't know.'

'Whatever it was had blood on it, though, didn't it?'

'Yes.'

'It *was* Patrick who put this *thing* in the horsebox, wasn't it?'

I dropped my gaze and nodded reluctantly. 'Yeah. But keep it to yourself. If he finds out I've sussed him—'

'As the grave, mate. But why did he do it?'

'I suspect it was simply to get rid of it, so it wouldn't be found in *his* car. It would take some explaining. Anyway, now you know it was Patrick, can I ask you a question? Any word going round he might be involved in gambling – probably cards?'

'I'm not the best person to answer that. A good chunk of my brass goes straight to my ex-wife . . . and daughter. None to spare to play silly buggers with. You can lose a lot – and I do mean a lot – gambling. But, come on, Harry. You know as well as I do, jockeys don't need encouraging to play cards.'

'OK, Keith, so who would be the right person to ask?'

He shrugged. 'Best thing would be to drop in at the stable's favourite watering hole. The lads generally use the Black Cat pub in Watersby.'

'Right. Are they likely to be there today?'

'A fair bet, I'd say, given the weather.'

'How about you point me in the right direction and I stand you lunch?'

Keith smiled. 'An offer I can't refuse.' Then his smile faded. 'But I can't promise you'll find anything out.'

'Either way, we need to eat. What do you say?'

The smile returned. 'Yes.'

The forecourt of the Black Cat pub was a slurry of churned-up snow, no longer white but discoloured by exhaust and oil leaks, across which ashes from the pub's fires had been scattered. Even as we drew up, a barman emerged carrying a wide shovel, stumped out a few yards, and hurled another load of clinker in a black arc. Seeing us watching, he raised a hand in acknowledgement and disappeared back indoors.

'Cheaper than buying salt,' Keith observed.

I nodded and crunched the car tyres over the latest offering.

Inside, it was sweltering. And the bar was packed with bodies. Keith had been right. The Black Cat seemed to be the gathering place for the whole of the county's stable staff. The noise level was amazing.

'What'll you have?' I bawled in his ear.

'You really have to ask?' He pointed to a sign over the optics that informed everybody that real ale was sold here.

Clutching our pints, we backed ourselves into the pool room where the noise level was considerably lower and the concentration on the baize absolute.

THIRTY-THREE

I gave the room a swift, surreptitious glance, but neither Patrick nor Rawlson was there. A knot of tension slid from my shoulders. Without their inhibiting presence, tongues would be more inclined to loosen.

Keith brushed my elbow. 'Jacko's playing – the bloke in a green jumper. He works for Patrick. He's winning an' all.'

I nodded and mentally wished the man well. Good luck, like liquor, expanded a man's confidence – and his willingness to chatter. Although he had his nose in front, his opponent was no pushover. To prove it, he won the next frame.

'Come on, Jacko!' one of the jeans-clad supporters roared. 'Get your arse in gear, man.'

I grinned and shot Keith a look and a raised eyebrow.

He nodded. 'Oh, yeah, there'll be money on.'

Jockeys themselves weren't allowed bets – not if they wanted to stay jockeys – but gambling among stable staff was rife. Hopes always ran high, but betting was mostly small-beer stakes – their wage packets took care of that. For that very reason, I knew the majority of these lads would be excluded from the sort of card games I was interested in. A fat income was needed to be able to indulge in the kind of action I suspected Nigel Garton had got entangled in. Although, from what Keith had said, it seemed Rawlson might have dipped a tentative toe in and got himself well wet. I took a long pull at my pint. It was nectar, and made ordinary beer seem vapid and mediocre.

'Good stuff, this.' I lowered the tideline dramatically.

'Told you, didn't I?' Keith had all but finished his pint.

The cheers and howls around the pool table increased in volume as balls found pockets – or not – and then, finally, Jacko made a superb long pot that clinched it. Two or three of the other lads came wading in with solid shoulder slaps of appreciation. No doubt, they'd be collecting up their winnings – on the way to the bar to sink them.

Jacko turned round, beaming at his supporters and noticed us. He nodded a greeting at Keith.

'Ay-up, see you're corrupting the top jock, here.'

'Good game, Jacko,' I said. 'Stand you a drink?'

'Yes, ta. Could do with a pint of Theakston's.'

We made our way back to the bar and tables. 'What's the food like? OK?'

'Good, yeah. Basic, but chef's a good 'un, knows what the lads like.'

'Well, we were reckoning on having some lunch. Join us if you like.'

Jacko grinned. 'Pint of real first, though . . .' he said slyly.

'Oh, absolutely.'

Keith went off to place a food order and returned with three pints of foaming ale. While the food was being cooked, we all settled down to fully enjoy our drinks and a crack.

I'd already decided to wait until after we'd eaten, and drunk, before I tried to probe. With a full belly, following on from his successful potting, Jacko was much more likely to be cooperative about giving out information.

And so it proved. Jacko forked up the last of his hot steak and leek pasty, stabbed the one remaining chip and wolfed them down. He gave a gigantic belch.

He grinned. 'Better out than in.'

'Considered to be a sign of appreciation, isn't it?'

'Dunno about that, Harry.' He wiped his mouth with the back of his hand. 'But you've got to give it to Martin. He's a damn good chef.'

I nodded. 'My fish was great.'

'Don't know how you get it down without chips.'

'The same way I get on the scales before and after a race: because I have to.'

'At least you make a decent living from all that abstinence. Not like us poor sods. We have to make *contingency* plans. Know what I mean, Harry?' He winked slyly.

'Hmm, not really, not unless you're moonlighting. In which case, when do you sleep?'

'Nah, after a day's graft in the stables I'm in no shape to do any more work. But cards don't count as work.'

'You could find yourself even worse off.'

'Not really. My mam came from Ireland – and you know what they say about the luck of the Irish. 'S'true.'

'One day, Jacko,' Keith cut in, 'you'll come a cropper. Luck's a tricky lady.'

'Yeah, yeah . . .' He grinned. 'Not when you've a touch of blarney to go with it.'

'Right.' Keith nodded cynically. 'And you're there to catch any backhanders, eh?'

Jacko shrugged. 'You've to get by, haven't you?'

'And if I wanted a game, how'd I go about it?'

'You've a wife and kid to support, ain't you?'

'Sometimes life gets a bit . . . stale. A card game might be just the thing to add some zap.'

Under the table I caught his shin gently with the toe of my shoe in acknowledgement of his attempt to steer the conversation where I needed it to go.

'You talking about a possible big return here, or just chicken feed?' There was a barely concealed sneer in his voice.

It was Keith's turn to shrug. 'Wasn't thinking chicken feed, seeing as I don't indulge much. But don't get me wrong; I'm not about to make it a hobby.'

It was time to make myself scarce. Keith would get a lot more information right now than I would. Jacko said nothing, simply upended his pint before setting it down on the table. I seized the chance.

'Can I get you another one?'

'Decent of you, Harry, ta.'

'Keith?'

'Yes, please, that'd be good.'

I left them to it and went over to the bar.

'Nice to see you in here, Harry.' The barmaid smiled beguilingly. 'You're a long way from home, aren't you?'

'A man can get a bit bored in this weather. It's good to catch up with some mates when you get the chance.'

'Would have thought Sundays might be more your style. You know, when the trainers and such are in.'

'Is that right?'

'Oh, yes, early Sunday evenings, they mostly drop in for a quick one.'

'And which trainers are they?'

'Well, let me think.' She put a red talon to her lips and posed. 'For a start, there's Mr Unwin. You know, from down your neck

of the woods. And, of course, Mr Brown – Patrick, that is. *Not
his dad.*' She giggled before sweeping her lashes down coyly. But
it was too late; I'd already caught the flash of desire in her eyes.
Mousey's suspicions regarding his son's liberal interpretation of
his marriage vows might well be justified.

'Anyone else?'

'Oh, yeah. Usually a couple of other men – posh, you know.
Dressed up in fancy suits. The older one always wears a cravat. I
teased him about it once and he said something like "I can't wear
it for business, so I wear it when I'm away from restraints". Like
I say, posh.'

'But you don't know their names, I suppose?'

'Afraid not,' she simpered.

'Thanks, anyway. Now, how much do I owe you?'

'Can we . . . I . . . look forward to seeing you on a Sunday,
then?' The lashes were now on piecework as she handed me the
change from a twenty-pound note.

'Possibly. But of course, it depends an awful lot on what
the weather is like.'

'Oh, of course,' she agreed earnestly.

'May I ask your name? You know mine, but I'm at a disadvan-
tage here.'

'Sherrie.'

'Most appropriate.'

'What?' And then the penny dropped and she screamed with
laughter. 'Oh, yes! I see what you're getting at. Because of my
job. Nobody's ever connected it before. You are clever.'

'Elementary, my dear Watson.'

'Eh?' She wrinkled her forehead.

'Never mind.' I smiled. 'Doesn't matter.'

I went back to our table. A third person, a young lad, had
joined the others. Jacko, who was talking to him, broke off his
conversation when he saw me coming.

'See you've met our Sherrie. You want to watch it, Harry. She
likes older men, especially if they're well heeled.'

'Too young for me.'

I started to hand the drinks out and was about to ask if the
youngster would like one as well when Jacko waved him away.
The lad took a couple of steps, then spun around, all but bumping
into me, rocking the table and spilling some of Jacko's ale.

'The money. Nearly forgot to give it to you.'

He reached over to Jacko with a handful of springy new fivers.

'Oh, right.' Jacko frowned. He grabbed them and reached inside his jacket for his wallet. But the ale had made his fingers slippery and the wallet fell from his grasp and landed on the floor.

I automatically reached down, retrieved it and gave it him back, but a loose piece of folded paper floated out and went further under the table.

'Oh, Gawd!' Jacko struck his forehead. 'I've bloody forgotten to give that to Patrick.'

'Important?'

He nodded. 'I'll say.'

'I'll get it.'

It wasn't an altruistic gesture on my part. It gave me a chance to read what the note said. The fact that it wasn't sealed inside an envelope told me it wouldn't reveal anything incriminating, but any snippet of information right now was more than welcome. The paper had slid right underneath the table, so I had to get off my backside and crouch down on one knee. It served my purpose. In that position, nobody could see what I was doing. Flicking open the note, I read the message and refolded it before getting to my feet.

'And who's sending Patrick love letters, then?' Keith commented casually.

As a detective's sidekick, he couldn't be bettered.

Jacko shrugged. 'Just one of the owners,' he said dismissively and stuck out a hand.

I gave him the note. Not that it mattered. I'd read the words – didn't understand them, but I'd work it out.

Thrusting the paper back inside his wallet, he turned his attention to supping ale.

'So, you going to tell me what it said?'

We'd left the pub and the warmth and were driving back through Watersby village.

'Sure, but I've no idea what the note means.'

'Well I might have.'

'OK. There were only a few words: *I want you there, Patrick, so don't let the snow stop you. Still, you'd better bring your water-wings, could get a bit choppy if it thaws.* Cryptic, or what. Any ideas?'

Keith nodded excitedly. 'Oh, aye. It fits with what Jacko told me while you were chatting up Sherrie.'

'Which is?'

'He was telling me whereabouts to meet up with the other men. He swallowed the story; thought I was serious about a card game. Basically, it's just up from the Watersby weir and before you get to the nursery and garden centre.'

'What does that tell us? A waterside property perhaps? One whose garden runs down to the river bank?'

'Nah.' He shook his head. 'Don't think so, Harry. There are private moorings along that stretch. I reckon the venue might be aboard a boat.'

'OK. Give me directions.' I patted the steering wheel. 'Let's go take a look.'

It wasn't that far; through the village, a swing right and a couple of hundred yards further on we came to the weir. Leaving it behind, following the river, sluggish and pewter-coloured between high banks of snow, we shortly came to the first of the moorings. There were about six or eight, each with an impressive-looking craft secured.

'You think it could be one of these, Keith?'

'Well, anybody owning one of these doesn't worry about paying his paper bill.'

'Yeah, very true.'

'Drop down. Let's see what the names are.'

I obediently went into second gear. Women's names seemed popular, along with *Flying Goddess* and *Queen of the Stream*. And then came the last one. Easily the largest of the houseboats, painted predominantly in red with a band of chevrons in black and white running along the top of the hull, it was a magnificent boat, commanding respect. It was named *The Winning Post*.

Keith stabbed a finger in my ribs at the same moment as I put both feet down and brought the Mazda to a stop.

'Got to be, hasn't it?' he said.

I nodded. 'I think I'll take you on as my official sidekick. You seem to have a knack for this stuff.'

'Coming from you, Harry, that's a compliment.'

'Some craft, isn't it?'

Keith frowned. 'Reminds me of something. Can't remember what, though.'

'Hmm . . .' I said, deliberately noncommittal. It reminded me of something as well. But right now I wasn't sure and didn't want to voice my thoughts. I could be very wrong. Logic told me I most certainly was, not to mention stupid for entertaining the idea, but gut instinct said, bugger logic, it *could be.* I prudently kept my mouth shut. But the now familiar tingle ran down the back of my neck. I'd check the theory out when I got back home. Half-baked ideas and hunches, as I'd discovered before, very often paid off.

'What are we doing now? Do you want to get any closer – see if the blinds are down on the far side?'

The blinds at the portholes along the left-hand side of the boat nearest the bank were all pulled down, obliterating any chance of looking inside.

'No. They're sure to be drawn as well. We'll make tracks back to your place, Keith.'

'Fair enough.'

I turned on the engine.

'I've got to say it's been a damn sight more interesting today than lying in bed with Sophia Loren.'

I laughed. 'Was she in the film you were going to watch?'

'Yeah, pathetic or what?'

'Come the thaw, you'll be busy enough.'

'They're forecasting it's on the way. Something to do with the wind changing direction.'

'Hope so. Just wish it would hurry up.'

It was a good job I didn't know then that that thought would come back and bite me – very hard – in a few days' time.

THIRTY-FOUR

I t was a long way back in miles from Yorkshire but it seemed to take little time at all. My mind had seized hold of the idea promoted by gut instinct and was going at it like a terrier scenting a rat. Logic was smothered by the possibility that my half-baked theory might just be the right one. If you dismissed credibility entirely and substituted supporting bits of the jigsaw, the picture took shape, albeit in a black-and-white skeleton rather than a fully fleshed Technicolor illustration. When I reached home, I would find out in a couple of minutes whether logic or gut was correct.

The rise of excitement within me wasn't so far removed from a Jack Russell's on scent. We both felt the thrill of chasing a quarry. I thought of Pen's words: *You're starting to talk like a private eye.* Getting involved in chasing murderers had never been up there on my radar in the past; in fact, I'd resisted until that blasted barrel had got me strapped over it with chains.

I winced. Could it be that Pen was on the right track and I was getting a taste for detecting? I might sound her out when I went over to dinner on Sunday. Mike, surprisingly jubilantly, had said he'd got a ten-pound turkey in the freezer waiting to be cooked and scoffed, and suggested including Pen's brother, Paul, to make it a foursome. I'd agreed automatically. Pen's prowess as a cook was a proven delight. Since Annabel had gone to live with Sir Jeffrey, home-cooked food was a treat I wasn't going to miss out on.

I felt surprisingly jubilant myself as I swung off the snowy lane – no such luxury as council gritters down here – and on to the gravel drive. But I had to slam on anchors because my parking space had already been taken by an Audi. My flash of annoyance dissipated as quickly as it had appeared. Annabel. My beloved Annabel was here. The kitchen door opened and she stood there, large ginger tomcat clutched to her bosom. I felt the grin split my face; couldn't stop it, didn't want to.

'Home is the sailor . . .' she said. 'Been fishing, Harry?'

'Yes, ma'am. I guess you could say that.'

'And what – if anything – have you caught?'

'Could be a red herring. Got to wait and see.'

'Noses out.'

I laughed. 'Not really. Just another of my hunches that could be horribly wrong.'

'Hmm. I know all about your hunches. They're seldom wrong. Even when the facts say otherwise. That's what gives you the edge over the others.'

'What others?'

'Oh, I don't know . . . Rebus?'

I shook my head. For an intelligent woman, sometimes she came out with the dippiest things.

'He's Ian Rankin's detective. He's not real. And he's retired.'

She nodded sagely. 'Cold-casing now.'

I took hold of her arm and propelled her back into the kitchen. 'Tea – gallons of it, scalding hot. And how is Jeffrey?'

'Last seen at eight o'clock this morning; he was fine.'

I nodded. 'Give him my best.'

'Will do.'

'So, who's looking after him right now?'

'Oh, Molly. You know, the private nurse? Nothing's too much to ask of her. She's absolutely dedicated to Jeffrey.'

I nodded. 'Sounds the ideal person.'

And my wildly orbiting hunch was successfully steered away from her thoughts and hopefully forgotten. If she had continued to dig, I might have found myself sounding out my theory on her and that would never do.

We repaired to the lounge with steaming mugs. I tossed a match to the waiting kindling and the fire obligingly caught and crackled. We sank back on to the settee to enjoy both. Leo gleefully spread himself over both our laps. He was a warm, vibrating bundle of fur.

'Little love,' Annabel said fondly and stroked his head.

'Hmm . . . can't hear yourself think when he purrs that loudly.'

'So, don't think. Just relax.' She sighed. 'I've missed him. Nothing like a cat to make a house into a home.'

'You've got Jeffrey.'

'I have, yes. But it doesn't stop me missing Leo.'

I risked it. 'Do you miss me?'

She glanced quickly sideways – our faces only inches apart. 'My honesty will get me into trouble one day.'

I waited. Annabel continued to caress the cat. When I'd all but given up on an answer and was sipping hot tea as consolation, she placed her hand over mine.

'I've never stopped missing you, Harry.'

I was about to interrupt, but she shook her head.

'We've never needed words. We both know without speaking how things are between us, don't we?'

It was true. Uncanny at times, certainly telepathic, we were thinking the same thing at the same time, drawing the same conclusions, our body language mirroring each other's and doing the talking for us.

I slid an arm around her shoulders, gave her a gentle hug. 'I miss you twenty-four/seven. I always will.'

She gave a little nod of acknowledgement. 'But it's different for me now.'

A mental picture appeared before me of Sir Jeffrey, surprisingly cheerful and adapted to his misfortune, sitting in the wheelchair.

'Of course it is,' I said. 'Jeffrey needs you, I know that.'

'But that's it; he *doesn't*.'

'What?'

She sighed. 'I care about Jeffrey; I couldn't be with him if I didn't. He was never a "convenience". When I left you, Harry, I didn't go to live with him simply to have someone. He was in love with me, yes. I knew that. But it's a powerful incentive to reciprocate the emotion and feel drawn to the person, to the love.'

I nodded. Annabel was a qualified psychotherapist. She would understand far better than the average person about the workings and impulses of the human heart and mind.

'And I did . . . do . . . care about him, probably more than he thinks I do.'

I remembered Jeffrey's words spoken to me in the hospital a few days after the car crash. *We still share her. I've got her affection . . . but you've got her heart . . . and soul.* And I knew she was right. Annabel was never a shallow, selfish woman – never could be; her whole persona was one of giving. She would never have made use of Sir Jeffrey either financially or emotionally. OK, so he was in love with her – I could well understand *that* – but on her side there had to have been strong feelings; otherwise she would never have chosen to spend her life with him.

'But since the accident, and his appalling injury, something's changed. Oh, not just physically changed; somehow he seems so much more self-reliant. I know that sounds stupid given his circumstances, but it's true. He seems to have reached deep inside himself and found a reserve of strength that he didn't have access to before the crash.' Her voice wobbled a little. 'He doesn't seem to need me anymore, Harry. He's running now on this new level of strength.'

'I'm sure it's not true, that he doesn't need you, Annabel. But the way he's accepted his condition and is dealing with it is absolutely amazing. I have to agree.'

We sat in silence for a few moments, each with our personal

impressions of Jeffrey. Then Annabel drained the last of her tea and seemed to recover her composure.

'Actually, the reason I came over, Harry, was to invite you for a meal with us. I suppose I could just have phoned, but it was a chance to touch base again, you know.'

'Oh, yes.' I nodded. 'See the cat . . .'

She laughed. 'That's right; put things into perspective.'

'Well, you know the answer to the question. Have I *ever* turned down a chance to eat one of your meals?'

'No.'

'There you are, then. When is this bunfight?'

'On Sunday.'

I groaned. 'Not this Sunday?'

'Yes, why?'

'I'm already having lunch with Mike and Pen . . . and probably Paul as well; Mike was going to invite him.'

'Oh, what a shame.' She made a face. 'But of course you must go to Mike's. We can make it another time to come over to us.'

'That would be good. I can't really let Pen down. It's a bit short notice.'

'And you mustn't. We'll just rejig ours.'

'If you're sure you don't mind; it's worked out quite well for me.'

'Oh, how do you mean?'

'Well, this way, I get to have a Sunday dinner cooked by Pen and then another one cooked by you. Got it made, haven't I?'

Annabel jokingly aimed the empty mug at me and I ducked.

'OK, then.' She stood up and tenderly placed Leo down on the settee. 'Best be going. I'll let you know another date when I've agreed it with Jeffrey.'

'Fine.'

She kissed me on the cheek. 'Take care of yourself, Harry. No undue risks, hmm?'

'The whole of life's a risk – you told me that yourself.'

'Just don't go looking for danger.'

'I don't go looking for danger, but it does seem to find me.'

'I'd noticed,' she said wryly.

I saw her out to the Audi and waved her off. Then I went back indoors, went to the lounge and ran a finger along the lower shelf of the bookcase. And found what I was looking for. A racing book, up to date and comprehensive, one that hopefully would give me the answer I needed: *Directory of the Turf.*

Among all the data it contained was a section on jockeys' silks. In particular, which colours were relevant to which owner. These colours were unique, allocated to just one owner, nobody else allowed to use them. These individual colours were required to be re-registered by that owner in the relevant month every year – cost sixty pounds – otherwise they would be re-allocated to a different owner.

I was looking for the specific colours of red with chevrons of black and white – the same colours in which the boat had been painted. It was a long shot, granted. They might have no relevance whatsoever and simply reflect the boat owner's taste. But Keith had been sure they reminded him of something. Admittedly, it was a jump to link the colours of a boat to the silks worn by a jockey, but those same colours had also seemed familiar to me.

I was sure I'd never worn them, which ruled out all the usual owners I rode for. But I could have ridden in a race where one of the other jockeys *was* wearing those colours and my subconscious had recognized them, triggered by seeing that boat boldly decked out in the same.

I sat back on the settee and turned to the correct pages. There were a lot of entries. If I ran down all of them, it was going to take ages. But there was one name I was looking for – and that wasn't going to take long.

It didn't – but it floored me. My hunch had seemed ridiculous, but Annabel had said, *Your hunches are seldom wrong.* And she was right. My hunches came not from cold logic based on fact, but from an inner knowing, impossible to explain, and not something you could call upon at will – you couldn't go to Tesco's and buy it straight off the shelf. It didn't work that way.

What I was aware of was that the more I got involved in the detecting of murderers, sometimes from the slimmest of leads, the more my hunches seemed to occur. Rather like a muscle, the more it was exercised, the better it functioned.

And, boy, had it functioned this time.

THIRTY-FIVE

I poured a large whisky and immediately downed half of it, welcoming the warmth that spread through me. Although I'd half expected this outcome, the confirmation had shaken me. This one piece of information filled in a lot of gaps towards the complete picture.

This, plus the sight of the piece of paper that I'd fished up off the floor in the Black Cat pub. I was sure nobody else had noticed anything. It had been fortunate I was down on one knee, my face hidden from view, when I'd retrieved the note. I had recognized the paper. The length of time I'd previously spent studying the cancelled IOU Victor's daughter had found in her husband Nigel's pocket had ensured there was no mistake. Both pieces of paper had come from the same source. It could not be a coincidence.

But somehow I couldn't quite reconcile myself to the fact that this man was a cold-blooded murderer. It seemed so unlikely. And then there was the one seemingly insurmountable problem of the piece of jigsaw that wouldn't fit. Just that one thing made a nonsense of even considering the man as prime suspect. For goodness' sake, his name didn't fit! Without another lead, it was hopeless.

I smacked a fist down on to the desk in frustration. It didn't help. All it achieved was barked knuckles. What I had to have was more facts, convincing facts.

So, I needed to speak to Edward Frame again, ask him if he'd found out anything further during his visit to the racing stables. Far too late this evening to consider haring off into the snow again. It was black outside. After the long haul driving back from Watersby in North Yorkshire, I wasn't inclined to venture out into the cold again.

I'd go over to Lincolnshire tomorrow. The roads would no doubt receive a scattering of grit and salt overnight. It made sense to drive over in daylight.

* * *

My assumption was wrong, as I found out when I drew back the bedroom curtains the next morning. The wind had obviously changed direction as the weatherman had predicted and, combined with a sun beaming in and out from scampering grey clouds, there had been a rapid rise in temperature. Most of the snow had disappeared. Persistent pockets remained in the shadows along the bottom of the hedges, safe from the sun's reaching fingers, but basically winter's icy grip had conceded big time.

Moisture dripped from every leaf and branch in the garden. The path was no longer a sheet of white but was now running with water. A blackbird was joyously bathing in the birdbath, flinging up spray with abandon. He brought a smile to my face. Nature never failed to remind you that the simple pleasures were often the most enjoyable.

But my smile faded when I considered the problem facing me. If Edward had nothing to report, basically I was pretty well stuffed. I had no further leads to follow – except . . . then I remembered. On Sunday evening I was supposed to be shadowing Nigel Garton from Lincolnshire. It was going to be much easier than I'd anticipated now I knew where he was headed – Watersby.

I needed to let Victor know. At least I had made some progress and I ought to telephone at the very least, report back to him. The little I'd found out wasn't going to be of much comfort, but he had to be told. At least he'd know I was putting in some effort on his behalf and he wasn't dealing with it on his own. In his shoes, I knew I'd be worried sick about the financial situation – not only for his daughter's sake, as he undoubtedly was, but also for his own future. He was an old man. Having a secure home to live in was paramount to his peace of mind. The not unreasonable fear of possibly losing it would be stressing him out.

I hesitated. I supposed I could leave it until there was more concrete news, but there were details I still needed to know ready for Sunday evening. I reached for my mobile.

Victor answered almost immediately. I pictured him sitting in the lounge, views from the east windows looking way out to sea, while he himself was warm and snug by the blazing fire. A beautifully appointed home. It needed to be appreciated with a peaceful heart and mind, not, as I was sure he was right now, racked with anxiety.

'Harry! My dear boy, d'y'know, I was just thinking about you.'

If you substituted the word 'thinking' and inserted 'worrying', it would be a much truer picture. But Victor was old-school, complete with the traditional British stiff upper lip.

'Hello, Victor. Got some news for you.'

'Good or bad?'

The swiftness of his reply confirmed my appraisal and I was suddenly very glad I'd decided to ring, although my offering was only just a crumb.

'I think I know where Nigel's headed on Sunday.'

'I think I won't ask how you've found out, Harry. Carry on.'

'It's near a village called Watersby, situated on the River Ouse. And the probable venue is on board a boat.'

'Good heavens.'

'I shan't know for sure until Nigel gets there on Sunday evening, of course. Do you have those details I need? His starting time from Lincolnshire and the car he's driving?'

'Yes. All furnished by Paula, of course. She's beside herself, y'know, Harry. Fearing the worst.'

'Yes, I'm sure she is.'

'However, I think I'll keep your piece of information just between us for now. Know what I mean? She's not a chatterbox, but the stress she's under could see her—'

'Don't worry, Victor. I understand perfectly. If you simply tell her I've got it well in hand, that should do.'

'She knows I've asked you to look into it, Harry. So that alone has to be reassuring for her.'

'Let's hope we can get a result this time.'

'Amen to that.'

'I'll ring you on Sunday night – don't know what time – let you know what's happened.'

'You do that and maybe I'll get to sleep through afterwards.' He gave a deprecating snort. 'Right now, it would be a novelty.'

'OK, then, take care, Victor.'

'And yourself. Bye.'

I went to the kitchen and fixed breakfast – scrambled eggs, toast and tea. I'd even got as far as hooking my foot around a chair ready to sit down at the table, but there was no chance of enjoying the food. A big ginger head pushed its way through the cat-flap, followed by all eight kilos of the cat himself. He leapt up on to my shoulder, bellowing a greeting. It might have been thawing outside, but Leo's fur felt icy cold against my cheek. He'd obviously been out all night, probably chasing down the neighbourhood queens.

I gave up the battle before it began and put my plate of scrambled eggs down on the table. Annabel was his devoted slave but, by God, I was running her a close second. After opening a tin of cat food and loading up his dish with smelly delight, I finally got around to eating breakfast myself. I was downing a second mug of tea when the mobile struck up. It was Georgia.

'Hi, Harry. Thought I'd update you before I head off to The Trug Basket.'

'Would this be about your night out with Lady Branshawe's cousin?'

'Yes. I promised I would.'

'Did you have a good time?'

'Great time. It was so interesting hearing how their lives had panned out since we all left university.'

'Uh-huh.'

'Elaine and Juliet are both married; somehow I didn't think they would be. We were all so driven at that last stage of our studies, you know. We'd each fixated on our choice of career, were determined to be successful. There didn't seem to be time to get to know any men in depth – casual friendships, yes, but nothing of substance. And I really was a dreadful swot, got my leg pulled rotten.'

'But you said Juliet and Jackson were a couple – at that time.'

'Yes, I know. And it's had a tragic effect. Juliet told me. Because she got pregnant and had that abortion, she's unable to have any more babies.'

'But she still got married.'

'Hmm. She didn't know until afterwards. It only became clear when they were trying to start a family . . .'

'So, it confirms what you told me.'

'Please don't say anything to her family, Harry. I mean, they're Roman Catholic . . . I would hate to be the cause of a rift, or worse. I feel bad about telling you because I promised Juliet I would keep it to myself. Seems like I'm piggy-in-the-middle.'

'Don't worry. As far as I can, I won't say a word. But I don't know where this trail's going to end, so I can't promise you.'

She sighed. 'I understand, but please try.'

'You know I will.'

'Thanks. And another update for you . . .'

'Hmm?'

'About Jackson. Elaine told me. Apparently, Lady Branshawe mentioned that after the piano recital he was off back to Ireland. His mother, Josephine, has a place in Wexford.'

'Really. Now that is interesting. What about his father? Was he going over as well?'

'Oh, no. Elaine said they'd have divorced ages ago if they hadn't been RC.'

'So they don't live together?'

'No. But it's his father who finances Jackson's training and career, via his mother.'

'Doesn't Jackson have much contact with his father, then?'

'Seems not.'

'Even more interesting.'

'People lead such convoluted lives, don't they?'

'Does his father know about the aborted baby?'

'Oh, Harry! Of course not. Can you imagine what a ruction that information would cause?'

'Instant turn-off of the financial tap, I expect.'

'Which would really leave Jackson . . .'

'. . . in the deep and sticky stuff.'

'Exactly.'

'Does his mother have a job at all? Or is she dependent on the husband?'

'I asked Elaine that question. Seems she's joint manager of a stud farm. She's not the owner.'

'Near Wexford?'

'Yes.'

'Curiouser and curiouser.'

'Well, I don't see it, but I'm glad to employ your grey cells.'

'If I said I see it, I'd be lying. Mainly it's guesses that either come across or don't.'

'I have to go, Harry. There's a shop in Grantham that needs opening up.'

'Off you go, then, do your daily duty. I'll ring you about having dinner one night, eh?'

'Lovely. Bye for now.'

I mashed another mug of tea to lubricate my grey cells and

mulled over what she had told me. The facts were indeed interesting. By the time I'd finished the drink, I had worked out what I could do to expand on what I knew so far. Going to my desk, I fired up my computer and keyed in 'stud farms in Ireland' – in particular ones in Wexford County. It brought up a whole clutch of them. One by one, I opened them up and checked out names. And then extended my search in the surrounding counties. Nowhere was the name Fellows mentioned.

But one of the names listed – Watersfall Stud – triggered my memory. The day when my breastplate gave way, the horse that won the race, the second favourite, who would surely have won without my competition, had come over as a yearling from Watersfall Stud in Wexford. I'd looked it up afterwards.

I keyed in Watersfall, followed by the name of the man to whom the red, black and white racing colours belonged.

He was listed as one of the directors.

Bingo!

THIRTY-SIX

One phone call to make – no point driving to Lincolnshire if he wasn't there. But Edward was at home – 'Come round straight away, I'll have coffee waiting.'

I closed down the computer, grabbed a jacket and locked the back door after me. I still couldn't take it in that this man I'd discovered could be a killer, but the insurmountable obstacle of his name had just been knocked on the head. Apart from my incredulity, the pieces of the jigsaw now fitted, showing me a picture – an unpleasant and incomplete one certainly, but one I could work with. There were gaps – some big gaps. But in none of the other cases where I'd tracked down a murderer had I ever seen a complete picture. Guesses and leaps of imagination always had to be made. And what I needed right now was something I couldn't buy: a large slice of luck.

A lot of time had been spent unproductively wondering about, analysing and discounting the people who had attended John Dunston's funeral. One of them had known I'd received that fateful first envelope. Their names and addresses would have been written on the mourners' cards, handed out at the crematorium. These cards were no doubt stored away alphabetically, probably by the undertakers, but I didn't need to see them. The people attending the cremation were familiar faces. But all I'd needed was just the one name.

Now, I knew. What a blind idiot I'd been.

The roads were free of snow and the traffic light. But before I'd cleared Grantham, the fitful sun had succumbed to heavy grey clouds sweeping across the sky and it began to rain. Lightly at first, and then increasingly heavily. It was still raining when I pulled up outside Edward's massive oak door.

He showed me into the lounge. It was beginning to feel familiar and I sat down on the same chair I'd used the last time I'd been here while he hastened to the kitchen to bring in the coffee.

'Help yourself, Harry. Cream, sugar . . . honey?' He raised eyebrows.

I smiled. 'Thanks, yes, I'll have a spoonful of honey.'

He nodded in satisfaction and pushed the jar closer to me. 'Now,' he said, without wasting any time, 'I've been up to Yorkshire.'

'You and me both, but to different parts, I think.'

'Hmm. The Old Rectory Stables are very impressive, I have to say. Patrick runs things very well by the look of it.'

I sipped the superb coffee and waited, letting him take all the time he needed to formulate his thoughts.

'He told me they were looking to expand, having some more stables built later this year. I managed to bring up the subject of losing his mother by saying I was sure she'd be proud of him for making such a success of the stables for his father. He was quite open about the fact that the money set aside for her private nursing care was now going to be channelled into the expansion. Said he was sure she'd be very happy to see the ongoing improvements at the stables. There was no sign of any financial squeeze whatsoever. O' course, he *could* have been bullshitting and up to his ears in hock, but I didn't see any signs of it.'

Edward slurped his coffee. 'I mentioned my visit to the snow racing in St Moritz, kept it very casual, low-key, you know, just chatty. Said I'd also been over there two or three years ago, not for the racing but for the concerts, and I'd seen the brilliant pianist Jackson Fellows perform. Asked Patrick if he knew him, had maybe heard him play?'

'And?'

Edward shook his head. 'Not a flicker. Denied knowing Fellows. I reckon Patrick would make a very good card player.'

The irony of his words wasn't lost on me. 'What about Sunday? Did you invite him out for a meal?'

'I did, yes. And the answer was a firm no. Said he was always busy on Sunday evenings. Which was a blatant lie, of course; I mean, even if he'd been racing in the afternoon, he'd be back for supper.' He frowned with frustration. 'So it doesn't seem as though I've helped you much, Harry.'

'The very fact Patrick purported not to know Jackson Fellows *has* helped. And he's confirmed he's busy this Sunday evening.'

'Is that important?'

'Oh, yes.'

Edward nodded. 'Well, I'm glad to have helped, even if it's only a bit. You do seem to go it alone, Harry. And let's face it, these circumstances you go into are damned dangerous. If you need back-up, any time, feel free to ring me, OK?'

'Thanks, Edward. I appreciate it.'

'Will you let me know the outcome?'

'Sure, maybe even by Sunday night, if I'm lucky.'

I stayed for a coffee top-up and the chat turned inevitably to racing and the horses Edward had committed to buying. Outside, the rain ran continuously down the windowpanes, obliterating the wide-sweeping views of the surrounding countryside. It was going to be a wet drive home. When I left, I did a quick run to the shelter of the Mazda. After the previous days of dry, frozen weather, the teeming rain was a sharp contrast. It continued as I drove over the county boundary into Nottinghamshire, and by the time I reached the cottage, it was absolutely siling down.

I parked and locked the car, hastened over the crunching gravel and pulled the big gate closed and slid home the latch. It was a day to go to ground if you got the chance – and I had the chance. I wasn't going anywhere else today.

Leo was still where I'd last seen him, sated by females and food, flat out and fast asleep in his cosy basket above the warm

Rayburn. He barely raised an eyelid as I dripped over the back doorstep into the kitchen and shrugged off my wet jacket.

'Don't blame you, mate. You've got the right idea. Definitely not weather for cats out there.'

Was it a sigh I heard? Probably, but it sounded a deeply contented 'do not disturb' kind of sigh. And I heated a tin of tomato soup and buttered hot toast without interruption.

The frost might be long gone, but with the coming of the rain, it was now bone-chillingly raw. I prodded the lounge fire into a blaze, drew up a low footstool right in front of the flames and sat spooning up steaming red soup. Delicious: exactly what I needed to thaw out.

Lunch over, I made a mug of tea, put on a Chopin CD and slobbed on the settee with the John Dunston file of notes. I started at the beginning, reading it coldly, keeping any emotion well out of it. I needed to assimilate everything, see the facts clearly, let nature's magnificent creation, the human brain, do the job it excelled at: finding solutions to problems. I just needed to feed in all the known details, then get myself out of my own way.

The fire crackled while the notes of the piano carried me away, and I simply read the file from beginning to end, absorbing everything but making no judgements, simply allowing the subconscious to seek connections that were beyond the grasp of the conscious mind. The CD tinkled gently to a close. I finished reading and laid the file down on my desk.

Then I went upstairs, ran a deep bath, stripped off all my clothes and climbed in. The water dispersed and eddied around me as I slid down and lay back. I closed my eyes, relaxed and mentally asked for answers. Lastly, I added the one other essential thing – complete trust.

Water was a wonderful medium. Famous writers including Agatha Christie and Dick Francis used it to work out tough plot problems. I'd used it myself, too. And I knew it worked. So I lay in the hot water and let my mind drift, confident that the answers I so badly needed would be revealed.

Sunday morning, eight o'clock and still lashing down with rain, I drove slowly, creating huge arcs of spray either side of the car, down the quiet Leicestershire country lanes to Mike's stables. He was expecting me to ride out at nine on a new horse, a grey gelding, Granite, which Samuel Simpson had recently bought. But the days of enforced rest due to the snow had left my muscles in need of toning up and an hour or so of mucking out was just what I needed to start the day. I wasn't unfit to the point of flabby musculature, but race riding was a sport for which a jockey had to be totally fit – racing demanded, as did the owners, a high level of stamina and strength.

Declining Mike's offer of tea or coffee before I started, I took myself straight down to the stable yard. Fifty per cent of Mike's workforce was already hard at it mucking out, refilling hay nets and water buckets, and I greeted them and happily joined in. Working with horses was not only a job and a way of life, but also a drug. Apart from the few stable lads who came into the business and swiftly left again, all these lads putting in the solid graft were committed to their horses – living, breathing, sleeping horses.

We all suffered from its hardships, knew it for the addiction it certainly was, yet we gave thanks for it and were grateful to be spending our young years working in a physically and emotionally satisfying job.

Inside White Lace's stable, I fell into routine and received a warm blow of hot air from the mare's flared nostrils. It was the equivalent of standing in front of a fan heater. I pulled one of her ears gently as I drew the body brush down her smooth, strong neck, and she harrumphed back at me, turning her head to nudge me in the shoulder. I felt some of my tension release where it had begun building up around my head and neck. Not for the first time, nor the hundredth time, did I wish myself a very long way away from the approaching confrontation.

Everybody's job is stressful these days – one of the blights of twenty-first century life speeding up and exacting demands. But the sure fact that in less than twelve hours I'd probably be facing down a murderer was over the top any way you looked at it. I deliberately squashed the unpleasant thought. Concentrate on the job you're doing right now, Harry, I rebuked myself. Mindfulness, the new buzzword for today, actually did work, but it also required effort. I swept my brush in long strokes from the mare's head to her withers. I cast a quick look at her. Her eyes were closed as she enjoyed the grooming and attention. She was clearly employing mindfulness herself, without effort. But it wasn't a one-way street: attending to White Lace had calmed me down, too.

Conversely, Granite, Samuel's new horse in the next stable, was looking like a taxing ride. Mike came into the stable as I was finishing tacking up. The horse had blown himself up as I tried to tighten the girth and it would mean walking him round the stable yard before I could fully cinch it up.

'Showing what he thinks of you, Harry?'

'Soon get rid of the flies when I get him out on the gallops.'

'Yes, thank God the snow has gone. They're all like a classroom full of kids that can't go outside to burn off the energy.'

'Hmm. Seems we've swapped the snow for rain.'

'That what you call it? More like a continuous monsoon, if you ask me.'

And indeed, it had been raining continuously for three days now – and it didn't look like stopping any time soon. Coupled with the melt from the ice and snow, the whole countryside was awash; flood warnings up in the red zone covered the nightly weather charts for the whole country on television, warnings that looked extremely severe for certain areas. The most notable ones were where rivers had burst their banks or were about to do so.

'We'll have coffee when you've ridden Granite, and you can tell me what you think of him. Samuel's well made up to have had the chance of buying him. Thinks he'll make a stayer. Must say, I'm in agreement there – I mean, look at the quarters on him.'

I did. Beneath the gleaming iron-grey coat, there was a ton of power in the spread of solid muscles.

I nodded. 'I'm inclined to agree, but let me ride him first.'

By the time we'd covered ground on the gallops and returned to the stables, I knew Samuel's instinct for sussing out good horses had, once again, not let him down. I made my way across the yard to Mike's house and shed my dripping coat.

'Well, what did you make of Granite?'

'He's an exciting prospect, Mike.'

I sat down in the warm kitchen and Pen pushed a steaming mug of coffee into my hand.

'Wrap around that, Harry. It's a pig of a day out there.'

'Hmm. Not looking forward to a drive to Yorkshire tonight, I have to say.'

'Yorkshire? It's a flood hotspot, you know.'

'I do know, but it's something that has to be done.'

'Whereabouts are you going?' Mike queried.

'Place called Watersby. Apparently, it's on the River Ouse.'

'Which is one of the rivers likely to burst its banks according to weather coverage on the television.' Pen frowned. 'You remember, York was flooded a year or two back? That's because the Ouse is fed from the upper reaches of other North Yorkshire rivers.'

Mike nodded. 'No loss of life, though, thankfully.'

'You *are* staying for lunch, Harry, aren't you?'

'Oh, yes, please. Home-cooked food isn't something I pass up lightly.'

Pen laughed. 'Twelve thirty on the dot. Turkey and trimmings do you?'

'Yes, very well.'

'Oh, and Paul's coming as well.'

Paul Wentworth was Pen's brother who lived in a nearby village.

'Is there any special reason for all this indulgence?'

She lowered her eyes and a blush spread over her cheeks. 'Well, actually, yes, there is . . . I was going to wait until we'd eaten and then tell you and Paul, but since you've asked . . .'

Mike chortled. 'Yeah, go on Pen; you know you're dying to tell him.'

'Oh, Harry' – Pen grabbed my hand, her face suffused with excitement – 'I'm expecting a baby.'

'Well! Congratulations, Pen.' I turned to Mike. 'You sly old dog, you kept that a secret, didn't you?'

'I was afraid it might come out. Remember John Dunston's funeral? Pen was taken really poorly, couldn't stop being sick. So, of course, I couldn't abandon her. That was the reason I didn't get to see John off with the rest of you.'

I smiled and shook my head at them. 'It's great news. I couldn't be more pleased for you.'

'And, Harry, wait for this . . . girl or boy, we'd love you to be godfather. What do you say?'

'What an honour. Thank you, I'd be delighted. I'd better make damn sure I survive the Yorkshire floods tonight, hadn't I?'

THIRTY-SEVEN

I lost sight of the black BMW as we headed north from York on the A19. It wasn't late, barely seven o'clock, but the night was black – no starlight, no moon – and the everlasting rain was still falling in torrents. There was only one person in the vehicle: Nigel Garton.

I'd been waiting in a big lay-by on the outskirts of Lincoln, one that curved between the entrance and exit with a plentiful growth of tall shrubs and trees that screened the centre curve from the road. I was confident Nigel was unaware I'd pulled out and was now following at a safe distance a couple of vehicles behind him.

Traffic, as expected on a Sunday night, was light and I was constantly monitoring my position, allowing one or two vehicles to overtake me. I was sure he'd not noticed my black Mazda. Talk about two black cats on a black night. Still, it made trailing him so much easier now that I knew where he was heading.

However, coming off the ring road, a bright yellow delivery vehicle had slipped between us and effectively blocked my view. If Nigel attempted a right-hand turn, fine, I'd see him come across. But I kept a sharp watch out for any left-hand turn he might decide to take. In the meantime, I assumed he was still somewhere ahead of me on the road up front.

The sparse line of traffic motored on, swishing through the rain. The hypnotic drone from the windscreen wipers was soothing but didn't stand a chance with my nervous system locked on to red alert. Some miles further on, the delivery driver called it quits for the night and swung off down a side road, and I caught a glimpse of Nigel's BMW on a bend now and again. It was enough.

I was sure Watersby would be his final destination, but another thought had occurred to me. The barmaid at the Black Cat had said the men usually called in for a quick one. Maybe Nigel intended to meet up with them there before going aboard the boat. If so, I had about ten minutes, less maybe, before he headed into the pub car park. We were getting so close now, I decided to take a chance.

One of the vehicles between the BMW and me peeled off to the right and I gunned the Mazda and overtook the next two cars and, with a clear road up ahead, continued on, overtook Nigel and swung left at the next junction. The country lane was winding but without any other vehicles in sight, I broke the speed limit and soon found that the lane eventually led to the village.

I headed towards the pub, did a swift spin around in their car park, noted the vehicles already parked and drove out again. I parked close by in a small cul-de-sac with the Mazda's bonnet pointing to the exit.

It was only a few yards to the pub and I walked smartly back. Tucking into the shadow of the wall, I waited. Not for long. The black BMW nosed into the car park and pulled up beside a four-by-four in the far corner. From where I was standing, I could see there was a side door to the pub. I made a quick decision. Take the enemy by surprise was a strategy that had worked for me before. I pushed open the door and went straight up to the bar.

'Hello, again. Pint of Theakston's, please.'

It was the same blonde barmaid, Sherrie, from the last time.

'Harry! Well, well, nice to see you.' Her smile was a full thousand watts as she reached for a glass and the beer pump handle.

But before she could pull the ale, a man appeared at my elbow.

'Got a taste for the real McCoy, then, I see.' He leaned towards Sherrie. 'Make that two, love.' He slid a note across the bar.

'Hi, Keith, thanks.' I must be slipping. I'd forgotten he'd been angling on my behalf for an invite to the card game. Not that I'd heard anything back from him either way.

'Let's take the drinks where it's a bit quieter, eh?' He nodded to the pool room, and I followed his lead. As we stepped through, I saw Nigel Garton enter the public bar. He didn't see us.

'I tried you earlier, but your phone wasn't on.'

'No. I was at a bit of a bash most of the day.'

He shrugged. 'Doesn't matter. Jacko didn't tell me I was in until middle of the afternoon. So, what's the game plan?'

It was my turn to shrug. 'Blessed if I know, Keith. Did Jacko tell you who else was going tonight?'

'No. Just that a couple had cried off, including Rawlson. Might be the foul weather. Not what you need for going boating.'

'Could be why you got the invite. Well, the bloke who walked into the bar as we came in here is headed for the boat. I've just trailed him up from Lincolnshire.'

'Right.' His eyes gleamed with anticipation. 'Knows you, does he?'

'Yes. He's the son-in-law of Victor Maudsley – you know, the trainer that retired some years back. I used to ride for him a bit.'

'Yeah, I know . . . wouldn't have thought a bloke in his position would go in for card games.'

I made a snap decision. Everything tonight was definitely a case of going with the flow. It was a situation where events could not be predicted. I'd been here before and it needed quick thinking at every moment to stay afloat. Exhilarating – or scary – depending on how you saw it. And sometimes you had to make things happen.

'Look, Keith, do you mind if I ask Nigel to join us?'

He pulled a face. 'That wise?'

'Probably not. But I ought to give it a chance.'

'What're you going to say?'

'God knows.'

I put down my pint and returned to the bar. Nigel was propping it up, staring moodily at his whisky. He did not look a happy man. I clapped him on the shoulder.

'Nigel. How are Paula and the boys?'

He jumped like a cow encountering a cattle prod.

'I–I . . . what are you doing here?'

'Appealing to your better judgement. I know where you're headed tonight.'

He lifted the glass and took a slug of whisky. 'Parents . . . you know . . . visiting the parents.'

I nodded. 'Wouldn't be playing cards – and probably losing another ten grand, then.'

He gaped, the colour leaving his face. 'How do you—'

'Know about that? Because Paula knows, that's how.'

'Oh, God!'

'She's in hell right now. Worrying about how much you'll lose tonight. And it's not just your wife; Victor is in a right old state, too.'

'Oh, God!' Nigel repeated.

'If you care anything for them, you'll pack the gambling in now, right now, before you get in too deep to stop. Because it happens.'

He finished the last of the whisky in one gulp.

'Come on, Nigel, think of the kids; you don't want to run the risk of losing the house – it's *their home.*'

It was possible his face turned even more ashen. 'Patrick's already done that.'

'*What?*'

'Not *my* house – Mousey's. He's already handed over the deeds for Mousey's house and stables. Hasn't told Mousey. Keeps hoping he can win them back, stupid sod. At least I didn't bet that much.'

'No, not much, only the odd ten thousand.'

He nodded morosely, his usual suave urbane manner totally absent. I could almost see common sense fighting the gambling urge. 'On the drive up, you know, I was coming to that conclusion myself: it's not worth it.'

'Good man.' I clapped him on the shoulder again. 'And tonight it looks like it might get a bit rough.'

'Really?'

'Hmm . . . wouldn't do your image much good. I mean, however innocent you might be, mud sticks.'

He nodded grimly and pushed the empty whisky glass back across the bar. 'I'm off, Harry, I'm going home right now. I needed a kick up the arse. Thanks.'

'Come clean with Paula and Victor, eh? Give Victor a call; he really is worried to death.'

'I will, soon as I get home.'

'Good man. Just one thing . . . before you go, can you tell me the names of the other players?'

He hesitated. 'Well, there's Patrick and—' He stopped short because the door to the public bar opened as a scowling Patrick walked in. He wasn't alone. The man with him was wearing a wide smile – and a cravat. Nigel took a deep breath. 'And . . . *him.*'

It was Jackson Fellows' father – his stepfather.

With Keith driving his vehicle, I sat scrunched up on the passenger seat with Tugboat taking up most of the space. We followed Patrick's SUV through the dark streets of Watersby, heading for the river. The two men in front were unaware they were being tailed. I wanted to keep it that way. It was obvious they were going to *The Winning Post*, but I'd no idea what was going to kick off.

There were gaps – gaps that I needed to fill in to see the entire picture. One of them was to do with Jackson. I knew Patrick had broken Jackson's fingers, but I didn't know why. I suspected Jackson was privy to some damning information because blackmail was involved. I also suspected John Dunston had met his death because he'd discovered something about Patrick. What was it? And then there was Alice Goode, the prostitute from Newark. A question mark hung over her death. Patrick had been in that neck of the woods the same day, at Southwell racecourse. The police weren't interested, but I needed to know the truth about what happened.

One thing I did know: it all came back to Patrick.

And a second was that there was no way I could call upon back-up this time. Previously, I'd relied heavily on Mike. He was my main man in a crisis and had saved my life more than once. But tonight Mike was safely tucked up at home with his pregnant wife. As it should be.

However, with Nigel gunning his way back to Lincolnshire, plus the two or three players who had declined to brave the rain and the floods, the odds were now pretty much even.

It left me and Keith facing the two of them – Patrick and Jackson's stepfather.

THIRTY-EIGHT

I couldn't see the weir as Keith drove slowly past through the black night, but I could hear the angry roar and imagine, only too well, the white topped waves whipped up into spray as they pounded over the weir to drop down to the level below. Not only was the rain tumbling down, increasing the volume of water in the river, but the Ouse was massively swollen with the waters draining down from the upper reaches of the other rivers that fed into it from North Yorkshire.

Involuntarily, I shivered and was given a comforting lick from a sympathetic Tugboat. Motoring on closer to where the boats were moored, Keith voiced what I was thinking.

'It's not bloody safe, you know. The river's barely holding. I don't fancy going on board. If the moorings go . . . it'll be straight down and over the weir.'

'You don't have to—'

'I can't leave you to go on board on your own.'

'Yes, you can, Keith. In fact, it might be better if you stay in the vehicle. Might be glad of a getaway driver if things get too hot.'

'Aren't they going to think it strange if I don't show up?'

'We got out of the pub without them seeing us. Since the other players have all cried off, it's logical that you might have, too. As far as they're concerned, you're most likely home, headed for your bed and an early night.'

'You reckon?'

I nodded. 'Let's face it, only a fool would be out on a night this bad.'

'Well, them two are out . . .'

'It's his own boat.'

'And Patrick?'

'I think Patrick hasn't any say in it. He jumps when he's told to jump.'

'Why?'

'That's what I'm hoping to find out – plus other things.'

We'd reached the upper stretch of the river where all the boats were moored. They appeared to have come to life. Snatching and tugging at their ropes, they bucked and rolled in the swell of the fast-running water. At the end of the line was the red, black and white boat, and I could also make out Patrick's car parked up on the tarmac road above the towpath. At least his vehicle was safe, unless the river did burst its banks. But safe or not, I needed to get on board *The Winning Post*, find out the answers to my questions.

'Drive on past, Keith. Drop me off near Patrick's vehicle and park close by.'

'OK.'

A light came on in the living quarters of the boat – a chandelier by the look of it – and without blinds down, I could see the two men.

'Right, I'll try to get on board without them hearing me. What happens then, don't ask me. I just need to find some answers. Wait here; I'll be back soon.'

'Watch yourself, Harry.'

With extreme caution, I made my way from the road down the slope to the towpath. Crossing the slippery gangway – a pretty hairy manoeuvre, clutching the rails to prevent losing my footing – I made it on board as far as the cabin door. Flattening myself against it, I opened it just a slit. There was no accusing shout. With the noise of the waves and rain beating against the boat, I hadn't expected them to hear anything, but my heart was thumping at top speed.

I took a look through the two-inch gap into the cabin. 'Palatial' wasn't too strong a word. Wood panelling cloaked the sides and it was carpeted with cherry-red, ankle-deep Axminster. The black, leather-covered seating was scattered about, with white cushions. The interior of the boat was colour coordinated all the way down the line to match the exterior – and the racing silks.

I barely had time to register the impression because Patrick began to bluster.

'OK, the bloody wimps have all cried off, so no poker. But we're here, so tell me, where's the goods? If they're not in your office, not at your home, where the fucking hell have you put them?'

'Somewhere safe.'

'Look, I only need them for twenty-four hours – maybe less.' Patrick waved both arms wide. 'Come on, man! Be reasonable. You have my word I'll hand them back.'

'But I'm holding them in my hands right now.'

'What the fucking hell am I going to tell the old man? He's worked up a head of steam already because he can't find the deeds. He only wants to check the bloody boundary line before we put in an application to the council to build more stables. I mean, how the hell did I know he'd ask to see them?'

The other man simply smiled.

I was riveted by their conversation. It was answering some of my questions without my asking them.

'Stall him. Go ahead, put in the application. Councils take for ever, and I should know; by the time they get round to considering it, circumstances may have changed.'

'How do you mean, *changed*?'

'Patrick, you're not that naïve. Mousey's an old man, an alcoholic – you're the one in charge of the stables. You're the one who, shall we say, *helps* my horses to win. And while I have the deeds, you will continue to do so. While your mother was alive, I was quite content to wait. There was no need to put pressure on you. You knew that, didn't you? As long as she was alive, I was prepared to be charitable. But she died, Patrick, along with Mike Grantley's wife. You're probably the only one who knows what happened over in Switzerland, whether or not it was an accident.'

'Of course it was an accident.'

I clenched my fists. So I had been right. The ring of truth in Patrick's words was all I needed to hear.

'However,' the man continued, 'now your mother's gone, circumstances have already changed. You probably think you're off the hook with me, don't you? But John Dunston didn't go to his death without talking. You see, I know you killed Alice Goode, the prostitute.' He held up a hand as Patrick was about to jump in. 'Yes, yes, I know, the police are perfectly satisfied they know who the killer was but you – and now *I* – know that's not quite the truth, is it?'

'You've no proof, no proof at all,' Patrick shouted. 'And he didn't say anything to sodding Radcliffe either. There was nothing in that letter I got back for you – nothing incriminating on either of us.'

The man shook his head sadly. 'It was a case of like father, like son, wasn't it? Both of you keeping it secret from your poor mother.' He laughed nastily. 'But you didn't know Alice was accommodating your father, did you? Not until that last time. And when you found out, it did your head in, didn't it? Knowing you were fucking the same woman. She had to go.'

'Some bloke had already battered and burned her. She was lying on the kitchen floor when I got there. The stink was foul.'

'But she wasn't *dead*. You finished her off, made sure of the job.'

'I just gave her one bash.'

'You killed her.'

'You can't accuse me of that. The other bloke had made a job of her first; she'd have died anyway. Because I turned up and gave her another good bash, it was probably a dead heat.'

I realized my nails were digging into the palms of my hands as I listened at the door. The callous, dismissive way Patrick was talking about poor Alice made me want to shoulder my way into the cabin and tear him in half. I drew in a massive deep breath and tried to calm down. I needed to hear whatever came next.

'Proving it might be difficult, I grant you, but I still know what you did, Patrick. Knowledge is power, don't they say?'

'And I know something you don't,' Patrick shouted, jutting his face forward to within inches of the other man. 'Your son – no, let's be accurate, your *stepson*, your precious piano-playing protégé – he knows you've got the deeds. Knows you're not squeaky-clean like the image you're so keen to show the world. He hates your guts – but he needs your money. But I know about Jackson – what *he* did.'

'What are you talking about? You don't know Jackson.'

'That's where you're wrong. Jackson was over in Switzerland when I was. He was pissing himself because we both saw the woman take a photograph. I told him not to be a prat. Nobody would recognize us – we were wearing shades.'

'I don't believe you.'

'And my brother was at university at the same time as Jackson. That's how I know all about it.'

'What are you talking about?'

'Ha, you'd like to know, wouldn't you?'

The civilized veneer slipped from the man's face and he grabbed Patrick's shoulders. 'Tell me.'

My heart lurched. Georgia's hope of keeping the abortion a secret was about to go out the window.

'Oh, I'll tell you right enough. It'll be a pleasure.'

The man drew in a hiss of breath. 'What are you talking about . . . what are you saying? What has Jackson done?'

'He got a girl pregnant and borrowed money for her to have an abortion.'

'What a load of tosh. You don't know Jackson. It's all lies.'

'Lies, is it, Mr Squeaky-clean pious Catholic? No way. It's not lies; it's the truth. Jackson borrowed the money for the abortion from me.'

'I don't believe it.' The man sank down on one of the black leather seats. 'It can't be true.'

'It bloody well is. Ask my brother, Ian – go on. He'll tell you. The girl's name was Juliet. And I never got my money back. Now tell me where those deeds are. I asked Jackson to get them for me but he fobbed me off, so I broke his fingers for a bit of encouragement.'

'You broke his fingers . . . My God, it was you . . . you . . . who stopped him playing the piano,' the man said with horror. 'If they hadn't healed right . . . he might never have played again. You bastard!' He launched himself up from the seat, reaching for Patrick's throat.

Patrick stepped to one side, snatched up a heavy brass table lamp from the side table and swung it with tremendous force at the man's head. The blow connected with a sickening crunch.

It happened too quickly for me to intervene. An arc of blood and matter spurted out, hit the wood panelling and trickled down the wall. There was no question it was a fatal blow.

Philip Caxton, the solicitor, lay where he'd fallen, his blood seeping into the red Axminster, and stared sightlessly up at the swinging chandelier.

THIRTY-NINE

I didn't wait to see what happened next. I quietly pushed the door closed and took a few steps away. Then I tapped in three nines on my mobile phone. And waited for it to be answered.

'Harry Radcliffe,' I whispered. 'Police, fast, there's been a murder. On board a boat, *The Winning Post*, on the Ouse, about three-quarters of a mile north of Watersby. The victim's name is Philip Caxton. Make it fast. I'm in immediate danger myself.' I cut the connection and put my phone to silent. No way did I want a return call alerting Patrick that his crime had been called in. I gave it a few minutes, then walked back to the cabin door – and knocked. I didn't wait to be admitted – I walked straight in.

'Am I right for the poker game?'

'You!' Patrick crossed the cabin in a couple of massive strides. 'Who told you I was here?'

'Keith Whellan decided against coming tonight, so I thought I'd give it a whirl.'

He'd been quick while I was making the emergency phone call. Caxton's body was now a hump lying along the edge of one side of the cabin, covered by a bed quilt. The arc of blood on the wood panelling was no longer trickling down the wall but had been reduced to a smear. He had started to remove the evidence and I'd disrupted the clean-up. I was under no illusions. Caxton's body would have been offloaded into the flood waters, and when it was discovered – if it was discovered – no doubt his injuries would be consistent with having hit his head and fallen into the river.

'Well, as you can see,' Patrick said, waving a dismissive hand, 'there's no one here.'

'So, no card game.'

'You got it. But I'm expecting Philip, the owner. He should have been here by now. Hope he's not met with an accident.'

Although my appearance had given him a shock, he was recovering fast, concocting stories to cover his back.

'Any chance of a game when – if – he turns up?'

Patrick shook his head vigorously. 'Oh, no. Wasted journey for you, I'm afraid.'

'So it seems.'

I needed to keep him talking, distract him. It was at least ten minutes since my emergency call. The police would be motoring up very soon now. If I could keep him here until they arrived, I might also walk away in one piece and still breathing.

'Anyway, it wasn't a long journey tonight – not like going over to Switzerland. Caxton was over in St Moritz for the snow racing this year. His first time, apparently. I'd hoped to see Jackson there – he never missed it, I was told. But he wasn't there this year. Odd, really – the only time Jackson didn't go was the year his father did. Don't you find that odd? Almost as though he didn't want his father to see him.'

'He's not his real father. His mother remarried after his natural father died. Jackson is Philip's stepson.'

'Right.' I nodded encouragingly. 'Caxton funds Jackson, doesn't he?'

'Apparently.'

'You know he does. Of course, Jackson needs every one of his fingers in good working order to pursue his dream.'

'What are you saying, Radcliffe?' Patrick's shoulders had drawn up with tension. 'Spit it out.'

'You broke two of his fingers trying to coerce him into getting

Mousey's deeds back for you before Mousey realized you'd gambled them away.'

'Don't talk such fucking rubbish.'

'Not rubbish, Patrick: the truth. But now Caxton's dead, you're sweating because you don't know where the deeds are. I shouldn't worry, though, I'm sure the Land Registry will have a record.'

'You know nothing.' Patrick snarled the words at me. 'You're just guessing.'

'Hmm,' I agreed, and moved closer to the mound on the floor, touched it with the tip of my shoe. 'And there isn't a dead body under this quilt, is there?'

He let out a bellow of rage and threw a wild punch at my chin. It was easy to sway to one side, let the force of his blow fetch him off balance. I moved in, planted a solid right fist into his solar plexus, waited for his body to fold, followed it with a stiff fist to his jaw and then kneed him viciously in the groin. He rolled on the carpet, gasping and gagging.

'That's for Alice,' I gritted.

I headed for the cabin door, opened it and went up on deck. The rain was still siling down. Patrick's car was still parked in the same place. Keith, however, had moved to within a few yards of the boat. However, there was no sign of any police vehicles. I peered desperately down the road to Watersby, but it was totally empty of traffic.

It was then I felt an arm encircle my neck, dragging me backwards across the pitching deck. I jabbed a savage elbow behind me, felt it connect, heard his grunt of pain and back-kicked, wrapping my left leg around his, dropping us both on to the slippery wet deck. I grabbed for his ears, raised his head, twisted and brought it down with a crack. He let out a high scream of pain and I felt a warm wet flow gush over my hands. Teeth and nose gone, at the very least I knew. But the blood plastered my hands and I couldn't maintain my grip.

Patrick eeled around beneath me and was on his feet before I could reach for him again. He booted me in the head and I must have blacked out briefly. Muzzily, I felt his arms dragging me to the side of the boat, my ribs grated on the metal rail briefly and then I went overboard.

I fell with a hell of a splash into the freezing floodwaters of the Ouse. I was barely conscious and swimming wasn't an option

– the current saw to that. My only chance was to try to keep afloat, keep my nose and face above the water. And then I heard another massive splash. In forcing me over the side, Patrick must have lost his balance and followed me into the river. I was too concerned with trying to battle the blackness inside my head that threatened to pull me down into unconsciousness, equally as deadly as the waters, to give him any thought.

The water rolled me around like a log, dragging me down, closing over my head. In desperation, I kicked and kicked for the surface with legs that all but refused to work. I felt terrifyingly weak and my struggle was futile against the might of the river. I felt my body rising on the waves, breaking the surface. I snatched a gasp of life-giving air before I was sucked below the surface again. I was all but out of it, my clutching hands meeting nothing, my legs gone altogether now. My lungs were burning for air, finding none.

And then my left hand connected with something that wasn't water. Hair, it was hair. Somebody's head – somebody's hair. Whoever it was, they were actually swimming at the side of me. I dug my fingers in, grasped the thick hair, found flesh and bone beneath. I locked my fingers and simply held on for my very life.

FORTY

I could hear voices. They were vague, far away, then very close. I tried to concentrate to hear what was being said, but it was too much of an effort. There was a heavy metal band playing very loudly in my head, with a manic drummer using my head as the drum. I slid unprotesting into the darkness behind my closed eyes and allowed myself to drift. How long for, I have no idea – could have been minutes, hours, even longer, before the band toned it down and the darkness began to lighten.

I heard a familiar voice, close by – in fact, right next to my left ear.

'Stop hogging it, Harry. I don't know. What some people will do to avoid working.' And I opened my eyes. 'Hallelujah!' Mike Grantley said, looking down at me, eyes filled with concern. 'And about bloody time, too.'

'Mike,' a familiar female voice remonstrated. 'Don't give him a hard time.'

It hurt too much to turn my head, but I swivelled my eyes across at her. And felt my lips curve automatically. Annabel.

'Where am I?' I managed to say.

'Hospital, I'm afraid, Harry.' Annabel leaned over and kissed my cheek.

I closed my eyes again and floated happily. Just a great pity I was incapacitated. It would have been bliss to draw her closer, kiss her in return.

'And your next couple of questions . . .' Mike grinned, relief lighting up his face. 'What day is it and how did I get here?'

'Yeah.'

'Tuesday, mate. You've totally lost Sunday night and Monday for ever.'

'You've been out cold, Harry.' Annabel squeezed my hand. 'Everybody thought you were a goner. The number of calls that have been burning up the telephone wires . . . Pen, Georgia, Victor, Edward Frame . . . you're a popular guy. Just shows how many people are concerned for your safety.'

I squeezed her hand back.

'They phoned each other because you hadn't phoned *them* on Sunday night. After you'd told Victor's son-in-law it was going to get rough.'

'And all the time you were in hospital, hogging some sleep,' Mike said.

'What happened? I don't remember much . . .'

'The doctor said you've probably got partial amnesia, but not to worry about it. Your memory will come back. What you've also got, though, is concussion.'

'And you're going to have to take it steady for a week or two,' Annabel said.

'But what happened? How did I get here?'

'Ah, that. Well' – Mike cleared his throat – 'you damn nearly drowned in the River Ouse.'

Even as he said the words, a flicker of memory returned. 'I was holding on to someone's hair. Patrick's hair?'

Mike shook his head. 'No, you weren't, mate. Patrick left you to drown, took his car and scarpered.'

I looked at him. There was a blank look in his eyes.

'The river had burst its banks, lower down. Flooded the road, covered it with debris, silt and mud, a right mess. He tried to drive straight through, get on to a bit of higher ground.'

'But?'

'Didn't make it. His car skidded off the road completely, ended up in the river. He was the one who was drowned.'

I drew in a shuddering breath, reliving the terror I'd felt as the water closed over my head, drawing me back down. Not something I'd wish on anyone, not even my worst enemy. 'So,' I said shakily, 'how the hell did I survive?'

'Oh, that's quite simple,' Annabel said. 'Keith sent his Newfoundland dog, Tugboat, in to get you when he heard a scream. 'Course, Newfoundlands are bred for river rescue. They're enormously strong and they've got webbed feet. You got hold of the dog's thick ruff. He pulled you to the bank and Keith did the rest. Called for an ambulance and back-up and . . .'

'And here I am.'

'Yes. Here you are, thank God.'

'Absolutely,' I said with feeling.

EPILOGUE

Three days later, Annabel collected me from hospital. Mike had protested: it was his day job, he said. But she was adamant. I didn't mind who won as long as I escaped the clutches of the hospital and got back to Harlequin Cottage and normality.

She drove carefully at a sedate speed.

'You need to keep that head as steady as you can for the next few days. Give it chance to heal. The doctors weren't sure if you'd sustained a faint hairline fracture. It wasn't entirely clear from the X-ray. And they've given me instructions to make sure you take it very easy for a while.'

I didn't try to nod. I'd tried that one before – not recommended. And I didn't tell her, but I felt as grotty as hell. Right now, I was sure Leo was a damn sight stronger than I was. And feeling weak was annoying in the extreme. Weak didn't get to ride racehorses.

Arriving at the cottage, she parked up on the gravel by the back door and helped me out. A familiar ginger cat streaked across the garden and launched itself. He landed on Annabel's shoulder this time. I breathed a sigh of relief. Leo's solid body weight – eight kilos plus – hitting the side of my head might have been more than I could take right now. He was so pleased to see Annabel, however, that he decided to bestow on her the 'welcome home' honour usually reserved for me. Annabel nuzzled her face into his ginger fur – the pleasure was obviously mutual.

Later, with a roaring fire in the hearth, stretched out and comfortably packed around with pillows on the settee in the lounge, I was delighted to accommodate a thunderously purring Leo. His pleasure was doubled having both of us home. Mine, too, come to think about it.

'Can you stay a bit?' I asked, gratefully accepting a mug of hot tea.

'I think you could say so.' Annabel buried her face over her own tea. 'If you really want me to.'

If I wanted her to! Right now, I couldn't think of anything in the world I wanted more.

'Believe it. I really, really want you to stay.'

She lifted her head. 'Well, there's nobody to consider, at the flat.'

I frowned. 'What flat? What are you talking about, Annabel?'

'The flat above my office in Melton Mowbray. I . . . I don't live with Jeffrey any more, Harry.'

'*What?*' I couldn't take in the meaning of the words she herself was having such difficulty in saying. 'You've left Jeffrey?'

'Yes.'

'Why, on God's earth, why? After all we three have been through, all our sacrifices for each other, how could you do such a thing to him?'

I had to put the drink down on the coffee table my hand was shaking so much.

'You know the old saying, women fall for their doctor, men fall for their nurses? Unfortunately, I have found out it's true.'

I simply stared mutely at her, completely floored by what she was saying.

'It's simple, Harry. I did tell you I was surplus to Jeffrey's needs now, but you didn't believe me. I hoped I was reading it wrong, that it was my imagination in overdrive, but it wasn't. He told me. Asked me to forgive him, but it wasn't something he had any control over. Jeffrey has fallen deeply in love with Molly, his live-in nurse.'

I was totally shocked. Could hardly credit what she had said.

'He's not the same man any more, Harry. The accident has changed him completely.'

'Could it just be a fling?' It sounded stupid to me even as I said it.

'No,' she said sadly. 'He really is very much in love with her. I'm sure it began because he was totally dependent on her nursing skills, but it's gone a long way beyond that.'

'And Molly?'

'She feels the same about Jeffrey.'

'My God.' Even in a constantly changing world, it was still the last thing I ever expected to happen.

'Sorry it's such a shock, especially with the state you're in, but you did ask and you are entitled to know. When I asked you to come for a meal with us, actually it was Jeffrey who asked me to invite you. He felt he needed to break it to you himself in a civilized way.'

I sat slumped in my seat. The sadness I felt for the way things had turned out was deep and enervating.

'Where does this leave us?'

It was a question I couldn't answer myself. Why I should think Annabel would have the answer, I don't know. And she didn't.

'No idea, Harry. None at all. But for now you need looking after. And it's always the priority, isn't it – whichever one of us has the greatest need. Right now, it's you.'

'And you could stay here and look after me?'

'Until you're a bit stronger, yes.'

We sat and stared at each other. The unbreakable connection was still there between us – we both knew it. It didn't need expressing in words and we didn't try.

'OK.' I took a deep breath and then added, 'I'd like you to stay – until I'm a bit stronger.'